Acclaim for Cathy Bramley:

'It's impossible not to fall in love with Cathy Bramley's
feel-good stories'
Sunday Express

'Heartwarming and positive . . . **will leave you
with a lovely cosy glow**'
My Weekly

'Books by Cathy Bramley are brilliantly **life affirming**'
Good Housekeeping

'This is **delightful!**'
Katie Fforde

'As **comforting** as hot tea and toast made on the Aga!'
Veronica Henry

'Thoroughly **enjoyable**'
U Magazine

'This book **ticks all the boxes**'
Heat

'Reading a Cathy Bramley book for me is like coming home from
a day out, closing the curtains, putting on your PJs and settling
down with a huge sigh of relief! Her books are **full of warmth,
love and compassion** and they are completely adorable'
Kim the Bookworm

'Full of **joy and fun**'
Milly Johnson

'Perfect **feel-good** loveliness'
Miranda Dickinson

'I **love** Cathy's writing and her characters —
her books are **delicious**'
Rachael Lucas

'The **perfect** tale to **warm** your heart and make you smile'
Ali McNamara

'Between the irresistible characters and the desirable setting, *Wickham Hall* is **impossible to resist**'
Daily Express

'Delightfully **warm**'
Trisha Ashley

'A **fabulously heart-warming** and fun read that will make you just want to snuggle up on the sofa and turn off from the outside world'
By the Letter

'Another absolute corker from Cathy Bramley. **She just gets better and better** – creating beautiful locations, gripping and lovely storylines and fantastic characters that stick with you a long time after reading'
Little Northern Soul

Cathy Bramley is the author of the best-selling romantic comedies *Ivy Lane, Appleby Farm, Wickham Hall, The Plumberry School of Comfort Food, The Lemon Tree Café* and *A Match Made in Devon* (all four-part serialized novels) as well as *Conditional Love, White Lies & Wishes* and *Hetty's Farmhouse Bakery*. She lives in a Nottinghamshire village with her family and a dog. Her recent career as a full-time writer of light-hearted romantic fiction has come as somewhat of a lovely surprise after spending the last eighteen years running her own marketing agency.

Cathy would love to hear from you! Find her on:

 Facebook.com/CathyBramleyAuthor

 @CathyBramley

 www.CathyBramley.co.uk

Cathy Bramley

A
VINTAGE
SUMMER

CORGI BOOKS

TRANSWORLD PUBLISHERS
61–63 Uxbridge Road, London W5 5SA
www.penguin.co.uk

Transworld is part of the Penguin Random House group of companies
whose addresses can be found at global.penguinrandomhouse.com

Penguin
Random House
UK

First published in Great Britain in 2019 by Corgi Books
an imprint of Transworld Publishers

A CIP catalogue record for this book
is available from the British Library.

ISBN
9780552173957

Typeset in 11.5/13pt Garamond MT by Jouve (UK), Milton Keynes.
Printed and bound in Great Britain by Clays Ltd, Elcograf S.p.A.

Penguin Random House is committed to a sustainable future
for our business, our readers and our planet. This book is made from
Forest Stewardship Council® certified paper.

1 3 5 7 9 10 8 6 4 2

To Snowy Arbuckle with all my love

Chapter 1

'There you go, Gladys, all nice and neat again.' I brushed the specks of loose soil from Mrs Wheatley's slate plaque and dropped a handful of faded pink azalea petals into my wheelbarrow. 'Weed free and blooming beautifully. Ready for your husband's visit tomorrow.'

I stood up and circled my shoulders. Only nine o'clock in the morning and the June heat was already beginning to build within the walls of the Garden of Remembrance. It would be a sunhat and sunscreen sort of day, a bit hot and sticky for me, working outside all day, but nice for our visitors to be able to say their farewells in the sunshine.

We had a full schedule today in the chapel of rest and on days like this, people would often linger for a while in the garden. It was the prettiest part of the North London Crematorium, in my opinion. The rest of the grounds around the chapel and the car park were laid to lawn and it always reminded me of the *Teletubbies* set: perfectly landscaped, beautifully green but with their man-made undulations and newly planted trees it was all a bit artificial. Nothing like the countryside where I grew up in the Derbyshire village of Fernfield, all woods and hills, streams and farmland. I suppressed a sigh and swallowed a pang of homesickness. I needed to stop thinking like this; home was here now, in London. With Harvey. I was lucky to have a job at all, not to mention one that allowed to be me outside in the fresh air.

Next stop the lovely yellow climbing rose. The ashes of a man called Shaun were scattered here. Killed in a motorbike accident, so his twin brother had told me.

Every part of this garden was special to someone: each plant, bench, wooden archway and stone ornament held treasured memories for people, the place where a loved one's ashes had been sprinkled. And it was my privilege to care for them all. My working day was calm, ordered and, most of the time, entirely predictable. In fact, this garden was the only place in the world where I felt in control at the moment.

I picked up my watering can and made my way to Shaun's rose bush. I got all sorts of odd requests from relatives; I was used to it by now. In this case, Shaun's brother had asked if I would mind singing a particular song to him every now and then. I looked over my shoulder to make sure my colleague Alan wasn't in earshot. I spotted him a little way off, going around the lavender bed with the edging shears. Mind you, even if he did hear me serenading the rose bush he would just shake his head fondly. Unlike my boss, Paula, who was very keen on remits and rotas and being discreet in public areas. She was all right, really, just a bit of a stickler for the rules. Singing and dancing were definitely not part of my job description.

But if it gave some comfort to Mr Wheatley to know that I had a chat with Gladys when I weeded the azalea he'd planted in her memory, where was the harm? And I'm sure Shaun's rose bush had been perkier since I'd been singing his favourite Queen song to him. I began watering and cleared my throat before breaking into song.

'Bom, bom, bom, another one bites the—'

'Lottie? Can I have a word?' came a voice from behind me.

I whirled around, sending a plume of water into the air that landed with a splash on my boots. Paula was picking her way across the soft green turf towards me in her court shoes. My heart sank as swiftly as her heels in the grass.

'Sure.' I put down the watering can. *As long as the word isn't 'P45'*. Thank goodness I'd only been singing quietly. 'What can I do for you?'

'Can you spare me five minutes?' she said with a jerk of her head. 'My office.'

And without waiting for an answer she spun on her heels and marched back towards the main building so fast that her flesh-coloured tights made a zipping noise where her thighs rubbed together.

'I'll just tidy my tools away,' I called after her.

'Now you're for it.' Alan looked up from his clipping, knocked his cap back off his forehead and winked. 'Another one bites the dust, eh?'

'Don't joke.' My stomach swooped. 'I really need this job.'

I'd worked for my dad as a tree surgeon before moving to London, but there'd been nothing like that on offer locally when we'd come south last December so that Harvey could set up his own personal training business in the capital. 'Let's follow the money and move to London,' he'd said, grabbing my hands, his eyes gleaming with pound signs. 'I've got a mate with a flat we could rent.'

Everyone in London could afford personal trainers, he'd reckoned. Punters were cash-rich and time-poor and would be falling over themselves to hand over said cash to be put through their paces. It would be a piece of low-fat, low-sugar cake to set up his own fitness consultancy down south. In fact, he'd said with a swagger, he'd probably have to take on staff within the first year. And it would do me good, he'd added in a tone laced with mock rebuke, to finally cut the apron strings and stand on my own two feet.

I'd been so proud of his ambitions and his self-assurance that I'd been swept along with it, not really thinking through what I'd do when I got to London. As it turned out, the streets hadn't been as richly paved with gold as he'd assumed and it had been impossible to find enough wealthy clients to make ends meet so when the gym he'd joined advertised for staff, he took the job to tide him over. He was still there. And the tiny flat that his friend had rented to him as a stop-gap was scarcely more than a bedsit and, although Harvey insisted on paying for it himself, I suspected the rent was triple what my sister Evie and her husband Darren's mort-gage cost for their three-bedroomed house in Fernfield. Needless to say, we were still there.

But Harvey had been right about one thing: it *had* been time for me to leave home. Dad and I had become too re-liant on each other. He took on a business partner when I left; a man who could do the aerial cutting that I'd always done. And although I wouldn't go so far as to say I was deliriously happy right now, I'd managed to survive six months in the capital, living and working with someone other than a family member. Not bad for a confirmed home bird like me.

I stowed my garden tools safely where they couldn't cause injury to the public and scurried after Paula. I caught up with her just as she reached the 'authorized personnel only' door in the side of the building and pulled it open for her.

'Good weekend?' I asked, using my question as an oppor-tunity to scan her face for clues as to what sort of mood she was in.

She stopped and leaned on the door frame to flick clumps of mud from her shoes. I took the hint and wiped my wet boots on the mat.

Paula sighed. 'The weekends are never long enough, are they? No sooner do we finish on a Friday afternoon than . . .' She clicked her fingers. 'Snap. Monday morning rolls back round and we're off again. Noses to the grindstone.'

'Too true.' I tried to smile rather than grimace. I daren't tell her that just lately my weekends had stretched to an interminable length as Harvey had become increasingly bad-tempered and – yes, I was going to admit it to myself – erratic. One minute he'd be squeezing the living daylights out of me, declaring that I was his soulmate and he couldn't live without me, the next he'd fly into a huge sulk after I made an innocuous comment about a work colleague. It was a relief to come back to work every Monday, knowing that because of my early starts and his late finishes at the gym, it would be Saturday before I had to spend many waking hours with him. And if I was lucky, he'd be doing the weekend shift and I could have a few hours to myself.

After I'd helped him design leaflets and deliver them to several hundred houses in the neighbourhood, I'd run out of things to do and had wanted to look for a job. Harvey said he felt humiliated that he couldn't afford for me to stay at home, and I remember kissing him and saying with a laugh that it was no longer the nineteen fifties and I didn't expect him to bankroll me. I think that was the day of our first row.

A temporary job as grounds maintenance at the crematorium had been the only thing I could find that came close to my skills and experience. I knew I was on borrowed time until the person whose job I was doing came back, but now I hoped my time wasn't up yet. Without something to get me out of our poky little flat every day, I'd go bonkers.

Paula ushered me into her office and shut the door behind me. My spirits sank a little lower; shutting the door was never a good sign. She removed her navy blue suit jacket to reveal a short-sleeved white nylon shirt which crackled with static and hung it on the back of her chair.

'Sit down, Lottie.' She waved me to her visitor's chair and plonked herself down behind her desk.

'Thank you.' I sat on the plastic chair, tucking my hands underneath my thighs to stop me waving them about nervously.

'How long have you been with us now?'

'Four months.'

'And what would you say is our primary function, here at the North London *Crematorium*?' She leaned forward on her desk, head cocked to one side.

'Our primary function is funerals,' I said, wondering if this was a trick question. 'And making the loss of a loved one as painless as possible.'

'Funerals,' said Paula, glossing over my second point. 'Specifically what type of funerals?'

'Well, cremations. Obviously.' I shrugged.

'Exactly. Not burials.' She pursed her lips. 'Cremations for . . . ?'

Oh God. A tremor of dread flooded through me. Suddenly I knew exactly where this was heading.

'People?' I muttered weakly.

Her gaze held mine as she reached for a glass of water on her desk. 'People, Lottie. *Humans.*'

'Okay, I can explain.' I untucked my hands and pressed them on to her desk. 'I know I shouldn't have dug a grave for that hamster in the south corner by the hedge. Nor made a little cross from two lollipop sticks. But the little boy had travelled such a long way on his own on the bus with a shoe-box containing what was left of Biscuit. It was the least I could do and it only took a few minutes. He'd written a eulogy and everything. Biscuit was his best friend. And he'd tried burying it in his garden but the dog had dug it up twice. The poor thing had already lost three of its limbs. I didn't have the heart to send the poor boy packing.'

Paula choked on her water and closed her eyes for a second.

'You acted out of kindness, I understand that.' She let out a long breath. 'But it's against the rules, Lottie. The Health and Safety Executive would crucify us.'

'It won't happen again,' I promised.

'And what about the singing?'

'You heard that?' I cringed, feeling the heat rise to my cheeks. 'I never was very good at Queen songs.'

'Queen?' She stared at me. 'I'm talking about your rendition of Frank Sinatra's "My Way" with an old lady, complete with high kicks.'

I gulped. 'How do you know about that?'

'CCTV,' she said, pointing to a small screen on a bracket high up on the wall of her office.

Oh no.

'I thought that was just for at night, when the security team is here,' I said in a small voice.

'Nope. We see everything.' Her nostrils flared but I thought – hoped – I could see a glimmer of amusement in her eye.

'Look, I'm sorry,' I pleaded. 'I know I'm supposed to be just gardening, but my motto is to always be kind. And I find it hard to say no when people ask me to do stuff. Always have. My sister Evie says I'm a pleaser.'

I once admitted to Evie that I took my inspiration from Paddington Bear who always did the kind thing. When she'd finally got her breath back from a fit of laughter, she said the fact I'd chosen a cuddly, duffel-coat-wearing, marmalade-sandwich-eating teddy bear as a role model explained a lot about the scrapes I got myself into.

'I can see that.' Paula cocked her head to one side. 'And while it does mean that you bend the rules to the point of snapping, kindness is something from which we can all benefit, from time to time.'

I let out a breath. 'I'm so relieved. I thought you were giving me a warning.'

'I am. Unofficially. But you've brought a zest for life to this crematorium, Lottie; not just to the gardens, but to the team too. We've never had a member of staff who's had so much interaction with our visitors before. I'm not, however, condoning the pet burial, or you joining in with ceremonies to sprinkle ashes, or sitting on the bench under the cherry tree going through that old lady's wedding albums.'

I winced; she really had paid attention to that CCTV.

'Now. Next week . . .' Paula sat back in her chair and steepled her fingers. 'There is good news and bad news.'

My heart sank again. 'Please can we start with the bad?'

'Lisa, whose post you've been filling, has been declared fit for work from Monday. Great for her, but it would mean that your last day should be this Friday.'

'*Should* be?' I held my breath.

Paula beamed. 'I'm delighted to say that another opening has cropped up . . .'

Ten minutes later I stumbled from her office and back outside to the car park hardly daring to believe what I'd just heard. A promotion. Me. To grounds maintenance supervisor. More money, longer hours, paid holiday, a pension even – I'd never had a pension! Dad would be pleased for me; he worried, I knew, that we were hardly making ends meet at the moment.

But Harvey: what would he have to say about it?

My stomach churned at the prospect of broaching the subject without him taking it as a personal affront, without him accusing me of prioritizing my job over our relationship, and making him jealous that my career was taking off when coming to London had been his idea, his dream. A few months ago it wouldn't have crossed my mind to worry about his reaction, but since he'd been at that gym he'd changed. I knew if I failed to pick the right moment there was every chance he'd fly into one of his rages followed by days of seething silence. By the time I'd reached the Garden of Remembrance to pick up where I'd left off, I was in a cold sweat. Hot acid rushed from my stomach to my throat. I was going to be sick. I dashed behind a row of conifers and coughed into shrubbery.

What a mess.

Chapter 2

Harvey Nesbitt was the most handsome, charismatic and devoted boyfriend I'd ever had. Not only that, his enthusiasm, energy and go-get-'em attitude had captured my imagination and ultimately my heart after we met through a dating app last year. He was a trier, was Harvey, and I'd been bowled over by his optimistic outlook on life. He thought nothing of changing careers, taking up new challenges, moving city ... He seemed to take it all in his stride.

Not like me. I'd had grand plans once upon a time. I even left home for a year to take up a place at university to study Media. Then Mum had been diagnosed with terminal cancer and my degree went out of the window. I came home to help Dad look after her and six months later she passed away. Evie tried to persuade me go back to uni. I was only twenty, it wasn't too late and it would open doors, she'd said, give me independence, a future. Three years older than me, she'd already finished her degree and had got a good job as an accountant in Manchester. But for me the moment had passed. I'd changed. *Everything* had changed. Spending three years with a load of carefree twenty-somethings whose biggest dilemma was which pub sold the cheapest drinks no longer held any appeal. I'd lost my mum and somewhere during the last few months of her life I'd lost my way too. Mum had been the sunshine in our lives and she and Dad had been blessed with one of those fairy-tale marriages which no one in their company could fail to be touched by. He called her 'blossom' and brought her a tea tray complete with her favourite china cup and a fresh flower in bed before he left for work each morning. She tucked paper hearts and love notes in his lunchbox and told him every day that he was her soulmate. If I could have even a fraction of their happiness when I eventually married, I'd vowed long ago, I'd be a happy, happy woman.

Immediately following Mum's funeral, Dad took early retirement from the fire service and I spent the next year trying to coax him out of the house. In the end, a friend begged him to help him get rid of a tree which had come down blocking his drive. To my relief, Dad found he quite enjoyed being active again. A month later Allbright's Tree Services was born. Dad took a course and obtained his chainsaw licence and, because I had nothing better to do, I became his assistant. All those years of climbing trees and making dens finally paid off. I became a dab hand with the shiny new shredder too, making bark chippings from the chopped-down branches, which we sold for ten pounds a sack.

Evie moved back to Fernfield, married a lovely man called Darren, successfully set up her own home-based accountancy business and sadly *unsuccessfully* tried to start a family. One devastating miscarriage and countless tests on both of them had taken their toll on the relationship and last time Evie phoned she admitted that she was beginning to think that they'd fallen out of love with each other. I re-assured her that this would be a temporary blip but it tore me apart to see them both suffering; they made such a lovely couple.

It was twelve years since Mum died and Dad had stayed single all this time. He eschewed all advances from members of the opposite sex, though as his tan deepened and his body grew leaner from all his physical work, there were plenty of offers. Now in his early sixties, he decided last month to retire properly, sell the business to his partner, rent his house out and travel around Europe for a year on his own.

I cried when I heard the news. Not because I didn't want him to go, but because this adventure had always been their plan for retirement: Mum and Dad's, together. I was both proud of him for going ahead by himself and heartbroken that he had to.

As for me, boyfriends had drifted in and out of my life, mostly out; they were all, without exception, pleasant enough. I even lived with the last one before Harvey for a couple of months. But none of them made my skin tingle or my heart leap when their name flashed up on my phone screen. None of them made my stomach fizz when they turned up at my door to collect me for an evening out. None of them ever called me 'blossom'. Until I met Harvey.

From the moment our flirting graduated from online chat to meeting in real life, Harvey charmed me. He charmed us all, actually. Dad thought he was just the type of young man to make me push my boundaries, Evie thought he was sexy as hell, and even Darren thought he was a top man and took him for the odd pint at the pub. When Harvey called me 'blossom' on our fifth date and brought me flowers, it felt like the sign I'd been looking for; maybe I'd finally met 'the one'.

A year down the line I still loved him, but the fairy-tale romance I'd signed up for had evaporated somewhere along the M1 between Fernfield and Tottenham. And I wasn't sure what to do about it.

That evening, when I let myself into our open-plan flat, Paula's words came back to me: 'You've made me realize that in certain instances, a kind word to a grieving mother or a consoling pat on the arm to a widower is valued far more than our usual policy of discretion and invisibility. Please give serious consideration to this promotion. I'd really like to have you on board permanently.'

Permanently.

I wandered across to the kitchen area, remembering the

panicky feeling that Paula's job offer had given me. Her eyes had been twinkling with confidence after she'd imparted her news; so sure was she that I'd snap her hand off. I felt terrible watching her smile slip when I told her I'd think about it.

I wasn't even one hundred per cent sure that I'd thanked her. I must have; I'd have done it on autopilot before standing up, shaking her hand and fleeing her office.

Until Paula uttered the 'permanent' word, I hadn't realized how much I cherished the freedom that my temporary job afforded me.

Did I really want to commit to the crematorium, or even to London, I thought as I washed up the dirty crockery Harvey had left on the kitchen breakfast bar. I poured hot water and washing-up liquid into the pan he'd used to make his mountain of scrambled eggs to let it soak for a few minutes while I made myself a cup of tea. He was on a high-protein, low-fat diet these days, which might be having an incredible impact on his body shape, but not using butter made a right mess of the pan.

The even bigger question was, I admitted to myself: did I really want to commit to Harvey?

A quiver of lust darted through me at the thought of his toned abs. He'd had a lovely body when I met him: slim and athletic. His last job before taking his personal training qualification was selling private medical insurance but he'd felt trapped and lethargic working in an office. Now he was well and truly 'ripped'. Since he'd been working at Muscle Works gym in Tottenham he had virtually doubled in size: his biceps were like boulders and his thighs were rock solid. Even his neck seemed to have grown. I was a bit leaner too. Partly because of my long hours at the crematorium, but mostly because of the healthy diet Harvey insisted was as good for me as it was for him.

Once the kitchen was clean, I chopped a mountain of vegetables and chicken ready for a stir-fry as soon as Harvey got in. Then I tidied the rest of our fourth-floor flat, which, due to the fact that it was barely bigger than my bedroom at home, took me all of five minutes. He'd be home soon and my stomach was already jittery with nerves. I decided to practise announcing my good news on my sister. I perched on the window sill and dialled her number.

'Supervisor at a crematorium, hey?' said Evie with a giggle when I told her. 'Every young girl's dream. At least it'll be quiet.'

'But it's a green space,' I said, gazing absentmindedly through the living-room window at the concrete jungle below. There were some lovely parts of Tottenham; unfortunately, our street wasn't one of them. 'You don't know how precious that is around here. Plus, we'd have a bit more money coming in.'

Although me earning more than Harvey would go down about as well as a hog roast at a vegetarian barbeque.

'Sorry,' she said, chastened. 'And well done on being promoted so quickly; they must really value you. Not that I'm in the least bit surprised; why wouldn't they? Although . . .' She tailed off with a sigh.

'Although what?'

'Forgive me if I'm overstepping the mark, but it doesn't seem to me as if Harvey's personal training business has taken off as planned, has it?'

That was an understatement. So far he'd only managed to recruit one client: an old lady who lived a forty-minute tube ride away and conducted her exercises from her armchair. And even that had fizzled out when her son had found out how much Harvey was charging her. Of course, I wasn't going to tell Evie that; it seemed disloyal.

'Give him a chance; it will,' I said, 'and now he's working at the gym, it puts him in a good position to pick up private clients. He certainly looks the part; he's got muscles on muscles these days.'

'Hmm,' she said, sounding unconvinced. 'I half hoped

you wouldn't like it in London and you'd come home. If you take the promotion it feels more permanent. I miss you, Lottie.'

My throat tightened; she'd inadvertently hit the nail on the head. At the moment I was on a zero hours contract: no commitment on either side. This new role would be harder to walk away from. If I needed to. I gave myself a shake.

'I miss you too,' I said with a catch in my throat.

And Dad, although he'd be off on his travels as soon as he'd found a tenant to rent the house. But I missed the village. I missed being part of the community. I missed people smiling at me in recognition in the pub, I missed bumping into my mum's friends who'd been so kind to us after she died. I even missed people knowing my business. Here I was no one, I *had* no one. Except Harvey. And although in our first few months, we'd had great fun living together, the honeymoon period seemed to be over.

'I can't win, though, can I?' I continued, forcing humour into my voice. 'You encouraged me to move out, start a new life away from the village. And now I've done it, you want me to chuck in the towel and come back.'

'Touché,' said Evie with a bark of laughter. 'Anyway, I'm being selfish. I bet Harvey's pleased.'

'He doesn't know yet. He's not back from work.'

'You didn't call him when you found out?'

'No, I . . .' I hesitated, feeling heat rise to my cheeks as I concocted a lie. 'He's not allowed to take personal calls at the gym.'

Something – maybe pride, or possibly even shame – had prevented me from telling my family how things were going between Harvey and me. As far as they were concerned, he was still the golden boy, the one who'd finally persuaded Lottie to fly the nest. I'd thought they might get suspicious when we didn't come home for Christmas. I'd really wanted to spend a few days with Dad and Evie, especially as Evie had hinted at problems between her and Darren, but

Harvey thought we should celebrate our first Christmas alone. We'd only just moved in together and he sweetly said it felt like we were on honeymoon; going home would just spoil the mood. He didn't have any family, so perhaps he hadn't understood what a big sacrifice it was for me not to see mine at Christmas and it had been on the tip of my tongue to point that out. But then he had painted such a romantic picture of our day – champagne breakfast, a frosty walk along Oxford Street to peer in shop windows and see the lights, followed by a movie in front of the fire, curled up together – that I'd been unable to resist him.

There was a pause down the line.

'O-kay,' said Evie eventually.

Oh sod it, why didn't I just tell her? I'd never kept secrets from her before. And Evie wouldn't judge; if anything she'd be upset I hadn't shared my doubts about Harvey before now.

I took a deep breath, my pulse racing as I built up to it. 'Evie—'

'Actually, I've got some news too,' she blurted out in a rush. The urgency in her voice made me forget all about my own worries. *Please say she was pregnant.*

'Go on, tell me then.'

'I'm going to apply for us to become foster parents,' she said, exhaling as she spoke.

I pushed aside my disappointment; it was still brilliant that they were taking positive action as a couple.

'That's amazing, I'm thrilled for you both!' I cried, my face breaking into a huge smile. 'See, I told you Darren would come round in the end. He just needed time!'

This had been the bone of contention between them for months. Darren had wanted a child but, according to Evie, he wasn't interested in going down any route other than the biological one. Evie wanted a child any which way she could.

'I haven't told him yet.' I heard my sister swallow hard and my heart plummeted. 'I thought I'd go ahead and fill in an initial form online. And then I'll tell him. Ideally I'd like to adopt, but he's not sure how he feels about that. At least with fostering we can practise looking after children without a long-term commitment and if it goes well . . . who knows?'

'Does this mean that things between the two of you have improved?' I asked hopefully.

I heard her groan softly. 'Not so as you'd notice. That's why we need to do something positive, something that moves us forward.'

'And you definitely can't consider other options: sperm donors, egg donors, IVF?'

There was a silence down the line.

'I would but Darren . . . Well, let's just say it's not an option. Which is why I'm ruling out being a biological mother. No,' I heard her suck in a breath, 'fostering ticks a lot of boxes.'

I bit my lip, worried that this approach was more likely to push Darren further away. 'I don't think you should get too far into it before you talk to him about it.'

'But I want to go ahead,' she said with a wobbly voice. 'I want to be a mum more than anything.'

'More than being Darren's wife?' I asked softly.

I thought about Mum and Dad and the loving role models they'd been for us. If anyone had been shown how to get it right, it was Evie and me. And yet look at us: I was having doubts about the man I'd fallen so madly in love with and she was going behind the back of a man who up until now had done everything in his power to make her happy.

'How did it come to this?' I murmured half to myself.

'That's simple,' said Evie sharply. 'I got pregnant against the odds and lost it and now because of our problem, Darren and I can't have the family we wanted, but it doesn't have to stop us completely, does it?'

Our problem. Evie had never revealed which one of them had fertility problems. She and Darren had simply told everyone that the chances of them conceiving were one in a million. No blame on either side. I totally respected their decision not to go into detail, but it did make this sort of conversation difficult.

'No, no, of course not. That wasn't what I meant,' I said, annoyed with myself for upsetting her. 'I meant . . . I was talking about me.'

'You? What's up, Lottie? There's something you're not telling me, isn't there?' she asked, her tone suddenly alert. 'I could tell. I could sense it in your voice.'

The relief at finally being able to open up to her made me almost weep. At that moment the front door crashed open, sending a shot of guilt through me.

'Harvey's home,' I said quickly. 'Got to go.'

He walked in and dumped several heavy-looking carrier bags on the breakfast bar.

'But why—' Evie began.

'Don't I get a hello?' Harvey pulled open the fridge door, took out the carton of milk and gulped at it, looking across at me quizzically.

'Sorry, I really have to go,' I said. I got a rash on my throat when I was nervous. I couldn't feel it, but I knew the signs; the blotches were appearing now. I hated that I did this: finished a call with my friends or family just because Harvey turned up. But it was easier that way. It wasn't that he didn't like me having contact with anyone, it was just that . . . well, I wasn't sure really. I just knew I needed to go.

'Okay, but call me soon. I love you.'

'I love you too,' I said, ending the call.

Harvey walked towards me, a look of bemusement on his face as he wrapped his arms around me and gave me a cuddle. 'Should I be worried?'

He moved like a panther these days, his shoulder muscles rippling under his T-shirt. His cropped black hair glistened with styling oil. 'Only, dinner's not ready and I catch you telling someone else that you love them.'

I forced a smile and threaded my arms around his neck, breathing in the smell of him: a faint hint of deodorant and fresh mint chewing-gum breath.

'Silly,' I said, kissing him. 'That was Evie. She and Darren are having problems. And dinner's not ready because you like your stir-fry still crunchy so I couldn't start until you got back.'

He nodded slowly, smoothing my hair back from my face, his thumb tracing the faint scar at the end of my eyebrow where a silver birch branch had once flipped up and scratched me.

'I'm surprised they're still together; it can't be easy living with the knowledge that your wife is barren. A man wants a woman who can bear his kids. Darren's still young enough to meet someone else and Evie, well, maybe she'll get a cat or—'

'What are you talking about?' I pulled away from him, shocked. 'That's a terrible thing to say. What about marriage vows? In sickness and in health, for better, for worse?'

'Sorry, that was a bit harsh.' Harvey grinned, released me and walked back to the kitchen. 'But I just think if someone doesn't keep their side of the bargain, the deal's off. Let's get dinner on; I'm starving.'

'Marriage isn't a *deal*, it's a commitment, a declaration of love,' I said crossly, folding my arms. 'And we don't even know if the medical issue is on her side.'

'Oh, Lottie, look at these.' He bent over the vegetables I'd chopped and shook his head. 'You know I don't like massive chunks of onion. I'll have to do it again. And the peppers. Look at the size of them.' He scooped up a handful of my perfectly acceptable strips of green and red pepper and then dropped them in disgust.

'Please yourself.' I poured myself a glass of water, still fuming over his comment about Evie but glad he seemed to have changed the subject.

He picked up the knife and bent over the chopping board,

slicing the veg into slivers so fine they were almost transparent. I suppressed a sigh. I liked them chunky; you could taste them properly, appreciate the different textures.

'Anyway, of course it'll be Evie's fault. Women's plumbing is complicated. Men are simple creatures.' He winked boyishly.

I raised an eyebrow at that but stayed quiet.

'He shoots, he scores,' Harvey continued. 'Simple. No irregular cycles, no blocked tubes. Just in, out, shake it all about.'

He thrust his hips forward comically in a deliberate attempt to make me laugh. It worked. I shook my head, smiling at him.

'It's got me thinking, though,' he went on idly. 'I wonder if it runs in the family?'

'What?' I set cutlery and plates out on the breakfast bar.

He slid the wok on to the hob and lit the gas. 'Being barren.'

I frowned. 'Will you stop saying that word? And of course not, otherwise neither Evie or I would be here, would we?'

'Think about it.' He dropped a blob of coconut oil into the pan and swirled it around. 'You're thirty-two. And you've never got pregnant.'

I laughed in disbelief. 'Well no, because I've never tried and we take precautions.'

Contraception was Harvey's department. He'd read an article last year about how prolonged use of the birth control pill could have an adverse effect on a woman's fertility rate. 'I'm thinking of you, and the future,' he'd said at the time. 'Come off the pill; let's use condoms, you can trust me. I don't want to be a dad yet.'

It was thoughtful of him to care about my health and to volunteer to take on the responsibility; in the past, boyfriends had just left it up to me to take care of that side of things. He'd been so sweet about it that I'd happily complied.

Harvey glanced sideways at me now before tipping

vegetables into the wok. It sizzled and a cloud of steam rose from the pan. 'Yeah, but we've had the odd accident and you've never caught.'

Caught. An unbidden image of a mousetrap popped into my head.

'Have we?' This was news to me. 'Why did you never say?'

'Didn't want to worry you,' he said with a shrug. 'And there was nothing to worry about; we've obviously dodged the bullet.'

'So you shot, but didn't score,' I teased. 'So maybe you've got a problem with your simple plumbing?'

'No!' He pointed his spatula at me, his jaw taut. 'There's nothing wrong with me.'

My heart thumped. This was what happened these days; one minute we were having a friendly chat, the next his temper flared and I had to talk him down.

'I was only joking,' I said, reaching out to stroke his bare arm. 'Shall I put this shopping away?'

Harvey took a deep breath. 'Yes please. I bought some more of that protein powder you like. Chocolate flavour this time. We can have it in our breakfast shakes tomorrow.'

'Yum,' I said, hoping I sounded convincing.

Every night he measured out our protein shakes ready for the morning. Fruit, kale and protein powder. All I had to do when I got up was add almond milk and blitz.

He thought I drank it on the way to work when what I actually did was pour it down the drain outside and then go to the Polish supermarket around the corner and buy myself a fresh pecan Danish pastry.

Five minutes later Harvey tipped our dinner on to the plates and pulled a stool out from the breakfast bar. He sat down and began to eat.

'Hey.' His eyes lit up. 'I meant to tell you. A guy walked into the gym today and asked about personal training. He had all the gear on and he was jingling car keys with a

Mercedes key fob; I could tell he was loaded. I gave him my number and told him I could do a bespoke programme. And I said if he came directly to me, it'd be cheaper than paying the gym for sessions. He seemed really keen.'

'Great!' I sat down next to him and smiled. It occurred to me that Harvey's methods might not go down too well at the gym, but seeing as I'd had my knuckles rapped today for not following the rules in my own job, who was I to criticize? 'Fingers crossed for you.'

Harvey shovelled his stir-fry in and swallowed it down. 'This could be my lucky break, Lottie. I only need a couple of regulars and I'll be earning enough for both of us. I'd really like it if you didn't work for a bit, stay at home, maybe do some leafleting again for me. I hate you leaving before me in the mornings. And I don't like you travelling on your own on the tube. I want you to be here where I can look after you.'

'Oh Harvey,' I said weakly.

'That's settled, then,' he said, mistaking my tone for happiness. He leaned forward to kiss me. 'I love you, blossom.'

I didn't want to tell him about my promotion tonight. I'd do it tomorrow.

Chapter 3

The next night after work, Harvey came home in a bad mood. The man with the Mercedes had been back in to book some sessions directly with Harvey. Unfortunately, he'd arrived before the start of Harvey's shift and had been served by the boss instead. When she found out that her new instructor had proposed cutting Muscle Works out of the deal, she'd bawled Harvey out in front of two other members of staff and given him a formal warning for effectively stealing from her.

'The idiot!' he spat, pacing up and down the flat, more like a caged animal than ever. 'I told him to phone me first, not just turn up. What was he thinking?'

I smiled sympathetically from my perch on the window sill, knowing he didn't want me to actually speak.

'And that bitch, humiliating me like that. Who does she think she is?'

Your employer? I thought.

'Now she's watching me like a hawk; daring to say I can't be trusted. She should be grateful I didn't walk out; I'm the only one with two brain cells to rub together in that place.'

Maybe this was my opening. If he did walk out, he'd have to accept that I needed to increase my earnings to compensate.

'Then leave,' I said, catching hold of his hand and forcing him to look at me. 'Go back to trying to build your own business. You'll be much happier and don't worry about money,' I laughed self-consciously, 'because—'

'No, I won't give her the satisfaction of walking out, but I will increase my efforts to pick up my own clients. I know!' he said, grabbing the laptop. 'Let's knock up a website! That way more people will find out about me.'

'Good idea,' I said, not mentioning that when I'd suggested that five months ago he'd said that websites were 'old hat' and nobody looks at them any more.

For the rest of the night, we sat together on the sofa building a simple site and scrolling through pictures of Harvey looking manly and muscular to persuade people that no one knew more about becoming the body beautiful than my boyfriend. It had been quite fun in the end; he did have a beautiful body and he knew just how to hold it against me.

On Wednesday evening, I'd only been talking to Evie on the phone for a couple of minutes when Harvey arrived home. She'd told me that she'd sent off for some information about fostering from social services that afternoon and was full of it. I got up from the sofa and walked over to him in the kitchen, watching him to try to gauge his mood. His face gave nothing away and I kissed his cheek.

'Who is it?' he asked, twisting my hand so he could read the screen.

'Evie,' I whispered.

He rolled his eyes.

'They're crying out for foster parents!' Evie said, sounding happier than I'd heard her for ages. 'I'm so glad we're doing this.'

I was still concerned that she was keeping Darren in the dark but this was her life, not mine. She'd been through enough and I would support her whatever she decided to do.

'Just tell Darren what you've told me,' I said, turning my

back on Harvey, determined that he wasn't going to make me feel guilty for talking to my own sister tonight.

He started banging about in the kitchen and I moved as far away as I could to the window.

'Let him know that you really want to go through with this,' I continued.

'Go through with what?' Harvey looked up.

'Tell you later,' I said, unwilling to get into a three-way conversation.

'I will, I will,' Evie said vaguely. 'But I want to take the first steps on my own. I think once I've got that far, he'll see how much it means to me.'

'I'm sure he will,' I said, although secretly I wasn't convinced. My heart tweaked for them both. Darren would have made a good dad; it was so sad that they were at loggerheads.

'Hmm,' she said glumly, 'the last time we talked about it he said he didn't want to see a constant, ever-changing stream of kids come through our house, and also that he thought that fostering wasn't for me.'

'Why not?'

'He thinks I'll get too attached.' I heard the note of doubt in my sister's voice. Not easy given that Harvey was recreating the show *Stomp* that we'd seen last year with our saucepans and a ladle. 'That when it's time for the children to leave our house, I'll get upset. He said that I'd feel the loss too deeply.'

I bit my lip; Darren might have a good point there. I looked across to Harvey who was now dropping bananas into the smoothie maker. I thought about going into the bedroom so I could continue our conversation in peace, but he'd probably accuse me of keeping secrets from him or something silly.

'Anyway,' she said brightly, 'for now, I'm keeping my fingers crossed. It's so exciting, Lottie. Our little bedroom could have a child in it in only a few months. Imagine!'

Just then the harsh whirr of Harvey's smoothie maker

took over and neither of us could make ourselves heard. I promised to call her soon and finished the call.

'What's the latest?' said Harvey a couple of minutes later, wiping a yellow banana-y moustache from his upper lip. I crossed the room to the sink, picked up a cloth, wiped up the milk he'd spilled and put his banana skins into the bin.

'Evie's applying for them to be foster carers.'

'Jeez.' Harvey pulled a face. 'Has she lost the plot?'

'I think she'll be good at it,' I replied defensively, although secretly I thought the same as Darren: that Evie would miss the children terribly when they left her, worrying about what was going to happen to them next.

He looked repulsed. 'Who'd want to bring up somebody else's kids?'

'Luckily lots of people do,' I said, hiding my shock at his heartlessness. 'Although according to Evie not enough.'

'Not surprised,' he muttered. 'I wouldn't let strangers' kids into my house. You don't know what bad behaviour they might have picked up from their parents.'

'They're children, Harvey, who've probably had a difficult start in life,' I said. I don't know what made me say it, but suddenly I was fed up of his narrow-minded opinions. 'It's a lovely thing to do. I'd foster kids too if I couldn't have any of my own.'

He choked on his smoothie. 'You what?'

'Why not?' I shot him a cheeky smile as I whisked past him to take some turkey mince from the fridge but he tweaked my ponytail and stopped me in my tracks.

'Harvey!' I said, half-laughing. 'Let me go, I was only teasing.'

He wrapped my hair around his hand to pull me closer.

'Not funny.' As he spoke I could smell milk and banana and felt myself gag. I held my breath.

'Let me go, I feel ill,' I said shakily.

He narrowed his eyes. 'What's wrong with you? Time of the month? Do you feel sick?'

Sick of you behaving like this. I shook my head. 'Just a touch of stomach ache. And anyway, you're hurting me.'

'I'm sorry. Poor baby.' He kissed my cheek and released me. 'Hey, I picked up a flyer today for a new café opening this weekend. I thought we could go try the brunch menu on Sunday, what do you think? My treat.'

His face was full of remorse and he looked so eager to make up for his outburst; at moments like this, I saw the Harvey I fell in love with. Unfortunately, lately such moments were few and far between.

I swallowed the lump in my throat. 'That sounds lovely.'

'You know, it's probably stress,' he said, glancing at my stomach. 'You work too hard. Perhaps you should go part time? I can cover the rent on my wages, you know.'

I excused myself and went to the bathroom to splash water on my face. I couldn't mention my promotion tonight.

After work on Thursday I let myself into the flat, set my shopping in the kitchen and popped the bottle of Sauvignon Blanc in the fridge which the man in the supermarket assured me would best complement the sweetness of the pork on tonight's special menu. We didn't often have wine; Harvey was convinced it killed your brain cells. He mostly stuck to water and smoothies these days anyway, but I was pulling out all the stops this evening.

Before I started cooking I opened all the windows wide. The sky was heavy with thick dense cloud, the air was humid and the heat oppressive; a storm was coming. My stomach churned. There'd quite possibly be a storm in here tonight; I had to give my answer to Paula tomorrow. Either I was out of a job on Monday or I'd be the new grounds maintenance supervisor. Hence me making an effort with dinner. My plan was to show Harvey that me working didn't mean that I didn't have time for us.

I caught sight of myself in the mirror. My cheeks were more flushed than usual and there were dark smudges under my green eyes. My dark brown hair was escaping from the habitual ponytail I wore for work, a look that might suit some, but just made me look bedraggled. I hadn't had a hair-cut since I'd been in London and the ends were dry and split. Despite the suntan I'd got from being outside all day, I didn't look healthy; I looked tired and older than my thirty-two years. I felt tired too, and could have happily slid under the covers and slept for a week. I opened the little silver locket on the chain around my neck and looked at the photo of my parents taken on their wedding day.

'Oh Mum,' I said under my breath, 'I can't work out what I want any more. I've always wanted to find a man who loved me as much as Dad loved you. Harvey adores me, but . . .'

My voice tailed off. He did love me, I was sure of that, but I was beginning to wonder whether his love was conditional on me fitting in with his beliefs, opinions and plans. And the way he'd pulled my hair last night worried me. He hadn't hurt me, but there was something domineering about it that was disturbing.

'Anyway, Mum, don't worry about me, I'll sort it out.' I closed the locket and brought it to my lips where I kissed it. 'Tonight. No excuses.'

The storm broke as I was making the paprika fat-free yogurt accompaniment for the goulash that was already simmering gently on the hob. The sky had darkened to an eerie blue-grey glow. The thunder came first: a distant rum-ble which built to ear-splitting cracks directly overhead. Then the sky lit up, time and time again, illuminating the flat with flashes of brilliant white. Lastly came the rain, lashing down and blowing in through the open windows. I dashed across to shut them, marvelling at the monsoon conditions outside, and when I turned back round, Harvey had appeared, dripping wet and panting.

'I got drenched!' His T-shirt had stuck to him, water was running down his face and he was grinning broadly as he pulled off his trainers. 'I sprinted back. Really enjoyed pounding the pavements and powering through the rain. What a buzz!'

I handed him a towel, my heart leaping with joy to see him in such a good mood. 'You look very sexy,' I said, kissing him. 'And you smell of fresh rain.'

'I feel really alive.' He rubbed his hair and his face, his eyes sparkling, and he returned my kiss fiercely, wrapping his arms round my waist and dropping the towel to the floor. 'How long have we got until dinner?'

I reached a hand out and turned off the hob. 'As long as we want.'

'Good.' He scooped me up into his arms, making me squeal with laughter, and carried me to our bedroom. 'Because this could take a while.'

The evening couldn't have gone any better, I thought later on, gazing over at him as I handed him a plate of goulash.

We hadn't just made love, we'd laid in each other's arms, limbs entangled in the sheets, listening to the rain drumming against the window, just talking about nothing in particular. It had felt like the early days when he'd been so tender and attentive, seemingly captivated by every word I said. The rain stopped, but the sky had stayed dark and eventually our hunger had driven us from the bedroom.

'This smells fantastic,' said Harvey, bending down over his plate. He scooped up a spoonful of yogurt. 'And is this definitely fat-free?'

'Yep,' I said, pleased with my efforts. 'Would you like wine?'

I unscrewed the bottle and held it poised over a glass. He looked at it and wrinkled his nose.

'*White*? With goulash?' He gave me a pitying smile. 'Oh Lottie, I know you've tried, but the clue is in the paprika. You need something full-bodied to go with goulash.' He grinned slyly. 'Like yourself.'

'Hey!' I said, feigning mock affront when, in truth, I was a bit offended. I could have countered that I'd sought advice in the supermarket for the best wine to accompany our meal but there was no way I was going to let anything ruin the mood tonight. 'Nothing wrong with child-bearing hips.'

'I bet that was what Darren thought about your Evie; how wrong could he be?' Harvey sniggered.

I counted to five under my breath. 'So, do you want wine or not?'

'Go on then,' he said, sighing. He winked. 'You could have one too, seeing as you've burned off all those calories.'

I chose not to rise to the bait. I'd have been having a glass for Dutch courage with or without our bedroom workout.

'I intend to,' I said, pouring some for us both. 'I think we should celebrate all the small things in life.'

'What are you calling small?' said Harvey, waggling his eyebrows.

'I had a really good day at work today,' I said, ignoring his innuendo, and taking a seat beside him.

Harvey eyed my large glass of wine and then stood up and poured us both a glass of water. 'At a crematorium?' he said sceptically. 'I'll take your word for it.'

'A steel band came to play at the service for one of their own musicians. They played "Amazing Grace" on the drums as the congregation filed in. The sound was incredible. Everyone stopped to listen. Even Paula came out of her office to watch.' My eyes pricked with tears at the memory and I shook my head. 'It was such a celebration, so joyous. Then afterwards, Lisa came in. She's the one whose job I've been covering. She's better now and—'

'Good.' Harvey shovelled in a forkful of goulash. 'That means you'll be finished at that death camp.'

I cleared my throat. 'Actually—'

'I've had a good day too,' he went on, swigging his water and then sipping his wine. 'I was manning the gym's shop when this woman walked in, all fake tan and fingernails.

29

She ordered five hundred quid's worth of food supplements and vitamins. Five hundred! And then she bought a load of sports gear, said she needed a whole new wardrobe before she could come to the gym. Daft mare.'

'Gosh,' I widened my eyes. 'Imagine having that much spare cash.'

'Thanks to the commission on that lot, I will have a bit more cash,' said Harvey, smiling broadly. 'So I was thinking, I might volunteer to work in the shop more often and then I can start putting a bit away, start saving for our future.'

Bloody hell, he wasn't going to propose, was he? Not that marrying Harvey was such an awful proposition, obviously, I corrected myself, feeling my face heat up. He was hard-working, good-looking and so in love with me that he liked to keep me all for himself. How many women would love a bit more attention from their men?

'Save?' I said weakly, aware he was waiting for some sort of response.

He nodded. 'For a holiday later in the year. I thought maybe Scotland?'

'That's a lovely idea! And so romantic,' I said, a little over-eager with relief that wedding bells weren't on the cards after all. 'I've always wanted to see the mountains and the lochs.'

'Great.' He nodded as if that was settled. 'I can go fishing and you can, I don't know, read or something.'

No way was I going all the way to Scotland to witness my boyfriend standing up to his nether regions in a lake getting more and more angry when he didn't get a nibble. I'd gone fishing with him once and never again.

'Or,' I said slowly, 'why don't I help save up and we might even manage a holiday abroad?'

Harvey's face fell. 'So you *don't* want to go to Scotland?'

'It's ages since I've been on a plane,' I said. 'And we've never been abroad together. And from Monday, I've got the chance to earn a bit more too.'

'How come?' He frowned. 'You said that other woman was coming back.'

'I've been offered a promotion to supervisor!' I said brightly, despite the quiver from my insides. 'Isn't that good news?'

He clenched his jaw. 'Management? You've only been there five minutes. You're not even a qualified gardener. Who did you have to sweet talk to get that?'

'No one! Paula just offered it to me; I was as shocked as you on Monday when she—' I gulped as he narrowed his eyes.

'You've known for *three days*?' He looked down at his plate and pushed it away with a bark of laughter. 'Nothing says guilty conscience like a posh dinner and a bottle of wine. Trying to butter me up, were you?'

'Harvey, I don't need to butter you up.' I straightened my spine. 'I've been selected for this job – which, I hasten to add, I haven't accepted yet – based on my performance. I'm not the least bit guilty and it would be nice if you congratulated me instead of accusing me.'

'Well, congratulations,' he said sarcastically.

My gaze softened. 'Thank you. It came as such a surprise, nothing had been advertised and—'

He raised a hand. 'Sorry, but have you thought about how this makes me feel?' He stared at me. Both his fists were clenched so tightly that his knuckles were white. He'd never laid a finger on me, not really, but now he had a look of fury in his eyes and I was worried he could erupt at any second.

'I hoped you'd feel proud.' I slid my hand over his but he shook it off.

'I brought you to London to support me, to help me become a successful personal trainer, not to start building your own career behind my back. You make me look like a failure.'

'I do support you,' I said. 'Completely. You're not a failure at all; I believe in you. It takes time to build a reputation,

31

that's all. And I haven't done anything behind your back. I'm allowed a career too.'

'You've kept this a secret from me since Monday.' He stood up abruptly and scraped the remains of his dinner into the bin. 'I bet you've told your sister.'

I opened my mouth and the slight hesitation told him all he needed to know.

He nodded curtly, glanced around the kitchen for his phone and put it in his pocket. 'I'm going out.'

'Harvey, please, let's discuss this,' I said, clasping my hands together to stop them from shaking. 'I don't even know if I want the job. But the alternative is to have no job, to start again, register with the recruitment agencies and look for anything. Anywhere.'

He looked at me coldly. 'Do what you want. You usually do.'

After he'd gone I poured myself another glass of wine and contemplated ringing Evie or my dad and telling them what a predicament I'd got myself into. In the end, I decided against hearing their advice; this was something I needed to work out on my own. Instead, I sat in the dark, tears sliding down my cheeks, wondering what had happened to the bright and bubbly Lottie Allbright I used to be and when I'd become so weak. I pressed a hand to my heart; she was in there somewhere, I was sure, and maybe it was time to find her again.

Chapter 4

The next morning, the storm clouds had cleared and so had my head; I knew exactly what I would say to Paula: I needed to do the right thing for *me*.

When Mum died, I'd gladly given up my university place to be at home with Dad. When he started up the tree surgery business, I'd been happy to join him. We'd had fun, him and I, working together. Every year or so, he'd check that I didn't secretly wish I was doing something more exciting. I'd always assure him that I didn't. Then Harvey had come into my life and shaken it up like one of those little glass snow storms and changed everything. And although I'd never had a yearning to live in London, I'd been swept along with his zest for adventure and had happily followed him.

I got up for work, creeping around the bedroom as usual so as not to disturb Harvey, who'd reappeared around midnight last night worse for wear, crashed around in the bathroom, before collapsing in his boxer shorts on top of the bed. I paused, leaning on the door frame to study his face in slumber before I left. His forehead smooth, long lashes brushing his cheeks, his lovely full lips pouting slightly with every out breath; he looked serene and calm, no trace of the demon within that had become the third person in our relationship.

'Goodbye, Harvey,' I murmured.

I blew him a kiss he'd never know about and slipped from the flat down to the street below, still quiet at this hour, not even bothering with the pretence of taking my protein shake with me today.

By mid-morning, I was jittery and restless and barely able to concentrate on feeding and weeding the large rose bed; Paula had asked to see me at noon and I couldn't wait to get it over with. The centre of the bed was full of standard roses: tall and neat with their foliage pruned to maintain the perfect shape. They weren't my favourite, I liked the more free-spirited ramblers which climbed walls, found neighbours to mix with and searched for the sunniest aspect. I worked backwards with my hoe, turning over the soil, chopping the tiniest weeds with the blade and stooping every so often to yank out any larger offenders. I was straightening up when out of the corner of my eye I spotted the swish of bright fabric. A woman in her late fifties had settled on to a bench a few metres away, her hands clasped in her lap.

'Lovely morning, isn't it?' I said, turning to smile at her.

I never said more than that; in my experience, if visitors wanted to talk they would.

She wore a red polka-dot dress with a full skirt, matching nail varnish on fingers and toes, and high-heeled wedge sandals. Her glossy caramel-coloured hair hung in waves to her shoulders and although she was wearing sunglasses which covered a large part of her face, contentment radiated from her.

'Glorious,' she said, returning my smile. 'I love the sun. My late husband Raymond didn't. He liked winter. Says it all, really; we were chalk and cheese.'

She gave a self-conscious laugh and I turned back to my hoeing.

'I had that birdbath erected in his memory,' she said after a few moments.

I looked across to the bed of stone chippings dotted with alpine plants. To one side was an engraved stone column with a shallow dish on top of it.

'That's charming,' I said. 'I like the fact that there are lots of different textures in the garden. It means that there's always something to look at, whatever the season. And it's lovely to attract birds.'

'I chose it because it seemed fitting,' said the woman, smiling with mischief. 'Stone is hard and unyielding just like him; as opposed to a flower, which would bloom and grow and enjoy the sun. Also, he used to take pot-shots at the birds in our garden with his air rifle. I thought it was karma.'

There was clearly a story here, but it wasn't my place to ask questions, no matter how tempting it might be.

'This is my last visit to see him,' she said, standing up and coming closer. 'I've met someone else now. Someone who makes me happy. Raymond hadn't done that for a long time.'

She gazed into the distance, her smile gone.

'But you were happy once?' I said softly.

A look of pain flashed across her face. 'At first, yes . . . Do you know what a narcissist is?'

I leaned on the handle of the hoe. 'I think it's someone who only values their own opinion, who views the world in terms of how it affects them, am I right?'

She exhaled. 'They're a lot more dangerous than that. They tell you what you want to hear, they'll pursue you relentlessly and make you feel loved like no one else ever has. And once you return that love, bit by bit, day by day, they cut you off from your friends and family and from who you used to be, moulding you into the person they want you to be.'

I stared at her. That was almost the exact thought I'd had last night, when I'd wondered what had happened to the old me.

'At the time I didn't even notice it,' she continued. 'Or if I did, I loved him so much that I made excuses for his behaviour: mistaking his jealousy for love, telling myself that his controlling ways were simply because he wanted to care for me, do what was best for me.'

My heart rate began to gallop; this all sounded too familiar. Why had I never realized this about Harvey before? A single tear rolled down the woman's cheek. She wiped it away and I gave her a sympathetic smile.

'I'm so sorry,' I said, not sure what else I could say.

'I'd have loved to have had children, but every year he came up with another excuse: we couldn't afford it, he didn't want to share me with anyone, he'd booked us an exotic holiday which would be ruined if I was pregnant. And then I went through an early menopause when I was forty and the door closed on that dream for ever. For years I felt like I was simply existing instead of living.'

A shiver ran down my spine. Would this be me in the future? I took a fortifying breath and gritted my teeth. No it wouldn't, I decided, I wouldn't let it.

'Why didn't you leave him?' I asked without thinking.

She sucked in air sharply and then slid her sunglasses up to the top of her head to reveal pretty blue eyes with a lattice of fine lines at the corners.

'Forget I asked that,' I said, glancing over my shoulder on the off chance someone was in earshot. Asking that sort of question would not go down well with my boss. 'It's none of my business.'

She smiled sadly. 'It's fine. I tried to leave him, but I was never quite brave enough. I should have made a complete break, no lingering goodbyes, no contact. The trouble was both of our families lived close by; if I'd left him, I'd have been forced to leave my parents too. They were elderly, they couldn't have managed without me – nor me without them, really.'

I bit my lip, tears blurring my vision. 'That's so sad.'

She looked at me, startled. 'Hey, are you okay?'

I shook my head. 'You could have been describing my boyfriend just then. The controlling behaviour, the gradual cutting me off from my family. Like you, I've been making excuses for him. It's got to the point where I'm censoring everything I say and do.'

She looked at me appraisingly for a moment. 'That's not good. You poor love.'

'I haven't wanted to admit it to anyone, even myself, but I've just been existing too.' I rubbed my forearm across my face, wiping away the tears. 'I don't know what to do.'

'Okay; first, don't panic.' She took the hoe from my hand and led me back to the bench she'd been sitting on. 'Let's talk this through.'

I perched on the edge, conscious of the CCTV. 'I'm sorry, you've come here to pay your respects, you shouldn't be—'

She shook her head. 'Nonsense. I'm glad to help. I'm Vicky, by the way.'

'Lottie.'

'Do you have children, Lottie?' She handed me a tissue from her handbag.

'Thank you.' I dabbed my eyes. 'No. Thank heavens. He'd probably resent my relationship with a child. He's jealous of everyone I come into contact with.'

She sighed. 'That does sound like Raymond. Do you have family nearby?'

I shook my head. 'I'm from Derbyshire. We came down here last year for his work but I miss my dad and my sister very much.'

She laughed but it was without humour. 'Let me guess: he doesn't like them to visit and complains if you contact them?'

I pulled a face. 'He doesn't encourage it.'

She listened silently while I went on to tell her about Evie's one and only visit. We'd planned that she'd come down on the train on Saturday morning and stay until after lunch on Sunday. But when I told Harvey, he claimed that he'd got theatre tickets for Saturday night as a surprise because he'd assumed Evie would only be here for a day. Besides, the flat was so small, he'd argued, there wasn't room for her. I'd waved that away, confident that Evie wouldn't mind a night on the sofa. I was delighted that he'd bought the tickets, it was so thoughtful of him. But I made the mistake of suggesting that she and I take the tickets seeing as it was her first trip to London to visit me. He'd been mortally offended that I didn't want to go with him and it had taken me three days to persuade him otherwise. In the end, Evie came for the day and Harvey took me to see *Stomp* that night. It had been good, but all the way through I couldn't help thinking how sad it was that my sister had been forced to cut her trip short.

Vicky frowned thoughtfully. 'How would you feel about giving up this job?'

I laughed half-heartedly. 'Harvey would love it.'

She looked at me sternly. 'Forget his opinion. I'm asking you.'

I blinked at her; she was right. I'd got into the habit of always considering what Harvey would think about something before I allowed myself to consider my own feelings. I felt disgusted with my own weakness.

Vicky patted my hand. 'I can tell by your face what's going through your mind. But stop blaming yourself. Harvey has had a lifetime of practising this behaviour; you're only just learning his tricks.'

I nodded. 'You're right and actually today's my last day doing this job.'

I explained about the promotion and the agony I'd had deciding whether to take it or not. When I finished, Vicky blew out a breath.

'Okay. Two minutes ago, you asked me what you should do,' she said firmly. 'I'll tell you, but it's going to take bravery.'

I nodded. 'This is the mad thing, I've always been quite brave, you should see me up a tree with a chainsaw.'

Vicky laughed. 'I like your spirit. Okay, listen, it's easy to give advice; it's much harder to take it. But if I was in your shoes, I'd go. Today. As soon as you can.'

My eyes widened. 'Seriously? Leave the flat and him and just . . . disappear?'

'Yes. Don't hang around to give him long explanations, just go, he won't let you leave him without putting up a fight, he'll do everything in his power to win back your love. So don't give him the opportunity. Cut off all ties, block him from your phone, move back to your family. Cold turkey.'

My heart started to thump. I'd been planning on accepting the promotion. I knew I could do it and I wanted to show Harvey that I wouldn't be bullied into turning it down, even if it would make life uncomfortable while he got used to the idea. But the job would be permanent and I'd have to give a month's notice if I wanted to leave. Whereas today . . .

'I could do my last shift, catch an evening train and be back in Fernfield before he even knew I'd gone,' I said softly. On Fridays, Harvey started work at noon and didn't finish until eight. Plenty of time. If that was what I wanted.

Vicky touched my arm. 'Lottie, the easiest course of action would be to stay exactly as you are and accept that this is just the way he is. Is that what you want?'

I shook my head. I deserved more than that.

'Thank you, Vicky,' I said, giving her a hug. 'You've given me the courage I needed.'

'I'm so glad,' she said, patting my back. 'One last thing: before this all has a chance to blur in your mind, write down the reasons why you left him, so if you're tempted to come back, or if he comes looking for you, you'll have something to remind you why you mustn't. Ever.'

I nodded and then shuddered with dread; I wouldn't put

it past Harvey to try to get me to change my mind, he never liked to lose at anything. 'Right, I'd better go and tell my boss what I've decided.'

Vicky smiled and stood up, pulling me to my feet. 'That would be my sister, Paula. I'll come with you. She hated Raymond so much she almost banned me from sprinkling his ashes here. When she hears about Harvey, she'll understand; in fact, I'll go as far as to say she'll help as much as she can.'

I shook my head in amazement; today was getting odder and odder. 'I feel like I've met my fairy godmother!'

Vicky was right: half an hour later, Paula had sorted out my employment paperwork and had decided to give me the rest of the afternoon off as a farewell gift. She'd been brilliant about me turning down the promotion and agreed with her sister that the sooner I got out of my toxic relationship the better.

I left her on the phone to a recruitment agency to advertise for a new supervisor and Vicky walked me to the exit.

'Thanks for listening,' I said, giving her a last hug. 'I thought I was going crazy. I thought I was being oversensitive. You've helped me make sense of it all.'

'It's weird, you know,' she said, looking puzzled. 'I hadn't planned to come to the crematorium today, but something propelled me here. I just couldn't get away from the idea that I needed to come. I think it was to see you. To stop you making the same mistakes I did.'

'I'm glad we met.' My hands were shaking as she took them in hers. 'I'm sick with nerves, to be honest, but now I've made the decision, I just want to get on with it.'

Her gaze held mine. 'Living, *really living*, is about more than just breathing in and out. You have to make each breath, each moment count. Life really is too short to merely exist. Do this for you. And for me.'

'I will,' I said. 'Enjoy the rest of your life with your new man.'

'I intend to,' she said with a coy smile. 'And don't let Harvey put you off men for too long, they're not all the same, you know.'

True, they weren't all the same, I thought, as I hurried away from the crematorium for the last time. But I wasn't interested in heading into another relationship any time soon; I had a feeling it would be tricky enough extricating myself from this one.

My legs felt shaky on the walk from the tube station to the flat and my stomach was in knots as I weighed up my next move. I was heading back to Fernfield, that was a given, but did I ring Evie or Dad and warn them, which would unleash a torrent of questions, or should I just turn up and tell them the news when I got there? A simple text message this afternoon might work best, I decided, that way I could let them know I was on my way but still keep it brief.

I'd text Dad, tell him I'd got a couple of days off and was paying him a flying visit. That should do it. I pulled my phone out of my bag and found that there was a missed call from him plus a text from Evie.

So last night I confessed to Darren that I'd been looking into fostering. I told him how much it means to me to be a mum. He said I'd be a great mum but it wasn't for him. I might have said that he was being selfish. He disagreed saying he wasn't going to stand in my way and it was better if we split up. So he's moved out and gone to stay at a mate's. So that went well. Please don't me call back, I can't talk about it just yet without sobbing xxx

Oh God. Poor Evie. What a nightmare. Was this my fault? I'd been the one urging her to tell him the truth. I felt sick at the thought. I texted her back.

My darling girl, I'm so, so sorry. I'm coming home. Sending massive hugs and see you soon xxx

There's no need, I'm better off alone x

I'm coming anyway

Thank heavens

I wondered if that was what Dad was calling about and called him next.

'Hello, love! Lunch break?'

I hesitated. 'Sort of. Is everything okay? How's Evie?'

'Evie?' He sounded confused, which meant he didn't know yet. 'Fine, I think. Now, I'll keep this brief as you're on your mobile.'

'It's fine, Dad, honestly.' He was always convinced that calls to mobiles cost an arm and a leg.

'If you say so,' he said warily. 'It's just that Adam has proposed to his girlfriend.'

'That's great!' This was lovely news; Adam was Dad's new business partner and his girlfriend Nicky was the receptionist at the village doctor's surgery.

'They both still live at home at the moment but they've decided to move in together,' Dad continued.

'Okay.' I waited for him to get to the punchline, he would never normally call to update me on this sort of stuff.

'And they've asked to rent our house – I mean, my house – while I'm on my travels.'

'Oh. That's good.'

My spirits sank. I hadn't got as far as thinking about my living arrangements, but somewhere in the back of my head, I'd thought maybe Dad would let me live there while he was away.

There was a pause on the line.

'So now I can get going sooner than I thought. I've

planned a route, bought some travel books and . . . Well, you don't need to know all that.'

'I'm happy for you Dad, really. And I think Mum would be really proud of you for going.'

I'd turned into our street now and without realizing it I was walking close to the buildings, staying in the shadows, pressing myself into doorways just in case Harvey hadn't gone to work for some reason. Which was ridiculous because Harvey had never had a day off sick since I'd known him.

'Thanks, love. The thing is, I need to clear your room to put everything in storage. Is there anything you particularly want sending on, or can I box it all up?'

My heart leapt; if I'd needed another sign to convince me that leaving London today was the right thing to do, this would have been it.

'Tell you what, Dad, I'll do it myself.'

'What? There's no need to do that. Besides, I don't have time to hang about. Adam and Nicky want to move in on Monday.'

'Then I'll come tonight. No arguments, I want to. I'll text you when I know what time the train gets in.'

'Excellent! Well, if you're sure?'

'I'm sure,' I said, growing more confident by the second. 'See you later.'

A flicker of excitement warmed my insides as I turned my key in the door and found the flat empty just as it should be. It was really happening.

It only took me ten minutes to pull my two suitcases from under the bed and stuff my belongings into them. It took me twice as long to compose a kind but firm letter to Harvey.

Dear Harvey,

I have come to a very difficult decision to end our relationship and leave London. I know that my decision will hurt you and you will be disappointed that I'm writing this down and leaving without telling you but I want to explain my reasons why.

For a while now I've felt that things between us haven't been right and I've felt pressured into doing things your way: behaving in a certain way to please you, avoiding speaking to my family when you're around, even eating and drinking things you approve of. This week, your reaction to our conversation about fostering and the way you lost your temper when I told you about my promotion upset me. You are a big strong man and when you get mad, it frightens me.

The last six months have been an adventure. You've taken me out of my comfort zone and I'll always be grateful to you for that. Living in London is great for you. With your energy and enthusiasm and irrepressible drive, I know your business will be a great success.

But you have such an assertive personality that sometimes I've felt swallowed up by you and your plans and lately I've lost a sense of myself and what I want out of life. Since the crematorium gave me the chance of promotion, I've realized that a permanent life in London isn't for me. I'm a country girl at heart. I'm used to space and quiet, where people know me and I can feel part of a community. I want to build a home, somewhere peaceful, where I can feel safe and loved and that's not going to happen here, with you.

I'll always remember the good times we had together and I wish you every happiness for the future. I hope that you can find someone else who

shares your dreams, but I know that that person can never be me.
  With love
  Lottie x

I left the letter, along with my door key, on the kitchen work surface next to the fridge where I knew he'd go first. And then, before I could change my mind, I transferred my cases to the communal hallway and closed the door firmly behind me.

Goodbye, London; I was going home.

Chapter 5

I passed through many tiny stations on my way home, but none as pretty as Fernfield, I thought, smiling at the guard who kindly handed my cases down to me. Colourful hanging baskets were dotted along the platform, trailing braids of purple petunias, gaudy geraniums and wispy ivy. Glass window panes were sparkling, the wrought-iron benches and railings were painted to glossy perfection, and in pride of place, on the wall outside the ticket office, was a shiny plaque commemorating a visit by Prince Charles when he was on one of his 'Aren't British farmers just the bees' knees?' campaigns.

But it wasn't the quaint features of the station that caught my attention this evening; it was the sight of Evie and Dad standing near the exit.

As soon as Evie saw me she dashed forward. 'Lottie!' she yelled.

My sister had inherited Mum's build: petite, dainty and as slender as a blade of summer barley. Her chin-length blonde bob perfectly framed an elfin face from which shone huge, intelligent eyes. Now, though, her eyes were red-rimmed and puffy.

She flung herself at me and almost suffocated me with the strength of her hug and I could feel every notch in her spine. She'd been through so much, and I hadn't been there for her. I'd make up for it, I vowed silently, hit by a fierce rush of love for her.

'It is so good to see you,' I said, returning her embrace. 'I'm so sorry about you and Darren.'

'Don't.' She mimed zipping her lips. 'Not yet. But you couldn't have come at a better time. I really need my sister right now.'

'Ditto,' I said, swallowing the lump in my throat. 'Does Dad know?'

She grimaced. 'Told him on the way here. Poor bloke almost cancelled his trip. I hope I've convinced him I'll be fine.'

We pulled back to look at each other at the same time; both of us had tears sparkling in our eyes.

'Will you?' I asked.

'Eventually,' she said huskily. 'Something needed to happen, it's been like living in a pressure cooker in our house for the last couple of months. I'm just sad that the "something" had to be us splitting up.'

Her gaze lowered to my two large suitcases, which by anybody's standards were excessive for a flying visit. She looked quizzically at me but before she could ask questions, Dad wrapped his arms around both of us. I'd inherited Dad's height and dark hair, but luckily not his broad-shouldered, muscular frame, although there was a lot more of me than Evie.

'Is this a private teary reunion, or can anyone join in?' he said, giving us whiskery kisses and tickling us with his wiry beard. We giggled and wriggled away, just as he'd known we would, as we'd been doing for the last thirty-odd years.

Finally, we broke apart. Dad picked up both my cases and Evie insisted on carrying my handbag to his van, which was parked in the waiting zone outside the station.

'Now, seeing as I've got both my girls to myself for a change,' he said, once we were all belted up in the front of the van, 'I'll treat you to dinner. It's either back home for sardines on toast or down to the pub for fish and chip Friday.'

'Oh God,' said Evie with a shudder. 'Pub. No contest. Besides, I need a drink.'

'Me too,' I added, and the relief at being back in Fernfield hit me with such force that I had to stare out of the window and take a few deep breaths.

The Royal Oak was always busy on a Friday night, but we placed our order, managed to find a reasonably quiet table and sat down with our drinks. I was feeling utterly drained by the events of the day and my head was starting to ache, so I only ordered water in the end. I was feeling nauseous too, partly due to hunger, but also due to the ticking time bomb in my stomach that was on countdown to when Harvey arrived home to find me gone.

I needed to find the right moment to tell them that I was back for the foreseeable future, but first I wanted to know more about the situation between Evie and Darren. I waited until Dad went to the loo and took Evie's hand.

'Do you want to talk about it?' I murmured, holding her gaze.

She groaned and gulped at her wine.

'I'm just going to blurt it out quickly, okay? Because I'm permanently this close to tears.' She demonstrated with a tiny gap between her thumb and forefinger.

I nodded encouragingly as Evie began to tell me what had happened.

She said last night she'd tried to explain how she felt to Darren: that a part of her was missing, that if she hadn't had the miscarriage she'd have been a mum by now and that she didn't think she'd ever stop grieving for the baby they'd lost, but that she still wanted motherhood – parenthood – to be part of their future. Darren couldn't even discuss it.

'He just clammed up,' she said briskly, blinking away her tears. 'He said he didn't feel the same and that if that was what I wanted he wasn't going to stand in my way. And then he packed a bag and I watched him leave, thinking that maybe this was the only logical next step.'

'I'm so sorry.' I swallowed the lump in my throat, not wanting to set her off in public. 'And how do you feel now?'

She blinked mournful big eyes at me. 'Exhausted, shell-shocked. But there's a sort of relief in things coming to a head. We couldn't continue as we were.'

'Fish and chips?' The waitress hovered over us with brimming plates and set them down just as Dad came back. Evie and I plastered on smiles, passed the condiments around and the conversation bumbled along for a few minutes while we tucked into our food.

'Thanks for coming home at such short notice,' said Dad, sprinkling more salt over his chips.

I felt the familiar prickle of rashy heat at my neck. 'Actually, there are some things I need to tell you about me and Harvey.'

Evie looked up sharply. 'Go on.'

And I told them how happy Harvey and I had been when we'd first moved to London. How much fun we'd had setting up home together. And then, as time went by, how his love had turned from affection to possession and he'd started to become suspicious of everyone I spoke to, jealous of anyone I spent time with other than him, and that he'd tried to persuade me not to see my family. In fact, all he wanted was to keep me for himself, preferably in the flat 24/7. I didn't tell them his negative views on Evie's decision to become a foster mum, that wouldn't achieve anything. Besides I could see from their faces, they'd already heard enough to change their opinions of him.

When I ran out of words there was a moment's stunned silence around the table. Finally, Evie reached across and hugged me tight.

'You poor lamb,' she said in a low voice. 'I'm so sorry you've been through that on your own.'

I smiled sadly. 'You've had enough to deal with without me adding to your problems.'

'I'll be fine.' She pressed her lips together and began to pleat her napkin. 'And anyway, I'd never be too busy to talk to you.'

Dad looked at us both and an expression of worry flashed across his face. Poor Dad. Two daughters in their thirties, both with man troubles, and him about to leave the country.

'Well, he had me fooled; I thought you'd found yourself a gentleman and that you were having a great time in London.' Dad sat back in his upholstered chair, frowning. 'I feel a right idiot for not noticing anything.'

'Me too,' I said, my voice shaky with relief that they'd believed me without question.

'He was lovely when you first met him,' said Evie. 'Even Darren said so, and he doesn't give praise lightly. We were all taken in.'

I noticed how naturally she dropped Darren's name into conversation. I hoped with all my heart that the spark between them was still alive. I had no intention of interfering, but now I was back, I was going to monitor that spark and if I did see an opportunity to fan the flames, I would do so.

Dad patted Evie's hand and sighed. He was very fond of Darren; I knew it must be hard for him to stand by and witness their break-up.

'You're well rid,' Evie added in disgust.

'I read up about narcissists on the train. Apparently that's their MO. They love-bomb you to start with, and once you trust them they gradually start wearing you down, undermining your confidence until you're so unsure of yourself that they can swoop in and control you.'

Evie shivered. 'Sounds horrific.'

'It wasn't all bad,' I said wistfully, thinking back to some of the happy times we'd had in London in the early days: our weekend jaunts to stroll round markets, brunch in Covent Garden watching street entertainers, boat trips along the Thames . . . fun touristy things. Harvey had been good company then, a little possessive at times, but I'd been too in love to notice.

Dad made a growling noise. 'And to think I encouraged you to go off with him.'

'I'd have gone anyway,' I said, squeezing his hand. 'I was totally smitten, I thought he was "the one". But he wasn't and now I'm home again.'

'Well, I feel sick to my stomach.' He frowned. 'I wish I hadn't ordered apple crumble now, I don't think I could eat another thing.'

I hid a smile as I looked at Dad's plate scraped clean: he'd demolished an extra-large cod, chips and peas before hoovering up my leftover chips and most of Evie's dinner. She hadn't done much more than push hers around.

'There've been a few times I'd suspected that you weren't happy.' Evie propped her elbows on the table. 'I could kick myself for not probing deeper. But I kept thinking that if anything was wrong you'd tell me.'

I picked up my glass and swirled the lemon slice around in my water. 'It took me a long time to realize that there was something wrong.'

'You've done the hardest part in leaving him, love,' said Dad, sipping his shandy. 'You can put it behind you and move on.'

'Absolutely,' I said with more confidence than I felt. It was eight o'clock; another half an hour and Harvey would be at the flat reading my note. I sneaked my hand into my bag, pulled out my phone and switched it to silent, setting it down on the table. 'All I need to do is find somewhere to live and a new job.'

'I'll drink to that.' Evie chinked her wine against my sparkling water and then against Dad's glass.

'If I'd known sooner, I'd have taken the house off the rental market and you could have moved back in,' said Dad.

I shook my head. 'You're counting on the rent to fund your trip.'

He dismissed that with a wave of his hand. 'Do you want me to tell Adam that he can't have the house? I'm sure he'd understand.'

Just then there was the sound of a champagne cork popping, followed by cheering and a round of applause. The three of us looked round to see Adam and Nicky surrounded by a circle of friends being toasted with full glasses of bubbly.

Evie winced. 'Although it would be a shame to rain on their parade.'

'Exactly. We can't let them down,' I agreed. 'It's not their fault I'm homeless.'

'Don't be daft.' Evie rolled her eyes at me. 'You can move in with me.'

I told her that I'd like that very much and then as we'd all finished our drinks, I nipped off to the bar to get another round in. When I returned, Dad was tucking into his pudding with gusto.

'Look at the two of us,' said Evie with a sigh, accepting a second drink from me. 'Spending Friday night with our dad, single again at our age. What a pair of saddos. I wonder what Mum would think of us.'

'Oi,' said Dad through a mouthful of crumble, waving his spoon at her. 'You make me sound like the consolation prize.'

'Not at all,' I said, wiping up the blobs of custard he'd dripped on the table. 'And above all Mum would just want us to be happy, whether we were single or not.'

'Of course she would. Like me.' Dad scraped the bowl clean. 'Single and happy.'

I shot Evie a knowing look. We'd suggested various women to him over the years, but he'd never been interested. I thought about Vicky earlier at the crematorium who'd had a second chance at love; perhaps it was simply a case of meeting the right person at the right time?

'I met a lovely lady today,' I said. 'She was a bit younger than you, Dad.'

'Single?' Evie asked, nodding unsubtly at him.

I shook my head. 'She's met someone. But she had been part of an unhappy couple. Actually, she gave me the push I needed to leave Harvey. She said that this time around she was going to make every moment count.'

'To making every moment count, good on her,' said Dad, raising his glass. 'You never know, perhaps I'll meet a sultry senorita in Spain.'

'Or a foxy frau in Frankfurt,' Evie put in.

'If you did,' I said more seriously, 'that would be all right with us, wouldn't it, Evie?'

'Absolutely. You deserve to be happy, Dad,' she agreed.

He set down his glass and leaned in closer. 'See that chap with the thin blond hair at the corner table over there near the fruit machine?'

We looked round to see who he meant.

'What about him?' Evie asked.

'Laurie, his name is. Had three wives and as for girlfriends – I think even he's lost count of how many he's had; he's always got a different woman on his arm. Now this spot just here.' He pointed to his left bicep. 'That was where your mum tucked her arm. Never the right. We'd walk with our hands clasped together, tucked into the big pocket of my Barbour coat. Snug as bugs. It wouldn't feel right having someone else on that arm. Like her side of the bed. I still look across some mornings and expect to see her.'

My throat constricted with a surge of emotion and, by my side, Evie picked up her napkin and blew her nose. Mum and Dad's love story never failed to move us.

'A love like that doesn't come along twice in a lifetime,' he said firmly. 'That would be too lucky.'

He was probably right; it hadn't come along at all for me.

At eight thirty-two my phone buzzed into life, vibrating against my unused spoon. Harvey's name flashed up on the screen.

'It's him,' I said, my heart pounding. 'He'll have read my note by now.'

Evie scowled. 'Don't answer it.'

'I'm not going to,' I said shakily. I tried to picture his face. Would he be upset or angry? I wondered. Or maybe he hadn't taken it seriously and thought I'd come back after I'd cooled down? Maybe he thought I was still in London at a friend's, although, thanks to his jealousy, I hadn't really made any friends. 'I've said all there is to say in my letter.'

'I've got plenty to say to him,' Dad muttered. 'Pass it here.'

'No, Dad.' I sent the call to voicemail. 'I've dealt with it. And you speaking to him would only make things worse. Let him sleep on it tonight and he'll calm down tomorrow.'

Which was about as likely as Eeyore winning the Grand National.

Dad harrumphed but let it go.

My phone screen lit up again: *You have one new voicemail message*.

We left the pub shortly afterwards and by the time I'd gone up for an early night a couple of hours later, the number of new voicemail messages stood at thirteen. I turned my phone off completely so it couldn't disturb me with its angrily flashing screen. Something told me Harvey wasn't taking the news very well at all.

Chapter 6

'This is it, then,' said Dad, giving us each a last hug and a whiskery kiss before climbing into the cab of his two-berth motorhome.

It was early on Tuesday morning, the three days I'd been back in Fernfield had flown by and already it was time for Dad to leave. He was dressed for his travels in shorts which he'd had for at least a decade and a straw trilby with a bent brim. His T-shirt was soft with age, but at least it didn't have any holes; we had a pile of those in Evie's garage bound for the tip. He started up the engine and raised a hand. 'Take care of yourselves, girls.'

'We will. Bye, Dad!' I blew kisses from the pavement, trying to ignore the empty passenger seat next to him.

'Remember to text us when you get to Dover,' said Evie, wagging a finger at him.

'Then again when you get to France,' I added.

His eyebrows flew up. 'And how much is that going to cost me from abroad?'

'You can't put a price on peace of mind,' Evie said sternly.

He chuckled and with a toot of the horn he pulled away from the kerb. And so began the grand tour of Europe which he and Mum had been planning all their married life. Evie and I waved and waited until the van was out of view.

'Bless him,' I murmured. 'I hope he'll be okay.'

'I've half a mind to run off and join him.' Evie sighed.

'The thought of escaping normal life for a while is hugely appealing.'

'*Normal*?' I arched a sceptical eyebrow. 'Where did you get that crazy idea from?'

'Good point.' She laughed softly and looped her arm through mine, leading us back inside.

We'd spent the weekend blitzing our family home. Dad had been clearing out in preparation for his trip for a while but there had still been plenty to do. Adam and Nicky were renting the house furnished, so we hadn't had to do anything with the furniture or appliances, thank heavens, but there had still been masses to load when the lorry arrived on Monday to take everything else to a storage unit on a nearby industrial estate.

Evie had been working, but I'd been on hand to help get Dad organized. He was understandably excited that the day was finally here, but I found it weird seeing the house stripped of all the little things that had made it home. Still, I didn't have time to dwell: Adam and Nicky were waiting further along the road with both sets of parents and three cars' worth of belongings and no sooner had the lorry trundled off than they pulled up on to the drive.

I'd transferred my two suitcases to Evie's spare room and Dad spent his first night in the motorhome, parked outside her house. It had been lovely being back with my family. I'd forgotten how easy life could be when you could speak your mind without having to censor it first for fear of someone misinterpreting the most innocuous of sentences.

Not that the last few days had been entirely without tension. Harvey had made his presence felt with numerous messages and texts, ranging from declarations of love and how he just wanted his favourite girl home to tearful pleadings for forgiveness, topped off last night with a furious rant that ended in 'GOOD RIDDANCE'.

I hadn't spoken to him once, but after that last message, I sent him one back.

Harvey, I'm sorry you're upset, but I've made my decision and I'm sticking to it. I've transferred some money to cover my half of the bills for this month and next, and now I'm blocking your number from my phone. I think it's for the best. I wish you well. Lottie

In truth, I wasn't entirely sure how much our monthly bills were; Harvey had put everything in his name, insisting I didn't want to be bothered with the details. Looking back, I should have seen this as another sign of his desire to control me, but at least he'd inadvertently made it easier for me to leave. After pressing send, I'd quickly added his number to my 'blocked callers' list and after that, Dad, Evie and I had been able to enjoy our last night together in peace.

'I ache all over from all the lifting and carrying I've done this weekend,' I groaned, circling my shoulders. 'My legs, my arms, my stomach – everything aches.'

'I think you need to relax for a few days now. You've been through a lot,' said Evie, eyeing me closely. 'And for someone who's been working outside for months, you look very pale to me.'

'I'm still sick with worry about Harvey,' I said, closing the front door behind us. 'And I can't shift this headache – I've had it since leaving London.'

'Hmm,' she said, frowning as we both gravitated to the kitchen. 'And did I hear you being sick last night?'

'I don't know. Did you?' I said flippantly.

I opened the back door to let the sunshine in and she began stacking the breakfast things into the dishwasher.

'I'd forgotten how annoying you can be.' She leaned against the sink and folded her arms. 'So what is it, a bug maybe?'

I had been sick several times over the last few days. But it was hardly surprising given the stress I was under. Plus, the two scones with clotted cream that our old neighbour had

baked for Dad as a going-away present hadn't helped. Dad had wolfed down three but Evie hadn't touched them.

'I'll be fine. You're probably right; I just need to relax. While we're on the subject of appearances,' I said, 'I've noticed you haven't been eating much and I think you've lost weight. Not that you've got any to lose.'

She gave me a wan smile. 'I've lost my appetite since Darren moved out.'

My heart went out to her. I was absolutely certain that finishing with Harvey was the right thing to do, but it was obvious that Evie still loved her husband. 'You don't think it's worth speaking to him again?' I suggested.

She shook her head. 'I've brought this on myself. We've been talking about our options ever since we found out that we had less chance of conceiving naturally than we had of winning the lottery. He refused point-blank to adopt, so I thought fostering might suit us: less of a commitment because if it didn't work out, we could stop at any time. He said no to that too. But I was convinced I could talk him round. I thought I'd call his bluff by telling him I was going ahead with fostering with or without him. I thought . . .' Her voice wavered and her blue eyes swam behind a layer of tears. 'I thought if he knew how much it meant to me, he'd cave in and agree. Turns out he'd prefer the "without" option too.'

I handed her a sheet of kitchen paper and she blotted her eyes. 'And now you're having doubts about fostering on your own?'

She wrinkled her nose. 'A bit. But I think it's the only way. Darren's made his feelings very clear. I want to comfort a child, read them bedtime stories, be waiting for them at the school gates to hear their news. I'm just going to have to accept that, to do that, I'll have to be a single mum. Do you think I'm being selfish?'

'Of course not.' I wrapped my arms around her thin shoulders. Although secretly I did think she needed to let

the dust settle on their separation before she made any major new plans. 'I'm just so sad for you. *And* Darren.'

Motherhood, for me, felt like a long way off. I was an old-fashioned romantic. I wanted the full works: the big romance, the down-on-one knee proposal and then, once we were married, I assumed we'd start thinking about a future that had children in it. I'd thought Harvey was my big romance; turned out he was my big mistake. Still, it was over now. It would take me a while to get over him and in the meantime, I could be here for Evie.

'It's great having you back,' she said, as if reading my thoughts. She rested her head against me. 'It's distracted me from missing him.'

'Well, I'm not going anywhere for a while and I'm going to look after you,' I said, pressing a kiss to her hair and releasing her. 'Starting with breakfast. You only had coffee when Dad and I ate. You'll need your strength if you're going to take on some foster kids. I can't imagine it'll be the easiest thing in the world.'

I slotted bread into the toaster for her and guided her to a chair. She took out her phone and scrolled through her emails while I laid out the butter and jam.

'I'm going to have to start work after this, I'm afraid,' she said.

'I'll make myself scarce. Take a walk around the village for an hour or so.'

She looked up and caught me rubbing my stomach. 'Just a thought, but why don't you register with the GP's surgery while you're out?'

I didn't need a doctor; no pill would take away the anxiety Harvey had caused. But it would be a chance to say hello to one half of Dad's new tenants: Nicky the receptionist. 'Why not?' I said. 'And I'll check Adam and Nicky haven't had any teething problems.'

Chapter 7

We were well into June now and the village was looking at its summery best. The grass verges were green, cottage gardens were a riot of colour, from poppies to peonies, and multi-coloured bunting zigzagged across the main street.

Fernfield was a large village on the fringes of the famous Chatsworth estate. It was peppered with charming gift shops selling everything from quirky mugs and locally made honey to beautiful woollen throws and cushions. It was a popular stop-off point for tourists as part of a day trip to Chatsworth House; consequently, the village was vibrant and bustling.

We were also lucky enough to have traditional shops serving our community, like the bakery, butcher and greengrocer, family-run businesses that had been here for generations. Of course, we still had a supermarket and a deli, several pubs, coffee shops and tea rooms, just like every other high street, but there was something special about Fernfield. If you squinted to block out some of the brighter signage, it wasn't difficult to imagine how it would have looked a hundred years ago. At the very heart of the village was a crossroads. Turn one way and you'd be in the market square: a cobbled, pedestrianized area which hosted different vendors every day. The farmers' market on a Friday, antiques on Sundays and second-hand books on Mondays; there was always something going on. Turn the other way and you found yourself in a narrow street, home to a lovely Italian restaurant, a pretty stone church set in its own tree-lined grounds and the flat-roofed doctors' surgery, which was my destination.

I headed down the street and was about to cross the car park when a vehicle pootled past me and pulled into the disabled bay nearest to the entrance. The driver yanked on the handbrake so firmly I heard it from the gates.

An old lady, slim built with fine white hair perfectly swept into a chignon, climbed out of the passenger side. She was elegantly dressed in a blouse, skirt and neat shoes with a gold buckle at the front. She made her way slowly around the back of the car, trailing a hand on the bodywork and opened the boot. As I drew level with her, I noticed she was trying to lift out a wheelchair.

'Can I give you a hand?' I asked.

The old lady turned. She had grey-blue eyes and although they were a little filmy with age, they were flecked with amber. She had a commanding presence now; she must have been a stunner in her younger days.

'Is that you, Pippa?' she asked, squinting at me. 'Your face has filled out a bit since I last saw you.'

'No, it's not, I'm afraid,' I replied, trying not to feel envious of Pippa's well-defined cheekbones. Whoever she was. 'We haven't met before.'

'Then kindly move along,' she said imperiously. 'Why the young assume that the more experienced generation can't execute the simplest of tasks without their input is beyond me.'

That was me told.

'I'm sorry, I was only trying to help,' I said, wishing I hadn't bothered.

Just then the driver's door opened with a creak and two exceedingly stiff and swollen legs, one with a large dressing on the shin, emerged clad in the most hideous pair of black shoes I'd ever seen.

'Perhaps she offered because she can see you've got arms like twiglets, Betsy,' said the owner of the legs.

The feet reached the floor and a short woman shuffled her bottom to the edge of her seat. She was wearing a pair of beige shorts which possibly could have been standard army issue in the days of the Raj and a polyester lavender blouse displaying an impressive stripe of what looked like egg yolk all down the front. Her hair was a mass of steel frizz and she had a mole on her chin of Nanny McPhee proportions but her eyes sparkled with mischief and she was wearing the biggest grin. To say they were an unlikely couple was an understatement.

With a series of grunts, she began to manoeuvre her generous frame out of the seat. I wanted to offer assistance but I'd already had my head bitten off once.

'Don't get out yet, Marjorie, for heaven's sake!' called Betsy in a shrill voice. 'I don't want to be scraping you up off the tarmac.'

Marjorie winked at me and rolled her eyes comically. 'Then let this young lady help you. The surgery will have closed by the time you've fiddled about.'

'Well, there's gratitude for you,' said Betsy, nonetheless standing aside to give me access. 'Anyway, it's scarcely nine. The place has only just opened.'

I lifted the collapsed wheelchair out of the boot. It was lighter than I'd expected. I set it down and tried to work out how to unfold it.

'Gratitude!' Marjorie hooted with laughter. 'It's not me who needs looking after.'

'That's quite enough airing of laundry in public,' Betsy cut in, putting a firm hand under her friend's arm.

I found the catch at the back of the wheelchair and released it.

'Thank you, dear,' said Marjorie, huffing and puffing as Betsy lowered her gently into the seat.

'I'll take it from here,' said Betsy, edging her way to the handles of the wheelchair.

Marjorie coughed ostentatiously.

'Thank you,' Betsy added.

I stood aside with amusement to watch their progress into the surgery.

'Onwards,' cried Marjorie, lifting her hand above her head. She pressed a button on her car key and the lights flashed, locking the vehicle. 'Straight ahead to the ramp and through the automatic doors!'

I followed them in, pausing to read the community noticeboard in the foyer. There was always something going on in Fernfield and this was the place to find it; well, this and the parish magazine. There were adverts for everything from holiday cottages to second-hand vacuum cleaners, babysitting services, coffee mornings, salsa classes and even Japanese lessons. I scanned it on the off-chance that someone was in need of an assistant tree surgeon, or a dog walker, or anything outdoorsy, but nothing stood out.

I took a photo of the details of a yoga class, thinking that Evie and I could both do with some relaxation, and then took my place in the queue at the reception desk. There was a kerfuffle at the head of the queue. An elderly man had spilled something across the counter which had leaked through to the receptionist's side. Two of the staff, one of whom I recognized as Nicky, had pushed back the sliding glass screen and were mopping up whatever it was with wads of kitchen roll. The other staff member had a nurse's uniform on

Behind the man was a woman with a small boy clutching her hand, desperate to see what the man had done and in front of me was Marjorie in her wheelchair, wheezing with laughter at the goings-on. Betsy was nowhere to be seen. I tapped Marjorie's shoulder and she wheeled herself round to look at me.

'What's happened?' I whispered, nodding towards the desk.

'Old boy hadn't screwed the lid on his sample bottle. Went everywhere.'

'Oh dear.' Nicky was shaking her head solemnly. She was

in her mid-twenties and kept her shoulder-length dark blonde hair tucked behind her ears. She was a nice sensible girl and her figure was what my mum would have called 'bonny'. She winked conspiratorially from beneath a ruler-straight fringe.

'We can't use that now, Mr Bradbury,' the nurse tutted. 'You'll have to do another sample.'

'No bother, Nurse,' said the old man, taking a new pot from her. 'There's plenty more where that came from. In fact, have you got a bigger bottle?'

'Oh, stop it,' Marjorie gasped, weak from laughing. 'At this rate I'm going to need one myself.'

The man shuffled off towards the toilets and Nicky gave a sigh of relief. 'Next please! And don't lean on the counter if you can help it.'

The woman and child moved forward, leaving quite a gap between them and Marjorie.

'Can you manage, or shall I push you forward?' I offered.

'No, dear,' said Marjorie, fishing a rather grubby hanky out of her bag and wiping away the tears of laughter. 'I'm not the patient. I've just brought my friend. She's in with the doctor now.'

I must have looked confused because she smiled and beckoned me to bend lower.

'Do you know Jensen Butterworth?' she whispered.

'No.' I frowned. 'Should I? Is he famous?'

Marjorie smoothed the front of her blouse down and noticed the yellow mark. 'Oh, look at that; I've spilled my egg. That's the trouble with this wheelchair. Food has such a journey from my plate, it's a wonder anything's still left on the fork when it reaches my mouth.'

'You were saying,' I prompted. 'About Jensen Butterworth.'

'Betsy's grandson,' said Marjorie, jerking her head in the direction which presumably Betsy had gone. 'If you're a friend of his, I daren't talk to you.'

I was intrigued. 'But I'm not, so . . . ?'

Marjorie's mouth twisted as if she was weighing up whether to confide in me. I smiled encouragingly. These two old ladies fascinated me; they were such characters and I found myself wanting to know more about them.

'Betsy's eyes aren't so good. My legs are pretty useless, as you can see. So we pool our resources and between us, we're a damn good team.' She smirked proudly.

'So I see. And what has Jensen got to do with it?'

'Lovely lad. Bright too. Some high-flying job in London. Betsy's so proud of him.' Marjorie sighed wistfully.

'Next please!' Nicky called.

'That's you.' Marjorie pushed herself out of the way. 'Go on, love.'

Nicky beamed at me, folded her arms and leaned forward to put her mouth close to the perforations in the glass screen. 'Lottie! Nice to see you.'

I looked at Nicky and back to Marjorie; I was dying to know more about the wonderful Jensen and why Marjorie hadn't wanted to talk to me if I'd known him.

'Yes, you too,' I said to Nicky. 'Excuse me, Marjorie. We'll carry on our chat in a moment, shall we?'

But Marjorie wasn't paying attention; Betsy had reappeared on the arm of a very handsome doctor and Marjorie was batting her eyelashes shamelessly at him. The doctor patted Betsy's hand and positioned her at the back of Marjorie's wheelchair.

'Tallyho,' cried Marjorie, raising her hand in a wave as the two of them set off for the exit.

'Marjorie dear,' said Betsy in a loud whisper, 'I don't mean to be indiscreet, but there is a distinct whiff of urine in reception. Do you need to visit the little girls' room?'

Marjorie hooted with laughter. 'Nothing to worry about; there's been a wee accident, that's all.'

Nicky and I exchanged amused looks.

'Never a dull moment,' she said, glancing at the large clock on the wall. 'And it's not even tea-break time yet.'

'So I see.' I leaned forward, about to rest my forearms on the desk and remembered just in time.

Nicky giggled. 'Believe me, it's had worse things on it than Mr Bradbury's green wee.'

Green? I winced and stood up straight. 'How was your first night in your new home?'

Her face went all gooey. 'Perfect. Just perfect. With that and Adam proposing to me last week, my head's in the clouds. I'm so in love I can't tell you.'

I felt a tiny pang of envy. 'I'm so pleased for you and I hope you'll be very happy.'

'We will,' said Nicky, blinking happy tears away. She picked up her pen. 'So did you want an appointment?'

'No. Well, possibly, I'm back for a while so I thought I should re-register.'

Nicky nodded and pushed a card under the gap in the counter.

'Put your new address on here—' She interrupted herself with a gasp. 'Oh blimey, I almost forgot! What am I like!'

She grinned goofily at herself and I looked quizzically at her.

'We had a visitor this morning looking for you. Tall, muscly, black hair. He turned up at the house just as I was leaving for work.'

My blood turned to ice: Harvey.

I swallowed. 'What did you tell him?'

She shrugged. 'I said you weren't here and as far as I knew you were living with your sister.'

'Oh God.' I pressed a hand to my chest, racking my brains to think whether Harvey had ever been to Evie's house. He had. I remembered one night last autumn having a Chinese takeaway for Darren's birthday. I could feel my heart thudding against my ribs as urgently as if I'd just sprinted a hundred metres.

'I'm really sorry. Did I say the wrong thing?' Nicky bit her lip. 'You've gone a funny colour. Do you want a glass of water?'

My head was spinning and I felt faint. Even if he had gone round to Evie's she wasn't in any danger; Harvey wasn't violent. *What about last week, when he wrapped your pony-tail round his hand and tugged it?* said a little voice.

'I've got to go,' I murmured and abandoning the GP's registration card, I stumbled back out of the automatic doors.

Outside the bright sunlight was such a contrast to the cool of the surgery that I had to stop, shade my eyes and take a few breaths.

I pulled out my phone and saw a text message from Evie. My hands trembled as I opened it, worried that Harvey was already there.

Exciting news! Lady from fostering agency is dropping in this afternoon for a chat. Am hoovering like I'm on speed!

Phew; at least Harvey hadn't turned up yet. I dialled her number to warn her but it was engaged. There was no time to waste leaving messages; if I ran fast I could be back at her cottage in five minutes.

So I ran.

Why was he here? Why couldn't he accept we were over? Maybe I'd done the wrong thing ending it with a letter, although that was the advice I'd been given and it had felt like the cleanest way to do it. What was I going to say to him? What sort of mood would he be in? I knew the answer to that – he'd be angry, very angry.

I stopped at the corner of Evie's street. On the drive was her little VW Polo and behind it, Dad's van which he'd lent to me while he was away. If Harvey had forgotten which number Evie lived at, the logo for Allbright's Tree

Services on the side of the van would have jogged his memory.

Completely out of breath and weak-kneed, I limped the last few metres to the house and knocked on the door.

Evie opened it instantly. Her eyes were wide and her mouth puckered with worry. 'I'm sorry, he didn't give me any choice.'

Behind her a broad shadow moved into view. 'Hello, stranger.'

The sight of my ex-boyfriend smiling contritely made my stomach quiver. He held out his arms as if expecting me to fall into them.

'No, I'm sorry,' I said, squeezing Evie's hand.

'You can do this,' she whispered so softly that Harvey wouldn't hear. 'Get it over with.'

I gritted my teeth and nodded, remembering what Dad had said in the pub: I'd done the hardest part in leaving him. Now I had to move on. And that was what I intended to do.

'Harvey,' I said, tilting my chin up, 'what are you doing here?'

I stepped into Evie's little hall and she put an arm protectively around my waist.

Harvey gave a laugh of surprise and came closer, hands extended as if he was going to hug me. 'What do you think I'm doing? I couldn't get through on the phone and I was worried about you. Dashing off like that. It's obvious you aren't thinking clearly at the moment.'

'I've never been clearer in my life. Excuse me.' I side-stepped him. 'I need a drink of water.'

I headed to the kitchen and I heard Evie persuading him to go in the lounge.

She followed me into the kitchen and closed the door behind her.

'He was hammering at the door,' she murmured, 'yelling that he knew you were in here. I had to let him in in case the fostering agency interviews the neighbours too. I couldn't risk them mentioning that I'd had an aggressive man trying to get in.'

'Don't apologize.' I hugged her swiftly. 'I'm sorry for putting you in this position and bringing trouble to your door.'

I noticed her glance at the clock on the oven. 'I'll get rid of him as quickly as I can.'

She waved a hand. 'Shit happens. Are you okay? You look clammy and red.'

I managed a laugh. 'Never run so fast in my life.'

'Are you going to leave me on my own much longer?' Harvey shouted from the living room.

'Tosser.' Evie gritted her teeth and shook her head. 'And to think I used to like him.'

'And *I* loved him.' I downed my water in one and wiped my mouth. 'Right, I'm going in.'

'Wait.' She grabbed her mobile phone. 'Let me ring Darren, he'll be straight over if we— Oh.' Her mouth opened and she blinked rapidly at me. 'For a second there I forgot and—'

We locked eyes for a moment and I squeezed her hand. Poor Evie, for all her brave talk of going it alone, I hoped she was beginning to realize how much Darren meant to her.

'I'll be okay on my own,' I said. 'You try not to worry.'

My sister gave me a look that said: *Yeah right*.

I took a calming breath and left the room.

Harvey was pacing up and down the length of Evie's living room. As soon as I entered, he dropped on to the sofa, perching on the edge, and patted the space next to him.

I headed for an armchair and sat back as if I was totally at ease with him. Inside I was quaking, but I was determined not to show it.

'Harvey, I appreciate you coming to check on me,' I said with an attempt at a warm smile, 'but as you can see, I'm fine.'

His brow furrowed. 'But you just left. No warning, no indication that anything was wrong.'

I felt so tired. Too tired to fight him. 'Oh come on, Harvey,' I said heavily. 'Things have been tense for months.'

He moved closer to my chair so that our knees were touching and reached for my hand. But I was too quick for him and snatched it away. He sighed irritably.

'Look. Whatever it was I said or did that made you run, I apologize. We can't let a silly little tiff come between us. We can sort this out, Lottie. Come home.'

I shook my head defiantly. 'I am home. I'm not going back to London.'

Or to you.

He threw his hands into the air and then slapped his thighs. 'So you won't accept my apology?'

I stared at him. 'It wasn't one single thing you said or did. It was everything. My promotion—'

'Oh, I get it.' He curled his lip meanly. 'This is about money. I don't earn enough to keep her Ladyship in frilly knickers.'

'It has nothing to do with money,' I jumped to my feet, breathing heavily, 'and everything to do with respect.'

'You talk about respect,' he spat, springing up to face me. 'Where was your respect for me when I offered to look after you so you didn't have to go out to work? Most women would kill for a gentleman like me.'

The heat in here was beginning to build, I needed fresh air. I crossed to the French doors which led out to the back garden and unlocked them.

'A gentleman doesn't pull hair like you did last week.'

'Oh, Lottie,' he groaned, 'how can you be so stupid? I love the feel of your soft hair and the smell of it. All fresh like flowers. I wasn't going to hurt you. I'd never hurt you. Come on.' He looked wounded. 'You're making out I was some sort of animal.'

I tried to open the French door but the handle was stiff and I was beginning to feel claustrophobic.

'I need air, I need to get out,' I muttered desperately.

'No you don't.'

I felt Harvey's hand on my shoulder and cried out as he spun me round. He took my face in his hands and his eyes burned fiercely into mine. He smelled of sweat and a wave of nausea rose in my throat.

'You and me, we're meant to be together. I'm good for you. You need me. You'll never get anyone who loves you like I do.'

I tried to shake my head but he was holding me too tightly.

'This isn't love; you want to own me, control me,' I stammered, trying to prise his fingers from my cheeks. Every nerve in my body wanted to scream for help, but I wouldn't give him the satisfaction of seeing me beg.

The door from the hall banged open and Evie appeared, my tiny guardian angel.

'Let go of her.' She had her phone in her hand and held it up to show us that the screen was lit. 'I've called the police. They're on their way.'

He released me with a push that sent me crashing into the glass behind me and I almost sobbed with relief.

'Hang up!' he shouted.

Evie shook her head defiantly. 'No way. Anyway, the location will already have been logged.'

'Harvey, don't!' I gasped as he lunged to tear the phone from her. Evie put the phone behind her back, holding it firm with both hands.

'Bitches!' Harvey roared, his face purple with fury. 'You're both stupid bitches.'

'Get out,' Evie yelled back.

'Lottie, that's it.' He stabbed a finger in my direction. 'I've given you your last chance.'

My head was spinning and I grabbed the curtains to steady myself. 'Just go. Please.'

'Don't worry. I'm out of here.' He shoved Evie so hard that she fell sideways and hit her head on the door frame.

She yelled out with pain and clasped the side of her head. I ran to her as I heard the front door slam.

'Hello. Which service do you require?' said a tinny voice.
We stared at each other, frozen with fear.
'Hello?' repeated the voice.
'Nothing. It's okay now,' said Evie, panting. 'He's gone.'
She ended the call and we sank to the floor and wept.

Harvey had gone and this time hopefully he'd gone for good.

Chapter 8

The next morning when I came downstairs in search of tea, Evie was already sitting at the kitchen table with a cup and her laptop in front of her. She was still in her dressing gown and had a towel wrapped around her head.

'Morning,' I said through a yawn.

'Morning, yourself. Sit down, I'll get you a mug, there's some coffee in the cafetiere.' She made to get up but I touched her shoulder.

'Tea for me,' I said. 'And I'll get it myself.'

'You're supposed to be my guest.' She smiled, but her face held a tension as if there was an emotion she was battling to keep at bay.

No prizes for guessing what was bothering her, I thought with a flicker of guilt. I cancelled the 'do not disturb' setting from my phone and refilled the kettle. The visit from the fostering agency had gone without a hitch yesterday. I'd gone out again to give Evie some space so I hadn't met the adviser, but Evie said that she had made all the right noises, approving the lovely light spare bedroom, which had originally been decorated by Darren as the nursery, and complimenting Evie on her small but pretty back garden, which could accommodate a swing or maybe a football goal if required.

But despite the positive outcome, the shadow of Harvey's less pleasant visit had hung over us and she and I had been jumpy all evening, twitching whenever we heard a sound outside and holding our breath in case there was a knock at the door. I'd heard her go downstairs again after we'd gone to bed and check all the locks and I'd felt awful. Me bringing my problems to her door was the last thing my sister needed right now; she had enough on her plate.

The only bright spot had been the couple of texts and a call we'd had from Dad. He'd got as far as Belgium and would be spending the next few days doing a tour of First World War landmarks. Evie and I had agreed that this stop probably wouldn't have been on the itinerary if Mum had been with him; she'd have headed straight for the sun, sea and glamour of the South of France. Dad had been as pleased as Punch that he'd had such a successful first day; there was no way we were going to spoil it by mentioning Harvey.

I sat down at the table with my tea. Evie peered into the mug and frowned.

'Black? You normally have your tea stewed but milky.'

I swallowed. 'Don't. Even the word . . . milky' – I said it fast – 'makes me feel queasy. I think you're right: I might have a bug.'

She stared at me. 'You're not pregnant, are you?' She managed to inject a hint of laughter into her voice but I wasn't fooled; it would be such a kick in the teeth for her if I'd got pregnant without even wanting to after all the heartache she and Darren had been through trying to conceive.

'Definitely not.' I shook my head. 'We took precautions and I haven't missed my period.'

A niggling voice reminded me that it was only a light one last time, but I pushed it away. Apart from the occasional accident which Harvey had owned up to, he was very careful about using condoms. There'd been one or two occasions when I'd been carried away and wanted to throw caution to the wind, but Harvey had insisted. He wasn't ready to share me with anybody else, he'd said, not even our own baby. I'd thought that was quite sweet at the time.

'Anyway, listen,' I said, placing my mug down away from her laptop and on top of the latest copy of the parish magazine, 'I've been thinking. It's lovely of you to offer me your *spare* spare room, but I'm going to look for somewhere else. I think I'm probably more trouble than I'm worth. Besides, if I'm going to hang around for a while, I might as well find a place of my own.'

I half hoped that Evie would protest; Harvey's appearance aside, it was lovely to be spending time together. But she gripped her own mug and gazed into it, not meeting my eye.

'It might be for the best,' she said quietly.

I plastered on a smile.

'Not that you're any trouble at all,' she added quickly. 'But given everything that's going on with me . . .'

'Exactly. And I wouldn't want Harvey to jeopardize anything.'

'It's unlikely he'll come back. Not after threatening him with the police. But . . .' She left the sentence hanging.

'I know. There might be children here next time he turns up,' I finished for her. 'And we can't put them at risk; I'd never forgive myself.'

Evie let out a breath of relief. 'Thank you. Nor me.'

The mention of police reminded me of something she'd said yesterday.

'Look,' I began tentatively, 'tell me to mind my own business, but your first thought yesterday was to call Darren.'

Her eyes flicked briefly to mine. 'Yes it was. It really hit me then, the reality of our separation. It was awful.'

'Do you think it might be worth ringing him? Telling him how you feel?'

'Don't you think I've tried that?' she said with a deep sigh. 'He's adamant that we need to have some time apart.'

'Then there's still a chance of reconciliation?' I said hopefully.

Evie lifted a shoulder. 'Except he doesn't want to foster kids. So unless I change my mind . . .'

I reached across the table and took her hand gently, my heart heavy with the injustice of it all. It was so unfair that some women could conceive effortlessly and others, whose arms ached to be filled with a new-born, could only dream about it.

We both picked up our mugs and sipped in silence for a moment. Sensing the need to change the subject, I opened the parish magazine and flicked through the pages, smiling at the outdated adverts for hairdressers, cleaners and handymen.

'I might advertise in the next issue myself,' I said, holding up a picture of a lady taxi driver. 'See if anyone needs a lady tree surgeon.'

I came to a page that had had the corner folded down. Evie cleared her throat.

'Ah yes. That.' She flicked a piece of fluff from her dressing gown. 'Interesting job for you maybe.'

I put my mug down and unfolded the corner so I could read it properly. I scanned the title:

Gardener/Housekeeper/Companion, Live-in (Contract length approx. six months, start date asap).

A job *and* a place to live, possibly with immediate effect. 'Gosh, you really are keen to get rid of me, aren't you?' I said, only half joking.

Evie pressed her lips together and a flash of determination crossed her face. I had a sudden rush of sympathy for Darren. She really was prepared to put her plan to be a mother ahead of everything else. I'd never seen this side of her before, so single-minded. I was both proud and envious of her.

'Don't be like that.' She lifted her mug to hide her face but I could see she was blushing. 'It was just a thought. Read on.'

I began reading again.

An opportunity has arisen for a capable, multi-skilled individual at Butterworth Wines, a small private vineyard located on the outskirts of the pretty rural village of Fernfield.

The position would suit an experienced gardener, familiar with large-scale gardening, with the ability to manage a team of part-time workers and, above all, a passion for the outdoors. The estate comprises a family home, ten acres of land, mostly planted with vines on a south-facing slope, the winery and stables converted into accommodation for the successful applicant. Duties to include some light housekeeping and companionship, although no cooking. A full driving licence is required as the property is located off the beaten track and the role may require some driving of the homeowner from time to time. Please send an introductory email, including a contact telephone number, to BottomsUp@ButterworthWines.com

'Well,' I said, not sure which bit to comment on first: the fact that someone, somewhere in our village, was producing wine this far north or the dodgy email address. 'Gardening, managing staff, housekeeping and driving . . . more commonly known as a dogsbody, I'd say.'

'But no cooking,' said Evie, pointing out the positive. 'And you could do the rest standing on your head.'

'Could I?' I arched an eyebrow doubtfully. 'I can't even manage myself, let alone others.'

'Didn't you say you'd been offered a promotion to supervisor at the crematorium?'

That was true. And if the staff were only part-timers, it might not be too onerous a task.

'I didn't even know there was a vineyard in Fernfield.' I wrinkled my nose. 'Don't you need Mediterranean sunshine to grow grapes?'

'No idea, you're the gardening expert, not me,' she said. 'I do know where it is, though: it's a couple of miles out of the village on the Buxton road. Set back behind a tall brick wall; you'd never know it was there.'

'Of course, the one major stumbling block is that I don't know anything about wine.' I shuddered, picturing the contempt on Harvey's face when I'd incorrectly served white wine with our pork last week.

'You like drinking it, that's a start. Besides, are they asking for wine knowledge? No.' She sat back and folded her arms. 'And it's only for six months. You could stick anything for that long and it would give you a chance to catch your breath and decide what to do next.'

I nodded thoughtfully. 'I suppose there's no harm in sending an exploratory email.'

Evie let out a long breath. 'Good because—'

She was interrupted by a call on my mobile. I picked it up and stared at the screen.

'It's a mobile number, not one of my contacts.' I looked at Evie, my stomach fluttering nervously. 'What if Harvey has bought himself a new phone, to get around me blocking him?'

'Then this will be his one and only call because you'll block him again. He won't be able to afford to keep doing that.'

I gulped. 'You're right. I'll answer and not speak.'

She nodded.

I touched the green button on the touch screen and set it to loudspeaker.

'Hello?' said a frail voice. Male. Possibly elderly.

Evie and I exchanged glances; either Harvey was playing games or it wasn't him at all.

'Hello? Oh, dash it, Roger, I think it must be one of those blessed answerphones.'

'Well, leave a message then, man,' said an impatient muffled voice in the background.

'This isn't Harvey,' I whispered. 'We're getting paranoid.'

We grinned at each other with relief; these two sounded completely harmless.

'Hello there?' I said. 'Sorry about the delay, I couldn't hear anything.'

'Can you hear me now?'

'Loud and clear,' I replied.

'Get on with it,' hissed the other voice.

'All right, all right.' The man cleared his throat. 'This is Godfrey Hallam. Calling regarding your application for the position at Butterworth Wines?'

'My application?' I stared at Evie whose eyes widened guiltily.

'I was going to tell you,' she whispered, 'and then the phone rang.'

'Well, yes,' said Godfrey, sounding uncertain. 'I received an email this morning. I have got the right number? This is Miss Allbright?'

'Yes, yes,' I said, a bit flustered. 'It's . . . I was . . . well, I suppose I wasn't expecting a response so soon. You're very efficient.'

Evie clapped her hands excitedly. I gave her a stern look. Wanting me to move out was one thing; actually applying for a job on my behalf was quite another.

'Why thank you!' said Godfrey, chuckling. 'One does one's best. I was the editor of a regional newspaper once upon a time, you know. And the urgency of working to a tight deadline never leaves you.'

'For heaven's sake, Godfrey, get to the point, she'll be here in a minute,' hissed the man I assumed was Roger.

'Keep your hair on, old chap.' Godfrey sounded like he had his hand over the mouthpiece. Then his voice became clearer again. 'Sorry about Roger. He isn't yet retired and hasn't learned to slow down and smell the—'

'Right, I'm taking over,' said Roger. 'Hand me that phone.'

There were some grunts and tussling noises for a moment and then a sharp voice came on the line. 'Miss Allbright,

Roger Cooper here. Are you available for an interview this morning at the winery at eleven, yes or no?'

The phone was still on loudspeaker. Evie shrugged and pulled a 'what have you got to lose' sort of face.

'Um.' I blew my cheeks out, still bewildered that I seemed to have landed an interview for a job I hadn't applied for and wasn't sure I even wanted. Despite that, I found myself answering that I was available.

'Excellent. See you anon.'

'Thank you, Mr Cooper, I look forward to . . .' My voice petered out as I realized I was talking to myself. I stared at Evie. 'He's cut me off. Roger is savage. I hope it's Godfrey who does the interviewing.'

'Well done! Day one of your job hunt and you've got an interview set up already.'

I gave her a withering look. 'You mean you've set me up.'

She waved a hand. 'Don't get all touchy. Now, what are you going to wear?'

'Easy,' I replied, getting to my feet. 'My gardener, house-keeper, companion, driver outfit, of course.'

Evie was right, I acknowledged later that morning: you'd never know there was a vineyard here at all. There was a tall sandstone wall edging the property which hid everything from view. I turned off the country lane through large open gates and slowed down to take in the view.

A valley had opened up before me: softly sloping land, lush and green as far as my eye could see. Immediately to my left and right, the fields were alive with ripening barley, rip-pling in the breeze, like a giant Mexican wave. I'd never seen a vineyard in real life before, but further ahead, the row upon row of neat parallel lines running downhill were unmistakable.

I wound down the window and inhaled the sweet sum-mer air; it was good to be out of London. And on a day like today, when the sky was blue and the sunlight made the leaves on the trees shimmer and the grass sparkle, there was nowhere I'd rather be in the world. Even the nightmare of yesterday was beginning to fade.

I inched forward, taking note of my surroundings. The driveway was rather rough and pitted, but edged with a rustic drystone wall along which wild red poppies grew, their cheerful scarlet petals seeming to wave me on.

The path narrowed ahead and became even rougher but to my right there was a tall beech hedge forming a perimeter around what I guessed must be the house and winery. A few metres further on, I came to a gap in the hedge and turned through it.

Ahead of me was a square concrete yard and to the left a large house, homely rather than grand, built from creamy yellow stone which lent it an air of faded elegance. With a deep sloping roof, pretty little windows set into the eaves and a beautiful climbing wisteria like frilly lavender bunting, the house had a fairy-tale quality to it. You couldn't fail to be happy living here, I mused.

Across the yard from the house were what looked like converted stables and finally, partially obstructed by several vehicles including a Land Rover and a quadbike, was a long single-storey building. This was much newer and more industrial-looking, with wide double doors standing open. Inside I could just make out some sort of stainless-steel construction and outside it was a forklift truck next to some pallets of bottles. The winery, I presumed.

A lean man with gingery hair and long legs and dressed in a tracksuit emerged from this last building and marched towards me, beckoning me forward with both hands like an air traffic controller. As I got closer, he started to wave me to the right, indicating I should park in the space next to the quadbike. I could probably have managed that by myself, I thought, but I gave him a thumbs-up to show I understood his instruction. At a guess, this was Roger.

A second man, shorter, rounder and balder than the first,

appeared and gave me a cheery wave. He walked with a slight shuffle towards my van as I climbed out.

'Miss Allbright?'

'That's me. Call me Lottie, please.'

He held out his hand. 'Godfrey Hallam.'

'It's a beautiful place you have here, Godfrey,' I said, shaking his warm pudgy hand.

'It's not his,' said the first man, smoothing his hair into place before extending his hand in greeting. 'Nor mine. I'm Roger Cooper, by the way; we spoke on the phone.'

Roger had a vice-like grip and I was glad when he released my hand.

'I spoke to you too,' said Godfrey, raising a hand timidly.

'I must say, I had my reservations when I read your email,' Roger said, casting an eye approvingly over my outfit. 'Given your age and, ahem, sex.'

'Oh?' I regarded him coolly, daring him to make a sexist remark.

'And I apologize for jumping to conclusions; you look very strong and capable.' He smiled at me as if he'd just paid me the greatest compliment.

'Thanks,' I said, inclining my head. 'I believe I am.'

Given the warmth of the sun today, I'd have preferred to be wearing a summer dress, but it would have done me no good given the practical nature of the job. So I'd opted for some heavy-duty canvas trousers I used to wear when I worked with Dad, a white polo shirt and my steel-capped boots, which I had to wear with thick socks. I reckoned it was about ninety degrees inside those boots right now. I looked down, half expecting steam to be coming out of them. So I might not look feminine and smart, but 'strong and capable' would probably win me more Brownie points.

'Come along, let's go and get settled into the winery before the ladies arrive.'

Roger looked left and right as if he was hiding from someone and then crept towards what I'd guessed was the winery, gesturing for us to follow him with an impatient flap of his hand.

'So you wouldn't be my employer?' I said, keeping pace with Godfrey who wasn't as nimble as Roger. 'I'm a bit baffled.'

Godfrey took out a large handkerchief and patted his shiny head. 'I'm sorry, my dear; it has all been a bit cloak and dagger, but all will become clear shortly. Trust me.'

'But there is definitely a job?' I narrowed my eyes, wondering if all this was a weird and wonderful wild-goose chase.

Godfrey hesitated. 'Roger and I believe so, yes. There's certainly a need. But the situation is – shall we say – delicate.'

'I see,' I said, although I didn't really. Maybe I hadn't found a solution to my imminent homelessness after all.

'So who does own this place?' I stopped in my tracks as we reached the open doors of the winery, intent on getting to the bottom of the mystery.

'Watch out for that pothole, dear girl!' a familiar voice called from the far side of the concrete yard.

'I know exactly where the pothole is,' tutted a second voice. 'And if you're not careful I'll tip you into it.'

I whipped round to see the two old ladies I'd met at the doctors' the day before: Betsy and Marjorie. Betsy as usual pushing the wheelchair and Marjorie shouting directions.

'They do,' said Godfrey, shaking his head fondly. 'The two Mrs Butterworths.'

Chapter 9

'Morning, Pippa,' said Betsy to me as she drew level, steering the wheelchair expertly through the winery doors.

'Actually, it's—' I began, before I felt Godfrey tug on my arm.

'Not yet,' he murmured.

Marjorie did a double take and then her eyes lit up. 'Why hello, dear!'

'Don't sound so surprised, Mar, Pippa spends more time here than you,' Betsy said, heading towards a hosepipe which lay across the floor.

'Taste this, Marjorie,' said Roger hastily, thrusting a glass of cloudy-looking wine into her hand as if trying to change the subject.

Unfortunately, Betsy hadn't seen Roger coming and so didn't slow down. She ran straight over the hosepipe causing the wine to slop down the front of Marjorie's blouse. She was in a bright pink one today, covered with yellow palm trees. She brushed at the spillage good-naturedly and sucked the end of her finger. I hung back at the doorway, unsure what to do. Nobody had corrected Betsy and I wasn't sure whether I was supposed to pretend to be Pippa or not.

'Ooh, yum scrum Betsy's bum, apple pie and chewing gum,' said Marjorie, smacking her lips and earning herself a poke in the back from Betsy.

'Very funny. We'll put that on the tasting notes, shall we?' said Betsy drily.

I laughed softly under my breath; these two were a hoot.

'Don't hover at the door, dear,' said Betsy, shielding her eyes and squinting in my direction.

She aimed the wheelchair towards a desk in the centre of the room which was overflowing with brochures, paperwork and rolls of self-adhesive labels, as well as a tray of wine glasses covered with a cloth. Godfrey did some subtle finger jabbing to indicate I should stand between two huge stainless-steel tanks.

'What are we tasting, Roger?' Betsy peered at the dribble left in the bottom of Marjorie's glass.

'The 2017 Pinot Meunier,' he said. 'Rather fruity, I think. From tank number ten.'

'Whatever that means,' said Betsy crossly. 'I can just about find my way round this room, but I'm darned if I know which tank is which.'

She turned Marjorie around to face us and sat herself down at the desk. I shrank back a little and Roger shot me a look of apology as Marjorie eyed me with pleasure but said nothing.

'Well,' Godfrey started to explain, 'tanks one to six are the original ones that Ted put in first. They're the little ones along the back.'

He was pointing towards the far side of the room at a row of upright stainless-steel tanks with flat lids and various valves and taps at the front; these tanks were half the size of the ones next to me. The room seemed to be divided into three sections and although there were open doorways to the left and right of me, I couldn't see what was beyond them.

'Yes, yes, I know all that,' said Betsy irritably. 'I was here when he built the place, remember? What I mean is . . .' She sighed helplessly. 'Oh, never mind. Someone pass me a sample of the Meunier. Just a small one, please.'

'And I'll have a splash more too,' Marjorie put in. 'And when I say splash, Roger, let's get it in the glass this time.'

Godfrey passed a clean glass to Roger, who filled both of them from a small tap set into tank number ten, to the side of a large circular valve. Both ladies then sniffed and slurped the wine, squelching it rather disgustingly around their mouths before swallowing it.

'Fruity, like you said.'

'But not as soft as some.'

'I like the gooseberry notes.'

I listened avidly; it was like another language. Just as well wine tasting wasn't part of the job remit. My descriptions were invariably on a sliding scale from delicious to absolutely rank.

'What do you think, Pippa?' Betsy looked up in my direction. 'Ted used to say you had a good nose. Oh, you haven't even got a glass. Come on, girl, stop dithering. I thought this was a tasting session.'

Roger and Godfrey nodded at each other, as if to say, *After you, no, after you.* Roger finally surrendered.

'We're not really tasting today,' he said solemnly.

Betsy tutted. 'But you said you had something to show us. Honestly, gentlemen. I could have been making some strawberry jam by now instead of wasting time in this black hole of Calcutta.'

Marjorie rolled her eyes. 'No way. Absolutely no way. Not jam.'

Betsy drew herself up in her chair, her spine ramrod straight. 'I have been making jam from my own strawberries since—'

'Since you could read the tiny numbers on your jam thermometer, yes I know,' said Marjorie affably. 'Only now you can't read them. Why don't you make a fresh strawberry trifle instead? Something which will leave you with a smile on your face rather than third-degree burns.'

'Here we go again.' Betsy set her glass down precariously on a sloping pile of papers and Roger grabbed it before it fell. 'Clipping my wings. I'd get more freedom in Holloway.'

Marjorie began to chortle, which made Betsy growl with frustration. Both Godfrey and Roger ran fingers uncomfortably around their collars.

'Without further ado,' said Roger with false jollity, 'there's someone we'd like you to meet.'

'Who? Where?' Betsy demanded, glancing at the door.

'Lottie Allbright has come to, er, visit,' said Godfrey, beckoning me to come forward.

I'd had two job interviews in my life: one for a Saturday job at the hairdresser's, which entailed the head stylist handing me a broom and telling me to get on with it; and the other at the crematorium, which involved completing twenty-eight forms in triplicate, two interviews, a personality test and a day's trial. Nothing had prepared me for this selection process, if indeed it was one. And yet I knew with certainty that this peculiar job, in this beautiful valley in Derbyshire, part of the most unusual team I'd ever come across, was, right now, the perfect move for me.

A surge of energy propelled me out of the shadows and directly in front of Betsy where I imagined her limited eyesight would have a chance of making out my features.

'Hello; we met yesterday at the doctors'. Pleased to meet you again.' I held out my hand and she shook it.

'You're not Pippa?' She looked puzzled. Her eyes were watery and she blinked them rapidly as if trying to clear her vision.

'No. I'm sorry for the confusion.'

'I thought you smelled different,' said Betsy with a sniff. 'Pippa usually smells of wet dog.'

Pippa was someone I couldn't wait to meet.

'This is a nice surprise.' Marjorie's eyes twinkled and she reached across for my hand, squeezing it in a friendly manner. 'Very nice.'

'Well, very nice or not, I'm afraid Butterworth Wines has never catered for visitors, neither do we sell to the public.'

'Nor to anyone at all presently,' muttered Roger wryly. 'Which is something else we need to talk about.'

Betsy frowned. 'If you gentlemen have nothing better to do than show a pretty young lady around, then be my guest, but you'll excuse me, Miss Allbright, if I don't come.'

'Of course.' I glowed at being called pretty before remembering that she was partially sighted and had already mistaken me twice for a sharp cheek-boned woman who smelled of dog.

'She's not here for a tour, Betsy,' said Roger.

'She's applied for a job,' Godfrey added.

'No vacancies at present. Send in your CV and we'll keep it on file,' Betsy reeled off as if she had to repeat herself daily. She gave me a brisk smile and stood up to terminate our exchange.

Godfrey clasped his hands behind his back and rocked on his heels. 'Actually I, well, Roger and I, have advertised for someone to come and help us out,' he said, stuttering slightly.

Betsy sat down immediately. 'I beg your pardon?'

You could have cut the atmosphere with a knife.

Marjorie poked me.

'See that big metal monster?' she said quietly, pointing at a huge horizontal machine with a funnel-shaped opening on the top. 'That's the wine press. Through that door is the wine store and through the other is where the bottling and labelling is done. Go and have a look around.'

I got the message and wandered off to examine the press; they clearly needed a private talk with Betsy. The trouble was that this place was like an echo chamber and I could hear every word.

'So is someone going to explain why you thought it fit to go behind my back and advertise for staff?' Betsy's voice wavered. 'I might be a widow, but I've only lost a husband, not my own mind.'

'Nobody's suggesting you have, love,' Marjorie soothed. 'But Ted worked all hours in the vineyard and now Pippa is your only member of staff.'

'And she's only part time,' Godfrey put in.

'And with Ted gone, well, everyone's at sixes and sevens,' said Roger.

'Everyone?' Betsy's voice lifted an octave. 'You mean me.'

'We mean all of us, dear girl,' said Roger softly. I glanced over to see him crouching down near Betsy's knees and taking her hand. Gone was the sergeant-major act, the impatient tutting. He obviously genuinely cared for her. My heart melted a little towards him. 'The vineyard needs managing. Someone who can coordinate the workload and look after Ted's precious vines. Take the pressure off you a bit. And us, we've all been doing more hours, but now it's time for someone to take over.'

'Has Jensen put you up to this?' Betsy asked sharply.

'Jensen doesn't know a thing about it. It was my idea,' said Marjorie. 'I asked Godfrey to put an ad in this month's parish magazine. We deliberately kept it off the internet in case, by chance, Jensen came across it. We wanted to surprise you.'

'You certainly did that,' Betsy scoffed. 'Good grief. So tell me about my vacancy, then.'

I went through into the wine store while the three of them outlined the job they thought needed doing, more or less repeating what I already knew from the advert. This part of the winery was much smaller than the main section but nonetheless took my breath away. I'd never seen so many bottles of sparkling wine in one place in my entire life. The walls were edged top to bottom with wine racks and every row was full. There was hardly any spare floor visible; the centre of the room was stacked with cardboard boxes loaded on to pallets and each box contained twelve bottles.

There must have been thousands of pounds' worth of stock in here, I thought. I wonder why none of it had been sold. I left the area and crossed the tank room again and into the third section. There were several machines in here, the largest had a conveyor belt, but what the other ones did was anybody's guess. There were more pallets of bottles here too, this time brand-new empty ones. Although judging by the layer of dust on the top box, nothing had been bottled recently. I re-joined the others.

'We all want you to stay in your own home where you're comfortable,' Marjorie was saying. 'And I'll visit as much as I can, but all the stairs in your house make it impossible for me to stay longer than one night.'

'I know that, Mar.' Betsy patted her hand. 'I don't know how I'd have coped without you this last month since Ted died.'

'We're all happy to carry on volunteering,' said Godfrey. 'Clare, Roger and myself. Pippa, of course, our youngster, is staff and does more hours; she'll always be here. And I know Matt is happy to help too when the time comes for bottling. But none of us can be here full-time.'

'Roger, you're a born organizer,' Betsy said, 'you be the manager. I'll pay you instead. There, sorted. No need to bring in strangers.'

'I'm still a PE teacher, Betsy,' Roger reminded her. 'I have a job. Viticulture is simply my hobby.'

'Still teaching? Good grief,' she muttered incredulously.

'I am only fifty-five,' he said huffily.

'It's a hobby for all of us and we love it, which is why we volunteer here,' said Godfrey. 'Since Ted became ill, we've all done extra hours, willingly. But with the grapes starting to grow, we need someone to take charge. Ten acres is a big area to manage, especially for me with my dodgy hip, and without Ted we can't cope. And perhaps – and this is in no way an insult – you can't cope either. Lottie, or whoever we recruited,' he added swiftly, 'would be able to help with some household chores.'

'Godfrey Hallam,' said Betsy imperiously, 'I am a strong capable woman.'

'We know that,' said Marjorie, 'but you've also got macular degeneration. Without Ted, who's going to read letters for you, or pay bills, or tell the difference between cheese sauce and custard?'

'That happened once, when I had a cold and couldn't smell it,' Betsy snapped.

'You're going to have to accept help,' said Roger firmly.

'No.' Betsy folded her arms and pressed her lips together, glaring at her three friends as if daring them to say another word.

The team seemed to be no closer to convincing her that she needed a member of staff at all. I glanced at my watch. The interview hadn't begun yet and I was beginning to doubt that there'd even be one. It had been too good to be true after all: an outdoor role with its own accommodation . . . Oh well, back to the drawing board. It was only day one of my job hunt. I let out a sigh, which had the unintentional effect of reminding everyone that I was still here.

'Lottie,' said Marjorie, smiling kindly at me. 'You've been woefully neglected. Roger, pass the lass a chair and let her tell us a bit about herself.'

Roger sprang up and found me a stool from underneath the desk.

'Sorry about all this,' he whispered under his breath as he set it down close to Marjorie's wheelchair but a little way away from Betsy who had now turned away under the pretence of sifting through the papers on the desk, although by all accounts, it seemed unlikely that she could read much.

'Thank you,' I said, taking a seat.

'The parish magazine deliveries only started this morning,' said Marjorie, stroking the mole on her chin absentmindedly. 'You applied very promptly for a job which we'd advertised with an immediate start date.'

'That's right,' I said, deciding not to mention that it was in fact my sister who'd stitched me up like a proverbial kipper.

'Which would lead me to conclude that you're in need

of somewhere to live and work.' She smiled encouragingly at me.

'The sooner the better,' I agreed.

Betsy didn't look up. 'That's all we need,' she muttered. 'Some desperado.'

I considered myself to be an optimistic person, someone who looks for the silver lining in every circumstance. I'd even carved a happy existence in a crematorium where I'd found myself surrounded by new grief on an hourly basis. But all of a sudden I felt something in me crumble. Over the last few days I'd been through a torrent of emotional and physical upheaval: the breakdown of Evie and Darren's marriage, my own escape from Harvey, waving Dad off on his solo adventure, enduring a frightening encounter with my crazy ex and today accepting that my presence in my sister's home threatened everything she held dear. And now, faced with these three kind people and Betsy's cold shoulder, I saw my one last glimmer of hope flicker and die.

'You're right,' I said, getting to my feet, a veil of tears rendering my sight as hazy as I imagined Betsy's to be. 'You don't need me in your lives.'

'Whoa, hold on,' said Marjorie, her face a picture of concern. 'Betsy didn't mean that.'

'Actually, she's right,' I said breathlessly. 'I'm a walking disaster zone. I've run away from an abusive man, and goodness knows when he might turn up again. I've had to walk away from a perfectly good promotion. Even though gardening in a crematorium might not suit everyone, I enjoyed talking to people and comforting them and chatting and singing to their relatives, or their memorials at least. I can't live with my sister Evie because she wants to start fostering and having me around – or rather the threat of a return visit from my ex – gets in her way. And my dad has sold his business and rented out the family home. So yes, Betsy is right: I am a desperado.'

They were all staring at me now. I even had Betsy's attention.

'Roger, Godfrey, it was lovely to meet you. Goodbye, ladies.' I swiped a stray tear on my cheek and trying to retain the tiniest shred of my remaining dignity I strode out of the doors.

My trembling hands were making it hard to get the car key in the lock and I was still fumbling when above the thunderous sound of my heart, I heard a voice.

'Wait.'

It was Betsy.

I stood in silence and waited, my throat so choked that I couldn't have spoken if I'd tried. I was expecting an apology and I was ready to wave it away. It wasn't her fault; I'd been foisted on her as a fait accompli. And not only that, she'd obviously been recently widowed, she was bound to be feeling a bit out of sorts. The apology didn't come.

'My sister-in-law and those two well-meaning buffoons in there are quite wrong when they say that I need help at home.' She shook her head in irritation. 'Outside these walls the world is one noisy blur, busy, fast and a little scary, and that's only in our village; heaven knows what it would be like if I had to venture further afield.'

'That was how I felt about London,' I managed to say in a gruff voice.

Betsy shuddered. 'Ghastly. Anyway, the point is that inside the walls which surround my property, I feel safe, I know where the potholes in the yard are, I know how many steps lead to my bathroom or down to the garden. I can, with a bit of concentration, still work the TV remote and I know what food is in my cupboards, the mix-up with the custard notwithstanding.'

'I can see that, Mrs Butterworth; your friends were trying to help, but I understand: you won't require my services.'

'No,' she confirmed. 'But it appears to me that you, young lady, are in need of a lucky break. And that it is, in fact, you who need mine. And do call me Betsy.'

I tried to laugh but it came out like a sort of yodel. I nodded instead.

'So how about this? You come and live in The Stables, across the way, and in exchange for a wage and your accommodation, you carry out a few tasks around the vineyard.'

'Really! That would be amazing!' Without thinking, I gave Betsy a hug and ended up sobbing on to the shoulder of her blouse. I half expected her to pull away; so far she had struck me as a stiff-upper-lip sort of lady. Instead, she rubbed my back. 'There, there,' she said under her breath.

'And The Stables . . .' I looked across the yard to the building with a traditional stable door. 'It is habitable in there?'

She gave a dry laugh. 'Fair question. Yes; it's nothing fancy, mind you.'

My heart thumped with relief. 'You don't know what a help this is.'

'Yes, well, it would only be for six months,' she said, with a return to her brusque manner. She produced a white handkerchief from her sleeve and handed it to me. 'Until after the harvest and then I'm going to consider my options. I can't afford to pay you a fortune, but I'll have a word with the accountant.'

'That's fine. More than fine.' At this point, I'd have snapped her hand off just for a fortnight's lodging. 'What sort of tasks did you have in mind?'

'Oh.' She waved a hand airily. 'Putting together a jobs rota for the volunteers to cover pruning, mowing, checking the vines for disease. There are always vine supports and fences to be mended, grass to mow and of course the garden at the back of the house too. And looking ahead, organizing supplies and workforce for the harvest. Oh, and a few household jobs which I struggle with.' She leaned forward, lowered her voice and wagged a finger. 'Do not under any circumstances tell Marjorie that I struggle. With anything.'

'Understood.' I nodded firmly.

'And the odd bit of driving. If Marjorie can't take me. That sound okay?'

'That sounds ideal.' And it was almost word for word

what the job advertisement had said, I thought, feeling my mouth twitch into a smile.

'That's better.' She patted my arm. 'Now, on you go. I'll see you tomorrow.'

'Tomorrow?' I said, surprised.

'I thought you wanted to move in straight away? No sense in dilly-dallying.'

'Oh, yes please.'

'That's settled then.' She looked innocently at me. 'Besides, the vineyard won't prune itself.'

Chapter 10

Twenty-four hours after starting my job hunt, I arrived at Butterworth Wines to take up my new position. I parked in front of the winery as before and removed my two suitcases from the back. It was only five days since I'd fled London with them, I'd packed them again on leaving Dad's on Monday and again this morning at Evie's. No wonder I was tired.

Evie had been a bit tearful when I left her house and I sensed she was beginning to feel out of her depth. Her application to become a foster carer seemed to be going full steam ahead, which was exciting on the one hand and terrifying on the other. I worried that she was rushing into this without giving herself time to grieve for the breakdown of her marriage but she wouldn't listen when I tried to talk about it.

Still, I was only a couple of miles away – close enough to be with her in minutes, but far enough away to keep the threat of a repeat visit from Harvey at bay. I'd text him later, I thought, let him know that I'd moved out of Evie's house so there was no point in him coming back in.

The stable door opened, breaking into my thoughts, and Betsy appeared.

'Lottie? Is that you?' She shielded her eyes with her hand although the sun hadn't yet put in an appearance and a slight breeze was keeping the temperature cooler than it had been for the last few days.

'Yes. Morning!' I called. 'Shall I bring my cases over?'

'Yes do,' she said, bending to lift a small white and brown dog into her arms. 'Welcome to Butterworth Wines, and specifically to The Stables.'

'Thank you, I'm very glad to be here.'

After hugging her yesterday I wasn't quite sure how to greet her: a handshake would have been too formal, but I got the impression that she wasn't normally a touchy-feely person. I held my hand out to the dog instead, letting it sniff me before daring to scratch it under the chin.

'Hello, little chap,' I said, guessing it was a male by the silver tag bearing the name Starsky hanging from his collar.

'Well, someone seems much brighter today,' said Betsy, regarding me with her head to one side. The little dog wriggled in her arms to be put down and she complied. I bent down, assuming that Starsky wanted to come and see me, but he scampered away inside.

'So you can . . .' I faltered, realizing that the question on the tip of my tongue was a bit personal, Betsy had a prickly side to her personality that I'd rather not invoke. 'Nothing.'

'Go on, spit it out,' said Betsy, grabbing the handle of one of my cases and lugging it over the threshold.

'Well, can you see my face properly?' I asked. 'Sorry, my dad used to say I was nosy. My mum encouraged it as natural curiosity.'

Betsy gave a bark of laughter. 'They're both right. And being interested in others is a far better trait than only being interested in yourself.'

That observation made me think of Harvey, who I now realized had only ever had his own interests at heart. I gave an involuntary shudder.

'I'd say I'm a people person,' I said, pushing the image of him with his hands crushing my face out of my head. 'And animals too.'

'Ted wasn't fond of pets, so we've only ever been allowed

97

one at a time. The first was a rescue rabbit when my daughter was eight, then a succession of guinea pigs, a cat or two and finally a dog who Ted fell in love with at first sight.'

'Quite a menagerie.'

'Indeed, but always called Starsky, which our friends found amusing.'

'Why Starsky?'

'Because the first Starsky came with his own hutch.'

We both laughed. Perhaps I'd been a bit harsh when I'd labelled her as prickly.

'And to answer your question, no I can't. Macular degeneration means that my peripheral vision is okay, but the centre is just a blur. So reading is a bind, particularly small print, and I can't rely on my sight to recognize people; I use my other senses instead, like smell and hearing and, in the case of handsome doctors, touch if I'm feeling brazen.' She pressed her lips into a secretive smile and I remembered her emerging from the consulting room on Tuesday on the arm of a good-looking man.

'And sometimes, like now, I get a sixth sense about a person. Yesterday you gave off a feeling of despair; today I'm getting happy vibes.'

I let out a breath and smiled. 'I *am* happy. I can't believe my luck landing on my feet like this.'

'Well, come on in, then,' she said impatiently. 'Can't stand here chatting all morning. I expect you'll be wanting a look round your new abode.'

I carried my other suitcase inside and found myself beside a small wooden table and two chairs. I set the case down on the quarry-tiled floor and looked around. The layout was open plan: behind the table was the kitchen area – one short run of units with a sink at one end and a cooker at the other and then further along was an L-shaped sofa on which Starsky had made himself comfy, the smallest log-burner I'd ever seen and a TV. A Henry hoover sat in the middle of the floor, plugged in with its cable trailing from the bedroom.

Directly facing the front door was another door through which I could see the end of a double bed. The décor was rustic and functional rather than fancy but the original beams had been retained and the whole place felt homely and inviting.

'Now it's only small but it should have everything you need.'

'I love it,' I said, unable to keep the squeak from my voice. 'And it's twice the size of the flat I lived in in London.'

Betsy opened all the kitchen cupboards in turn to show me where everything was. 'And I've put a few basics in for you, tea and coffee and so on. But you'll need to shop for meals.'

'Thank you. I'm tea only at the moment, I'm off coffee recently, I think I probably overdosed at my sister's. She mainlines the stuff.'

Evie had insisted on sending me off with a shopping bag and a cool box full of essentials, both of which were still in the car. So at least I wouldn't have to leave the vineyard again today. Today was about getting my bearings, meeting everyone and hopefully, later on, getting a chance to google how on earth one was supposed to look after vines . . .

'As long as you haven't gone off wine,' said Betsy. 'Because you won't be able to escape the smell of that here.'

I shook my head, opting not to tell her I probably couldn't distinguish a Chardonnay from a Chenin Blanc.

'Come through to the bedroom,' she said, leading the way.

The bedroom furniture was heavy and dark: mahogany bed, wardrobe, drawers and an old dressing table with a three-fold tarnished mirror on top of it.

'My mother's old stuff,' said Betsy. 'Old-fashioned, I know, but I couldn't bear to part with it. Particularly that dressing table. I spent hours at that going through her make-up and trying on her jewellery. I was always in trouble for tangling her necklaces.'

'It suits the room perfectly.' I smiled, imagining her as a

defiant unrepentant child smeared with rouge and bedecked in rows of pearls.

'Bathroom,' she said, opening a second door. 'Or rather, shower room. You'll have to manage without a bath, I'm afraid.'

'No problem,' I said, staring in wonder at the little room, all gleaming chrome, sparkling floor-to-ceiling tiles and a shower cubicle that looked brand new. 'I always like the idea of a bath far more than the reality.'

Betsy's lips twitched. 'Completely agree. All that time spent filling the thing and as soon as I'm in I'm too hot and bored and wonder how soon I can get out without feeling like I've wasted all that water.'

She left the room and I bounced my bottom on the bed to test it. It was deliciously soft, the duvet cover was a little faded but all the softer for it and it took all my will-power not to lie down but instead to follow Betsy back out.

I found her about to switch on the vacuum cleaner.

'I can't actually see if I'm sucking anything up,' she admitted, 'but I'm not taking any chances. The cottage has been empty since January; an entire army of spiders might have taken up residence in the place, for all I know.'

'Let me do it,' I said. 'I might as well start working straight away.'

'You are starting straight away,' she corrected me sternly. 'Pippa will be here in a few minutes; I've arranged for her to take you on a tour. Nice girl. Painfully shy but she was a big help to Ted in the early days.'

'Did Ted pass away recently?' I asked gently, glad of the chance to ask.

She sighed and sat down with a plop on the sofa. Starsky immediately pressed himself against her, his chin resting on her knee.

'A month ago,' she said, gesturing to the other end of the sofa for me to sit. 'From cancer. But he'd been ill for months before that. He kept it hidden from me at first – not wanting to worry me, he admitted at the end. My damn eyesight,' she said with a sudden burst of anger, smacking the arm of the sofa. Starsky made a whimpering noise. 'If only I could have seen properly, I'd have noticed, but my eyes are useless.'

I ignored her directions and sat next to her instead. 'I'm sorry.'

She smiled. 'Thank you for not trotting out the same old platitudes. You've no idea how much I want to punch idiots who say things like: "he's at peace now", or "you mustn't blame yourself", or my personal bête noire, "these things happen for a reason".'

'My mum died when I was nineteen, she was only forty-four and we had a lot of that,' I said. 'I think people feel the need to say something, you know, fill the silences. When really all I needed was someone to simply listen.'

Starsky heaved himself up from Betsy's lap and relocated to mine. I stroked his head and his ears. His fur was wiry, although his ears were velvety and close up I could see his silvery muzzle. He was an old boy with a melancholy demeanour.

'Poor mutt,' Betsy crooned, running her hand down his back. 'He was Ted's shadow. I'd never have believed that dogs could suffer from depression, but I think that's what it is. He's lost his lust for life. He doesn't know what to do with himself without Ted. You and me both, boy.'

A single tear dropped from Betsy's face into her lap.

'It's still all very new,' I said, squeezing her hand lightly. 'The best piece of advice I had after Mum's funeral was to just focus on getting from A to B then to C and not look any further than one step at a time. I hope that doesn't make you want to punch me.'

She snorted with laughter and wiped her cheek. 'It makes me glad you came to Butterworth Wines, child. Now yesterday you told me what you've run from, but what is it you want from this next part of your life?'

The question took me by surprise; it was such a change in direction.

'Me?' I thought about it for a moment. 'I want to feel safe and secure again, I— That makes me sound pathetic.'

She shook her head. 'It's honest. I like honesty. Go on.'

'I want to build a home. I think of myself as a homemaker at heart but somehow I've never had the chance to be that person. I want to build a home which will be a happy safe place for my own family one day.'

'My grandson used to call my house his happy place, where he felt safest.'

'Jensen?'

Her face softened. 'Apple of my eye. The irony is that he now thinks I'm not safe here and would really prefer it if I sold up and moved out.'

I bit my lip but decided not to comment. Jensen had a good point; there might be plenty of volunteers around in the daytime to keep an eye on things, but with her failing eyesight, how could Betsy possibly be safe at night on her own?

'I suppose he's just looking out for you; with your eyes being—'

'He doesn't know about that,' she cut in sharply. 'And I want it to stay that way. Understood?'

'Um, yes,' I said, taken aback. 'Understood.'

Her breathing had quickened but before either of us could speak again there was a knock on the cottage door.

'Come in!' Betsy called.

A slim girl in her mid-twenties with dark brown hair showing under a floppy sunhat edged timidly round the door and raised a hand self-consciously. She was wearing a floaty summer dress and trainers. She was pale and freckly with perfect cheekbones. It could only be Pippa.

'Pippa, come in and meet Lottie, our new vineyard manager.'

'Hi.' I smiled and waved before remembering that part of my role was the management of the staff. I'd never actually managed anyone before, but I was sure Betsy would expect a bit more from me than simply grinning inanely and waving. I jumped to my feet and strode towards this young woman, hand extended.

'Lovely to meet you, Pippa. Betsy has just been telling me what a big help you've been to Ted over the years.'

'Oh, I don't think so.' Pippa's hand fleetingly touched mine, she dropped her head and two fat tears promptly slipped down her face.

'Don't say that,' I said with a jokey laugh, 'I'm relying on you to teach me about growing vines.'

'Viticulture,' she said with a watery smile. 'That's what it's called.'

'You see,' I said, nudging her with my elbow. 'I've learned something already.'

'I'll leave you to get to know one another while I finish the hoovering,' Betsy said, hauling herself from the sofa.

'I think if it's all right with you, I'd like to see the vines first?' I guided Pippa out of the cottage. I'd been hoping to unload the rest of my things from the car, but that could wait.

'Sorry about that. What must you think of me, weeping when Betsy introduces us?' Pippa mumbled, pulling a tissue from her pocket and pressing it to her eyes.

'That's nothing,' I said, glancing sideways at her. 'I wept on Betsy yesterday during my interview.'

'Really?' she said, sniffing.

I nodded. 'I needed a job and somewhere to live urgently, and didn't think I'd have a chance of getting this one, given my lack of experience. I was so grateful that Betsy gave me the opportunity.'

'That makes me feel better. Ted was like a father to me; I'm permanently tearful at the moment.'

'Then it's only natural that you miss him.'

She smiled sadly. 'My own parents were quite old when I came along. And since they died, Ted filled the gap.'

'I'm sorry for your loss.'

She took in a shuddering breath. 'It breaks my heart to see his winery without him in it. He'd spend all day every day in there, just tinkering. It crossed my mind not to carry on working here, but he'd want me to, I know that really.'

'Gosh, you mustn't leave!' I clasped her arm dramatically. 'You're my only paid member of staff.'

A fact that I wanted to get to the bottom of soon: how could the business be running with such a tiny team?

She emitted a giggle and shook her head with amusement. 'Come on, I'll show you around.'

Pippa led me along a path that ran down the side of the house and we started to head downhill. To our left leading from the house was a large patio which must have a fantastic view across the entire valley. We went down some steps and through a delightful garden bursting with a tangle of pretty summer flowers: phlox, peonies, roses, aquilegia, cornflowers and a host of others I couldn't identify. She stopped to open a gate in the middle of a long stone wall which ran at least twenty metres in either direction. At the far side of it was a set of double gates, wide enough for a vehicle to pass through, and a line of tall conifers stood like a row of soldiers leading downhill.

'I was wondering how grapes would grow well enough to produce a decent crop this far north,' I marvelled. 'I guess this wall and those trees protect the vines from some of the worst winds.'

She smiled. 'Correct, plus we grow cool-climate varieties.'

We went through the gate and the breath caught in my throat.

'I've never been in a vineyard,' I said, whistling. 'It's quite a sight.'

The lush green vines were held in check by thick wires which ran horizontally from post to post and ran in perfect lines to the bottom of the hill. Stripes of long grass dotted with wild red poppies ran between every row and their natural beauty complemented the symmetry of the vines perfectly.

'Isn't it beautiful?' said Pippa with a happy sigh. 'It's such a special place for me; I love being here.'

I eyed her curiously. 'Did you not want the job of vineyard manager? Surely you'd have been the obvious choice rather than an incomer who knows nothing about winemaking or viticulture?'

She shook her head. 'All the volunteers asked me the same question but I didn't want the responsibility. Managing this place would have taken the pleasure out of it for me.'

'And you're sure none of the volunteers wanted it either?' I bit my lip. 'Because I don't want to be treading on anyone's toes.'

'You won't be,' she assured me. 'Butterworth Wines is a hobby for everyone else. They aren't here regularly enough to keep a handle on what needs doing and no one wants to take on the commitment.'

'And the vineyard can run on such limited help?'

Pippa pulled a doubtful face. 'The vines cover about ten acres and between us Ted and I used to be able to just about manage. The last few months have been a bit of a stretch for me. The volunteers have been great since Ted became ill, putting in extra time, but they all have their own lives to lead.'

'So no one is going to resent being managed by a complete novice?' I asked doubtfully.

'Godfrey rang me last night to tell me about your appointment. We're all really pleased. Believe me, you're doing everyone a favour.'

'That's good to know,' I said with relief.

Pippa pulled a small tube of suncream from her pocket and rubbed it on her bare shoulders. She caught me looking. 'Even with factor fifty on, I can burn, I'd love a nice tan like yours.'

'Ah, but one of us will look like a leather sole when we hit sixty and one of us won't,' I said with a grin. 'So tell me about the vines.'

We walked on and Pippa explained in quiet, economical sentences that the grapes grown here were Chardonnay, Pinot Noir and Pinot Meunier – the three varieties traditionally used to produce champagne. British producers weren't allowed to call their sparkling wine champagne, of course; the name was protected by the French. But Butterworth Wines had been perfecting their own brand of sparkling wine for years and according to Pippa, who'd had it on good authority from Ted, it was as good as anything to come out of France, and without the price tag.

Each row was eight hundred metres long with a break halfway down to allow easier access. I learned that there were ten thousand vines, roughly a third of each variety, and that it was possible for one mature vine to produce enough grapes for one bottle of wine.

'And these are mature, by the look of them,' I said, trailing my hands through the soft leaves.

'Most of them are about nine years old, so yes, fully matured,' Pippa confirmed. 'They've more or less finished flowering now, but there's still a few vines in flower in the cooler corners. Look.'

She lifted the leaves of a vine to show me a thumb-sized stem covered in tight green buds. Some of the buds had sprouted fine white threads which gave the bunch a fluffy effect.

'The white fronds are the flowers. And once they've been pollinated they'll form grapes and then these little bunches will hang downwards instead of facing up towards the sun.'

'They're much prettier than I imagined.' I bent to smell the flowers. 'Pear drops.'

'Exactly.' Pippa looked pleased. We carried on down the row, tucking overgrown tendrils back into the wires as we walked.

'This is where I spend my time when I'm here,' she said,

breathing deeply, 'just tidying and tucking in, checking for disease and, as summer progresses, plucking off leaves to let the sun get to the grapes. It's very calming. I used to bring Wiser with me, our – I mean *my* – old chocolate Labrador, but it's too far for him to walk these days, but I don't mind; I'm used to solitude. I heard you worked in a crematorium before coming here, so you must be used to peace and quiet too?'

'It was rarely quiet and although there was sadness, mostly there was a lot of love. It was quite a special place, actually.'

She sighed wistfully. 'There's love here, too. Ted lavished it on all his vines, now it's up to us to do the same.'

I wrapped a springy tendril around the wire and tucked the end in.

'I'll do my best,' I promised.

We headed back uphill towards the house after I'd seen all I needed to for now. Some of the vines were a little overgrown and I made a mental note to draft an action plan for a major prune as soon as I had the chance.

'So what do you do when you're not working here?' I asked.

'I've been the librarian at Fernfield library for ten years.'

'That long?' I laughed with surprise. 'You don't look old enough.'

She nodded. 'I started straight after my A levels. I was a shy girl, bookish, not brave enough to leave home. The job in the library was a natural fit. I've never seen you in there, though.'

I laughed. 'I never really got into books. I was always a doer rather than a reader.'

'I envy you,' she admitted, tucking her hair under her hat. 'I've done nothing with my life; I live vicariously through my books.'

'Oh, I don't know,' I said, sweeping my arm out to encompass the vines as we arrived back at the gate. 'This doesn't look like nothing to me.'

She gave me a reserved smile but didn't elaborate. She struck me as the sort of person who could sit next to you on a long-haul flight and never strike up a conversation. I couldn't even stand in the ten items or less queue at the supermarket without spilling my life history to the poor person behind me.

'Does the library have any books about vineyards?' I asked.

'Oh yes. We have an entire shelf on viticulture.' Pippa eyes sparkled. 'In fact, that's how Ted and I met. He came into the library and asked that very question. But you don't need to borrow books from the library. Ted has collected books from all over the world – ask Betsy if you can borrow some.'

We'd reached the yard again and I asked Pippa if she'd help me take the remaining boxes out of my car. Five minutes later I was all unloaded and dying for a cup of tea.

'So I've learned about the grape growing part of the business,' I said, inviting her into The Stables and putting the kettle on. 'Who should I ask about how the wine is made?'

Pippa took off her sunhat and ran a hand through her hair. 'Now that is the sixty-four-million-dollar question.'

I looked at her quizzically. 'Why?'

Pippa took a deep breath. 'Ted and his brother Ron used to make the wine together. Ron died five years ago in a motorbike accident. Marjorie was injured too, broke her spine, that's why she's in a wheelchair.'

'I had no idea!' I gasped. Poor Marjorie and yet I'd never met anyone so determinedly bright and cheerful. If I'd loved her before, now I was even more inspired.

'So that left Ted to do it by himself. And now . . .' Her voice faded and she shrugged. 'There's no one. Last year's harvest is sitting in tanks waiting to be blended and bottled.'

'So there could be ten thousand bottles' worth of wine sitting in the tanks?'

She nodded. 'Well, less than that, because we'll keep

some back for blending. And once it's bottled, it's another year before it's ready for sale, which means that the previous vintage is now ready for sale. Matt and Clare are the two volunteers who help out in the winery, but Ted handled sales by himself.'

'So another ten thousand bottles?' I stared at her.

'Then of course there's the new crop on the vines. It's only three or four months until harvest and we'll need those tanks for the next pressing.'

'What are we going to do?' I said, feeling desperately out of my depth already. I passed her a mug.

Pippa looked at me meekly. 'I don't know. You're the boss.'

That's right, I thought with a gulp. I am. The notion that the next six months were going to be a time for stress-free healing and gentle reflection was beginning to evaporate like a morning mist.

Chapter 11

I spent the rest of the day touring the estate on the quadbike with a pad and pen, making a note of urgent jobs and creating a logical schedule for maintaining the vines and getting to grips with the various pesticides and fertilizers, and the machinery for applying them, all of which I found in an immaculately organized shed behind the winery.

Godfrey had dropped by at three to check how I was getting on and gave me a potted history of the vineyard. Ted had been in the police force and in his spare time he'd learned how to grow grapes and make wine, taking Betsy on wine holidays across Europe and researching which varieties would grow in Fernfield's sandy soil. His dream had always been to establish a vineyard as soon as he retired. Planting had taken place over a period of years, with a team of workers from Belgium arriving each spring to do the hard work. Once the vines had matured enough to produce a viable crop, Ted got the chance to use his winery for the first time. Since bottling his first vintage seven years ago, making wine had become Ted's *raison d'être*. He'd always been an introvert: not keen on parties or socializing or even holidays if there wasn't an educational point to them.

From that first vintage, Butterworth Wines had become better and better until, according to Godfrey, the sparkling wine, made in the traditional champagne method, could give any French fizz a run for its money.

Before he left, Godfrey had written down the names of all the volunteers and their phone numbers and by five o'clock I felt like I was beginning to get to grips with the task ahead of me.

I went back to The Stables, poured myself a cold drink and sat down on the doorstep to gather my thoughts.

Butterworth Wines had always been a family business, but apart from Marjorie and Betsy, there didn't seem to be any family around to carry it on and although I'd never met him, I reckoned that that would have been a disappointment to Ted. Betsy seemed to have her mind fixed solely on the next six months; I wondered what she was planning to do after that, and what, if any, thoughts she'd had on what to do with the full tanks of wine needing attention in the winery right now. I finished my drink and got to my feet; there was only one way to find out.

I rang the doorbell but couldn't hear it chime so I knocked on Betsy's front door instead. I tried a couple of times but there was no reply. I knocked one last time for luck and was about to give up and walk away when I heard approaching footsteps.

'All right, all right, where's the fire?' Betsy chuntered crossly before opening the door.

She had a crease on one cheek and her hair, usually so immaculate, was fluffy on one side and had partly escaped from the clip at the back. She stretched her eyes as if adjusting to the daylight.

'I'm so sorry, did I wake you?'

'Good heavens, no,' she said, appalled. 'Asleep at four o'clock in the afternoon? Not me.'

'Oh good,' I said brightly. It was well after five; someone had had a nap and lost track of time.

'Well, don't stand on ceremony, come in.' She turned away and marched off through an open door, trailing her hand along the wall as she did so.

I stepped into a hall with wood-panelled walls and a lovely worn herringbone wood floor. Overhead was a huge Tiffany chandelier which even when it was not lit from within created rainbow patterns on the walls where the light hit it. The house smelled of vanilla, lemons and furniture polish and a faint hint of wood smoke; it was a welcoming home and I had the strange sense of being wrapped in a warm embrace. I smiled at my sentimental thoughts, shut the door and followed Betsy into a large old-fashioned kitchen. It was exactly how I imagined it would be: from the original deep butler sink with its lovely copper taps to the oiled oak work-tops atop cream cupboards with worn metal handles. A family-sized table and chairs stood beneath a large picture window that had views out across the patio and the vine-yard beyond. Bunches of dried herbs, a garland of garlic and a string of onions hung from a wooden drying rack which had a pulley system. But perhaps, unsurprisingly, the most dominant feature was the huge floor-to-ceiling wine rack which, next to a sturdy oak dresser, took up most of one wall.

'You have a beautiful home, Betsy.'

'Hmm, you should have seen it when we moved in. A pig-sty, in more ways than one. Sit down, I'll make you a cup of tea; it's just straightforward English – I don't hold with that herbal stuff.'

'Thank you. No milk for me, please.'

I took a seat at the table and inhaled the scent from a jug of sweet peas which sat in the centre on a small lace mat. Starsky trotted in, eyed me warily and then flipped over on to his back presenting me with a pink tummy to stroke. I obliged and he squirmed happily.

Betsy shook the kettle and topped it up at the sink. 'The kitchen was the first room I did up when we moved in. Needs redoing now, but I shan't bother.'

'I think it's lovely,' I said, meaning it, taking in the row of knives on a magnetic strip fixed to the wall and an earthen-ware pot with at least fifteen wooden spoons and spatulas of varying sizes and the orangey-red cast-iron pots stacked in the corner. 'It feels lived in and loved, like the heart of the home should be.'

Starsky rolled on to his tummy, curled into a ball and closed his eyes as if to prove just how much he loved this room.

'It was.' Betsy sighed so faintly that I barely heard her. Then she seemed to give herself a shake. 'I always hankered after a large range cooker. Ted promised me one, but then decided we needed a quadbike more. He said as soon as we started making a profit from the wine we could have a whole new kitchen. I'm still waiting.'

A little alarm bell rang; did that mean that the vineyard had never made a profit? Or that Ted had always found something better to spend the money on? I decided that I wouldn't ask those questions today, even if Betsy didn't mind that I was nosy.

I remembered Marjorie saying something about Betsy burning herself and joined her by the kettle.

'I'll pour the tea, shall I?' I said. The mugs she'd dropped teabags into were ringed inside with caffeine stains and looked like they could do with a good scrub.

'No need.' She took a small device from a drawer and clipped it on to the side of one of the mugs.

'What's that?'

'Aha! It's a magic alarm to tell me when I've poured in enough liquid. My eyes find it hard to judge the level of water. Stops me burning myself. Despite what Marjorie may think, I'm not an idiot; I do keep myself safe. You can pass the milk, though.'

I opened the fridge and a whiff of something off made me gag. On the top shelf was a half-eaten carton of peeled prawns which had a greeny tinge to them. The use-by date was last week. What should I do? Tell her and risk embarrassing her, or . . . let her smell them for herself? And what if she didn't, what if she ate them?

'I was going to have prawn sandwiches for supper, if you wanted to join me?' said Betsy. 'Hurry up with that milk, dear.'

The question startled me and I ended up slamming the fridge door harder than I'd intended.

'That's very kind of you,' I said, 'but I'm planning on doing some reading this evening. Pippa said there might be some books on growing grapes you could lend me?'

'Just a hundred or so,' she said wryly. 'I'll find you some later. Come and watch my magic thingy.'

I watched as Betsy poured the boiling water into the mugs until the beeping noise alerted her to stop.

'See,' she said stoutly, handing me my mug. 'Perfectly safe.'

'Indeed.' I wiped the hem of my T-shirt around the rim of the mug surreptitiously. I'd have to find a way of dumping those prawns in the bin, perhaps if she left the room . . .

'Do sit down, dear, you're cluttering the place up. I'll find us a biscuit to tide us over. Should be a tin of shortbread in here somewhere.'

I did as I was told, hoping that whatever she was looking for wasn't six months past its sell-by date. My stomach contracted at the thought. I wasn't sure I could even drink my tea after sniffing the contents of that fridge, let alone swallow a biscuit.

'This place was some sort of smallholding when we bought it,' said Betsy, opening a cupboard and squinting at the contents. 'A misguided couple from Birmingham had taken it on wanting a taste of the good life.'

'Did they have animals or grow crops?' I watched her run her hands over the tins and boxes and plastic Tupperware containers, seeking the biscuits by touch.

'Both. Pigs and garlic.' She let out a peel of laughter. Her fingers alighted on a square tin and she gave a triumphant sigh. 'Can you imagine a more pungent combination? Once they'd got the good life, they found they didn't like the taste after all. Nor the smell. Mind you, I'm not surprised. It took me six months to get the aroma of pig shit out of the stables where you're living now.'

'Goodness!' I raised my eyebrows. It was such a lovely cosy little place; it was hard to imagine it with pigs in. I opened my mouth to say so but she got in there first.

'Why the surprised tone?' she tutted. 'Because I said shit?'

'No, not at all,' I laughed. A scratching noise at the front door caught my attention and I turned my ear to the kitchen door to listen. It sounded like someone was sliding a key in.

'Honestly, why your generation thinks that swearing is the preserve of the young I'll never know. Even Shakespeare was fond of a good obscenity. My particular favourite is f—'

'Gran?'

'Jensen!' Betsy gasped. She dropped the tin and swept the little liquid alarm from the worktop mug into the drawer.

'Surprise!' A man bounded in, grabbed Betsy around the waist, lifted her from the floor and swung her round, pressing loud kisses to her cheek. I couldn't help but smile, seeing the usually buttoned-up Betsy being whirled round, her feet flying out. I'd never seen her so undignified; but she seemed very happy about it.

Starsky sprang up too, his little tail thumping against the leg of the table.

Betsy hooted with laughter. 'Good heavens, child, put me down.'

The 'child' was a man in his thirties dressed in smart trousers, polished shoes and a pale pink shirt, open at the neck with rolled-up sleeves just below his elbows. His dark blond hair was short at the back but the top was curly, flopping over one eye, giving him the look of a 1950s film star – charming with just a hint of mischief. He was taller than Betsy, which wasn't hard, and athletic-looking – a lean build, so much more natural than the ginormous shoulders and biceps Harvey was so proud of.

He lowered his grandmother to the ground and she pressed a smacking kiss to his cheek before patting her hair back into place.

'Silly boy,' she chuckled, her cheeks rosy. 'You gave me quite a fright.'

'I rang the doorbell, but no one came so I used my key.' Jensen spotted me at the table and smiled enquiringly. The dog couldn't contain himself any longer and jumped up Jensen's legs for some attention. He obliged, scratching behind the delighted dog's ears. 'Hello, boy.'

'Battery's dead and I couldn't find the right screwdriver to replace it,' said Betsy.

Jensen and I spoke at the same time:

'I'll do that.'

'I can sort that.'

Jensen turned his attention to me. 'My apologies, we haven't been introduced.'

Wow. Jensen was one of the most gorgeous men I'd ever seen. Piercing navy blue eyes, dazzling smile, lovely teeth. I felt an unexpected ping in my chest. If I hadn't been completely sworn off men after escaping Harvey's clutches I may well have embarrassed myself by morphing into a swoony giggling girl. As it was I managed to keep perfect control.

'I'm Lottie Allbright,' I said, getting to my feet and returning his smile.

'Jensen Butterworth.' He shook my hand. 'Lovely to meet you.'

Unexpectedly, the touch of his hand – warm, dry and somehow assured – sent the butterflies in my stomach into a tizz. Double wow.

'Likewise.' I swallowed.

His jaw had a hint of stubble and he smelled lovely; I probably smelled sweaty.

Why hadn't I got changed before coming across? Slipped into a dress, or a T-shirt and shorts. Anything other than this polo shirt, still hanging out from when I'd rubbed my mug with it and which must have shrunk because it never used to be this tight across the chest, and these hideous work trousers which were brilliant for keeping thorns and insects at bay, but probably equally effective at keeping male admiration at bay too. Plus, I was hot suddenly. Very hot.

'Lottie,' said Betsy, suddenly tight-lipped, 'is our new vineyard manager. Amongst other duties.'

He stared at me. 'Sorry, I, er, I wasn't expecting . . . Gran hasn't mentioned anything about you.'

I realized I was still holding on to his hand.

'Sorry,' I said, releasing it. Now I wasn't just hot, I was embarrassed too which meant a whole new level of attractiveness: my neck and chest had done its rashy thing.

'Lottie.' Jensen scratched his chin. 'Hello, pleased to meet you.'

'Clearly,' said Betsy, looking between the two of us and smirking. 'You've told her twice.'

Jensen pushed the dog off his leg and gave his grandmother a look somewhere between bewilderment and frustration. 'Can we talk in—'

'Tea?' said Betsy loudly, interrupting him. She marched back to the kettle, took out another mug, reached for the drawer and hesitated. Starsky retreated to his spot under the table and closed his eyes with a contented snuffle.

I knew exactly what she was thinking: that she couldn't use her magic alarm with Jensen there because he'd ask too many questions. I decided to come to her rescue just this once. I completely understood why she didn't want to admit any failings in her health to her beloved grandson; she didn't want to worry him and five minutes ago I'd have probably sided with her. Now, having smelled her fridge, I couldn't condone her deception. At this rate it wouldn't be too long before some sort of disaster occurred and I didn't want that on my conscience; coming to the Butterworths' was supposed to signal an incident-free time for me.

'You open the biscuits,' I said, handing her the tin, 'I'll make Jensen his tea. Or would you prefer coffee?'

'Coffee please,' said Jensen, jingling coins in his pockets. After his exuberant entrance his demeanour had changed completely: his smile had been replaced by a weary frown. 'Gran—'

'I didn't hear your car on the drive,' said Betsy, blatantly ignoring him and wrangling ineffectively with the lid of the tin which I could see was sealed with clear tape but she presumably couldn't. 'Such a lovely treat to see you. To what do I owe the pleasure? Oh, this infernal lid!'

Betsy shoved the tin at Jensen who caught my eye with a flicker of amusement.

He picked at the end of the tape, peeled it off with a flourish and prised off the lid.

'Could have sworn I'd already removed that,' said Betsy innocently.

I turned away, spooning coffee into Jensen's mug to hide my smile.

'My car doesn't make much noise. Come and look, Gran.'

He beckoned her to the window at the far end of the kitchen which overlooked the yard.

'What am I looking at?' she said, pressing her face to the glass.

'My new car. Just got it last week. What do you think?'

'Very smart,' she said, 'and it's my favourite sort.'

Jensen laughed. 'So you know what it is then?'

'Of course. Silver,' she retorted, turning from the window, she caught my eye and mouthed, 'Help!'

I crossed to the window to see for myself. The car *was* smart: a silver Mercedes, which if I wasn't mistaken . . .

'Is that an electric Mercedes?' I asked, handing Jensen his coffee.

'Thanks. Yes, it's a hybrid.' Jensen nodded. 'A new initiative at work to be more eco-friendly. My idea. If we've got to

118

be on the road so much, it makes sense to reduce our carbon footprint as much as possible.'

'What do you do?' I asked.

He sipped his coffee. 'I work for a global firm of architectural engineers.'

I looked at him blankly and he smiled.

'So, for example, we're working on an infrastructure project in Scotland and a sports stadium in Singapore. And I'm a project manager, tasked with integrating all the different pieces of software into each building so everything talks to each other.'

'He's very clever,' Betsy put in.

'It's true,' Jensen said, deadpan. Then his lips twitched. 'The world of digital systems would collapse without me.'

'I'm impressed,' I said, raising an eyebrow. 'And talking about being eco-friendly, I was looking in the shed today where the fertilizers and pesticides are kept and I was wondering how you'd feel if I looked into some organic alternatives?'

'Fine by me,' said Betsy, with a wave of approval.

Jensen frowned. 'Gran, we probably should discuss the vineyard's cash flow before we start spending any money.'

'Says the boy with the flash new car,' said Betsy crisply, biting into a shortbread finger. 'Stop worrying and have a biscuit. That always used to work when you were a little boy. Do you remember coming into my room in the middle of the night, Mr Rabbit tucked under your arm, to tell me you'd had a bad dream or wet—'

'Gran, please!' Jensen raked a hand through his hair.

'Sorry, darling, didn't mean to embarrass you.' Betsy didn't look the least bit apologetic, she was smirking. I was beginning to get the measure of this old lady; she was devious and mischievous and I already loved her to bits.

'That's a company car, which cost me nothing,' her grandson continued. 'I've been promoted.'

'Well done!' Betsy said in a wobbly voice. 'Oh, your granddad would have been so proud. And so am I.'

Jensen sat beside her and held her hand. 'Thanks, Gran.'

The two of them sat lost in their thoughts for a few moments and it crossed my mind that I was intruding and by rights should disappear back to The Stables, but I'd come over to borrow some books and really wanted to get on with some background reading this evening. I'd just have to wait for a suitable opening in the conversation, fetch the books and leave them to it. In the meantime, I ran some hot water in the sink, added some washing-up liquid and began scrubbing the mugs and teaspoons.

'And the reason I've called in is because I've got a meeting in Newcastle tomorrow morning and I thought I'd drive up to surprise you and take you out for dinner. Oh, that reminds me, I've left something in the car.'

Her head lifted swiftly. 'Out?'

'Just a plate of pasta at the Italian in the village, nothing fancy. I'll be right back.' He kissed her hand and excused himself to go back outside.

A look of panic crossed Betsy's face.

'Oh bother! This is the last thing I need,' she hissed. 'I can't read a menu unless I take my huge magnifying sheet with me. I won't be able to find the lavatories, or even navigate a bumpy floor without someone telling me where I'm walking. What am I going to do?'

'What do you normally do?'

She looked stricken and my heart went out to her.

'I insist on eating at home, but that packet of prawns won't be enough for his big appetite.'

'And actually I think they're out of date,' I said, glad to have had the chance to tell her.

'Damn. Quick get rid of them before he finds them; he'll have me signed up to Meals on Wheels before you can say salmonella.'

I held my nose as I disposed of the putrid prawns and had

just taken a deep breath when Jensen reappeared with a bouquet of flowers.

'These are for you,' he said, kissing Betsy again. 'You sounded a bit glum on the phone when we last spoke. I thought you might need cheering up.'

'Seeing you is enough to brighten my day,' she said, visibly choked up.

'Let me put those in a vase for you,' I said softly.

She smiled up at me, her eyes hazy with tears. 'You're very kind.'

'It's my job, remember.' I smiled back.

'It is,' she said slyly as if something had just occurred to her. 'And I'll need you to come to dinner with us too. Because there are some things I'd like to discuss about the vines while we eat. Why don't you go and get ready and—'

'Oh, but Gran!' Jensen sucked air through his teeth. 'Lottie, I don't mean to be rude, but there are also things I need to discuss, about, well, me actually.' He laughed awkwardly.

Both of them gave me pleading looks. I felt torn. And also tired. The last thing I wanted to do was go out to dinner, especially when I wasn't wanted by fifty per cent of the rest of the party.

'It's a lovely offer, Betsy,' I covered my mouth to shield a yawn which was only half fake, 'but it's been a long day and I'm sure Jensen would rather not share you.'

'Oh, very well.' She shot me a filthy look and I felt dreadfully disloyal.

'If the carbonara is on the menu, I highly recommend it,' I said, hoping Betsy would realize I was dropping hints to help her out with the menu. I also hoped this would help earn her forgiveness. 'And the bruschetta to start. And if you want dessert there's—'

Jensen held up a hand, grinning. 'Thanks for the tip; I think we'll find our way around the menu, thank you.'

'Of course. In that case, I'll, er . . .' I cleared my throat. 'I'll leave you to it. Lovely to meet you, Jensen.'

'You too,' he said.

'Well, bye then.' I didn't quite know how to take my leave and ended up doing a weird arch shape with my hand like a windscreen wiper and cringed all the way across the yard.

At least I was bound to have made a lasting impression on the lovely Jensen, I thought pragmatically, the question was: what sort?

Chapter 12

Back inside, I hooked open the top half of the stable door to let the warm evening breeze blow through and set to work unpacking. I was arranging my toiletries in the bathroom when my mobile rang. It was Evie in a high state of excitement.

'Oh my God, Lottie, you'll never guess who's just called.'

'Dad?' I said, catching a glimpse of my face in the bathroom mirror. There was a streak of mud under my chin which Jensen couldn't have failed to see. I sighed. 'Oh great.'

'Well, yes, actually he did call,' said Evie, sounding confused. 'What's wrong with that?'

'Nothing,' I said, not wanting to complicate matters further. 'Sorry, I was talking to myself. How was he?'

'Having a ball, by the sound of it. Said he'd met loads of women.'

'Really?' This was so out of character for Dad that I abandoned my packing and walked through to the living room to sit down and give Evie my full attention.

'You won't believe this.' Evie snorted. 'He had a flat tyre and got rescued by a choir of Belgian nuns on their way to Lourdes for a concert who dropped him off at a garage to get help. He said he felt like an extra on the set of *Sister Act*.'

We both laughed, imagining Dad squashed in the back of a minibus singing hymns with the Belgian sisters. My heart twisted with love for him. I wished I'd had more time at home with him before he'd left on his adventure; I'd barely seen him this side of Christmas. Still, I was glad he was enjoying himself.

'I told him you'd got a new job and moved out,' she went on.

'You didn't mention anything about Harvey turning up?'

'God no,' she said with a shudder in her voice. 'I didn't want to worry the old boy.'

I breathed a sigh of relief.

'Anyway!' The excitement in her voice was back. 'You'll never guess who else has phoned *and* asked me to dinner at the Italian in the village?'

'Who?' I crossed my fingers . . .

'DARREN!' she squealed.

I laughed. 'And I take it you're pleased about that?'

'Very. I've got a really good feeling about it. What if he's come round to the idea of fostering and he wants us to try again?'

'You still really love him, don't you?' I said, thrilled that there was still a chance for them.

'I do,' she said softly. 'I know we've had our ups and downs, but when Harvey turned up on Tuesday and I went to call Darren, I realized what a huge hole he has left in my life. It broke my heart. If he wants to move back in I swear I'll jump on him at the table.'

'That I'd love to see,' I said. 'In fact, I could have seen it. I was invited out to dinner there myself this evening.'

'By whom?'

'Jensen Butterworth, Betsy's handsome grandson.' I could feel my cheeks lifting as I talked. 'He turned up out of the blue this evening in his brand-new car, smelling divine and with the loveliest bouquet—'

Evie squealed again. 'You fancy him; I can tell by your swoony voice!'

'If I wasn't so metaphorically bruised and battered by my ex, I probably would; but let's face it, Evie, I need a break from relationships for a while. So don't encourage me.'

She conceded that I had a point and we discussed her

outfit possibilities for a few minutes before ending the call. I closed my eyes and allowed myself to slump down on the little sofa. I stretched my arms to the side of me and planted my heels on the rug to anchor me. I suddenly had an image of me and Evie doing snow angels in deep fresh snow outside our back door in our pyjamas. We'd thought Mum would go mad, but she'd run to fetch the camera and took pictures of us instead. Giggling to myself, I replayed the motion again now, my legs and arms flailing like a starfish.

'Lottie? I've brought you— Oh, sorry, I'm interrupting . . . something.'

My eyes flew open to find Jensen hanging over the open half of the stable door, looking startled.

'Yoga. Helps to release tension from the spine.' I jumped to my feet, pressed my hands together in prayer over my heart and did a small bow, hoping to disguise my burning face. 'Namaste.'

'Namaste,' he replied, clearly amused, one blond eyebrow arched. His eyebrows were lighter than his hair, I noticed. Sun-bleached almost. His face was tanned too; I bet he'd had freckles when he was younger. My first boyfriend had freckles. Everywhere. I used to trace them with my finger across his tummy. I wondered if Jensen had freckles left anywhere . . .

He coughed politely and I realized I was still in prayer mode. I dropped my hands, swung them around a bit and then settled them on my hips.

'You brought me something?'

'Gran sent you these,' he said, holding out a stack of books. 'She's gone to get changed before we go out.'

'Oh, thanks.' I took them from him and set them on the kitchen table. The cottage was so small I could do this without taking more than a couple of steps.

A normal person would have opened the door and let him in. Not me. I just let him stand there on the other side of the stable door, like we were two horses sharing a nose-bag or something.

He rubbed the back of his neck. 'Look, this is a bit awkward.'

I nodded, smiling; he was here to apologize and beg me to come out with them, I could tell. I bet Betsy had told him off for his bad manners.

'It's fine, don't worry. And I really am tired; I've had a lot to learn today and there's still loads more to go at.' I gestured to the books. 'So if your grandmother really wants a third person I suggest you try Marjorie.'

Jensen frowned. 'That wasn't what I was going to say.'

'Oh.' My face was so hot even my eyes were burning.

He took a deep breath. 'Lottie, you seem like a lovely girl.'

I widened my eyes.

He flushed. 'Sorry, *person*. And I'm sure under different circumstances you'd make a great vineyard manager – I presume you've had a lot of experience with vines—'

'Well, I . . .'

'Anyway, that's not the point. The point is—'

'Jensen?' Betsy called from across the yard. 'I'm all dressed up with nowhere to go here, come along.'

He exhaled with frustration. 'I'll have to catch up with you at another time. This weekend hopefully.'

'Hopefully,' I found myself echoing.

He looked confused and turned to go and then hesitated. 'Hold on a sec.'

He zapped his key fob at the car and it lit up. 'Get in, Gran,' he shouted.

'How do you think she's doing?' he said, his blue eyes boring into me as if they were trying to read my soul not just my face.

'Well, I've only just met her, so . . .' I said, flustered and absolutely determined not to drop her in it and mention her sight.

'But do you think she's coping okay without my

grandfather?' He looked over his shoulder. 'I want an honest answer. I can't ask any of the others, including Marjorie, because they're all so protective of her. As if at the slightest sign of trouble, I'd whip her off into a home or something.'

'And you wouldn't?' I said, watching his features carefully.

He took a deep breath. 'I love my grandmother more than anyone else in the world. I want her to be safe. But most of all I want her to be happy. That's my priority.'

I felt my throat tighten. That had to be the most adorable thing I'd ever heard.

'Then you probably know her better than anyone,' I said kindly. 'Watch her tonight, gauge for yourself how she is. I think she's . . .' I swallowed.

Jensen's eyes narrowed. 'Yes?'

'I think she's very lucky to have you.'

The horn of his car sounded loudly and we looked across to see her waving impatiently at him.

'She was my rock when I was a little lad,' he said fondly.

I reached across the stable door and touched his arm. 'And now it's your turn to be hers.'

He gave me a dubious look.

'But don't tell her that,' I added and we both laughed.

I waved them off as they drove out of the yard and marvelled at what an unusual day I'd had. Life with the Butterworths was not quite the low-key summer I'd had in mind. Still, I was happier than I'd been in a long time and maybe, I thought with a flutter of hope, I'd finally found somewhere to call home, at least for the summer.

Hours later, a loud insistent knocking at the door woke me with a start. I blinked myself awake. There were no lights on, and with the stable door fully closed, the cottage was dim. The knocking started again, this time with more urgency.

My pulse raced; something might have happened to Betsy in the night. And I was the only one here. I stumbled to my feet and a heavy book crashed to the floor; I must have fallen asleep reading one of Ted's books.

'Coming!' I yelled.

I dashed across the room and flung open the door. 'Sorry, I was— Oh!'

Jensen stared at me grimly, feet planted, arms folded.

I pressed a hand to my chest, breathing heavily. 'Is everything okay, is Betsy all right?'

'Gran's fine,' he said. 'But I'm not. I need to talk to you.'

'It's the middle of the night!'

He shook his head in disbelief. 'It's eight thirty; it's not even dark.'

As my eyes adjusted to the light, I saw he was right.

'Oh, right,' I said. 'I'm very tired at the moment, a lot has been going on and I haven't been sleeping—'

'Can I come in?' he said, stepping into the cottage and sweeping past me into the kitchen area. There was no point answering that.

'Tea? Coffee?' I asked instead, closing the bottom half of the stable door, but leaving the top half open so that Jensen's hot air could escape. 'Cold water?'

'No.' He caught my eye and looked away again guiltily. 'Thank you.'

'How was your dinner?'

He rubbed his forehead, leaned against the worktop and folded his arms again. 'The waiter told us the specials and Gran repeated each one like it was some sort of memory test, which I thought was odd.'

'Oh?' I had an inkling where this was leading. Of course, I'd expected him to guess. What I hadn't bargained on was this obvious anger.

'Yes.' His blue eyes held my gaze, but rather than the dazzling smile he'd given me earlier, now his fierce stare bore into me like a laser. 'And she held her menu upside down and pretended to peruse it until I turned it around for her.'

'Lucky she had you to look after her,' I said softly.

'Yes, I was there then. But I'm not here most of the time,' he said through gritted teeth. 'I had no idea that Gran can't see!'

'She can see; her vision is simply impaired,' I corrected.

'If you can call it vision,' he muttered. 'Once I'd tackled her on it, she admitted that she's had macular degeneration for a couple of years, but her optician confirmed that it's deteriorated a lot recently. The doctor recommended some vitamin supplements the other day, but the loss of sight is irreversible.'

So that was why she'd been at the surgery when I bumped into her and Marjorie.

'Poor Betsy,' I said. I picked up the book that had fallen and stacked it with the others. 'Do sit down.'

He raked a hand through his thick hair. 'I can't, I'm too wound up. I don't understand why you weren't honest with me. I don't understand why Gran has employed you and I am not at all sure about your motives.'

His long legs started to pace the length of the tiny space and something inside me snapped; this was like watching Harvey build up to one of his rages all over again. I was not going to stand for it.

I got to my feet and stood in his path, forcing him to stop pacing.

'I have to tell you,' I said, chin tilted, 'that I don't respond well to bullying. I've recently ended an' – I stopped short of admitting that it had been abusive – 'an unhappy relationship and will never again tolerate that sort of behaviour.'

Jensen's jaw dropped. 'This isn't about *a relationship*; this is about you taking advantage of an old lady who's recently been widowed.'

'I resent that remark,' I said, folding my arms. But a small voice in my head was already beginning to worry. Had I taken advantage of her? She hadn't even advertised for staff, that had been Godfrey and Roger. And if I hadn't burst into tears, she probably wouldn't have changed her mind and I wouldn't be here now. Had I taken advantage of her kindness? I swallowed nervously, doubting my own intentions.

'Lottie,' Jensen said, exhaling deeply as if trying to control his temper, 'my grandmother can't see properly! How can she possibly remain in this big house alone, not to mention in charge of ten acres of vines and a winery?'

He cared about her, I reminded myself; he was angry because he was worried, that was all. I touched his arm tentatively.

'Jensen, I completely understand how you feel—'

'Do you?' he snapped, shrugging me off. 'I doubt that very much. My job is really high pressured. I work in London at the moment and if things progress how I think they might over the next few months, I'll be even further away. I wouldn't be able to relax knowing that at any moment, Gran could have an accident.'

'And is that what is the most important thing here: you being able to relax?' I stared at him, challenging him with my eyes.

He looked away and massaged his forehead.

'Yes. No. Of course not! But I do have a duty as her grandson to make sure that she is living her best possible life and any idiot can see that living here, being responsible for a business, which by the way has cash flow problems to rival a small African country, is impossible.'

He finished his little tirade and appeared to run out of steam, dropping down on to the sofa with a thump and clasping his head between his hands. 'Hell fire, what a bloody mess.'

My legs were shaking from a combination of tension and tiredness and I was about to sit on the opposite end of the sofa when a voice from the door made us both jump.

'Jensen, my dear boy, I think we need to get a few things straight.' Betsy stood framed in the open part of the stable door. She looked like a wise old angel in her white blouse with the pink of the setting sun forming a halo around her white hair.

'Gran!' Jensen looked across to the door and groaned.

'Apologize to Lottie this minute.' Betsy reached inside, fumbled with the door catch and let herself in. 'The poor girl has been through enough and she does not deserve getting short shrift from you.'

I shot her a smile of thanks, even though I wasn't sure she could see my features clearly. She steadied herself by holding the back of the nearest dining chair.

'I'm waiting,' she said imperiously.

Jensen gave me a sulky look. 'I apologize.'

'Well, that was full of sincerity,' said Betsy sternly. 'I thought you had to leave for Newcastle, shouldn't you be on your way?'

He stood up and stifled a yawn. 'I can't go now, not until I get some answers to my questions.'

Betsy stiffened her spine and drew herself up to her full height. I glanced at Jensen to see if he realized there was a torrent of ire heading his way. He did.

'Gran,' he began, holding his palms up in defence.

'Here's a question for *you*,' she said. 'Did Granddad's will mention anything about you being in charge?'

He frowned. 'No but—'

'Or about me having to defer decisions to you?'

'Well, no but—'

'Precisely. Which means that you have absolutely no right to be demanding answers.' She glared at him and he shifted his gaze from the floor to me and back again. He looked so uncomfortable that I was beginning to feel sorry for him. 'From either me or my staff. Now, I'm prepared to discuss my plans with you, but under my terms and without feeling harangued. Understood?'

'Fine,' said Jensen flatly, looking like a beaten man. 'But I'm going to need some coffee first to wake me up, I've had a long drive up from London.'

Betsy's icy demeanour melted instantly. 'Oh my poor boy, of course you have and I'm causing you more stress.'

'I'll put the kettle on,' I said, pleased to be able to do something positive.

'Proper coffee,' Jensen added, eyeing up the jar of instant on the worktop.

Betsy caught my eye and gave me an amused wink, har-rumphed and turned back to the door. 'Oh, for heaven's sake. Back to the house, city boy, and I'll make you some fresh.'

'Goodnight,' he said to me, stifling another yawn as he trooped out of the cottage and stomped across the yard.

'Typical,' Betsy said with a tut. 'Just as hot-headed as he was as a boy.'

'It's just because you're his favourite person in the world,' I said, 'he told me.'

'Oh, the dear child.' She sighed. 'But be that as it may, he's deserted me. Would you mind walking me back to the front door? I haven't brought my stick and my eyes are worse when the light fades.'

'Sure.'

Jensen's yawn was infectious and once I started I couldn't stop.

'Excuse me,' I said, covering my mouth.

She tucked her hand through my arm as we made our way slowly back to the house, dodging the potholes.

'Don't tell me we're boring you,' she whispered, her eyes twinkled mischievously.

'There is no chance of that.' I laughed softly. 'Anyway, tell me, did you enjoy your Italian?'

'Oh yes,' she chuckled, 'once I'd memorized the menu. Although there was a young couple at the table next to us having a bit of a domestic. Such a shame. Apparently, the man threw money on the table and walked out, leaving her in tears.'

My heart thumped in horror.

'Are you all right from here?' I asked once we'd reached her front step. 'Because I'd like to go and phone my sister.'

She bade me goodnight and I sprinted back to my cottage. My pulse was whooshing in my ears as I rang Evie's number. It might not have been her and Darren that Betsy overheard arguing, but it seemed too much of a coincidence not to be.

My heart sank as her voicemail kicked in.

'Hi, Evie,' I said, careful to keep the worry from my voice, 'just wondering how your evening went? Call me back. Love you.'

Two minutes later, a text message flashed up on my screen.

Awful. I got it all wrong. He doesn't want us to try again, he wants a divorce. Don't call me back, I don't want to talk tonight. Evie xx

Poor Evie. And Darren. My chest felt tight with sorrow for them both. I sent Evie a text sending my love and urging her to call me any time, night or day, as soon as she felt able to. Ten minutes later I crawled into bed, exhausted; the first night in my new home. Despite feeling more tired than I'd done in my whole life, my brain kept replaying the drama of the week and I couldn't stop asking myself a million questions. What could possibly have gone so wrong on Evie and Darren's date for it to end in the threat of divorce? And what would that mean for her chance of fostering; would she have to sell the house? What if Harvey came back for me and found me here? I wouldn't want any trouble for Betsy. And finally, what if Jensen was right and the vineyard really was in financial trouble? Suddenly, the simple life I'd envisaged back in Derbyshire was looking less simple by the hour . . .

Chapter 13

It was Sunday morning and even though Betsy had insisted that I work normal Monday-to-Friday hours, I had no intention of lazing around. I felt full of energy for a change after a twelve-hour sleep last night so I went for a walk around the vines, tucking in and tying back wherever I saw a wayward frond. I was already getting to know the different varieties and learning which rows got the most sun. That very sun was warm on my face and after an hour my shoulders were beginning to burn and my head ached. I decided to head back inside for a bottle of water and some sunscreen. Hopefully the winery would be open by now too. Roger had spent a couple of hours here yesterday and had told me that I might catch Matt and Clare in there today: the only two regular volunteers I hadn't yet met.

On the walk back up to the cottage I sent Evie a quick text to check she was okay and got a 'thumbs-up' back. Phew.

I'd met her for a drink at the Royal Oak on Friday night, the night after her disastrous evening with Darren, and she'd poured her heart out. We'd sat outside in the corner of the beer garden where she could cry unobserved if necessary. It had been going well, or so she'd thought, until she'd reached across the table to stroke his hand, taking a chance that that was what he wanted too. But he'd folded his arms, looked down at the table and told her that he'd found himself a solicitor, that he was prepared to make everything as painless as possible and that she could keep the house. Evie had been so shocked that he wanted such a quick end to their marriage that she'd burst into tears. Things had gone downhill from there, which must have been the point at which the commotion drew Betsy's attention.

Since then Evie had thrown herself into redecorating the spare room and by Saturday evening she'd been feeling bright enough to invite me round for pizza and wine. I'd declined, telling her that I was enjoying my research into viticulture so much courtesy of Ted's extensive collection that I couldn't drag myself away.

'You've never read a book in your life,' she'd laughed.

This was true; while she'd been addicted to Judy Blume and all things *Sweet Valley High*, I'd been climbing trees and trying to train earthworms to go round an assault course I'd built in a shoebox. It was surprising we got on as well as we did, when you thought about it . . .

'I've just never found one I've been interested in before, that's all,' I'd retorted.

So I'd been propped up in bed by nine, with a giant bag of Minstrels, a bottle of sparkling water – my new obsession - and a beginner's guide to grapes from around the world. And this morning I was reaping the benefits.

The doors to the winery were open and a pick-up truck and a tiny hatchback were parked outside. I dashed back into The Stables, slathered my arms and shoulders with factor thirty, grabbed a bottle of water from the fridge and headed to the winery. After three nights of reading about it, it was time to add some liquid knowledge to all that theory.

'Okay, ready!' called a bright female voice from the depths of the winery.

'Right you are,' shouted a deep masculine voice in reply.

A mechanical whirring noise followed, which reminded me that I had a headache and I swigged at my water in case I was dehydrated.

I headed to the back of the room and found a man and

woman working at different steel tanks, a thick hose running between them, connected at the base of the tanks with large chrome valves. The man, roughly my age, was crouching crablike, elbows resting on knees. He had long dark hair tied in a ponytail and huge biceps bulging from a faded black T-shirt. The woman had shoulder-length, highlighted hair with a heavy fringe, a wrist full of tinkly silver bangles and wore a long apron over a coral shirt and tight cropped jeans.

I coughed gently so as not to make them jump and the man looked up.

I waved. 'Hi, are you Matt?'

'The one and only.' He grinned, getting up from his crouched position. He was tall and broad and looked somewhere between a pirate and one of those American wrestlers with comedy names like Warrior and Crusher. 'Wait up, Clare, we've got company.'

The woman dried her hands on her apron and clasped them together in prayer. 'Please say you're Lottie?'

I nodded.

'Yes!' She punched the air.

'Pleased to meet you both.' I smiled back, delighted to get such a warm welcome. Even though Pippa had insisted that no one else wanted to take on the top job, I was still half-expecting to meet resistance from someone. It didn't look like it would be Clare.

Her Adidas trainers squeaked on the floor as she scurried over, smiling broadly to reveal a gap in her front teeth. I stuck my hand out for a handshake and she took it in both of hers and squeezed gently, finally releasing it with an affectionate pat.

'We are so thrilled that Betsy agreed to employ someone. What a bloody relief!' she said, pretending to mop her brow. 'Now we can get motoring again.'

She had perfect nails, I noticed, and they were painted the exact same shade as her shirt. How did people manage such casual coordination? I thought I was doing well if I put red nail polish on at Christmas. And by Boxing Day most of it was chipped off.

'Hope you don't mind me interrupting but I've come for a lesson in winemaking, if that's okay?'

Matt loomed over me and took my hand next, pumping it up and down in his big hands. 'If only we had someone who knew what they were doing, eh, Clare?'

'You tease.' She punched his arm. 'Ignore him, honey. We'll happily show you around.'

We chatted for a few minutes, introducing ourselves. Matt ran a pub in a nearby village with his girlfriend but they had grand plans to move to France and open their own guest house one day; and Clare, who I guessed to be in her late forties, seemed to split her time between the vineyard and the gym, and was involved with lots of committees to keep herself busy now that her children had left home. Despite Matt's comment, they both seemed very knowledgeable about Butterworth Wines.

For the next twenty minutes or so I helped them with 'racking off', which I learned meant filtering the wine to get rid of the sediment by transferring it from one tank to another.

'This is last year's Pinot Meunier,' said Matt. 'It's been in the tank for eight months now.'

'When will it be ready for bottling?' I asked.

Clare pulled a face. 'We've never had to make that decision; it was always Ted's job.'

'But I think it's there, as near as dammit,' said Matt, rubbing the dark stubble on his jawline.

'And can you handle the bottling when it is ready?' I asked.

'Bottling is no problem.' He sniffed, puffing out his chest. 'I can work all this kit with my eyes shut.'

'It's blending that's the tricky bit. The 2017 vintage has all got to be blended first before bottling to make our three wines,' Clare chipped in, chewing her lip. 'None of us are confident enough to do that. It's a massive responsibility.'

I nodded; Pippa had said something similar last week. It

seemed to me that a winery manager was needed as much, if not more, than a vineyard manager.

Matt agreed with Clare. 'Get the blend wrong and that's an entire harvest down the drain.'

'All our lovely new tanks are full.' Clare pointed to the row to our left. 'These are the Meuniers, the Chardonnay is at one end and the Pinot Noir is at the other.'

'New?' I said, taking in the long line of gleaming stainless-steel vessels.

She smiled sadly. 'Ted was so excited to make the first sparkling wine from these tanks this year. So sad he'll never get to taste it.'

'Surely between us, we can carry on without him?' I said. But looking at the doubt on their faces, perhaps not. 'Or is that impossible?'

'Truth is, the only person who really knows, or should I say *knew*, how to create the perfect wine was Ted.' Matt folded his arms and flexed his biceps one at a time. 'We've got to find a way to do him proud. I owe a lot to that guy. This wine's not leaving Butterworth's until it's as good as he'd have got it. Not if I've got anything to do with it.'

'We all owe a lot to Ted,' said Clare, giving his arm a motherly pat. They shared a sad smile. 'Now, why don't we give Lottie some wine to try?'

'Do I have to make slurpy noises?' I asked, remembering how Marjorie and Betsy had sloshed it around.

Matt laughed. 'The point of rolling the wine around your mouth is for your tongue to get the full effect. The tip of your tongue tastes the sweetness, the sides get the acidity and the alcohol hits the back of it. Slurpy noises strictly optional.'

Clare fetched three wine glasses. 'Matt, will you do the honours?'

He walked to one of the Pinot Noir tanks, turned on a small tap one third of the way up and squirted half a glass of wine into each.

I watched them hold the glass to the light, swirl it round and plunge their noses over it. I followed suit. It had a golden tone and smelled fresh and earthy and full of minerals. I lifted the glass to my lips and took a big sip. Matt and Clare squelched it around their mouths making 'Mmm' noises and nodding to each other. I rolled the wine self-consciously from one side of my mouth to the other before swallowing it.

'Well?' Matt raised an eyebrow. 'What do you think?'

'You go first,' I said, in case I'd got it completely wrong.

'Light on the nose,' said Clare.

'I'm getting honeysuckle and fruit,' Matt agreed.

'Maybe raspberries?' I suggested.

Matt nodded enthusiastically. 'Exactly. Well done.'

Clare smiled fondly. 'Clever girl.'

'So if you know how all the machinery works, Matt, why can't you blend the wines?' I asked, trying not to show how pleased I was with their compliments.

'See that little cubbyhole in the corner?' He was pointing to a small area that had been sectioned off with softwood panels. 'That's Ted's lab. All the refractometers, hydrometers, test tubes, packets of everything from yeast to oak flavourings are in there. And that was where he used to do his blending. He made notes on every wine he ever made but we think the notebooks must be in the office in the house. Until we get those, we don't know what proportions of each variety he used in the past.'

'But even with the notes, blending isn't straightforward,' Clare put in. 'Every vintage has its own characteristics, its subtle nuances. To make good wine, it's not just a case of following a recipe.'

'Hmm.' I frowned. 'Can't you just start from scratch, make a blend that we all agree tastes good?'

'I wish,' said Matt with a laugh.

'It's not that simple,' Clare explained. 'Butterworth has a house style for each wine; customers know what to expect and we need to be consistent. I think this is nearly done, Matt.'

We left Clare to finish off the filtering process and Matt led me through to the wine store.

'Ted has always made three different wines.' He picked up a bottle from the uppermost shelf and another from a lower shelf further along.

'This is the Butterworth Classic Cuvée, our best seller. One bottle from 2015 and the other from 2016. It's got almondy-brioche flavours which customers love. Imagine if this year's ends up tasting flinty with a hint of gooseberry? We'd get complaints.'

'And I'm guessing that's hard to achieve?' I doubted my taste buds would ever be able to decipher the flavour of French pastry.

'Without an experienced winemaker, it's impossible.'

'Gosh,' I said with a sigh, 'and I thought the biggest problem was going to be keeping the grapes alive until harvest.'

Matt chuckled. 'You're right, actually; that's impossible too.'

'Thanks for the encouragement,' I said wryly. 'I don't know whether I need a lie-down or another drink.'

'If in doubt, always go for another drink,' he said, winking a dark brown eye at me.

I held my palm up. 'I'm actually heading back out in the sun, so maybe not. And I certainly don't want to drink that.'

I pointed to the bottle from 2016 which wasn't labelled and had a thick sludge of sediment inside.

Matt laughed. 'Don't worry. This one isn't finished yet, what you can see is the dead yeast, called "lees". The 2016 vintage is ready for the next stage now, called *dégorgement* and *dosage*. It'll be crystal clear after that.'

I winced. 'That sounds like a medical procedure.'

'It's French for blasting out the old yeast and topping up the bottle with a *dosage* – a mix of wine and sugar. Great fun. *Then* you can drink it.'

'In that case, count me in to help with that.'

'Getting the *dosage* right is a delicate process too, and something else that Ted was brilliant at.' Matt frowned. 'If we get it wrong, it could ruin us.'

'I'll have a look for Ted's notebooks as soon as I get the chance,' I said.

'That would be a start, thanks.' Matt smiled grimly, shoving his hands into the back pockets of his jeans. 'Clare asked Betsy to look for us, but she got short shrift. Godfrey thinks it's because she doesn't like admitting how bad her sight has become. Whatever the reason, we've put off asking her again. But now we're running out of time.'

I promised to do my best and as we carried on the tour of the winery, Matt told me how he and Ted had met eighteen years ago. Matt had been living rough, he confided, and Ted had still been in the force.

'I'd been nicked a couple of times for shoplifting. Ted sat me down with a cuppa and gave me a talking-to about life choices. Then he helped me get a job at a pub and, long story short, I'm now the landlord of my own pub, The Golden Arrow in Flittham. As soon as he got the winery up and running, I asked if I could get involved. If I didn't come here I don't know what I'd do with my spare time.'

'You never wanted to work here full time?' I asked, thinking what a good manager he'd have made.

'Nah. The pub is doing well, my girlfriend runs the food side and I've got a great team of bar staff. It's busy, noisy, hectic and I love it. Coming here is like the antidote to the pub and a few hours here, tinkering with the tanks, with nobody to manage, is like therapy, but I like the balance as it is. I'll leave the management of this place to you.'

'Me? No!' I laughed. 'I couldn't manage the winery; I don't know the first thing about wine.'

'I'll pretend I didn't hear that,' said a smooth voice from the doorway.

I turned to see Jensen, leaning on the door frame, arms

folded and a wry smile on his face. My stomach flipped; was I destined to say or do something idiotic every time he saw me?

'Oh, hello!' I felt the heat from my earlier sunburn turn up several notches. 'What I meant was—'

'Lottie's too modest,' Matt interrupted. 'She's not got a bad palate, actually. She'll probably know as much as any of us within a fortnight.'

'I take it back.' Jensen cocked an amused eyebrow. 'Seems you've made a good first impression.'

'The feeling's mutual.' I smiled at Matt and then held Jensen's gaze, wondering what sort of impression I'd made on him.

We stared at each other until Matt broke the moment.

'Good to see you, Jensen.' He crossed the gap between them and gave him a manly thump on his back.

'You too, Matt,' said Jensen, returning the bigger man's greeting with a more reserved pat. 'How are you getting on here?'

He looked past Matt to the tanks.

'Well . . .' Matt sucked in air.

'The winery isn't part of my remit,' I jumped in, 'but we urgently need to talk to Betsy about a plan of action. No one has the experience to progress the wine from tank to bottle.'

'She's right.' Matt's brow furrowed. 'And we can't seem to get through to your gran how important it is.'

Jensen stroked his chin pensively. 'I thought as much. The wine business was Granddad's domain; I don't think she can face it without him.'

There was a loud gasp as Clare noticed Jensen's arrival.

'Jensen!' She flew across the winery, arms wide and kissed him. 'I haven't seen you since the funeral. You look tired, have you been eating properly?'

He did look tired, now I looked at him properly.

'I'm fine, thank you.' Jensen laughed, prising her hands from his face. 'A bit tired because I've had to work this weekend, but I like to be busy.'

'You'll get used to this.' Matt cupped a hand to his mouth and pretended to whisper to me. 'Clare mothers everyone whether they like it or not.'

'It's true. Can't help it,' she said with a giggle, giving Jensen's cheek one last pat. 'My daughter, Frankie, is in Australia, married with a beautiful baby, and my son, Ben, is in the army currently posted to Afghanistan, so I've got no outlet for my maternal love.'

'I'm sure you manage to show them you love them across the miles,' I said. It took all my will-power not to offer myself up as an 'outlet'; Dad was the best dad ever, but even he had been no substitute for a warm and comforting hug from my mum.

Clare looked wistful. 'I do my best. And I have all of you to look after and that keeps my mind off things. Although I miss fussing over Ted.'

'I miss Granddad more than I thought possible,' said Jensen softly. There was such raw emotion on his face that it brought a lump to my throat.

Matt hooked an arm around Jensen's neck, which was more like a rugby tackle than a sign of endearment. 'We all miss him. He was the life blood of Butterworth Wines.'

Jensen acknowledged Matt's heartfelt words with a smile. 'He was a man of few words, my granddad, but he was a good judge of people.'

Clare perched her bottom on the desk and sighed. 'I'll never forget the time he caught me crying over my shopping trolley in the breakfast cereal aisle. All emotional because I'd automatically put a seventy-four pack of Weetabix into the trolley for our Ben before remembering he'd be waking up in Kabul and getting goodness knows what for his breakfast.'

'What did Ted say?' I asked.

'He produced a hanky from his pocket and said the key to enjoying my new freedom was to find a hobby. Then he asked me if I'd like to learn how to make champagne and he's been paying me in Butterworth sparkling wine ever since.'

'Me too,' said Matt. 'I usually go for the Blanc de Noir.'

'Talking of which,' said Jensen, giving himself a shake, 'Gran has sent me over to grab a couple of bottles for tasting with lunch.'

Matt held up a finger. 'Take the 2015 Classic Cuvée. It had a year on its lees and it's now had six months in the bottle since *dosage*. Six months.' He stressed this last bit before jogging into the wine store to retrieve the bottles.

Clare chewed her lip. 'He means we need to sell it, Jensen. Sales have ground to nothing since Ted became ill. And your gran doesn't seem interested. We've all offered to go through the emails, but . . .' She shrugged.

Jensen winced. 'I'm on it. I hadn't realized quite how bad her sight was. I think now that's out in the open things will get easier.'

He looked sideways at me and I felt a flush of relief that I didn't have to keep that particular promise to Betsy any more.

Matt wiped the dusty bottles on his jeans and handed them over.

'Thanks.' Jensen looked at me. 'Lottie, Gran would like to know if you'd care to join us for lunch. My great-aunt is here too; they're both on the terrace. There are things about the vineyard I'd like to discuss if you've got the time?'

My face had cooled down a bit since he'd first arrived but I was still conscious that I was in a grubby vest top and shorts whilst he was immaculately dressed in soft indigo jeans and a pale blue linen shirt which brought out the colour of his navy eyes. From nowhere my stomach churned with nausea; possibly too much sun, although my head felt better.

'You've gone as white as a sheet.' Clare peered at me. 'Do you need to sit down?'

I breathed deeply and shook my head. 'I'm okay, thank you.'

'Not the most enthusiastic response to a lunch invitation I've had from a woman,' Jensen teased. 'Are you sure you're okay?'

I produced a smile. 'Absolutely, but would you mind if I just joined you for a drink, rather than lunch? I don't have much of an appetite at the moment.'

We left Matt and Clare to finish off what they were doing and lock up the winery for the day and we set off across the yard. Jensen did a double take when we reached the centre and stopped by a patch of new cement.

'Someone has filled in that big pothole.'

'I did,' I said lightly. 'I googled it and worked out how to fix it. I didn't want your grandmother to fall down it. Nor your great-aunt's wheelchair, come to that.'

His eyes slid sideways to me. 'You're full of surprises, aren't you?'

I shrugged. 'That's nothing. You should see me twenty feet up a tree with a chainsaw.'

He laughed, assuming I was joking, and I just smiled sweetly, not bothering to correct him.

'I'll just be a few minutes, I'm going to freshen up,' I said, pointing to The Stables.

'Not on my account, I hope?' Jensen said, glancing casually at my shorts and vest top. 'You look nice as you are.'

'You don't believe women dress to impress men, do you?' I said, pretending to be shocked and veering off towards home.

'No, no, of course not,' he spluttered after me.

Inside, I peeled off my clothes and ran to the bathroom. Right, five minutes to make myself presentable. For Betsy and Marjorie. Naturally . . .

Chapter 14

A few minutes later I approached the terrace at the rear of the house in a black T-shirt dress. The three dresses I'd rejected had made me look busty, butch and bloated respectively, but this one – with a scoop neck and short sleeves – covered up the bits that were feeling a bit bigger and emphasized my tan. Perhaps I should have had those protein shakes for breakfast instead of the morning pastry, I thought ruefully. The diet starts tomorrow. Again.

I'd only got as far as the side gate when I heard raised voices. I lifted the latch and hesitated, not sure if I should intrude.

'Over my dead body!' That was Betsy sounding most affronted.

'I'm just saying, Gran, we need to face facts,' Jensen replied calmly.

'Here's a fact for you: Granddad left the house and his ninety per cent share of the business to me,' Betsy continued crossly. 'Your great-aunt Marjorie, of course, owns the other ten per cent. As a zero per cent shareholder, you don't get a say.'

'What your gran means to say is that she loves you dearly,' said Marjorie carefully, 'but she'll ask for help when she needs it.'

I smiled at that; Marjorie had probably been playing the role of peacekeeper for the hot-headed Betsy for years.

There was a patter of paws followed by the appearance of a wet black nose under the gate as Starsky sensed my presence.

'Come on through, Lottie!' Betsy shouted. 'You can be on my side.'

I opened the gate, stopped to give Starsky some fuss and headed to the large wooden patio table shaded by a huge canvas parasol. The back doors to the house were open and a delicious smell of cooking wafted in the air. Marjorie patted an empty chair beside her and I sat down. She'd transferred from her wheelchair to a wooden armchair and looked comfortably ensconced, with cushions under her bottom and behind her back. She was wearing a voluminous grey T-shirt with the Harley-Davidson logo across her chest and shorts which looked like they'd once been a pair of jogging bottoms. Betsy, by contrast, looked dressed for a garden party at Buckingham Palace in a neatly buttoned tea dress, pearls and her trademark swept-up hair-do.

'We're *all* on your side, Gran,' said Jensen wearily, sending me a pleading look.

On the table were two ice buckets and a tray of champagne flutes, a bowl of little salted crackers and a stack of papers.

Jensen pulled a bottle from the ice and began peeling off the foil cap.

'There is absolutely no need for me to up sticks and move,' said Betsy crisply. 'I'm managing perfectly well, especially with your help, wouldn't you agree, Lottie?'

'Well,' I began, conscious that whatever I said I'd annoy somebody, 'we did have a good sort-out in the kitchen on Friday afternoon, and I've written labels in large print and stuck them on tubs of things to make it easier to identify their contents.'

I'd also thrown away all the food that had passed its sell-by date – an entire bin's worth – but I thought it best not to mention that. Unfortunately, Marjorie felt no such loyalty.

'Don't tell me you've finally chucked that commemorative tin of Marks and Spencer's biscuits from the royal wedding,' she said.

'It was a wrench,' Betsy admitted, not meeting my eye.

We'd had words about that. The biscuits, like that tin of shortbread from the other day, hadn't been opened, but even so, they wouldn't have been out of place on the *Antiques Roadshow*.

'Wonders will never cease.' Marjorie helped herself to crackers and pushed them in my direction. I took a few and ate them. The saltiness was exactly what I needed and I had a couple more before sliding the bowl away.

Jensen sighed as he eased the cork from the bottle with a twist. The contents gave a pleasing pop and we all whooped politely.

'If you've still got biscuits from 2011, Gran, I think the first toast should be to the fact you haven't given yourself food poisoning.'

'Just a small one for me,' said Betsy, holding up a glass to him. 'Don't be silly, Charles and Diana got married much earlier than that.'

The look of horror on Jensen's face was a picture. Marjorie slapped her thigh and burst out laughing and I popped some more crackers in my mouth to hide my mirth. Betsy remained po-faced, but she couldn't quite conceal the twinkle in her eye.

'To go back to your suggestion, Jensen,' she said, 'I love you dearly, but I'm afraid the answer is no. N O spells no. I won't move out, so I'm toasting independent women. Cheers!'

'Lottie, have this.' Marjorie wisely changed the subject to the Butterworth 2015 Classic Cuvée in our glasses, handing me a sheet of paper containing the tasting notes.

'You'll notice the wine is probably not as chilled as you'd normally get it. But cold masks the flavour. To appreciate it properly, professionals always taste at room temperature,' she explained.

I glanced through the page to see what it was I was looking for. According to the tasting notes, the drink I'd got in my hand was an elegant dry sparkling wine, a pale straw colour characterized by a steady stream of minute bubbles. It claimed to have an aroma of biscuit and nougat. I smelled it and was delighted to get a whiff of toasted oats. I read on: a creamy mousse on the palate with hints of baked apple and frangipane. The finish was crisp, fresh and moreish.

'What do you think of it, Lottie?' Jensen was studying me closely.

'I get the creamy mousse part and I can taste fruit, but nothing more accurate than that,' I admitted. 'Sorry. I'm not a big drinker. I'm willing to learn, though.'

'And a quick learner too, according to Roger.' Betsy nodded regally. 'He said the timetable you've done for next week is as good as anything Ted produced.'

'High praise indeed from Mr Bossy,' Marjorie chuckled, brushing spilled wine from her bosom.

I raised my glass to my mouth to cover my proud smile.

'Thank you. How much does it retail for?' I took another gulp and I swirled it round my mouth as delicately as I could.

'Thirty quid a pop,' said Marjorie.

I coughed and choked. 'Gosh! I've never drunk anything so expensive in my life.'

'Ted's wines are award-winning,' Betsy said. She slurped at it. 'This is very good. Do we have much stock of it?'

'An awful lot,' I told her. 'And Matt says it's ready to leave the winery.'

Betsy sniffed. 'Ah, yes, I suppose it would be. Ted always dealt with the orders. I . . . I'm afraid I've rather let things slide.'

Jensen caught my eye.

'Gran, I'm sorry to have to mention this . . .' He reached for her hand. 'Granddad sent me some cash flow reports for my advice a few months ago, but I got side-tracked with work and by the time I got round to reading them and realized how precarious the business's finances were, he was ill and I decided it wasn't the right time to bring it up.'

'How precarious?' said Marjorie, sitting forward.

'Those new tanks he bought last year?' said Jensen.

Betsy's face looked pinched. 'He had big plans for expansion; he reckoned this year's harvest was going to be huge and he'd need more capacity. I wanted him to slow down, do less, but he wouldn't listen.'

'He used all the company's cash reserves to do it rather than take out a loan,' said Jensen softly. 'And according to the last quarter's accounts, there wasn't enough to cover the outgoings. The cost of the pruning team alone in January took up all of the bank account's overdraft facility. I would have advised him differently and I feel very guilty that I didn't give him help when he first asked for it.'

I wondered if this was the reason for the dark smudges under his eyes: not from working too hard, but from guilt that he hadn't intervened while his granddad had been alive.

'So we're badly overdrawn.' Betsy pursed her lips. 'So what? We'll survive.'

'Why didn't you say? You must have received letters from the bank?' Even Marjorie looked shocked.

Betsy withdrew her hand from her grandson's and folded her arms. 'Have you seen how minute the print is on those things?' she huffed. 'You need a microscope to make any of the letters out, let alone a pair of reading glasses.'

Jensen groaned. 'I'd have helped.'

'You've got enough to do.' She waved a hand. 'I didn't need to read them anyway, I'm not colour blind, everyone knows a red letter means trouble.'

'No, a red letter means it needs urgent attention,' Jensen replied firmly.

'Top-up?' said Betsy, ignoring him. She picked up the bottle and waved it at Marjorie who directed it into her glass.

'I'm not quite sure what we should toast this time,' said Marjorie, 'the patron saint of overdrafts, maybe?'

Betsy gathered herself up as if she'd had a brilliant idea. 'Let's toast Lottie,' she declared. 'Ted would be thrilled that you've joined our merry crew.'

'Motley crew, more like,' said Marjorie.

Betsy ignored her. 'When Ted became very ill, I was too preoccupied to think about Butterworth Wines and then after he died I was so overwhelmed with everything that needed doing and didn't know where to start.'

'You hid it very well.' Marjorie blinked at her sister-in-law. 'I've been in awe of your composure.'

'I know I was foolish not to confide in anyone,' Betsy admitted, 'but I was scared I was losing my grip. Now with Lottie here I'm already feeling more confident about staying put and seeing the next harvest through without Ted.'

Jensen rubbed his forehead. 'But Gran, you were always trying to get Granddad to leave this place, now when you have the choice, you won't. I don't understand?'

'Not leave permanently, just once in a while,' she huffed. 'When we came here I thought making wine would be a hobby, but it took over his life. Ted made excellent sparkling wines and I'm proud of him for what he managed to achieve so far north when most vineyards are on the south coast. But I resented the fact that there was a whole world out there to see and the only view I had of it was from our boundary wall down to the bottom of the valley. Now he's gone and you're right, there's no reason for me to stay except that for me the world has now become a hazy place, where I don't feel safe, where I can't find my way—'

She broke off and took a napkin from the table, twisting it between her bony fingers. The rest of us remained silent and I felt a knot of sadness in my chest for her.

'And there's another reason too. Ted was convinced that the harvest we're going to have this autumn will be our best ever. He asked me to stay and gather in the crop for him one last time, one last Butterworth vintage.' She looked up with watery eyes. 'How could I refuse?'

'You did the right thing, Gran, but the problem is that without Granddad here, there's no one with the know-how to run the winery. So . . .' He blew out a breath as if psyching himself up. 'I strongly recommend we try to find a buyer for the business as a going concern. Someone who can hit the ground running and get straight to work. There's a lot that needs to happen before the next crop is ready.'

'Lottie, what do you think?' Betsy looked at me, willing me to side with her. 'Can we manage by ourselves?'

My heart thumped. 'Well, I—'

Jensen held up a hand. 'With respect, Gran, by her own admission, Lottie knows nothing about wine.'

'Shush, don't be rude. Go on, Lottie.'

I shot Jensen a look of apology. 'Your volunteers are all lovely and willing to do as much as they can. But Jensen's right, Betsy, no one has Ted's expertise and without that, last year's wine can't be blended and the previous year is waiting for two things beginning with "D".'

'*Dosage*,' Marjorie supplied. 'And *dégorgement*.'

'Exactly,' I continued. 'No one has been able to get your input, Betsy.'

She winced. 'Yes, that's probably my fault. I've been a bit crotchety since Ted's funeral and Clare caught me at a bad time and asked me a question about Ted's notebooks. I bit her head off and told her I didn't want anyone ferreting through his things. They'll be in his office somewhere. I should look for them, I suppose.'

I could feel my stomach working up to an almighty rumble and just about managed to cover it up by grabbing a handful of crisps and crunching into them.

There was a beeping noise through the open window.

'That's the oven timer; I'd better go and check on lunch.' Betsy swallowed the last drop of sparkling wine and pushed her chair back from the table.

'Would you mind if I had a look in Ted's office?' I asked.

152

'Perhaps I can locate the notebooks? And if it's all right with you, I'd like to check the computer for orders too?'

She hesitated. 'Ted was very particular about his office.'

'I understand,' I said meekly.

'Betsy, don't you think it's time you let others help you?' said Marjorie gently. 'If you want to get this next harvest in for Ted, Lottie's going to need access to his notebooks and if there are orders stacking up . . . ?'

Betsy exhaled and her shoulders sagged. 'Of course, I'm being ridiculous. Please help yourself to what you need, Lottie.'

She unhooked her walking stick from the back of the chair and set off inside.

'I'll show you where everything is,' said Jensen, getting to his feet. 'Excuse me, Aunt Marjorie.'

'Take your time, love,' said Marjorie, refilling her glass. 'I'm going to have another search for those baked apples.'

Jensen ushered me into a small room stuffed with filing cabinets, shelves bowing under the weight of thick reference books and, in the centre, a long wooden desk hidden under heaps of papers. He shut the door behind us and raked a hand through his hair.

'What the hell am I going to do?' he said in a low voice. 'The sensible thing would be to move her into an assisted-living apartment and sell the business on but I can't see her agreeing to that.'

'What would Paddington do?' I murmured, reaching below the desk to turn on an elderly computer.

'What did you say?'

'Er . . . I said I don't envy you,' I replied, hiding my warm face behind my hair. 'Look, give me an hour while you have lunch and I'll see what I come up with. You never know, there might be an answer staring us in the face.'

'Thanks.' He turned to go and I caught his arm.

'And, Jensen? I know your heart's in the right place and I don't envy the position you're in, but leaving here would be the end of so many things for your gran. Not just the house and the land and wines but her memories of happy times too. And it would be the end of her independence.'

'So what are you suggesting: that we leave things as they are?'

I shook my head. 'Things definitely have to change. For a start off there are thousands of bottles of wine to get moving and bills to pay. What I'm saying is that we have to do the kind thing, which is not necessarily the most sensible.'

His lips twitched. 'How about kind *and* sensible?'

'I'll do my best,' I said, miming pushing up my sleeves. 'Now, no more arguments over lunch; it'll give you indigestion.'

'You're bossier than Gran.'

'You ain't seen nothing yet.' I gave him a mock stern look and I heard him laughing all the way along the hall.

Honestly, I thought an hour later as I scribbled a few notes, I was wasted as a gardener slash vineyard manager, I should have been a private detective. I'd uncovered all sorts of nuggets of information that could change everything. I'd even found an old photograph of Betsy and Marjorie with two men I presumed were their husbands and another man who, according to a note on the back, was called Sidney. They were standing in a row of vines holding glasses of red wine aloft in a country that definitely wasn't England. A bit more digging through old emails had not only unearthed Sidney's full name but also revealed that he had given Ted advice in the early days of Butterworth Wines. If Sidney was still alive he could be a big help to Betsy this summer. But the best find was Ted's meticulously kept notebooks. He had two sets: one for the vineyard, in which he noted everything from hours of sunshine to the exact location of frost patches on winter mornings, and the other for every blend of wine he'd ever made. His writing was scratchy and hard to decipher and what bits I could read didn't mean much to me, but I was certain that the books would be a great help to us all over the coming season.

Ted's desk hadn't been touched for several months, judging by the pile of unopened post, the unanswered emails and an answerphone which had stopped taking messages because it was full.

There were condolence cards too, stacked on one end of the desk, opened but still in their envelopes; the thought of Betsy sitting at Ted's desk trying to read them with her magnifying glass made my heart ache. I picked out the correspondence that needed the most urgent attention to pass to Betsy and Jensen and made my way back outside to the patio.

My insides were fizzing with more bubbles than a glass of Butterworth Classic Cuvée; I had the beginnings of an idea and if I could get Jensen on side, it just might save the vineyard.

'Someone looks like the cat who got the cream,' said Marjorie, looking up from her bowl of trifle as I joined them.

'I have had one or two ideas,' I said, sitting in the chair which Jensen pulled out for me. 'How would you feel about a party?'

'A party?' Betsy gasped.

I could have kicked myself for my choice of words. It was insensitive of me to suggest something so frivolous so soon after losing her husband.

'I mean an open day,' I said quickly. 'We could offer tours, tastings and perhaps give some bottling demos in the winery. The main aim would be sales, of course, and we could have special offers on bulk purchase of our wines. It would be a great way of generating some instant cash flow.'

Jensen and Betsy said nothing, just stared. I began to doubt myself; perhaps it wasn't such a good idea after all.

'Have some pudding, Lottie. Trifle or just strawberries?' said Marjorie, her hand hovering over the two serving dishes.

I chose strawberries without cream; they were home-grown

and looked refreshing and luscious. I bit into one and tried to guess what the others were thinking. After another few seconds of silence I felt obliged to fill it.

'Ted has a big mailing list with lots of wine societies on it. And there have been loads of messages and emails from people wanting to buy from us. This would give us a chance to reduce stocks and save ourselves the hassle of arranging deliveries in one fell swoop. And,' I looked directly at Jensen, 'if the vineyard were to come up for sale in the next year or so, an event like this will help raise the business's profile.'

He raised his eyebrows. 'It's a thought.'

'A party would cheer me up no end,' said Betsy, her eyes sparkling. 'And if it will help get us out of a financial hole, even better. I think it's a splendid idea.'

'Agreed,' said Marjorie, looking rather pink-cheeked. She drained her glass and lifted it up. 'I'll be in charge of the bar.'

'We could get one of those gazebos and put it just down there in the space between the wall and the start of the vines. Matt's good at that sort of thing,' said Betsy, pointing southwards towards the vineyard.

'I'm so glad.' I breathed a sigh of relief. 'I couldn't see any reference to previous events so I wasn't sure if it was something you'd consider.'

'There weren't any,' said Marjorie. 'He was a private man, was Ted.'

'Wine societies were always making enquiries to visit but Ted never wanted the public here,' Betsy explained. 'In his words, he didn't want to turn the place into a circus. Occasionally wine merchants were allowed in, strictly by appointment, but apart from that, all his sales were done by phone or email.'

'But needs must,' said Jensen. 'And whatever happens in the future, tackling the high stock levels is a priority. I'm all for it.'

'Excellent,' I said, 'because I thought you could head it up, as a Butterworth.'

He opened his mouth as if to argue but his grandmother got in there first.

'Oh yes, Ted would have loved you to be involved. He always hoped one day you'd take an interest in the wine business and take over from him.'

'I didn't know that.' A shadow passed across Jensen's face and I guessed he was still feeling guilty about not helping Ted out when he'd asked.

'He didn't mind, of course, it was only a dream,' she reassured him. 'And he was very proud of your career.'

'Then of course I'll be there,' he said, squeezing Betsy's hand. 'Lottie and I can discuss dates and details later. But there's still something we need to sort out: how are we going to finish off Granddad's wine without his expertise? According to Matt and Clare, the 2017 needs blending and bottling and the 2016 vintage is ready for its *dosage*.'

'I think I might have a solution to that,' I said cautiously.

Jensen grinned at me. 'Don't tell me; you googled it and worked out how to do it yourself.'

'Sort of,' I said, pulling the old photograph from my pocket. 'How about asking for help? From Sidney Buxton?'

'I remember him.' Jensen took the picture from my hand to examine. 'It's Granddad's old school friend!'

'Sidney Buxton,' Marjorie chuckled. 'Now there's a blast from the past. Married a French girl and together they took over her father's vineyard just outside Reims. Why didn't we think of him before?'

Betsy frowned. 'He was a regular visitor at one time, and helped Ted no end when he was setting up the vineyard. I've not heard from him for a while, although I think he and Ted kept in touch by email.'

'We invited him to the funeral but he didn't come,' said Jensen. 'I phoned the number in Granddad's address book myself and left a message on a French answerphone.'

'He wrote me a lovely condolence card,' said Betsy, 'and sent his apologies for not attending.'

'If Ted were to trust anyone to blend his wines, it would be Sidney,' said Marjorie. 'He makes wonderful champagne.'

'It's a fabulous idea, Lottie.' Betsy clapped her hands together. 'Let's see if he can spare us some of his expertise. I knew it was a good idea taking you on. Jensen, aren't we lucky?'

'It certainly looks that way.' He smiled and it lit up his whole face and the warm glow it gave me touched my heart.

My happiness lasted all day and it was Jensen's face I saw as I drifted off to sleep that night. There were lots of things to be happy about with my new job, and Jensen Butterworth was definitely one of them.

Chapter 15

After sorting out a date with Jensen for the last Saturday in July (he had a packed diary – business meetings all over the place – but, I'd noted, by reading over his shoulder, no mention of a girlfriend anywhere), the plans for the inaugural Butterworth Wines open day took shape with surprising speed.

For the next month, the team pulled together, throwing themselves into the preparations. We'd settled on ten pounds a ticket, which I thought was excellent value for a glass of award-winning sparkling wine and a full day's entertainment.

In the run-up to the event, Marjorie had been pressed into office duty, going through emails and collating all the orders that had been missed. We had already made a dent in the stock of 2015 vintage that had been sitting in the wine store gathering dust. I gave the job of phoning around some of Ted's wine society contacts to Betsy. I'd written a list of names and numbers in black marker pen so she could read it and she spent many hours in conversation with wine lovers all across the country, laying it on thick about how unique the open day was going to be. Heart-warmingly, she received many compliments about Ted's wines from well-wishers who were thrilled to hear that the vineyard was opening to the public for the first time.

Matt had been beyond excited about the event, offering us the use of several marquees and a pop-up bar, complete with a couple of barmen to man it, a fact that had thrilled Marjorie no end. He'd even set up a free prize draw on the bar of the Golden Arrow – first prize being a bottle of Butterworth's finest – using the promotion to advertise the open day.

We'd also managed to decipher from Ted's notebook some details about the *dosage* he had used for the last two years and after a bit of experimentation, Matt and Clare decided they felt brave enough to do a trial with the 2016 vintage so that our open day visitors would get to see our production line in action. It would be another year before this batch of sparkling wine would be ready for sale, but we'd be taking pre-orders and hopefully avoid a repeat of the stock build-up situation that we were currently in.

Roger, Godfrey and Pippa had spent every spare hour with me in the vineyard. The vines were rampant at the moment now summer was in full swing; leaves were green and lush and new shoots seemed to appear overnight, stretching across the rows to try to join tendrils with the vines opposite. It was a constant battle to keep them in check. The grapes were still in tight green bunches but so far we hadn't lost any to bad weather or disease. We'd had only the teensiest bit of mildew and that had been in the lower area nearest the stream which ran along the bottom of the property. Thanks to a quick response from Roger, we'd nipped the rot in the bud by treating the affected vines with bicarbonate of soda.

The trio weren't just vineyard focused; they'd each got their marketing talents too. Godfrey had exploited all his old newspaper contacts, sending out a press invitation along with the promise of a free bottle of fizz to any journalist who turned up. Pippa had printed the event details on bookmarks and put one inside every book that was checked out at the library. Roger had come up trumps too. At his school's Sports Day, he'd grabbed the loud hailer from the head teacher and told all the parents to come along.

What's more, he'd persuaded a group of boys from the first-eleven cricket team to act as car-park stewards for us on the day.

Only Jensen hadn't been involved with our preparations, although to give him his due, he had spoken to the bank on Betsy's behalf and arranged for a temporary extension on the overdraft. And, as he explained to me on the phone one day, his company was involved in the biggest pitch in its history and he couldn't get away but he promised to be with us on the day.

And now it was the evening before the Butterworth Wines open day. The sky was blue and cloudless and the sun to the west was beginning to sink, bathing the tops of the vines in honeyed light. The volunteers had gone home exhausted and excited for tomorrow and Betsy was inside watching the television at full volume. She said it helped to have it up loud: it compensated a little bit for not being able to see much of it.

I did one last circuit, taking in all the little details that would make tomorrow memorable for everyone – not just for our visitors but for the Butterworths too. The barrels Matt had borrowed from the brewery to act as little tables; the colourful bunting we'd strung across the courtyard, borrowed from the library; the huge pots of fuchsias and geraniums I'd planted up and dotted everywhere; the trays and trays of polished glasses on loan from Matt's pub – it all looked so inviting. Even the Portaloos we'd hired were posh ones decorated to look like a row of pastel-painted beach huts.

We'd achieved so much as a team, I thought with a rush of pride, in just a few short weeks. The site was almost unrecognizable from the unloved and untidy place it had been when I'd arrived. The vineyard was immaculate and the winery was pristine and worthy of a visit from royalty. Back at the cottage, I caught sight of myself in the mirror – my flushed cheeks and the twinkle in my eyes – and I realized I'd achieved something for myself too. Gone were the circles under my eyes and the worry lines on my forehead and the tremor in my stomach at the sound of Harvey's key in the door. Butterworth Wines was far more than just a job for me; it was my home, my haven and my happy place. I felt part of something incredibly special and tomorrow, if the open day went well, maybe Jensen would fall under its spell too . . .

The open day officially began at noon and our three young car-park attendants were under strict instructions to keep the gates closed until then. At eleven forty-five, I gathered everyone else together on Betsy's terrace. I'd had some smart black polo shirts made for the day with the Butterworth Wines logo emblazoned on the chest and we'd all paired it with either shorts or jeans. Matt had had to roll the sleeves up on his because his biceps were too big. Clare and I had opted for a size larger than normal, she wanted to wear hers over leggings, I was just feeling bloated at the moment and wanted comfort. Godfrey's strained a little over his stomach whereas Pippa and Roger, who were both slim and athletic, looked perfectly at home in theirs. We were an assorted bunch, I thought fondly, but already they felt like family and they'd worked so hard these last few weeks. Ted must have been quite special to have engendered such loyalty.

'Is everyone happy with their roles for today?' I asked.

Marjorie was overseeing the bar while Betsy would remain ensconced near the refreshments on the terrace to talk to people and Jensen would be a floating pair of hands, acting as host and fielding business enquiries as needed.

'Absolutely,' said Roger, rocking on his heels. 'Can't wait to get cracking.'

Clare raised her hand. 'If anyone with an outside job has had enough of the sun, feel free to ask me to swap later.'

'I might,' said Godfrey, dabbing his pink forehead with a

hanky. 'And if you spot a journalist, please point them in my direction.'

Pippa tugged her cap down lower over her face. 'Definitely. I don't want to talk to the press. I don't want to talk to anyone, really. My plan is to keep as low a profile as possible.'

I reassured her that she wouldn't be expected to give tours, but just to be on hand to help as needed. It was a shame she was so shy; she was such a lovely girl and more knowledgeable about the vineyard than the rest of us put together. Still, there was no way I was going to force her to do anything she was uncomfortable with.

'I've put a thousand bottles of 2016 Blanc de Blanc through the gyropallet,' said Matt. 'So they're riddled and ready to go.'

This was the big cage machine which joggled the bottles gently until they were upside down and all the dead yeast formed a plug at the bottle neck, ready to pop out.

'Great.' I gave him the thumbs-up. 'And you're confident you can do the *dégorgement* and *dosage* in front of an audience?'

'Sure.' He folded his arms across his broad chest and grinned. 'What's the worst that can happen?'

I shuddered. 'Don't tempt fate. We don't want any equipment malfunctions today.'

He and Clare exchanged amused looks; a valve on a tank had failed a few days ago resulting in Clare getting an impromptu hosing down with several gallons of the Cuvée.

'And I'm going to follow on from Matt's demo with the labelling machine,' Clare put in. 'Putting the foil caps over the corks and attaching bottle labels.'

'I've put a cool box with bottles of water for us at the top of the vineyard and another just inside the winery.' Pippa glanced at my bare head. 'It's hot and exposed out there, Lottie; make sure you find a hat.'

'Good thinking,' I said, making a mental note to borrow something from Betsy.

I was going to be giving tours of the vineyard and talking

through a year in the life of a vine. I had some flashcards in the pocket of my shorts with some statistics on in case I forgot; I'd never been very good with numbers.

'Has everyone got sunscreen?' I continued. 'Roger, Godfrey, you should be mostly under cover, but even so.'

The two men were handling sales and wine tastings between them in an open-sided marquee next to the bar.

'Slip, slap, slop,' agreed Roger heartily, taking a tube of suncream from his pocket and offering it round.

'It's going to get even hotter later,' I said, shielding my eyes and taking in the view from the terrace, to the bushy green vines and to the verdant valley below, 'but I think the good weather will mean we get more visitors; people like being outdoors in the sunshine.'

'Ted's smiling down on us today,' said Godfrey softly. Pippa patted his shoulder affectionately.

'I couldn't sleep last night, I was so excited,' Clare admitted, wafting her face with one of our open day leaflets.

'Nature sounds,' Godfrey advised. 'I fall asleep to the sound of running water. Works a treat.'

'Wouldn't work for me with my bladder,' Clare laughed.

'Wine is a diuretic, you know,' Matt teased. 'That'll be your problem.'

'Oi, you. I don't drink that much!' Clare jabbed him with her elbow. 'I have hot milk, honey and a sprinkling of grated nutmeg in bed, I'll have you know. Ian brings it up with him after the news.'

'Nutmeg is supposed to be like Viagra for women,' said Pippa.

Clare smiled serenely. 'It is.'

There was a beat of silence while we all stared at her in surprise.

'You go, girl,' said Matt with a snort.

'Hello, everyone, sorry to keep you waiting,' said Betsy, appearing in the doorway on Jensen's arm.

'Not at all,' I said, smiling at them both.

164

I felt my heart speed up at the sight of Jensen. I'd tried to stay awake so that I could casually bump into him in the courtyard when he arrived last night. But I must have dozed off on the sofa because when I woke up his car was there and there were no lights on in the house. 'Thanks for joining us today,' I said, catching his eye.

'Wouldn't have missed it for the world,' he replied. We grinned at each other. We both knew that wasn't entirely true but I was too happy to see him to point that out.

He helped his grandmother down the step and out on to the terrace. Even in jeans and a company polo shirt, he was the epitome of sartorial elegance, I thought, doing up the button on my shirt, which kept popping open. Perhaps I should have gone for an even bigger size.

The kitchen door opened and Marjorie appeared with a bottle of sparkling wine wedged between her knees. She pushed herself down the ramp and handed the bottle to Matt. 'Do the honours, please.'

'I was late because I was looking for my brooch,' said Betsy. 'Ted gave it to me when we opened the vineyard all those years ago.' She stroked the brooch that was pinned to her dress. It was a cluster of tiny red stones in the shape of a bunch of grapes, the delicate stems and leaves made of gold.

'It's beautiful,' I said, taking her hand and tucking it through my arm.

I'd become very attached to the old lady over the last few weeks; I'd never known my own grandparents and listening to Betsy's stories, reading recipes books aloud to her or helping her find her way to pick flowers and herbs from her garden had felt like spending time with family and not like work at all.

'He looked after me well, my husband,' Betsy acknowledged with a sad smile.

'Your husband looked after all of us, in different ways,' said Roger gruffly.

I'd heard everyone's else's tale of how they'd met Ted. Including how Godfrey had been sitting on a bench in the churchyard after his wife died, feeling lost and lonely, when from nowhere, Starsky had jumped on to his lap. A few moments later an anxious and breathless Ted had arrived and quickly snapped a lead on to the runaway dog's collar. The two men got talking, Godfrey confiding that he and his wife had been inseparable and he was struggling to fill the void her death had opened up in his life. Twenty-four hours later, he was given a pair of secateurs, a reel of wire and a row of Chardonnay vines to prune. He'd been a regular ever since.

It was only Roger's link to the vineyard I hadn't heard.

'How did Ted look after you?' I asked him while the others were preoccupied, handing round glasses, finding sunhats and applying suncream.

Roger's brow furrowed. 'We've been friends for a decade. I represented my school on a community committee and Ted was on it too. We hit it off straight away. Then about seven years ago I went through a rough patch with my marriage, we split up and I had a bit of a breakdown. Ted let me talk and talk. He just listened without judgement and when I'd poured my heart out he asked me to do him a favour. There was a parcel of Pinot Meunier vines in the centre of the vineyard which weren't thriving and he told me to work out what they needed.'

'And what did they need?' I asked, making a mental note to check that they were still all right.

His face softened. 'What we all need: some TLC, someone to have faith and invest their time in them.'

There was a restrained pop as Matt expertly twisted the bottle and the cork away from each other. Jensen stepped forward with glasses, Betsy asked for just a small one, and soon we were each holding a glass aloft.

'To Ted,' said Jensen. 'My granddad. For creating Butterworth Wines and bringing us all together.'

'To Ted!' we all chorused and took a first sip.

'And to all of you, for your hard work over the last few months, and more recently, Lottie.' Jensen turned to me, his eyes as vivid as the summer sky and a gentle smile playing at his lips. 'Today wouldn't be happening without your energy and determination. On behalf of Gran, Aunt Marjorie and me, I thank you. To Team Butterworth.'

We all raised our glasses a second time and then Betsy thanked everyone for their efforts, insisting that we each take home a crate of wine of our choice as payment. And then everyone began talking excitedly. Except me. I was trying to look anywhere but at Jensen.

He was suddenly standing so close that the fine blond hairs on his arms brushed my skin and sent every nerve ending into a spin and his aftershave seemed to be doing something to my pulse rate. My sense of smell had become more sensitive recently and I now detected base tones of wood and spice with a top note of vanilla and rose. Whatever it was, it was intoxicating and I had to fight the urge to inhale him.

'You look miles away,' Jensen murmured close to my ear.

'No, I'm here,' I said, rousing myself from my secret sniffing session. 'Which is exactly where I want to be.'

'That's lucky, then,' he said, scrunching his face up as if trying to contain his laughter.

'Isn't it just?' I said, my voice catching.

This wasn't supposed to happen. I wasn't supposed to fall for the boss's grandson. For one, he lived in London, I'd been there, done that, and I had no desire to repeat the experience. Two, from what I'd seen so far, he was one of these driven types who feel like they're skiving if they put in less than a hundred-hour week. And three, I was just getting used to being independent and not having to consider other people's plans alongside my own. I was enjoying it and I wasn't ready to think about anyone else but me for the time being.

Not that he'd indicated any interest in me; all he'd done was point out that I was daydreaming.

I rolled my eyes at myself just as he touched my arm as if to lead me aside. 'Lottie, can we—'

Before he could finish his sentence the side gate crashed open. 'Mr Cooper, Mr Cooper!' A lanky boy bristling with excitement appeared wearing the hi-vis jacket which Roger had insisted all the boys wear. 'We've opened the gates and there's a minibus on its way up the drive. And cars. People are coming!'

Clare began collecting in our glasses and Roger and I ran out into the yard. Sure enough, the minibus was being waved into position by one of the other boys and a line of cars was snaking its way towards us.

Roger rubbed his hands together. 'Looks like we're in business. Action stations, everyone!'

'Right,' I said briskly. 'I'm on tour duty, I'll see you later.'

'What should I do?' Jensen asked hurriedly.

'You,' I said with a fleeting glance, 'need to make everyone fall in love with your granddad's vineyard so they buy lots of wine to take home with them.'

'Oh dear.' He pulled a face. 'I don't have the best track record of making people fall in love.'

I found that hard to believe.

'Never mind,' I said with a grin. 'Just offer them a drink. That will work just as well.'

From that moment on and for the next few hours, I only saw Jensen from a distance. The open day was a much bigger hit with the folk of Derbyshire than we could ever have anticipated. There were wine societies from miles away who had hired minibuses and organized day trips, and they left with cases and cases of wine and receipts for their pre-orders of the next vintage. There were old contacts of Ted's who were part of an online support forum who offered to lend a hand in the winery at harvest if we needed it and excitingly there were several brides-to-be who'd decided to select our sparkling wines for their weddings. Godfrey had been delighted with the press turnout: he organized an on-air tasting for the reporter from the local radio station, Betsy and Jensen gave an interview to the *Derbyshire Bugle* and I lost track of the number of photographs I posed for with wine bloggers who promised to give us a glowing review.

At half past three, I was beginning to flag, and as much as I had enjoyed the day, I was looking forward to four o'clock when the event was officially over.

I spied a free chair next to Betsy and went to join her on the terrace to have a sneaky rest. There was a plate of fresh scones on the table in front of her and I realized how long it had been since I'd eaten. Perhaps I'd have a cup of tea and a scone and catch my breath for a few minutes.

By the time I'd reached her, Betsy was talking to a red-haired woman in a brightly coloured floral dress, plimsolls and a floppy straw hat.

'I am so ready for a sit-down, mind if I join you?' I said, as much to let Betsy know who I was as anything.

'Oh Lottie, it's you!' said Betsy. 'I'd like you to meet Olivia from . . . um . . . ?'

'Hi. Olivia Channing, English Wine Board.' Olivia beamed and shook my hand. 'Mrs Butterworth says you'll give me a tour, do you mind?'

'Lottie Allbright. And it'd be my pleasure,' I said, eyeing the plate of scones regretfully. 'Follow me.'

'Butterworth's has created a lot of interest in the industry in the last few weeks since you announced this event,' said Olivia as we headed down the rows of Pinot Noir. She stopped every so often to examine the grapes which were starting to swell now, the first hint of redness appearing in their skins. 'Ted Butterworth was an enigma. Reclusive, almost, as far as the world of wine was concerned. A talented winemaker but—'

She stopped herself and looked hesitant.

'Go on.'

'Everyone knew his sparkling wines were his passion, but beyond perfecting his blends, he never seemed interested in developing the business. That was as far as his ambitions lay. We tried countless times to get him involved with national ventures, consumer campaigns, export trips even, but his focus was always on the wine and not the consumer.'

'And that's wrong?'

'Oh no, not at all!' she insisted with a smile. 'Not wrong; his business, he could run it how he pleased. Unusual, maybe. Our job is to promote English wine – high quality wines – to a wider audience, both at home and internationally. He always resisted our advances. Perhaps now's the time to reconsider.'

I nodded thoughtfully. 'It wouldn't be my decision but I'll talk to the family about it.'

Ted's illness had taken everyone by surprise, including him. I still hadn't got over the fact that all those orders had been sitting on his computer unopened, the messages on the answerphone unanswered. We'd already converted orders into cash, which had pleased the bank manager no end. Perhaps Ted's business had simply grown out of his control: he enjoyed the practical side of making wine but not the sales and marketing aspect of it. But maybe with Olivia's help it wasn't too late to take it to the worldwide stage?

What we really needed, I thought, was to hear back from Sidney. If he could help us with our blending problem, great; if not, we were in trouble. Everyone had agreed it had been a good idea of mine to contact him. I'd sent emails which I could see had been opened, but had had no response. I didn't want to push it too much; if he couldn't or wouldn't let us have the benefit of his experience, there wasn't a lot I could do about it.

Olivia and I walked back up to the marquee where Roger was holding a group tasting session. I picked up a bottle of the chilled Classic Cuvée and poured her a glass.

'Great colour. Pale straw.' She held it to the light, swirled it round and then blinked. 'Oh. Not joining me?'

I hesitated. 'Of course.'

I poured myself a small amount and positioned a spittoon discreetly on the barrel table.

She slurped the wine, making little noises of pleasure before swallowing it. 'Honeyed oats, nice creamy mousse, plenty of fruit – quince and almond. Delicious. Definitely falls into the category of high quality that I'm looking for.'

I did the same, aiming mine neatly into the spittoon rather than swallowing it.

'You are good.' Her eyes twinkled. 'I've booked a cab to pick me up; my first visit to Butterworth Wines was such a good opportunity that I wanted to make the most of it.'

I walked her across to the winery. 'I only have a few steps to make it home,' I said, pointing to my little abode as we crossed the courtyard. 'The Stables comes with the job.'

'That's handy,' she said thoughtfully. 'You know, you could look into wine tourism if you can offer accommodation too. People will pay to stay there and work for free.'

I laughed in surprise. 'People do that?'

She nodded and waved an arm around at the crowds which had thinned now as the event was beginning to wind down. 'Half of your visitors will go home tonight and dream about starting their own wine business. It's right up there with running your own guest house or restaurant. Aspirational. And international interest in English wine has never been so high.'

'Really?' I bit my lip. 'I'm ashamed to say I'd always been a bit snooty about it until I came here.'

She leaned closer. 'Believe me, even the French are sitting up and taking notice of us these days. In fact, I'm hosting a delegation from Russia later this year, maybe I could include Butterworth Wines in the itinerary.'

'I always think of Russia as a nation of vodka drinkers,' I said, making a mental note to google it later.

'They were.' She nodded sagely. 'But Moët hopes to double their Russian exports of champagne in the next five years. My job is to convince Russian buyers that an English sparkling wine will fit the bill just as well.'

'Oh, it will,' I said confidently.

Olivia shook my hand and laughed. 'That's exactly the spirit we're looking for at the English Wine Board.'

I left her in the winery with Clare who automatically pressed the poor woman's arms to check for sunburn and headed back outside.

Wine tourism, exports and a place on the international wine stage . . . I stifled a yawn; I was exhausted just thinking about it. I was planning my escape to The Stables when I spotted Jensen waving off a minibus-load of ladies from the Flittham Wine Society.

'Lottie, do you have a minute?' he called.

'Sure.'

We wove our way through the parked cars towards each other. He looked as cool and fresh as he had done at noon. I felt hot and bedraggled in comparison.

'I need to leave soon,' he said. 'I've got a party in London tonight.'

Of course he did, I thought enviously. I bet where he lived in London was a world away from the place I'd rented with Harvey. He probably had an amazing apartment overlooking the Thames with a pool, a gym and an underground car park. He'd mix with crowds of rich, successful and handsome people just like him and have strings of drop-dead gorgeous women trailing in his wake at all times. Whereas I was a slightly plump and extremely clammy labourer for his gran.

'Lottie?' He bent down to peer at me and his bemused laugh brought me out of my reverie. 'You really are tired, aren't you? You didn't hear a word I said.'

'I did, you said . . .' My mouth had gone dry and I swallowed. 'I am a bit weary, now you mention it.'

He placed his arm loosely around my shoulders. 'Come on, let's find a seat. You're trembling. Have you eaten anything today?'

I shook my head, realizing that I might be on the verge of tears. I wasn't sad, but he was being so kind and I realized suddenly how much I'd missed being held by someone. He spotted a rogue tear on my cheek and looked horrified.

'Oh God, did I do that?'

'No, you've been very kind.' I wiped my eyes. 'I always do the Paddington thing myself, but when the tables are turned, I can't cope with it.'

'Paddington. Right,' said Jensen, clearly mystified. He steered me to two chairs and a small table which our young car-park attendants had set up for themselves under a parasol and we sat down. Alarmingly there were a couple of empty bottles under the table; I hoped the boys had gathered up empties as part of their rubbish-collecting duties and not drunk them themselves. Our knees were touching and I wondered if Jensen was as aware of the sensation as I was.

I gave myself a little shake and then wished I hadn't because I really did feel quite light-headed.

'You were saying,' I prompted, 'about the party with the gorgeous women?'

'I was?' He looked puzzled. 'Actually, it's my boss's fortieth wedding anniversary.'

'Ah yes, I remember,' I said vaguely. Everything had gone slightly hazy and echoey.

'Look,' he shifted in his seat, 'I'll get to the point. Can I have your number? I'd like to call you.'

'My phone number? To call me?' Did this mean he was attracted to me the way I was attracted to him? And if so, should I really be encouraging it? He seemed nice and fun and he was definitely good-looking, but I'd only been single for six weeks or so, I really wasn't looking for romance.

Jensen's eyes sparkled. 'That is the usual reason.'

'Sure.' I swallowed nervously. 'The thing is, I'm not in a great place right now. I've just split up with someone.'

'Fair enough.' He rubbed his chin and cast his eyes down. 'But I'd like to get progress reports from you: whether Gran is all right; how sales are going; what's happening in the winery. That sort of thing. I'll give you mine too, in case you need to get hold of me.'

I just about managed not to groan out loud. He wanted my number for professional reasons; of course he wasn't asking me out.

'Good idea.' I recited my number to him and watched him tap it in.

'All my numbers are on here.' He passed me a business card. 'And perhaps when you're in a . . . better place, you'd consider having dinner with me.'

This was obviously part of his checking-up activities.

'Thank you.' I beamed, thinking how long it had been since I'd been to a restaurant with a man who wasn't my dad. 'That would be lovely.'

He shook his head, bemused. 'I've never been good at reading signs from women, but I think I'm getting mixed messages. Am I?'

I stared at his face. The first time I saw him, when he'd bounded into Betsy's kitchen and swung her around, he'd seemed so exuberant and confident. Seeing him less certain of himself all of a sudden was new to me, and it made me like him even more. I felt a tug inside and itched to lean across the gap between us and kiss him. Could I do that? I wondered.

'Yes,' I found myself saying.

He laughed softly. 'Yes to dinner, or yes to mixed messages?'

I didn't get the chance to answer because a taxi pulled to a squeaky halt in the yard just inches from our chairs and a spritely old man got out and slammed the door. In a creased ivory linen suit, cravat and crumpled panama hat, he looked like he'd come straight from a game of cricket with Jeeves and Wooster.

'Jensen? Young Jensen Butterworth?' said the old man. His face was tanned, but his eyes were bright and his top lip sported an enormous twirly white moustache. 'Is that you?'

'Yes? Mr Buxton? Good grief!' Jensen leapt up to greet him, laughing in disbelief. 'Lottie, this is my grandfather's friend, Sidney Buxton.'

'Absolutely delighted to meet you, Lottie.' Sidney lifted his hat to reveal a perfectly bald head then did a delightfully old-fashioned little bow.

'What a lovely surprise!' I got to my feet, shocked by the turn of events, and felt my head spin.

The world tilted as if I was on a fairground ride and I staggered forward into the metal pole of the parasol. My legs crumpled and there was an echo of someone shouting my name as I hit the ground.

The noise of my alarm clock was hideous. Why wouldn't it stop? And what on earth had happened to my pillows? They were really uncomfortable. I flapped my arm to try to turn it off, but someone caught hold of my hand. The skin was dry and exceptionally soft and I recognized it as Betsy. The knowledge that she was there brought a rush of tears to my eyes.

'Look, she's coming round now. Thank God,' said Betsy, sounding relieved.

'Still, it's best to let the paramedics check her over.' That was Marjorie.

The noise had stopped, thank goodness. It wasn't my alarm at all, I realized; it was an ambulance siren. *I'm fine*, I wanted to say, but couldn't quite muster up the energy to speak.

A friendly male voice took charge. 'All right then, folks; can you make some room for us please.'

'Who have we got here?' The second voice was female.

'Lottie Allbright,' said Jensen. 'She stood up too quickly

and stumbled forward, hit her head on that metal pole, I think, and fell back on to the concrete.'

'Then she was sick.' That sounded like one of the boys.

I groaned inwardly. That meant everyone was probably standing right by my vomit. Great.

'I thought she looked peaky earlier,' Betsy said. 'I shouldn't have asked her to do that last tour. I feel awful now.'

There was a crash as someone stumbled and knocked over the empty wine bottles.

'Looks as if someone's been celebrating,' said the male voice.

'*Has* she been drinking?' asked the female.

There was a humming and hawing.

'Yes, but not a lot,' said Jensen eventually.

'I see.' The woman gave a weary sigh and picked up my wrist, checking my pulse. 'Lottie? Can you hear me?'

I opened my eyes and blinked blearily at a huge crowd of faces peering back at me. 'Urgh.'

'Step back, give her some space please, folks.'

Nobody moved at first.

'She might be sick again.'

That worked.

Jensen took my other hand, his face etched with worry. 'Hi, is there anyone you want me to call?'

I shook my head, too mortified to look at him. Two minutes after him asking me to dinner, I'd thrown up in front of him. Nice one, Lottie . . . I wondered where Sidney had gone? What a welcome I'd given him. This was too awful for words. What I really wanted to do was crawl off to bed and sleep and have nobody staring at me.

'We'll take her in, check her out for concussion or alcohol poisoning.'

'Not drunk,' I croaked pathetically. 'Just want sleep.'

'I'll go with her,' Clare offered as one of the paramedics fetched a stretcher. 'My son played rugby; A&E was our second home when he was a boy.'

176

I smiled weakly at her, thinking that a hug from Clare was possibly all the treatment I needed.

Jensen tightened his grip on my hand. 'Thanks, Clare, but I'll go; the Butterworths are her employers after all and this was a work-related injury.'

'Good idea,' said Betsy. 'We'll get Sidney settled in; you look after Lottie and phone me as soon as you have news.'

Someone sucked in air, Godfrey I thought, and a muttered conversation started up about insurance claims and compensation. I wanted to tell Betsy that she needn't worry on that score but just then the two paramedics transferred me to a stretcher and wheeled me towards the back of the ambulance.

Sidney loomed into view. 'And I'm so sorry. I feel responsible.'

I tried to shake my head but it wouldn't move. 'Not your fault. Thank you for coming.'

Then I was on a ramp being pushed into the ambulance.

Jensen patted Sidney's back and climbed in beside me.

'No. Party,' I murmured, remembering something about Jensen needing to be in London with gorgeous women. 'Party.'

The female paramedic chuckled. 'The party's over for you, I'm afraid, Lottie.'

Chapter 16

The journey to the hospital took around fifteen minutes, but I only remembered two things about it: that the female paramedic, whose name was Julie, put something on my forehead which stung like hell and that she flirted shamelessly with Jensen the whole way there.

As the paramedics wheeled me along a brightly lit corridor, lined with seats full of waiting patients and smelling strongly of disinfectant, Jensen walked alongside, his face alternating between over-bright smiles and concerned frowns when he thought I wasn't looking. On the other side of me was a nurse whom my male paramedic was bringing up to speed with my ailments.

'Head injury to the rear and bruising to the left side of forehead, blood pressure low, vomiting, possible concussion, possibly had a few too many sherbets.' He winked at me. 'That's a technical term.'

The nurse asked me for my personal details. I gave her my full name and date of birth easily but I struggled with my address. It was the first time I'd ever had to list it as the vineyard, which was weird enough, and the nurse exchanged glances with Julie the flirt when I couldn't recall the postcode. Luckily, Jensen knew it, which seemed to act as confirmation that we were a couple. We reached the end of the corridor and arrived in a noisy open area with telephones ringing, staff dashing about and lots of injured and ill-looking people slumped in uncomfortable plastic chairs. Out of the corner of my eye, I saw two policemen trying to control a man who was doing his best to lash out at everyone, despite being hand-cuffed to both of them. He was covered in mud and had a large bloody gash on the side of his head.

'This is ridiculous,' the man drawled drunkenly. 'Police harassment. You should be out there nicking real criminals.'

'Being drunk and disorderly is a crime,' said one of the officers.

The other officer gripped the drunk under his arm and led him away. 'So is assaulting a police officer. And if you carry on like this . . . Oh Jeez.'

The man threw up on the floor.

'I think I'd like to go home,' I said, closing my eyes. 'I'm not ill enough to be here and you're obviously busy.'

'We'll put you straight into a cubicle,' said the nurse, pat-ting my arm. 'Your boyfriend can come too.'

The cubicle was tiny and no quieter than the main wait-ing room but at least it was a little more private with the curtain drawn round us. The nurse took my blood pressure, which was low, while Jensen sat beside me giving me encour-aging smiles. Once she'd gone, I flailed about, trying to push myself upright.

He looked over his shoulder warily and back at me. 'Is that wise?'

I shrugged. 'I don't know, but being sick whilst lying down definitely isn't.'

The effort of not flinching away from me was written all over his face and if my head hadn't been throbbing so much I'd probably have laughed. Despite his reservations, he hooked his hand under my arm, eased me forward and propped me up with pillows.

'Better?' he asked, placing a cardboard sick bowl on my lap.

I nodded, barely moving my head. 'Much better. I really don't think I'm concussed. Shall we just go? It's so busy here, we could sneak off and no one would probably even notice.'

The curtain was whisked back and a smiley-faced doctor in a fraying white shirt with pen marks around the breast pocket appeared. 'Not thinking of absconding, were we?' He grinned. 'Tut tut. I'm Dr Zarzycki, but you can call me Toby, pleased to meet you.'

He closed the curtain again and shook my hand.

'I don't want to trouble anyone,' I said.

Jensen stood up and shook the doctor's hand. 'She's very determined, I'm afraid. Once she sets her mind to something, she keeps going until she gets it.'

Despite my wooziness, I felt quite proud of that.

'Laudable,' said the doctor, 'in most circumstances. But I wouldn't be doing my job if we didn't check you over thoroughly.'

He scanned through the notes on a clipboard sitting at the end of my bed and I sighed, resigned to spend several hours here only to be told I was fine and could go home, while Jensen missed out on his boss's party.

'I'll phone my sister Evie to come in,' I said to Jensen, pressing a hand to my forehead to suppress the pain. My fingers brushed against the dressing; I must have looked awful. 'Then at least you don't have to waste your evening.'

He opened his mouth to object just as I retched without warning and spat into the cardboard bowl. Jensen took it from me, put it in the bin and handed me a tissue and a cup of water.

'See,' he murmured. 'I'm not wasting my time, it's like having a second doctor in the room.'

Toby shot him an amused glance. 'In that case there's a chap in the cubicle next door with a boil that needs lancing, how are you fixed?'

Jensen held up a hand. 'Sorry. I'm strictly a one patient at a time sort of doctor.'

Toby snorted. 'That's called a private hospital.'

After lifting up my eyelids and testing my vision, the doctor perched on the edge of my bed.

'Right. Before we start any tests, Lottie, there's a standard question we ask all women of your sort of age: any chance you might be pregnant?'

'Um.' I swallowed, determinedly avoiding Jensen's eye. 'Technically there's a chance, I suppose. I mean, I'm not a . . . I am, I have been sexually active.'

I tried to think calm thoughts to quell the rising heat to my face. On a scale of one to ten, with ten being the most excruciating, I'd just passed eleven . . .

'So is that a yes?' Toby pressed me for an answer.

'No. Unlikely.'

'No. Okey-dokey.'

Jensen was now examining a leaflet about head injuries very closely. I wondered who was the most uncomfortable with this discussion. Not Toby, that was for sure.

'According to the notes from the paramedics,' he said, scanning the sheet on the clipboard, 'you stood up too quickly and fainted.'

'It's all a bit vague,' I said. 'Sorry.'

'I was there, Doctor,' said Jensen. 'It looked as if she was losing consciousness as she stood up, she hit the parasol first and then fell backwards.'

He nodded. 'Hot day, low blood pressure, it figures. Had you been feeling ill prior to this?'

I hesitated. The truth was that I'd been feeling off-colour since leaving London: loss of appetite, headaches, tiredness, nausea . . . but I'd put it down to anxiety, particularly after Harvey's unexpected appearance at Evie's house.

'Not really,' I said uncertainly.

'Hmm.' Toby narrowed his eyes. 'We'll do a urine test, take some bloods. Then check that head out. Okay?'

Jensen went to fetch a cup of tea while a nurse took me to the toilet in a wheelchair to produce a urine sample. When we got back to the cubicle I convinced her that I was feeling well enough to continue sitting and she left me in a chair while she vanished with my pot of wee.

It was ages before anyone came back and I'd just felt

myself nodding off when Jensen appeared with two cups of tea and a big bar of chocolate.

'Sorry,' he said, handing me one of the cups. 'I needed to make some calls first, let people know I won't be there tonight. Have I missed anything?'

I took a sip of tea and sighed with pleasure. 'I think they've forgotten about me. This is heaven.'

Despite being from a vending machine, the tea was exactly what I wanted. I hadn't drunk tea with milk in for weeks, but now I couldn't get enough of it, swallowing it in three big gulps.

'So I see.' He laughed and disposed of the cup for me before leaning against the empty bed. 'I thought it might sober you up.'

'Hey, I am not drunk!' I protested. 'I didn't seem drunk to you when you asked me to go to dinner with you, did I?'

His lips twitched. 'A little vague, maybe.'

'Oh well,' I waved a hand, 'that's normal for me.'

'Okay, Lottie.' Toby whisked his way back into the cubicle again, clipboard in hand. 'I've got the results of your urine test.'

Jensen stood up straight. 'I should probably go outside for this bit.'

I grabbed the sleeve of his polo shirt. 'No need, you can stay. You're my second doctor, remember?'

I was confident that this wasn't about to turn into an episode of *Embarrassing Bodies*; there was nothing wrong with me.

'Well, if you're sure.' Jensen looked a bit doubtful but resumed his position anyway.

'I'm sure.' I looked at Toby. 'Go on then, Doctor, what did you find? Scarcely any alcohol, I bet.'

'No, no, the alcohol levels were negligible.' The doctor maintained a neutral expression. 'But I can confirm that you're pregnant.'

*

'Pardon?' I said stupidly, even though I'd heard him perfectly.

'You are expecting a baby.' Toby's mouth formed a wary smile.

I stared at him. I was pregnant. With Harvey's baby. A sob escaped from my throat. There was a baby growing inside me.

Jensen crouched down by my chair and touched my arm. 'Are you okay?'

'Not really,' I managed to croak.

'I take it this wasn't planned?' he asked.

I shook my head, meeting his eye. 'Like I said, I've just come out of a relationship.'

Jensen exhaled, his eyes full of concern and something else I couldn't put my finger on, but he looked sad.

'So you two aren't a couple?' The doctor waved a finger between us.

Jensen shook his head. 'We're just friends.'

There was a flat tone to his voice that made me think that after today we might not even be that. He cleared his throat. 'Lottie, I'm not sure I'm the right person to help you deal with this.'

I swallowed. 'I understand.'

'Shall I ring your sister?' he asked.

'No! Oh God, no!' I burst into tears. 'Evie'll be devastated.'

Jensen took my hand. 'I'm sure that's not true.'

'It is! You don't understand. She'll hide it and pretend that what's important is my health and what I want but inside she'll be heartbroken. This couldn't have happened at a worse time for her. And it's all my fault. What am I going to do?'

There was a moment of stillness in the cubicle where both men looked at me and the only sound in my ears was the thumping of my heart. Toby's face was calm and patient, giving me time to absorb the news. Jensen . . . well, I couldn't read his expression but I bet he was wishing he'd accepted

Clare's offer to come with me and had left for his party as planned.

Toby handed me a wodge of tissues and scribbled some notes. 'I'll write a letter to your GP and you'll need to make an appointment with the midwife,' he said softly. 'Find out how far along you are. And then you can consider your options.'

I nodded but even in my numb state, with a million thoughts running through my brain, I knew my options were limited. Despite this being Harvey's baby and unplanned and all the obstacles which I'd no doubt have to overcome, I couldn't have a termination. It might be practical and right for other people, but for me it would seem too cruel when my sister so longed for a baby. It would seem like flaunting not only my fertility but my ability to choose whether to have a baby or not in her face. Then again, how would she cope with seeing me getting a bigger and bigger bump over the coming weeks?

What a dilemma. I groaned with the shock of it all and dabbed at my tears.

Unless I didn't tell her, of course . . . But I couldn't think about this now, there was too much to take in, my head ached and all I really wanted to do was sleep.

Toby was waving a hand in front of my face. 'Lottie?'

Jensen squeezed my fingers. 'The doctor asked who your GP is.'

'I'm registered with one in London. But I'll go to the surgery in Fernfield.'

Jensen glanced sideways at me. 'Is that where the father is, London?'

I shuddered. 'Yes. Please, I don't want to think about him now.'

'You'll have to tell him; he has a right to know.'

'I'm aware of that,' I snapped.

He held his hands up. 'Sorry, none of my business.'

Harvey. I'd hoped he was out of my life for ever, but if I was to go ahead and have this baby, he and I would be eternally linked. What a depressing thought.

'I'm so sorry you've got dragged into this.' I shut my eyes.

'You've got nothing to apologize for.' Jensen put his arms around me and rocked me from side to side, resting his chin on my head. I'd never been so glad of human contact in my life and leaned into him, soaking up the feeling of comfort.

'I'd like to go home now please, Doctor,' I said firmly, peeling myself away from Jensen. 'Apart from being pregnant and having a very sore head, I'm fine and I feel awful for leaving the clearing up to everyone else at the vineyard.'

'Fine. But no clearing up for you.' Toby looked at Jensen. 'Make sure she does nothing but rest and drink plenty of fluids.'

'You hear that, Lottie? Doctor's orders,' said Jensen sternly.

'I've drunk more fluids in the last month than in my entire life,' I told the doctor. 'Unfortunately, a lot of it was sparkling wine. The poor baby is probably pickled.'

I pointed to the logo on my polo shirt.

'Ah. You'll need to cut down your alcohol intake immediately,' said the doctor, 'and please get yourself booked in for a scan as soon as possible.'

It took a further ten minutes for the paperwork to be completed and for me to be officially discharged. The nurse we'd seen when we came in advised us to go up to the main entrance where we'd find a taxi. I didn't have any money with me and promised to pay Jensen back, but he waved my protests away. He offered me his hand as we stood up to leave the safety of my cubicle and I took it gratefully.

I wasn't just weak from my fall; I was in shock from finding out I was going to be a mother. Or perhaps I was already a mother, simply by being pregnant? I'd never thought about it before. And I don't know if it was psychosomatic, but I felt oddly aware of my tummy suddenly, with an urge to shield it from the other patients as we walked along the corridor.

'You've been so kind.' I squeezed Jensen's hand lightly.

'Not at all.' He pressed a feather-light kiss to my cheek. 'I'm sorry this hasn't been a happier occasion for you.'

His tenderness nearly undid me. If only someone like him had been the father of this baby and not Harvey. But Jensen wasn't the father; I was on my own. Until today I hadn't given much thought to how my first pregnancy would pan out, but I was pretty sure that being single with a violent ex, a temporary job (one which involved a lot of alcohol) and a temporary home wouldn't have figured in my master plan. And what was worse, what tugged at my heart the most, was that poor Evie and Darren, who would have made wonderful parents, weren't able to do what I'd done accidentally. Why was life so unfair?

My eyes pricked with tears. 'Life has a funny way of throwing curve balls in our faces, doesn't it?'

'Oh yes,' he said with meaning. A shadow crossed his face, which made me wonder.

'Do you want children?' I blurted out.

He blinked. 'Um. Yes, eventually. I . . . well, I've never said this out loud before, but I planned on focusing on my career until I was thirty-four and then marrying and starting a family from thirty-five.'

'That's very organized. How old are you?'

'Thirty-six.' He smiled ruefully and shrugged. 'Best-laid plans and all that.'

Out in the main reception area, the drunken man we'd seen earlier was still flanked by two police officers. But the fight had gone out of him and he looked like he was asleep. Actually, now the blood had been cleaned from his face and he was no longer flailing about, he looked very familiar.

As we drew level with him, I slowed down.

'Darren?' I gasped.

My brother-in-law opened his eyes and rubbed them. 'Nope. It's not me. Don't tell your sister, because it's not me.'

'It's not the normal you, admittedly.' I don't think I'd ever known him drink enough to get drunk. This was a first. I caught the eye of one of the officers. 'I *am* family, I promise. What's he done?'

'Cut his head in a fight outside the Royal Oak,' said the officer, looking distinctly fed up.

Darren struggled to sit up. 'That shit-fer-brains Tommy Dawson asked me if I'd mind if he had a crack at Evie now we've split up,' he grunted angrily.

Jensen pressed my arm discreetly. 'Are you going to introduce us?'

'Yes of course, how rude of me.' I felt my face flush.

This was just perfect. My family and I were making one hell of an impression today; first an unwanted pregnancy and now a drunk and disorderly . . . 'Darren, this is Jensen Butterworth, my boss's grandson.'

'Pleased to meet you,' said Jensen, he extended a hand automatically before realizing that Darren was handcuffed to two officers. He patted his shoulder instead and looked at me. There was a strange expression on his face: somewhere between intrigued, horrified and amused.

'And Darren is my sister Evie's husband.'

'Soon to be ex-husband,' Darren chuntered. 'What are you doing in here anyway?'

'I hit my head at work,' I said, which was the truth, but all the same, I couldn't quite meet his eye. Not that there was anything to worry about there; his eyeballs seemed to be looking in different directions.

Suddenly there was a commotion at the reception desk and we all turned to see a diminutive blonde demanding to see someone in charge.

'Oh no, it's my sister,' I hissed to Jensen, looking for a way out. But it was no use; a nurse was already pointing at us.

His eyes widened with curiosity, I could only imagine

what he'd be telling Betsy later on. This was getting worse by the second.

'Darren, what the hell?' Evie yelled, taking in the sight of her usually law-abiding husband wedged between two policemen. 'I've just had a call from the landlord at the Royal Oak. What's going on? Don't tell me you really picked a fight with that lunatic Tommy Dawson? And why did you call Lottie and not me? Hello, sis.' She took a breather from yelling at Darren to kiss me and raise her eyebrows at Jensen and me holding hands. Then she did a double take, noticing the dressing on my forehead.

'I didn't, she's ill too,' Darren protested.

'Bloody hell, Lottie.' She stared at me. 'Are you okay?'

I swallowed. 'Fine. Absolutely fine. This is Jensen.'

'Hi,' she said, flicking her eyes to him briefly and back to me. 'You don't look fine. What happened to you?'

'Nothing.' And then, without thinking, I did something for the first time, something that from then on I'd be doing approximately once every five minutes for the next few months: I placed a hand protectively on my tummy.

With the sixth sense of someone who had been enviously watching other pregnant women for years, Evie noticed the move straight away. The blood drained from her face.

'You're . . . Oh my God, you're pregnant, aren't you? Are you pregnant?'

My mouth went dry; so much for not telling her.

'I'm so, so sorry, Evie.'

Chapter 17

When our taxi pulled into the drive leading up to Butterworth Wines, Pippa, Clare, Roger and Godfrey were waiting for us.

'You've got a welcome committee,' Jensen murmured. 'The returning heroine.'

I looked away, cursing the tears that threatened to fall. Again.

'I've let everyone down, cast a shadow over our lovely open day, made you miss your party and driven away my only sister. Hardly heroic.'

'Here, this is my last one,' he said, handing me a tissue. 'Lottie, give yourself a break. You've had a traumatic day and a big shock. And I know it was a big shock for your sister too, but it's okay to put yourself ahead of others once in a while. Gran is forever singing praises about your kindness. And look at this lot.'

The welcome committee were waving wildly, except Roger who was doing his air traffic control impression for the taxi driver, pointing out a parking space.

I looked at my lap. 'You don't understand. My sister has got a lot of stuff going on.'

'Try not to worry.' Jensen squeezed my hand. 'I'm sure she knows you need support and I bet she'll be over here like a shot as soon as she's free. After all, she's going to be an auntie. If you decide to keep it, that is.' He looked uncomfortable. 'Sorry, I shouldn't assume.'

'I'm having it,' I said staunchly. 'Decision made.'

He released my hand as the taxi came to a halt and hugged me to him. 'I admire your certainty.'

'Or craziness,' I said, undoing my seat belt. 'Depending on how you look at it.'

It had been awful leaving Evie so distraught at the hospital, but Darren had been called into one of the booths to be seen and she'd ended up arguing with a nurse because the police wouldn't let her accompany him. I'd sent her a text and left her a message but she hadn't returned them. Goodness only knew what opinion Jensen must have of me and my family. Whatever it was, he was very discreet about it; he'd simply held my hand all the whole way home, kept me topped up with tissues and hadn't once bombarded me with questions even though he must have been dying to ask some.

The taxi stopped and before I'd even had a chance to open the door, Godfrey had pulled it open while Jensen got out of the other side and paid the driver.

'Well, my dear, how are you? You've been gone for hours,' said Godfrey, helping me out.

The others crowded round me.

'We've been worried sick,' said Pippa, wide-eyed and so pale it could have been her who'd had the accident.

'I'm fine, really,' I said flatly.

It felt like a lifetime since I'd left the vineyard and in that time my entire world had been turned inside out. I felt the lump on the back of my head, which had already started to go down a bit.

'Give her some room, old chap,' said Roger briskly, pushing past Godfrey. 'Lottie, take my arm.'

I did as I was told, although Godfrey insisted on hanging on to me too.

'Oh, love, you have been in the wars.' Clare flapped at the

two men to let go of me and wrapped me up in her arms. I felt myself relax against her. Jensen had looked after me well, but I was missing my mum and my sister so much and Clare's warm embrace was the next best thing.

'I feel like I've done five rounds with Muhammad Ali. This bit in particular stings like a bee,' I said, prodding my forehead.

'Matt had to go to work but he sends his love,' said Pippa, rubbing my arm. Her freckles had come out in force today and her nose looked a bit pink too. She looked fresh and young and carefree, in stark contrast to how I felt right now.

'I'm sorry to ruin the end of a good party and I'm sorry I wasn't here to clear up.' I managed a smile and looked around me. The visitors were long gone, the yard was empty except for our own cars, everywhere had been tidied up and only the bunting, flapping in the strong evening breeze, gave any indication that there had been a major event here today. Heavy clouds were beginning to gather and the temperature seemed to have dropped too.

'Don't be daft,' Clare said gently.

'You're all so kind.' I swallowed the lump in my throat. I was exhausted, mentally and physically; one sign of kindness and I was in danger of dissolving like a sugar lump.

'Let's get you sitting down,' said Jensen, touching my shoulder. 'Would you mind coming over to the house? I'm sure Gran and Marjorie would like to know you're all right.'

My stomach flipped; what would Betsy say when she found out I was pregnant? The phrase 'you're fired' sprang to mind. Who wants a pregnant woman in charge of a vineyard? I released Clare reluctantly and fell into step with Jensen as he walked across the yard.

Betsy and Marjorie were sitting on a bench on the terrace looking out across the vines and didn't see us approach. Starsky spotted us; he didn't move, but his tail thumped happily on the flagstones. The sky was more dramatic from here without any buildings blocking the view and far away in the distance I caught a flash of lightning.

'Did you see that?' I pointed it out to Jensen. 'I hope the grapes will be okay if the storm reaches us.'

'Godfrey checked the weather earlier; we're in for some rain, but the hail and worst of the storm is expected further south so it should miss us.'

'Let's hope so.' I wasn't convinced; the sky looked full of mischief to me.

Hail could cause untold damage to grapes, bruising the most exposed bunches and ruining their skins. Pippa had told me that they once lost seventy-five per cent of their crop in a single day. 'Because I don't know what I'd be able to do to protect the fruit.'

He raised an eyebrow. 'See? Even now you're worrying about something else.'

'It's my job and it's important to me.'

He stopped dead and touched my arm, his deep blue gaze holding mine. 'I understand that, but things have changed now, haven't they?' he said earnestly.

I blinked at him. This was disappointing; somehow I hadn't expected him not to be on my side.

'I'll be working for months yet.'

He cleared his throat and looked away. 'Let's join the ladies.'

'Here she is,' Marjorie cried, raising a glass with what looked like a triple measure of amber liqueur in it. 'The woman of the hour!'

'Me?' I said, smiling to myself as I took in her rosy cheeks.

'And her knight in shining armour,' Betsy piped up. She got to her feet tipsily and kissed both our cheeks. 'Hello, darlings. We've been so worried about you.'

'My blood pressure was a bit low, that's all,' I reassure them with a smile. 'Nothing serious.'

Jensen looked at me pointedly, sending a flock of energetic butterflies into action in my stomach.

'Gran, do you mind if I stay the night?' He checked his watch. 'I'd rather not drive back to London now; I want to be on hand for a while to make sure Lottie is okay.'

Betsy and Marjorie exchanged triumphant looks. It didn't take a genius to work out that there'd been some speculation about our relationship. Not that there was likely to be one now; finding out the girl you'd asked to dinner was pregnant with another man's child had to be up there as one of life's most effective passion-killers. Still, now was hardly the time to be thinking about romance; not now that motherhood had plonked itself on the horizon.

'That's kind of you, Jensen, but it's really not necessary,' I said, flicking the tiniest of glances his way. There, I thought, you are officially absolved of responsibility.

'Of course he'll stay!' said Betsy, waving away my protests. 'No arguments.'

Jensen laughed. 'Gran's word is law, Lottie, so that's that.'

'Sit down,' said Marjorie, patting the bench beside her. 'You look dead on your feet.'

'I'll be fine after a good night's sleep,' I said weakly. Or rather I'd be fine once I'd got used to the fact there was another human growing inside me . . .

Betsy and I both sat down and Jensen pulled up a chair from the patio table to sit next to us.

'Jensen, you'll have to take the little room; your Aunt Marjorie is in the put-up bed downstairs and Sidney's in the big spare. He's gone to bed early too, exhausted, poor chap.'

'Gosh, Sidney! I'd forgotten about him,' I said. 'How lovely of him to turn up out of the blue.'

Marjorie harrumphed. 'Not sure his son would agree.'

Betsy pursed her lips. 'Hmm. Sidney is recovering from a heart attack and was under doctor's orders to rest. That's why he didn't come to Ted's funeral and didn't want to worry me by mentioning it in his condolence card. His son and daughter-in-law practically had him under lock and key.'

'So that's why I wasn't allowed to talk to him!' I said. 'At least he got my messages, though.'

Jensen gave a bemused smile. 'How did he get here?'

Marjorie laughed. 'The old devil waited until they'd gone out this morning and ran away! He enlisted a friend to drive him to the airport, then took a train and taxi here.'

'He sounds a bit of a character.' I couldn't wait to meet him properly although, I thought, stifling a yawn, I was glad it wouldn't be until tomorrow.

'Just what this place needs: another rebellious pensioner,' Jensen muttered with a comical look of despair.

'He's exactly what we need; he's such good fun,' said Betsy with glee. 'I made him phone his son to let him know he was safe. It was quite a colourful conversation, I can tell you. Anyway, Lottie, back to you; what did the hospital say?'

'Oh, nothing much,' I said vaguely. 'They told me off for not looking after myself properly. But luckily the blow to my head didn't do any major damage.'

I turned round so Betsy could feel the egg-shaped lump.

'Crumbs, that's quite a bump.'

Nothing compared to the bump I was going to get, I thought wryly.

'That's good news,' said Betsy, reaching for her glass.

'Who's ready for more good news?' said Marjorie, beaming. 'We've only just finished cashing up and I can tell you, the bank manager is going to be very pleased with us all. Very pleased indeed.'

'Yes,' Betsy chipped in. 'Thanks to everyone's hard work, we sold over a thousand bottles of wine of the 2015 vintage today.'

'Amazing!' My eyes opened wide; the retail value of that would be around thirty thousand pounds! We still had several thousand bottles to sell, plus a decent quantity from the previous year, but it was great news and fingers crossed would be the start of good things to come.

'Not only that,' Marjorie continued, 'we took lots of

pre-orders on the next vintage and had over two hundred visitors in total, some of whom have promised to re-order next month.'

'That's really encouraging,' said Jensen brightly. 'Well done, Lottie, the open day was a great success.'

'It was a team effort but thank you, I'm so pleased!' I said modestly. I was filled with pride; I'd never organized anything like it, hadn't even thought I was capable, but I'd done it. It was only an open day on a small vineyard, but a few weeks ago my self-esteem had been at rock bottom and now look at me: learning and doing new things every day.

'This calls for a celebration,' said Marjorie.

There was a small table next to her with a bottle of brandy and two clean glasses. She picked up the bottle and poured brandy into both of them and handed one to me.

Jensen was watching me like a hawk as I took it. I felt my mouth dry up.

'I think I'd rather make myself a cup of tea if you don't mind,' I said. Decaff, or herbal preferably . . .

'Of course,' Betsy said kindly. 'Alcohol is the last thing you'll want after a bump to the head. We should have thought.'

Jensen stared into the bowl of his glass and swirled the brandy round and round. I was grateful to him for not giving the game away, but I felt a sudden urge to tell them myself. I should probably have waited until I'd had my scan, or at least seen a midwife, but after Evie's reaction I craved some female comfort and these two lovely ladies were becoming as dear to me as family.

'It's not just that . . .' I took a deep breath. 'The thing is, I've just found out I'm pregnant.'

Marjorie choked on her brandy and banged her chest hard. 'Bloody hell.'

'Pregnant?' Betsy's jaw dropped.

I nodded and gripped my glass, resisting the urge to gulp it down. 'It's come as a bit of a shock. As you know, I split up from my boyfriend – the baby's father – before I started here and I have no idea when it's due,' I said, letting the words come tumbling out.

I wondered when I had conceived; that last week I'd been with Harvey probably. I wasn't showing yet, so I couldn't be that far along. Although my clothes had been getting tighter, especially around the chest. And all the little things that had been happening to me made sense now: going off milk and tea, the tiredness, the upset tummy.

'If I hadn't gone to hospital today I wouldn't have known,' I continued. 'I haven't got used to the idea yet, I'm not sure what I'm going to do and I'm very sorry to let you all down.'

'Why on earth would you think you've let us down?' said Marjorie, staring at my tummy.

'Your boyfriend was a bit of a rotter, as I recall.' Betsy grasped my hand between hers. 'Well, listen, whatever you decide to do, whatever you need, we'll be here for you. Won't we, Mar?'

Marjorie confirmed it and even offered to run me to appointments if I needed her to. Their kindness melted my heart and I leaned my head against Betsy's shoulder. 'Thank you both.'

'So now we'll need to have a rethink.' Jensen ran a hand through his hair. 'The vineyard, the very manual job Lottie does . . . She can't continue as she is. No offence.'

Nothing is guaranteed to offend me more than adding that particular phrase to an unsolicited opinion. I sat up straight and gave him my sternest stare. 'Despite you announcing that you were a second doctor in that cubicle today, you don't know what you're talking about.'

He blinked at me, startled. 'Excuse me?'

'Providing Betsy is happy for me to carry on working here, that's what I intend to do.'

'Course she is,' Marjorie answered for her.

'But what if you had another accident?' Jensen frowned. 'I'd never forgive myself.'

'But I'm not your responsibility, so no forgiveness needed. I'm young, fit and strong,' I replied, laying a hand on my stomach, 'and quite capable of delegating when necessary. Besides, Betsy offered me this job for only six months, so I'll be out of your hair by the time the baby arrives.'

Jensen gritted his teeth. 'You're twisting my words.'

'Are you suggesting Lottie leaves us, dear boy?' Betsy looked appalled.

He knocked his brandy back. 'Gran, we agreed that you'd stay here for the time being on the basis that Lottie would keep an eye on you and help you out. Not only in the vineyard, but in the house as well. Lottie, you might not be my responsibility, but Gran is.'

'Good grief, boy.' She stared down her nose at him. 'She's only having a baby. If Emmeline Pankhurst could give birth to five children while leading the fight for the emancipation of women, I'm sure Lottie can look after a few grapes and one old lady.'

Marjorie sniggered and topped up her and Betsy's glasses. 'To women's rights!' She raised her glass. 'Cheers!'

Jensen groaned and dropped his head into his hands. 'I'll go and make that tea.'

I watched him stride away into the kitchen. Oh dear, I had a feeling that offer to take me to dinner had been well and truly rescinded.

Chapter 18

'Experiment, taste, make plenty of notes and then taste again,' said Sidney, burying his nose deep into a glass and inhaling. 'That's the way to make the best blend.'

'According to Ted's book, the 2016 Classic Cuvée had exactly the same proportions as our option two, but it tastes completely different,' said Matt, scratching his head with the end of pencil. 'I can't figure out why.'

It was Wednesday afternoon and Sidney had asked me to join him, Matt and Clare in the winery. For the last few days, while I'd been getting to grips with being pregnant, he'd been getting to grips with the contents of every one of Ted's bottles and tanks and working out what needed doing and when. This morning, the three of them had concocted five different blends of the 2017 wine still in the tanks, made from grapes picked last autumn – Ted's last harvest.

'It said in his notebook that the 2016 harvest was late and the grapes were small,' I remembered. 'Whereas in 2017, there was a much warmer September and October. Do you think that could have affected the flavours?'

'Top marks for Miss Allbright,' Sidney said with a twinkly smile which I couldn't help returning. He folded his arms and crossed his legs, a gesture I already recognized as his I'm-going-to-tell-you-a-story pose. 'Frost, rain, drought all make their presence felt in the finished wine . . .'

We'd all fallen under Sidney's spell instantly. For a man in his seventies, and who was recovering from a heart attack, he was bursting with energy and had wasted no time in getting to work. His passion for wine was infectious and his presence and guiding hand had put a new spring in everyone's step; for the first time since I'd been here, it felt as if everything might be okay, as if we could carry on Ted Butterworth's legacy. And heaven knows, I needed something to go right, I thought, tuning back into Sidney's lecture. He gave us a lot of lectures.

'The length of time on the vine is one of the key factors in taste. And judging when to harvest is a minefield. Pick the grapes too early and the wine will be too acidic, too late and the wine will be flabby.'

'Yuck. Reminds me of my reflection in the mirror at the gym this morning.' Clare pulled a face.

Sidney chuckled. 'Flabby just means not acidic enough. And you, my fair lady, are neither flabby nor acidic.'

Clare and I exchanged fond looks; he was so charming and gentlemanly and we'd previously agreed we both wanted to adopt him to be our granddad.

Matt scratched his head again and sighed. 'So is our 2017 harvest acidic or flabby?' He looked completely bamboozled. Either that or he'd been forgetting to use the spittoon again.

'It will be neither.' Sidney stood and turned to the winery desk. On it were five glass jugs, each containing half a litre of clear liquid. In front of each jug was a slip of paper on which was written its precise contents – the proportions of Butterworth's three grape varieties plus some tiny additions that I couldn't make out. Option two, which Matt had been talking about, was made from 55 per cent Chardonnay, 12 per cent Pinot Noir and 33 per cent Pinot Meunier. The others were all slight variations on those quantities.

He worked his way along the samples, from option one to five, pouring a quarter of a glass of each, holding it up to the light and examining it, before inhaling deeply and lastly tasting it. He drew air in over his tongue, pushing it around his mouth.

Finally, he nodded and turned to Matt. 'Rightio, young man. Let's do an option six. As option four but lower the Noir by one per cent and increase the Meunier by the same.'

'On it.' Matt jumped up and set to work and once the blend was done and the proportions written down on paper, he poured Sidney a small glass of it.

I held my breath as Sidney tasted it.

'Well?' said Clare, unable to contain herself.

The blissful smile on Sidney's face said it all. He lifted his glass up and addressed the ceiling. 'Ted Butterworth, my dear old friend, we're going to do you proud.'

Matt poured some for the rest of us and we all tasted what would become Butterworth's Classic Cuvée 2017. Clare and Matt made appreciative noises, smacking their lips while Sidney made notes and I took my time, practising my wine-tasting skills, rolling it around my tongue with my eyes closed, identifying its unique notes, spitting it out into an empty glass. My ability to detect flavours had improved a hundredfold since being at Butterworth's, as had my confidence to say what I tasted.

When I opened my eyes, Sidney was looking at me warmly. 'Does it pass muster?'

I nodded. 'It smells delicious: baked apples and caramel, and I tasted sharp fruit, but not too acidic. But most of all—' I stopped, realizing that I was about to head into fairy-tale territory.

Sidney leaned back on the desk and twirled the end of his moustache. 'Most of all?'

Matt and Clare were listening now.

'Well, it's magical,' I said, feeling silly. 'I know it's just a glass of wine, but when I taste it, it conjures up a picnic on an English summer's day, with sunshine and cakes and laughter and games of rounders. And, well, it makes me happy, that's all.'

Matt swallowed hard. 'That's exactly the sort of thing Ted would have said,' he said gruffly.

'Oh honey,' said Clare with a sniff, 'I think you've summed it up perfectly.'

Sidney's eyes sparkled. 'Ladies and gentlemen, not only have we found our blend today, I think I may have found my new apprentice.'

Matt and Clare raised their glasses to that and I smiled at my lovely new friends. I was falling in love with life at the vineyard. In an ideal world, I'd love to be an apprentice, maybe even go back to college and take a course in viticulture. But the reality was very different; this was a summer job and Betsy had only promised Ted that she'd stay here long enough to gather in this year's harvest. And then there was the small matter of my pregnancy; I was putting off making any firm plans, or even vague ones, until I'd seen the midwife tomorrow. But despite the transient position I found myself in, I really couldn't imagine giving the baby up. Which meant by winter I'd be about to bring a child into the world, which was hardly the best time to start studying. Plus, I'd be jobless and homeless too. And the thought of that was breaking my heart.

The Thursday antenatal clinic was very busy, but thankfully I didn't bump into anyone I knew; even receptionist Nicky, Dad's tenant, wasn't there. I wanted more information about this pregnancy before I started passing the news on to others. After introducing myself to Issy the midwife and answering some questions, it was time for my first weigh-in. I glanced at the dial and gulped.

'Okay,' said Issy, making a note on the computer, 'you can get down now and put your shoes back on.'

I stepped off gladly and slipped on my trainers. What a

201

shocker! I'd never been so heavy in my life and my pregnancy wasn't even showing yet. At this rate, by the time the baby was due, I'd need one of those weighbridges they use to measure lorries before they get on ferries.

'Do you know how far on I'm likely to be?' I asked her.

She shook her head, making her ponytail swing from side to side. She was probably younger than me, had grey-blue eyes, a round face, a bulky watch on one wrist and a tattoo of a bumble bee on the other.

'Not just by looking at you, no,' she said. 'And because you have carried on having periods, we can't even work it out. But I'd say definitely less than nine months.'

'Very funny,' I said, liking her instantly. 'I've read stories about women who give birth without even knowing they'd been pregnant, and I thought they were made up. I feel bad now.'

Issy strapped a cuff around my arm, popped her stethoscope on and pumped up the blood pressure monitor. She let it down with a hiss of air and nodded. 'Normal. Excellent.'

She began typing information into the computer.

'So you said you've been sick quite a bit, you went off certain foods and have been feeling more tired than usual.' She said it without a hint of irony but I couldn't believe how I'd missed the signs.

'I've been such an idiot,' I groaned. 'When you put it like that it's obvious, but recently I've moved house, changed cities and generally been under quite a bit of stress; I thought it was that.'

'It's more common than you think, especially if it's not planned.'

'Harvey and I always played it safe, he took his duty as chief contraceptive officer very seriously.'

Issy raised an eyebrow approvingly. 'Good man. He sounds like a keeper.'

I cleared my throat. 'We've split up, actually. So I'm flying solo.'

'Whoops, me and my big mouth. Sorry.' She winced. 'And not entirely solo, I'll be here.'

I smiled, trying not to think about Evie and how much I wished she was here with me too. 'Do most women already know their due date when they come to see you for the first time?'

'Some do.' She shot me a conspiratorial smile and carried on typing. 'I shouldn't say this but my favourite ladies are the ones who had no idea – the happy accidents.'

I puffed out my cheeks. 'This is definitely an accident; the jury's out on whether it's happy or not.'

'Oh crumbs, sorry.' Issy looked distraught. 'Never assume, my dad says. It makes an ass of "u",' she drew the letter in the air, 'and me. Only not you,' she added hurriedly. 'Just me. I'm the ass. Nearly always.'

I couldn't help but smile at her earnest face. 'It could certainly have come at a better time, that's all, and with a better father.' I swallowed. 'I wish my mum was still alive to talk to about it.'

'Of course.' Issy nodded. 'Have you got someone to support you: a friend, family?'

I didn't want to get into the situation with Evie right now so I said I did.

'Okay, now first things first, we'll get you booked into the hospital for a scan and find out when this baby is due. Then you can work out what to do next. Sound like a plan?'

I rubbed my face with the tissue and stood up to leave. 'Do you know how long it will take for an appointment?'

She shrugged. 'A couple of weeks, maybe more.'

'Good,' I said with a sigh of relief. By then, I was hoping Evie would have answered my calls and we'd have made up. I could manage by myself if I had to, but I'd much rather have her by my side if she could bear it.

'In the meantime, eat plenty of fruit and vegetables and steer clear of booze. Oh and one more thing: I don't have your address on the system?'

'Well, the fruit and veg isn't a problem,' I said with a grin. 'But I live on a vineyard, I work for Butterworth Wines.'

Issy's eyes twinkled. 'I get the feeling you and I are going to be friends.'

I almost hugged her; little did she know I could use a friend right now.

Chapter 19

It was another ten days before I saw my other new friend again. It was Saturday afternoon and I'd just emerged from The Stables when Jensen pulled his car into the yard.

'Wow, look at you.' Jensen's deep blue eyes crinkled at the corners as he greeted me with a kiss. 'I didn't realize blooming was an actual thing before. But you are definitely blooming.'

'That'll be my permanently red cheeks. Not to mention,' I continued, waffling to cover up the fact that I was quite shocked with how pleased I was to see him again, 'that blooming is another way of saying that I'm bursting out of my clothes.'

I didn't know whether it was psychosomatic, but in the two weeks since I'd found out I was pregnant, I'd ballooned. My stomach didn't look any different, but my face looked like a full moon, my waist had disappeared and all I could get into, bra-wise, were a couple of sporty crop tops I'd bought when I was going through a yoga phase. At this rate, there'd be no need to break the news to the rest of the team; they'd have to be blind not to notice there was a lot more of me than there'd been when I'd arrived at the vineyard eight weeks ago.

Jensen's eyes flicked momentarily to my enormous bosom. I coughed.

'Um. I hadn't noticed,' he said, running a hand through his floppy curls. 'But you're feeling okay?'

'Well . . .' I hesitated.

Physically I was fine, I'd stopped being sick and after weeks of needing early nights and having to drag myself out of bed in the morning, I had more energy than I knew what to do with. Mentally, however, I was still struggling: with a pregnancy I hadn't planned and with worrying thoughts about Harvey and what he was going to say and do when he found out I was carrying his child. And then there was the rift between Evie and me. I'd phoned and sent numerous messages which she hadn't returned; I'd even been to her house but if she'd been in she didn't come to the door. I missed her so much; we'd always been there for each other and I didn't know how to make things right.

'Yes. Perfectly okay,' I confirmed finally, opening the gate and waving him through to the terrace. 'And the vineyard is in tip-top shape too. Come and see for yourself, everyone is waiting for us and we've got loads to show you.'

Around the patio table, sheltering from the fierce glare of the August sun under the shade of a parasol, sat my team plus Sidney. The table groaned with tea things: a luscious Victoria sponge, a plate of scones, dishes of jam and cream, and a bowl of fruit salad, all courtesy of Betsy, who had sent her apologies but she and Starsky had an important engagement with Marjorie that she couldn't get out of. Alongside jugs of water there was an ice bucket containing two bottles of Butterworth sparkling wine and a tray of glasses.

'Right, all present and correct,' said Roger officiously, handing a pile of paper to Pippa, who sat on his left. 'So take an agenda and pass the rest on. Let's get going.'

'Just in time!' Clare beamed at us, pouring tea from a large pot. 'Betsy has done a separate pot of decaff, for some reason, if anyone would prefer it?'

I caught Jensen's eye and we shared a knowing smile. Betsy had been such a dear this last fortnight: suggesting all sorts of things she thought I might like food-wise and even offering me the use of her bathroom for a soak as The Stables only had a shower.

'Me please,' I said, taking the empty seats between Clare and Sidney. 'I'm on a health kick,' I said, in answer to her look of disbelief.

'Does that mean I can have your slice of cake?' Godfrey asked hopefully, dolloping cream and jam on to a scone.

'I'm only giving up caffeine, Godfrey. Cake is still on the agenda for now. Baby steps.'

I heard Jensen chuckle softly at my unintended pun; I didn't dare look at him.

Roger rapped a spoon on the table and Matt and Clare rolled their eyes.

'Talking of agendas.' He opened his notebook and wrote down all our names for the minutes. 'First item: welcome by Lottie.'

'Thank you, Roger; and thank you for coming this after-noon, everyone,' I said, spooning a small amount of fruit salad into a bowl. Despite what I'd just said to Godfrey, it was the thought of the sharp and sweet fruit rather than the cake that was making my mouth water.

'So much has happened since our open day two weeks ago, I thought it would be easier to update each other together. Firstly,' I said, smiling at Sidney and covering his hand with mine, 'a big thank-you to Sidney for helping us out in the winery. You've achieved so much for us, we've all learned a great deal and we couldn't have managed without you. We're really going to miss you.'

'Hear, hear,' said Roger, raising his teacup.

Sidney lifted his panama hat politely. 'Pleasure's all mine, dear girl. Only sorry I can't stay longer. I've been put out to pasture in our vineyard now by the young folk, it's been exciting to work on your wines. And good to feel useful again.'

His cardiac consultant had phoned two days ago and

issued instructions for him to return to France immediately *while he was still alive.* He'd booked his flight reluctantly and Jensen was driving him to the airport later this evening.

'Talking of exciting,' said Godfrey, rustling papers in front of him, 'I've got an update on our press coverage.'

'Hold your horses, we'll come to that shortly,' said Roger, tapping the agenda.

'And I want to tell everyone about the 2016 and 2017 wines Sidney has helped us develop,' Matt added, indicating the two bottles on the table. 'We could be in with a shot at winning awards with this lot, eh Clare?'

'Abso-bloody-lutely we could,' said Clare fervently. She took a lacy square of rose pink and ivory wool out of her bag. 'Excuse me if I carry on with my crocheting; I'm on a deadline and the blanket committee I'm on will go bananas if I don't hurry up.'

I suppressed a smile; I didn't know how Clare kept on top of all her social commitments. The blanket committee was a new one on me, but last week, she'd been involved in hosting a group of Latvian teenagers who were over here for a language summer school.

'Did that wine society come back to us about the bulk purchase of the Blanc de Blanc?' Godfrey asked me. 'They were very keen at our open day.'

I opened my mouth to answer but Roger jumped in first.

'Order!' he boomed, raking a hand through his fine gingery hair. 'Sales figures are item four. Really, I must insist.'

Marjorie had completely sorted out the backlog of orders, many of them dating from the months leading up to Ted's death, and we were on top of deliveries for the time being. But it wasn't a long-term solution. The trouble was that there just weren't enough hours in the day and none of us particularly liked working indoors.

Jensen put a calming hand on Roger's arm.

'Sorry to interrupt,' he said, pulling a business card out of his pocket, 'but before I forget, I have the details of a virtual sales office for you, Lottie. They'll collate phone and online orders, make sales calls to existing customers and send a daily summary through to you. It would solve the admin issue for the rest of this year at least.'

And then what? The 2017 vintage would be ready to sell. And the tanks would be full of the 2018 harvest, waiting to be blended and bottled. What *was* going to happen next year? I wanted to ask, but wasn't sure I wanted to hear the answer.

'I'll call them,' I said simply, taking the card from him.

Pippa put her hand up. 'If there's time, can we discuss a possible wine tasting at the library? My boss wondered if I could set one up. She's heard a few of our members talking about it and thought it might be a nice way to be a bit more interactive with readers.'

'Definitely!' I said, delighted.

Pippa beamed proudly as the rest of the group nodded their praise.

'*Veraison* is coming on beautifully,' said Sidney, twirling the end of his moustache. 'I don't think your harvest will be much behind ours in Reims this year.'

Veraison was the onset of ripening, when the grapes turned from green to black. It was still amazing to me that our black grape varieties – Pinot Noir and Pinot Meunier – produced white wine rather than red, because only the juice was used, not the skins. Unless, Sidney told me, the juice had too much contact with the grape skins, in which case we'd end up with rosé. Or in future, if we wanted to, we could leave the skins in the juice and make our own red wine. Except, I reminded myself with a pang of sadness, there wasn't a future for Butterworth Wines, was there?

'Our Classic Cuvée isn't far behind yours either.' Matt rocked back on his chair, arms folded smugly. 'You wait until you try it, Jensen.'

'Fingers crossed we don't get the wet weather we had last year.' Clare shuddered. 'Remember the rush we had to get the grapes in before the rain came down? And picking by hand is back-breaking work; I was exhausted. And my nails were ruined.'

She waggled her fingers. Today's manicure was dark purple with a glittery top coat. It would be, wouldn't it, I thought enviously, noting her purple linen dress and silvery espadrilles.

'Worth it, though.' Pippa pressed her finger into the last scone crumbs on her plate. 'We'll need to organize extra teams of pickers well in advance this year to handle the bumper crop Ted predicted.'

'Perhaps Jensen will help with the harvest this year?' Sidney regarded him intensely. 'Your granddad would have loved that.'

Jensen leaned forward and topped up his water. 'Um, I'll have to check my work commitments nearer the time. I might be away a lot by autumn.'

'I can't wait to get picking,' I said, trying not to show my disappointment at Jensen's lack of enthusiasm. I'd watched umpteen YouTube videos about harvesting grapes and the thought of bringing in our own harvest filled me with joy.

Sidney topped up my tea. 'Your job will be to direct operations from the winery and oversee the fruit going into the press.'

Jensen met my eye. 'Not bending down snipping thousands of bunches of grapes.'

I flashed him a look to shut him up. 'No way, I want to roll up my sleeves and join in at the sharp end!'

I grabbed a scone and sliced it in two, hoping the others wouldn't put one and one together and make three. Betsy had had to tell Sidney because I'd had dinner with them a few times over the past fortnight and he kept trying to ply me with alcohol. I wasn't ready to tell anyone else yet. Not until I knew how far gone I was. It was partly because I still needed to get used to the idea myself, but also, on a sadder note, because I was only too aware of Evie's experience. She had miscarried her baby at twelve weeks and if my pregnancy ended as brutally as hers, the fewer pitying expressions I'd have to face, the better.

'Sidney's right, Lottie,' said Roger. 'There's a lot to do at harvest: delivering empty crates to the vines, collecting full crates of grapes, checking the quality . . . The list is endless. We need someone to keep track of everything.'

'That was what Ted used to do,' Pippa said quietly.

Everyone fell silent for a moment.

'Look, sorry for jumping the gun, but I've got to show you these before I burst,' said Godfrey, passing printouts of blog posts and online reviews and a lovely article in the *Derbyshire Bugle* around the group. Roger made a grunting noise but I was grateful to Godfrey for stepping in just as the mood had started to dip. 'And there's another thing in the offing too, I'll keep you posted.'

'That's it!' muttered Roger hotly, jabbing a finger at the agenda. 'I want everyone to read through the agenda before speaking another word.'

I did as I was told. It had several points on it: vineyard yield, status of 2016 and 2017 wines, sales update, marketing activity, future events.

Matt scanned the page before casting it aside. 'Great, well, we seemed to have covered most of this, so without further ado, let's start with the 2017. Grab the glasses, Pippa.'

Roger folded his arms and looked away sulkily.

'Ooh goody.' Clare stuffed her blanket back in her wool bag. 'Spittoons at the ready for the drivers amongst us!'

Matt poured the team a small glass of option six, the blend we'd all agreed on. 'Now, this has got more Pinot Meunier in than last year, and slightly less Pinot Noir. Drink up, Jensen. What do you think, would Ted approve . . . ?'

As Matt began to tell everyone what Sidney had taught him and guided us all through the different options they'd considered, Sidney leaned over to me.

'I'd like one more walk through the vineyard before I go, would you join me?' he whispered.

I grinned at the lovable old man who had been so generous with his time and expert knowledge, not to mention he'd managed to put a smile on Betsy's face thanks to the constant trips down memory lane over the last two weeks. 'With pleasure.'

We took a detour via the shed for a pair of secateurs and took the side gate through the wall to the vineyard.

'This was Ted's favourite spot,' said Sidney, waiting while I secured the gate behind us.

'Mine too.'

We were standing on the highest point of the vineyard, under the dappled shade of the line of conifers. These trees shielded the western side of the vines from the harsh winds that whistled through Derbyshire in early spring, protecting them from losing their precious buds, and today provided Sidney and me with a welcome respite from the fierce midsummer sun. The sky was cornflower blue with just a few gossamer clouds on the horizon. The valley had never looked so beautiful: myriad greens in the fields and foliage and crops below, a flock of sheep way out to the east, and in the distance, a smudge of cottages and the curve of the river as it carved its way through the countryside.

'See that pink rose?' Sidney turned back and pointed to the house where a climbing rose smothered the back wall right up to the bedroom windows.

I nodded. It had lovely coral blooms with yellow centres. I'd admired it so much that Betsy had taken to putting fresh bunches of them on the doorstep of The Stables for me every couple of days; it smelled amazing.

'It's called "Summer Wine". Ted bought it just after he'd planted the first batch of vines a decade or so ago.'

I laughed. 'Wine really was everything to him, wasn't it?'

'Everything. Well, that and his family. It's a shame he was

never able to combine the two, like I've done.' He sighed wistfully and gave himself a shake. 'He'd be so happy that his good work is being carried on in his absence.'

'For the time being at least,' I said.

He frowned. 'I've been thinking about that. It's heartbreaking to think that the vineyard might fall out of Butterworth hands.'

'You can't blame Betsy and Marjorie for wanting an easier life, though,' I said reluctantly. 'And the only other Butterworth I've met is Jensen and he seems to love his job in London.'

We headed to the Chardonnay rows; there was a clump of vines which weren't thriving as well as the others and I wanted his advice before he left. He told me to thin out the foliage as much as possible and apply a little fertilizer to encourage growth and then we moved on to the next row.

Sidney had helped us so much in the last two weeks; I was going to miss our early-morning walks amongst the vines and the little lessons he'd been giving me in the winery about all the various flavours and enhancements that could be added to our wines to lift them from ordinary to extraordinary. Trawling through Ted's never-ending collection of reference books had given me lots of knowledge, but it was no substitute for the hands-on experience of an expert like his old friend.

'It was Betsy who found this place, you know,' said Sidney, as we took our snippers to a particularly voracious vine that had sent springy new shoots out to the row opposite. 'It came up at auction. He and I had scoured the South Downs in the hope of finding something on the same seam of chalk which runs from England under the Channel to the Champagne region where my vineyard is. Ted was adamant that would give him the best shot of recreating a sparkling wine to match champagne. Betsy had other ideas.'

'Why doesn't that surprise me?' I said with a laugh.

Sidney plucked a few leaves away from the bunches of ripening grapes, taking a moment to explain how removing some greenery would let the sun get to the fruit to ripen it, but still keep enough foliage to allow for photosynthesis to feed the plant. Then he continued, 'Her daughter, Samantha, and Jensen had not long moved back to the area after leaving Jensen's father. Betsy didn't think it was the right time to move away, she wanted her and Ted to be hands-on grand-parents and heaven knows, Jensen needed a decent male role model in his life.'

My ears pricked up; I didn't know much about Jensen's parents but it hadn't escaped my notice that Jensen was a Butterworth and obviously hadn't taken his father's surname.

Just like you, I said to the new life inside me. My baby would be an Allbright, Harvey Nesbitt was going to have nothing to do with it. With him or her, I meant. My heart gave a jolt, remembering Jensen's words in the hospital. *You'll have to tell him; he has a right to know* . . . But not yet, I wasn't ready to face him. Not without my family to back me up, and who knew when that was going to happen. I tuned back into Sidney's story, feeling decidedly uneasy . . .

'Ted knew when he was beaten; if Betsy didn't have her heart on a move to the south coast it would never happen. So Ted and Betsy came out here and met with the couple who were on their knees from trying to breed pigs and grow garlic and desperate to sell.

'Ted took one look at the mud bath and almost walked away but Betsy pitched it to him just right.' Sidney shook his head, laughing at the memory. 'She told him to think how proud he would be of producing top quality wines here in Derbyshire where he'd been born and bred. So he had the soil tested to see if it had the nutrients it needed. All it was lacking was phosphorous.'

'And that is easy enough to remedy,' I said, thinking back to the fertilizers we'd used at the crematorium.

He nodded. 'That's right. And so Butterworth Wines was born. Caused quite a stir in the wine world at the time; there were hardly any vineyards this far north.'

'There aren't many now,' I said, having done my research. 'A million new vines were planted in England last year, but only a tiny percentage of those were north of London.'

Sidney looked impressed. 'What else do you know?'

'Nowhere near as much as you.' I shrugged. 'But I know that some of the top champagne houses have cottoned on to just how similar the *terroir* is here and have been buying up land, so not only have land prices shot up, but the reputation of English sparkling wine is at an all-time high. We're winning awards all over the world, and countries like America are waking up to how good our products are too. It's an exciting time to be making wine in England.'

Sidney chuckled. 'You love this job, don't you?'

'Very much.' I took a deep breath, inhaling the delicate scent of the vines and wondering, not for the first time, how on earth this job had managed to find me just when I needed it, as if some mysterious force had had a hand in it. 'I keep having to remind myself not to get too attached. That it won't last.'

Sidney's smile dropped. 'Are you sure about that?'

We were in the centre of the vineyard now, in the wide path that separated the upper and lower slope. Sidney headed for a wooden bench, took off his hat and fanned his face. I lowered myself next to him and stretched out my legs.

'Betsy can't carry on here indefinitely and my job is only until the end of autumn. And even if it wasn't, I'll be taking some time off work when the baby is born. It's very sad, though, thinking that Butterworth Wines is nearing the end of its life.'

'Very sad.' He shook his head, tutting softly. 'When my wife, Sylvie, died, life was able to go on as before. Her family have owned vineyards for over a hundred years. She has a brother and a sister, between us we have six children and, so far, eight grandchildren. Even if half of them had no interest in wine, there are enough of the new generation to continue our wine story for decades to come. Ted and I were the same age; it's sobering when your health is under threat, you realize you're not immortal after all. There's a lot to be said for having your family close when times are difficult.'

'There is.' I had a sudden overwhelming need to talk to my own family. I resolved to try Evie again later and wished more than anything that I could just pick up the phone and talk to my dad. He was in Germany now. I'd only communicated by text with him for two weeks, worried that I'd mention the baby as soon as I heard his voice and until I could guarantee that I wouldn't burst into tears over the mess I'd got myself into, I didn't dare speak to him.

Sidney must have noticed something in my tone because he patted my hand.

I forced a smile. 'Is Jensen's mum not around?'

No one ever mentioned her, and I was aware I was being nosy, but if anyone was going to tell me it would be Sidney.

He pulled a face. 'Samantha? Yes and no. She's happily married and living abroad. She won't move back now.'

'Which just leaves Jensen,' I said softly. My heart sank. It was obvious he had no interest in taking over the family business, he'd just been promoted and his work meant a lot to him.

The old man nodded. 'Ted once told me that he hoped Jensen would take over here when he got too old. From what Betsy has said, Ted's illness took hold very quickly. I expect he didn't want to burden his grandson with the responsibility of the business when his career was taking off. And then time ran out and he never got the chance to talk to Jensen about it.'

'Time ran out for my mum too.' I swallowed. Even after more than ten years it was hard to talk to people outside the family about it. There were so many things she'd missed out on. She would have loved to have been at Evie's wedding and I knew she'd always hoped one day to be a grandmother. 'It makes me want to live life to the full in her honour.'

216

Sidney looked at me speculatively. 'I've been thinking about the future too. Do you think you and Jensen could give it a go? You seem to complement each other well.'

'No, I don't think so.' I looked down at my fingers, stained green with sap off the vines, my short nails caked in mud from pulling up weeds. So different to his clean office-boy hands. We were chalk and cheese. 'Actually, he did invite me to dinner but that was before we found out I was pregnant. He hasn't repeated the offer since, which is hardly surprising. And besides, he likes London, I hate it. So that's that.'

His lips twitched. 'I meant give Butterworth Wines a go. As *business* partners.' He lifted his hands. 'But romantic partners would make his grandmother and his great-aunt very happy.'

My cheeks flamed. 'Please don't tell anyone what I just said.'

He chuckled and mimed zipping his lips. 'Your secret's safe with me. Although why do you say it's hardly surprising? Any man would be proud to be stepping out with you.'

'Thank you, Sidney, you are such a gentleman.' I sighed. 'But it's hardly the ideal first date, is it? With a woman who's carrying another man's child.'

Sidney took a breath as if about to reply but he was interrupted.

'Lottie? Lottie? Where are you?' It was Jensen calling to me from higher up the slope.

'Talk of the devil.' I fanned my face quickly before replying.

'In the centre path sitting on the bench. What's up?'

I stood up as I heard Jensen running towards us. He appeared from the end of a row of Pinot Noir vines.

'You've got a very contrite visitor,' he said, out of breath. 'I've left him with Matt and Roger in the winery.'

Harvey? My mouth went dry. 'Muscly physique, short black hair?'

He shook his head. 'No, don't worry. It's Darren, your

brother-in-law. I almost didn't recognize him without his two burly friends.'

My shoulders sagged with relief. 'Is he, um, sober?' I asked, shooting an apologetic look at Sidney.

'I hope so,' Jensen replied, 'because he drove here. Although his van does have "Get Plastered" across the side of it. So who knows?'

'That's his business.' I was flustered, wondering what Darren wanted or if he had a message from Evie. 'Not as in to get plastered, but to plaster other things. Sidney, please excuse me.'

'And we need to be making tracks soon.' Jensen pulled Sidney to his feet and together we all headed back to the winery. Marjorie's car was parked in front of the house, which meant that she and Betsy were back in time to see Sidney off. Out of the corner of my eye, I saw Darren emerge from the doors of the winery and raise a self-conscious hand.

Sidney kissed both my cheeks and clasped my hands. 'Goodbye, Lottie. Think about what I said. English wine is about to enter a whole new chapter, one which I'm sure you're going to enjoy.' He shot a mischievous look at Jensen. 'And don't write this young fellow off too quickly; he's more attached to this place than he likes to let on.'

Jensen raised his eyebrows questioningly and I hugged the old man to hide my blushes. He was wrong about that, I thought sadly, as I crossed the yard to the winery; Jensen didn't love Butterworth Wines as much as I did, not enough to save it anyway.

'Sorry for just turning up,' said Darren, looking downcast. 'I didn't know who else to turn to.'

'It's really good to see you.' I hugged my crumpled brother-in-law and pushed thoughts of Jensen to the back of my mind; right now I had someone else's mess to unravel, which made a refreshing change from my own. 'Come inside and let's have a chat.'

*

'I love Evie so much.' Darren sat at my dining table, rubbing a thumb over the callused knuckles on his other hand, his nails split from their constant contact with plaster. 'I've made a hash of everything.'

'Why did you move out?' I handed him a can of Diet Coke from the fridge, poured myself a glass of water and sat opposite him. He looked terrible; despite the weeks of sunshine we'd had, he looked almost grey; he seemed tired, defeated and desperately sad. 'You told her you wanted a divorce.'

'Because I love her,' he muttered gloomily. 'I'll always love her, no matter what.'

I frowned. 'You're not making any sense. You told her the marriage is over; that's not the most obvious way of showing you love her.'

'I didn't mean any of it. I thought I was doing the right thing.' He dropped his head into his hands and groaned. 'I'm such an idiot.'

I touched his arm, my heart filling with hope. 'You two were always so good together. I know you've been through a lot, but it's at times like these, when you're both at a low ebb, that you need each other most. And if you still love her maybe it's not too late?'

He shook his head. 'No. She's hurting at the moment, but it will pass, she'll move on, get what she deserves and then she'll forget about me.'

'And what does she deserve?'

His eyes clouded with tears. 'To be free to start over again.'

'She doesn't want to be free, she wants a husband, she wants you.' I shook his arm. 'And a family. With you.'

He gave a hollow laugh. 'Until we found out my sperm swim so slowly they're almost comatose. It was a miracle Evie got pregnant once; it won't happen again.'

I blinked at him. 'I'm so sorry; I didn't know.'

He stared at me disbelievingly. 'Evie didn't tell you?'

I shook my head. 'She always said "we". She never said it was you. I don't think she wanted you to set her free, Darren.'

'Oh, Evie,' he whispered hoarsely, pressing his palms over his eyes. 'Once she started talking about fostering, I realized how important being a mother was to her. Until then I just thought having a family would be the icing on the cake for us as a couple. But it means everything to her. So I reckoned it wasn't fair of me to hold her back. There's no need for her to deny herself the chance to be a mum naturally. I thought if I walked away I'd be setting her free. There's no need for her to adopt, or foster, she can have her own babies naturally. She'll make a brilliant mum.'

'She will.' I hugged him tight. 'But you'll be a brilliant dad. Being a good parent can start from the moment you bring a child home, however that journey began. Evie wants you at her side every step of the way on that journey.'

'That's not what she said when she dropped me off at home after the police released me; she said I was a poor excuse for a man and it was just as well we hadn't had children if I was going to get hammered every time I had a setback.'

That sounded like my sister; I could imagine how furious she'd have been with him.

'To be fair, Darren,' I said, my lips twitching, 'you were a bit of an idiot that day. But I still think she'd like the two of you to properly consider the options and become parents together.'

His back straightened. 'Do you think? Because I've realized – and I know I'm a bit slow on the uptake – but I want us to be parents together too.'

My heart soared. 'That's the best news I've heard for ages, Darren. Evie is going to be thrilled!'

He eyed me doubtfully. 'Trouble is she hasn't taken my calls since that night at the hospital.'

'Mine neither.' I sighed. 'But she's got a lot to deal with:

220

you walking out on her and then finding out that I'm pregnant. She's bound to be upset.'

Darren massaged his brow and groaned.

'Oh Lottie, of course, I'm sorry I've been so preoccupied . . . I should have asked.' He glanced down but my stomach was hidden by the table. 'You're going through so much too. Evie told me how nasty it turned between you and Harvey. I wish I'd known, I'd have had some serious words with him.'

'You weren't to know,' I assured him. 'Besides, he wasn't always like that, was he? The four of us used to have fun together, once upon a time.'

'We did.' He nodded ruefully and we fell silent for a moment, thinking of happier times.

'And how do you feel?' He scanned my face.

'Physically I'm fine.' I hesitated and Darren raised an eyebrow expectantly. 'Mentally it has taken some getting used to; pregnancy was the last thing on my agenda. Particularly given my last encounter with the father.'

He winced. 'What are you going to do?'

'I'm going ahead with the pregnancy. No question,' I said. 'I've got my first scan next week; I want to find out when it's due before I make any more decisions.' I sucked in a sharp breath, not wanting to get distracted by my own problems. 'Anyway, back to you. What's next?'

He reached across the table for my hand. 'When that plonker Tommy Dawson started mouthing off about fancying Evie, I realized that I can't let her go; I love her too much to see her with someone else. I want Evie back, Lottie.'

'So what are you going to do?'

'I'm running out of ideas.' He shrugged. 'She won't take my calls, when I went round she wouldn't let me in. I've sent her flowers, written her a letter. I even tried my key in the door, but she's changed the locks. Will you help me – help *us*? Please?'

My heart ached for the two of them and I felt a flush of guilt for not trying harder to make up with Evie. I'd been so wrapped up in my own issues and coming to terms with being pregnant that I'd glossed over her trauma. Not only was she facing a future without Darren, she was possibly facing a future with a baby in the family, except not her own as she'd always wanted. We'd never gone this long not speaking to each other. I'd make it my mission to make amends as soon as I could, and maybe I'd be able to salvage her and Darren's marriage too.

'I'll do my best,' I promised, squeezing his hand. 'I want her back too and I'll tell her as much, even if I have to camp out on her doorstep.'

It had to be worth a try; I missed her so much and so, by the look of it, did Darren.

Chapter 20

The next morning was Sunday. I'd had a lie-in, a shower and a leisurely breakfast. Maybe later, I thought, selecting a sundress from my wardrobe, I'd pop into the nearest supermarket, choose the nicest bunch of flowers I could find and knock on Evie's door again.

I combed through my damp hair and twisted it up into a clip before I smoothed body lotion on to my legs and arms. Then standing in front of the bedroom mirror, I lowered my towel and examined myself in profile. I had the most ridiculous white torso and nut-brown arms and legs, thanks to working outside, but that wasn't what held my attention. There, below my tummy button, was a tiny bump. I laid a hand on my white skin. Yes, it was definitely there, I was *definitely* beginning to show. I smiled and my pulse speeded up; I was desperate to show someone else, to have someone place their hand on the roundness and marvel at my changing shape.

A pang of loneliness shot through me sharp as a needle and pricked at my eyes. Today was the day; I had to get through to Evie. Maybe all it would take was for me to make the first move.

There was a knock at the door.

'Who is it?' I called from the bedroom, throwing on my bra and dress, glad that I hadn't left the top half of the stable door open for once.

'Me!' shouted Jensen. 'We're being attacked and I don't know what to do.'

I darted to the door and flung it open. Starsky was there too, wagging his tail. 'What? By whom?'

He jabbed a finger towards the sky. 'Birds, hundreds of them.'

'Show me.'

We ran together across the yard with the dog scampering between us through the gate across the terrace and then stopped at the top of the steps, watching as a flock of black birds swarmed over the uppermost rows of the Pinot Noir vines. Starsky began to bark and the birds nearest us took flight only to land again further away.

'Incredible.' I was mesmerized and horrified at the same time.

I had read about this. When the grapes start to turn black and sweet they attract the birds and word clearly spread like wildfire in the bird world.

'Are the starlings back? Bloody nuisances! Clear off!' Betsy appeared at the kitchen door. She stepped on to the terrace, waving her stick. 'Ted tried everything.'

'And what worked, Gran?' Jensen stared at the sky.

'His shotgun. I'll fetch it! You go down and run around making noises, I'll fire some shots.'

Jensen snorted with laughter. 'Don't even think about it!'

'I used to be a crack shot, I'll have you know,' Betsy sniffed.

Jensen and I exchanged worried looks; presumably, that was before the centre of her vision had faded.

'Come on, they'll have stripped half the grapes off at this rate,' I said, jumping down the steps and letting a by-now-frantic Starsky through the gate and in amongst the vines. I'd never seen the little dog so animated but he seemed to know what to do, barking up at the sky and sending the birds soaring.

'Gran, stay out of trouble, bang some saucepan lids together or something,' yelled Jensen over his shoulder.

'Spoilsport,' I heard her grumble.

I charged at the birds, clapping my hands above my head. 'Shoo! Scram! Go on, off!' I yelled.

Jensen took the next row, letting out a war cry: 'YAHHHHH.'

'What do you think this is,' I shouted, waving my arms in the air, 'an all-you-can-eat buffet?'

In the next row, I heard Jensen burst out laughing. 'Flock off, birds, or I'll set my gran on you.'

'I heard that,' came a haughty shout from the terrace. 'Now, eat your heart out, Keith Moon.'

A hideous racket started up as Betsy clashed two large saucepan lids together. Whoever Keith Moon was, he didn't seem to be a particularly gentle influence.

'I love your gran,' I yelled to Jensen, getting a stitch from laughing and running.

There was a tiny pause. 'She's a one-off all right.'

And then we both set off again, yelling ridiculous insults at our feathered enemies. More and more birds took to the air, Starsky ran up and down the rows, beside himself with joy, barking and snapping fruitlessly at the air while Jensen and I ran to the end of our respective rows until we met, breathless, in the middle. We both collapsed, laughing and worn out, on the bench where I'd sat with Sidney the day before.

'They've gone,' I said, panting as hard as Starsky who flung himself down at our feet, a doggy smile on his little face.

'You can stop now, Gran!' Jensen shouted up to the house, shielding his eyes from the sun.

Betsy didn't hear him and carried on beating the anti-starling tattoo with her metal lids.

'She'll give up in a minute,' I said with a giggle.

'Let's hope the birds have given up for the day too.' Jensen scanned the skies. 'Perhaps you can see if there are any less labour-intensive bird-scaring methods?'

I grinned at him. 'I'll google it.'

I pressed a hand to my side and winced.

His smile dropped. 'What is it? Is it the baby?'

I shook my head, touched by his concern. 'Just a stitch. It's all this laughing; I haven't had so much fun in ages.'

'Me neither.' His blue eyes held mine. He lay his arm on the back of the bench behind my shoulders and it took all my self-control not to scoot next to him and snuggle into that hollow between his chin and his collarbone.

He jerked his head back towards the terrace. 'I think Dave Grohl can rest easy, Betsy Butterworth won't be stealing his thunder any time soon.'

'Thunder being the operative word.'

The clashing of saucepan-lid cymbals stopped and we heaved a joint sigh of relief.

Jensen examined the edge of his thumbnail. 'Sidney spoke to me on the way to the airport; he was asking me about the two of us.'

'Oh?' I willed my face not to give me away, although in all honesty I probably couldn't get much pinker after all that exertion.

'Yep.' He didn't look up. 'He thinks we'd make a good team.'

'He said something similar to me,' I said quietly.

Jensen sucked in air. 'The thing is, Lottie, if things were different, I think he might be right.'

We looked at each other and I was suddenly hyper aware of him, the smell of his skin, the rise and fall of his chest and the flicker of a pulse in his neck. If things were different, if I wasn't pregnant with another man's child . . .

'I understand.' I blinked at him. I hadn't expected anything less, but hearing him actually say the words brought me up short.

'The trouble is, Butterworth Wines is something my granddad created, it's his achievement. And it's great but . . .' He shrugged.

So he hadn't been thinking about 'us' at all; I didn't know whether this was a good or a bad thing.

'It was his dream, not yours,' I said, focusing on keeping my tone neutral.

'Correct.'

'So what is your dream?'

His jaw tightened. 'Dreams are for dreamers, people like my father. I believe in setting goals and then doing every-thing in your power to reach them.'

I looked at him sharply. 'You've never mentioned your father before.'

'Bill McKenna, everyone calls him Mac.' Jensen ran a hand through his hair. 'He was an artist; he might still be, for all I know. When I was a kid, he specialized in large-scale installation art for people with delusions of grandeur and too much cash. Whenever he got a commission for a piece, he'd be all fired up, convinced it was going to be the one that would finally make his name. And then he would uproot us from whichever temporary home we were in to go and "make a fresh start".'

The bitterness in his voice made my heart ache for him.

'Was he a successful artist?' I asked.

'Like I said, he was a dreamer,' Jensen scoffed. 'He'd have a vision in his head about how his creation should look but the reality rarely lived up to his expectations. More often than not, the project would take longer than planned, the client would begin to lose patience and faith and Dad would fly into a rage, declare he couldn't be expected to *create* under such oppressive conditions and abandon the project. We'd have to slink off under a cloud and wait for some other unsuspecting client with more money than sense to knock at our door. Dad never acknowledged it, but it was only because Mum did some part-time book-keeping that we were ever able to make ends meet. So no, in my eyes he wasn't successful,' he said wryly.

'Sidney said they split when you were a teenager?'

'They'd never actually married, which used to bother Mum, but made it easier for her to leave in the end. I think she finally got fed up of playing second fiddle. Dad wasn't deliberately unkind, but I've never met anyone so disinterested in the people who loved him. The last I heard he met a Native-American woman called River and moved to her reservation in Wyoming. That was about ten years ago.'

'Don't you keep in touch?' I asked, thinking of my own loving father and realizing how lucky I was to have such a caring man in my life.

'There's little point, I didn't get to know him,' he replied with a shrug. 'Not properly, I'm not even sure Mum did.'

'Sidney said she lives abroad now; you must miss her?'

'I do.' His face softened. 'She found happiness second time around with a golf professional called Victor. He's a good guy; I'm pleased for her. Victor was headhunted by a brand-new golf club in Shanghai and they live the life of Riley now. I don't get to see her much, but I know she's happier than she's ever been.'

At that moment, several starlings dared to swoop down on the vines just behind us. Starsky shot out from under the bench, barked furiously at them until they disappeared and then trotted back to flop down looking very pleased with himself. We both laughed at his smug expression.

'So,' I pursed my lips playfully, 'we've established that you have goals not dreams, so what is your goal?'

He laughed. 'Sorry, that was a long-winded answer. Am I boring you?'

'Not at all.' I shielded my eyes from the sun to study him. 'Your upbringing is a lot more exciting than mine, not that I'm complaining.'

He pressed a fingertip to my arm. 'I think we should get

out of the sun; you're going a bit pink. I don't want you collapsing on me again.'

I gave him a stern look. 'You're not trying to get out of telling me your ambitions, are you?'

'No, no,' he said softly, 'I'm just trying to look after you.' Which made me go a bit pinker.

'I'm happy to talk,' he went on. 'I want you to understand why I can't come back to the vineyard.'

He stood and offered his hand to pull me up. I took it gratefully; my legs felt heavy after all that running up and down and I was ready for a drink. He tucked my hand through his arm and with Starsky pottering beside us we walked slowly back towards the house using the thin line of shadow from the conifers as shade.

He paused when we got to the top of the vineyard and together we turned to admire the view.

It never failed to take my breath away and I glanced at Jensen's face, unable to believe he wasn't as in love with this place as I was.

'If I had the choice, I don't think I'd ever leave here,' I said, trying to keep the note of melancholy from my voice.

'It would certainly be a great place to raise a family,' he said with a faraway look in his eye.

I followed his gaze and tried to see my future self here, with a child playing alongside me as I tended the vines but I couldn't; I just couldn't picture myself as a mother yet. It all seemed so surreal. The thought that I was somehow failing at all this brought a lump to my throat and it took a moment to realize that Jensen was still talking . . .

'But despite having reached my self-imposed saddo deadline to meet *the one* and settle down by thirty-five, I'm single.' *He was single*. A flicker of an emotion I wasn't quite ready to name danced in my stomach.

'You're not *quite* past it yet,' I said lightly. 'There's plenty of time to meet *the one*.'

He grinned. 'I hope so. But the upside of that is that I can throw myself one hundred per cent into my career. Within the next five years my goal is to be my own boss.'

'You're planning on giving up corporate life?'

He lifted the latch on the wide gate and nodded. Starsky scampered off up the steps and disappeared into the cool of the house. We followed at a more leisurely pace towards my cottage.

'Right now I'm serving my time, learning everything I can, growing a network, and waiting for the right moment to set up my own consultancy. I'm with a good solid firm; they make sure their staff are at the cutting edge of the modern architectural world, they send us around the globe to learn the latest advances in building technology and pick up best practice. And most importantly, they respect me and I respect them. I'm fairly confident when the time comes for me to go it alone, they'll back me all the way and employ my services.'

Jensen's blue eyes glittered determinedly; I was in no doubt he'd be successful.

'Do you have a goal?' he asked.

'Not really.' I wrinkled my nose. 'Mine have all been short-term things. I'm not very ambitious; I've always been content to go with the flow.'

'You do yourself a disservice,' he said with a bark of laughter. 'Within your first month at Butterworth Wines, you'd whipped the vineyard into shape, restored confidence in the team and organized the company's first ever open day. We've sold more wine in the last two weeks than in the last six months. We've had press coverage, sales enquiries from all over the country and you somehow managed to get an old man with thirty years' winemaking experience to finish off the 2016 vintage and blend the new one. On top of all that, you've made it possible for Gran to carry on living here. Lottie, those are not the result of being *not very ambitious*.'

'Well, since you put it like that . . .' My chest swelled with pride. 'I guess my immediate priority is family. I've been so lucky. Two parents who loved me and my sister and loved each other. Family is important to me.' I automatically reached for my bump and Jensen didn't miss the gesture. 'And that was what I wanted for myself. I thought by the time I brought a child into the world, I'd have a loving cushion of family to fall back on.'

'And don't you?'

I told him about my parents' retirement plan to travel across Europe in a campervan and how my dad was now doing it solo. He already knew about the rift between Evie and me but I filled in the details of Darren's visit yesterday.

'Has your sister been in touch?'

I shook my head sadly as we crossed the yard and I opened the door to my cottage. 'I'm going to attempt to sort things out today. But it's not only Evie I'm missing; the baby's father is no longer in my life, so the poor thing won't have a dad, or paternal grandparents. My own mum passed away, and Dad has gone off travelling on his retirement gap year.'

I opened the fridge, took out a bottle of sparkling water and offered him some.

'Yes please. Look, there are worse things than being brought up without two parents, you know.' He pointed to himself and flopped down on the sofa. 'Better to have one who loves you than two whose relationship turns the air at home toxic. Case in point.'

'I know,' I said wearily. I sat beside him and handed him a glass. 'It's just . . .' My throat felt tight and suddenly I couldn't get the words out.

He placed a hand gently on my shoulder. 'What's wrong?' he murmured.

'I just didn't think I'd be going through this alone, that's all.' My throat was burning and from nowhere my eyes filled with tears.

'Hey, don't get upset.' He looked at me, alarmed.

'Ignore me,' I said, blinking rapidly. 'Raging hormones. I'm being pathetic.'

'Would you like a hug?'

His dark blue eyes radiated warmth and concern and it was all I could do not to dive on him.

'Very much,' I managed to croak.

He took my drink from me, placed both glasses on the coffee table and gently wrapped his arms around me. Gradually I felt my body relax into his embrace, relishing the comfort of another human being. It felt like an eternity since I'd been held and I wanted this feeling to go on for ever.

'You aren't alone.' His voice was soft and his lips brushed against my hair.

'But I am,' I argued, my tears making a wet patch on the collar of his shirt. 'It's my scan on Friday. I keep imagining that scene you see in films, where the mother sees her baby for the first time and the father squeezes her hand and they gasp in wonder and both whisper "hello, baby" to the screen and the dad gets a photo of the scan and shows it to all his friends.'

'Blimey,' said Jensen, 'you *do* imagine things in a lot of detail.'

'I suppose I do.' Despite my sadness, his tone made me giggle. 'But instead it will just be me, and the sonographer will glance discreetly at the door to check no one else is coming in and then give me a sympathetic smile.'

'Or—' He stopped abruptly as if holding himself in check.

'Or what?'

Jensen cleared his throat. 'Or I could come with you, hold your hand and say "hello, baby". If you like?'

I flicked at my tears and stared at him. 'You'd do that? You'd have time off work and come to the hospital with me?'

'Just call me your second doctor.' He grinned. 'Course I'll do it, it's no biggie.'

'It's big to me.' I kissed his cheek. 'Thank you so much.

But if it's okay with you, I'm going to have one last bash at my sister.'

'Sure.' He smiled. 'Good plan.'

'But will you be Plan B?'

'Of course. Lottie, I . . .' He paused, his eyes drinking me in as he touched my face. 'I'd really like to kiss you. May I?'

I didn't answer. Instead, I leaned in towards him and closed my eyes. My breath trembled as his lips brushed against mine, softly at first, gentle and exploring and then with more heat as we pulled each other closer, my hands in his hair, his at the nape of my neck, caressing me. I felt breathless and light-headed and completely and utterly captivated by the taste of him.

This, I thought distractedly, is the kiss of my dreams.

My head was racing ahead and wondering where this was going but the moment came to an abrupt end as a car came screeching to a halt in the yard outside.

Jensen's eyes shone. 'Damn, I was enjoying that.'

'Me too.'

He stroked my cheek, before going to the door to see who had arrived in such a hurry. I went to join him but before I'd taken a single step I heard a familiar voice. My heart leapt; it was Evie.

'Is Lottie here?' She sounded agitated and I rushed across the room to greet her.

'Yes,' Jensen answered. 'She's here, come in.'

'Evie?' I gasped.

Jensen stood back to let her in. She had mascara streaks down her face, her eyes were red and puffy and she was clutching a tissue.

'Thank God.' She ran into my arms and hugged me tight.

'What's the matter?'

'It's Dad,' she said through great gulping sobs. 'He's been in a motorbike accident in Germany.'

Chapter 21

'He's never been on a motorbike in his life!' I felt my pulse pick up speed. 'Is he okay?'

'I don't know.' She shrugged helplessly. 'He's in surgery now.'

Jensen touched my arm. 'I'll make tea.'

He filled the kettle and began clattering mugs and spoons while I led Evie to the sofa.

'Do you know what happened?' I pulled her down beside me, still clutching her hand and passed her a tissue from the box on the coffee table.

She dabbed her face. 'I know hardly anything. I had a call from a woman called Agnes who said she was a friend and that they had been on motorbikes around Munich and Dad had come off his, hit a car and landed awkwardly.'

'Bloody hell.' Fear gripped my heart. We'd already lost Mum; I couldn't bear it if anything happened to him. I shut my eyes tight. No, Dad, not you. Please be okay. I don't want to lose you.

'I called you as soon as I found out,' she said, rubbing my back. 'But you didn't pick up. I left messages and you didn't return them.'

'I'm so sorry. I haven't seen my phone; Jensen and I were outside.'

He handed us both a mug of tea.

'My fault,' he said, resting his hand briefly on my

shoulder. Evie's eyes followed his every move as if trying to work out what was going on between us. 'There was an emergency on the vineyard.'

'Oh no.' Evie glanced at me sharply. 'What sort of emergency?'

'Don't worry, nothing major.' Jensen held his palms up calmly. 'All sorted now.'

'Right. Good.' She took a sip of her tea before setting it down. I gulped at mine; I'd cut down on caffeine just recently, but this was hitting the spot. Jensen had put some sugar in it and it was just what I needed.

Evie gripped my knee. 'Lottie, when you didn't return my calls I thought you were ignoring me. And I don't blame you; I feel so ashamed of how I've behaved. I'm so, so sorry about the way things have been between us.'

'Don't apologize,' I said, taking her hand. 'I understand how hard it must be for you, knowing I'm pregnant. And I'd never ignore you.'

She cast her eyes down, her chin wobbling.

Jensen cleared his throat. 'I'll leave you two to talk. But if there's anything I can do, anything at all, let me know and . . .' He waited until my gaze was focused on him. 'I meant what I said about Friday; you probably won't need me but I'm here if you do.'

'Thank you.' I felt awkward suddenly. I wanted to get up and kiss him goodbye but there was no way I could do that in front of my sister. Not at a time like this. I did my weird windscreen-wiper wave, which made him smile, and then he was gone.

'Well.' Evie raised an eyebrow. 'He's lovely.'

'He is.' I allowed myself a small smile before turning my attention back to her. 'So. What do we do now about Dad?'

'I'm going to fly out there,' she said, tucking her blonde hair behind her ears. 'Tonight, if I can get a flight. Goodness knows where I'm going and where I'll end up sleeping but he should have family around him.'

'Okay, let's see what seats are available.' I got up to retrieve my phone from the bedroom. The home screen was full of notifications of messages and voicemails from Evie and I quickly scrolled through them and returned to the living room, opening up Google. 'I'll come with you.'

'Is that wise?' Her eyes flitted to my stomach. 'It'll be tiring and I don't know when I'll be back.'

'There's nothing going on here that I can't miss,' I said, not meeting her eye. 'So I'm coming. Here we go. Manchester to Munich . . .'

Together we looked at the details. There was a flight leaving at 6 p.m. and there were still seats free. Evie ran out to get her bag from the car and I stood up to put our tea mugs in the sink.

'Got it,' said Evie, dashing back in brandishing her credit card. 'I'll read the number out to you.'

I picked up my phone from the sofa to complete the transaction, but a new message pinged through.

Your dad's health is very important, but so is yours and the baby's. Whatever you do, please be careful and remember Friday, Jensen x

I was still mooning over the kiss at the end of the message when Evie peered over my shoulder.

'Lottie, what's happening on Friday?'

I snapped back to the moment. 'I've got my first scan. But it doesn't matter; I can be back by then, Dad needs both of us in Germany right now.'

She wagged a finger. 'Oh no. I'll look after Dad, you look after yourself and—' Her voice faltered. 'Your baby.'

I bit my lip. 'I feel so bad about being pregnant after all you've been through.'

She looked appalled. 'You don't mean that.'

'Sometimes I do. And then at other times I get this happy fluttering in my stomach when I think about what he or she

236

might look like and how it will feel to hold a baby in my arms.' I groaned, raking my fingers through my hair. 'My brain's all over the place. I don't have two consistent thoughts in my head.'

'This is my fault.' Evie moved closer to me. 'I'm ashamed of myself. My little sister is having a baby, no mum, no dad around, an absolute knobhead for an ex, and the *one* person you should have been able to rely on to be there for you – me – turned her back on you. I feel so guilty.'

'So do I!' I said, meeting her eye. 'I keep thinking, Why me? Why not you? You'd have made such a good job of it; you even have a bedroom to put a baby in.'

'Because life's not always fair. It's messy and complicated so it's no wonder your brain can't cope. Neither can mine some of the time.' She gave me a sad smile. 'Have you thought about what you're going to do?'

I shook my head. 'No. Not really beyond knowing I couldn't have a termination.'

Evie squeezed her eyes tight. 'Oh Lottie, I thought, with what's happened between you and Harvey, that you might be considering it.'

I pulled her close and hugged her.

'That's been the thing that I was most upset about; the thought that I wanted a baby so much and you didn't,' she went on.

'It's hardly ideal, though,' I reminded her. 'I'm in temporary accommodation, I have a short-term job and I don't even know if I can afford to bring a child into the world. A child whose father is Harvey, for goodness' sake. What if he wants to be part of the baby's life? I'd hate that.'

Evie sucked in air. 'I've been thinking about Harvey too. Does he know yet?'

I shook my head. 'I wanted to have the scan first, find out how far along I am before I tell anyone. Not even Dad knows yet.'

'Then you can't miss that appointment.'

'What if Dad's injuries are really serious?' I said solemnly. 'I don't want you to have to go alone.'

Evie bit her lip. I could tell she was torn; she didn't really want to go by herself.

'How about we try to contact this friend of Dad's again?' I suggested. 'Perhaps there'll be more news by now.'

Agnes had given Evie her mobile number and Evie tapped out a text message asking for an update. I made us some toast and more tea, decaff for me, and by the time we'd eaten the toast and the tea was cooling, we got a reply.

Your father had his operation. He sleeps but he is not dangerous. I give more news when he will be awake.

We collapsed against each other with relief.

'I think that must mean that he's out of danger, rather than being actually dangerous,' Evie said with a wobbly smile. 'Unless he's had a personality transplant when he hit his head.'

We shared a slightly hysterical laugh.

'Thank heavens,' I said, a sob catching in my throat.

'So,' said Evie determinedly, 'much as Dad would love to see you, I'm going to Germany on my own. I don't know how long I'll be staying and you need to be there at that scan on Friday.'

I opened my mouth to argue but Evie took my phone out of my hand and changed the number of tickets from two to one. 'I'm the eldest, so no arguments.'

'Yes, boss.' My stomach swooped as it hit me just how much I wanted to find out my due date so I could start to make some plans. 'But promise me you'll text me as soon as you get there.'

She hugged me. 'Promise. And don't worry about money or where you'll live. We can sort that out over the coming months. Everything will be okay; I'm here for you from now on.'

'Thank you.' I kissed her and she stroked my hair and I felt flooded with relief that, despite the awfulness of the event that had brought her here, I had my sister back in my life and, for that at least, I had reason to be happy.

As if she was reading my mind, she pulled back and smiled. 'I was going to come and see you today, even before I had that call from Agnes.'

'Snap! I was going to come to see you.'

'When I woke up this morning I gave myself a firm talking-to. I thought about you and then I asked myself what Paddington would do.'

'And what would he do?' I grinned at her.

'The kind thing, of course.'

We both laughed at that and she got up to go home and pack. She looped her arm through mine as I walked her to her car.

'You're showing, you know,' she said, looking at my stomach. 'Can I?'

I nodded and I felt a well of love and sadness as my sister gently pressed her hand to my tummy and whispered hello to her niece or nephew.

She got in her car and wound down the window. 'It's a boy,' she declared.

'How do you know?' I looked down at my barely-there bump.

She snorted. 'Your bum's already massive. Sure sign.'

I gasped with indignation. 'I take it back; I haven't missed you at all. Now go.'

She blew me a kiss. 'I'm going. Love you.'

'Auf Wiedersehen, pet.'

'Ha.'

I watched her car disappear down the drive and ran back inside. Evie didn't want to go to Germany alone and perhaps there was a way she wouldn't have to. I scrolled through the numbers on the phone until I found the one I wanted. He answered straight away.

'Darren? Are you busy?'

'No, why?'

'Get yourself to Manchester airport; Evie needs you and you've got a plane to catch.'

'What's going on?'

I quickly brought him up to speed. Darren had always got on well with Dad and without hesitation he said there was nowhere else he'd rather be than by his wife's side.

'And it's a two-hour flight, Darren; that should be long enough for you to tell each other how you really feel.'

'Oh God. I hope she feels the same as I do. Wish me luck.'

As soon as he'd rung off, I sank down on to the sofa and let out a weary sigh of satisfaction. Just one message to send.

You'll be surprised to know I'm being sensible. If the offer still stands, will you come with me on Friday? L x

A reply pinged straight back.

Best offer I've had all day. J xxxx

Four kisses, plus the one from earlier! Today hadn't been quite so bad after all. Now all I needed was to wait for Evie to check up on Dad . . .

I was getting ready for bed later that evening when Evie called; I grabbed my phone on the first ring, eager for news.

'How is he? Have you seen him?' I demanded.

'He's conscious, I've spoken to him, he looks like he's been hit in the face with a bag of spanners, and his right arm and shoulder are strapped up and plastered but he'll live.' Her voice sounded shaky.

'Thank goodness.' I flopped on to my bed, weak with relief. 'Give him a kiss from me and send him all my love.'

'I will. He asked about you and I said you wanted to come but your passport had expired. "Classic Lottie," he said.'

'Evie!' I rolled my eyes. 'What if I wanted to go and see him next week?'

'You'll have to say you got an emergency one. Sorry, but I was doing my best not to mention the baby and I panicked. Anyway, at least it made him smile.'

'Poor old Dad.' I so wanted to be there and hug him myself. 'So what happens now?'

'No idea. Agnes has gone to find out, but I think he'll be in for a few days.'

'Do you think I'll be able to talk to him tomorrow?'

'I'll try to sort something out, even if I have to smuggle my phone on to the ward. It's very hi-tech; the hospital is like a spaceship but the doctors and nurses all speak good English. It took us a while to find him and it's half past ten here now. Agnes has offered to put us up at her house, so at least we don't have to find a hotel. Apparently his motorhome is parked there already.'

Us. In all the excitement it had slipped my mind that Darren was with her.

'What's Agnes like?' All I knew so far about her was that she was German and rode a motorbike. In my head I had a picture of a Germanic version of Joanna Lumley: long-legged and glamourous, wearing leather trousers and red lipstick.

'She's fab. She's like a twinkly-eyed little koala bear: tubby, short with wiry grey hair.' Evie giggled and lowered her voice. 'Goodness knows how she gets her leg over a motorbike.'

I heard a low male voice in the background followed by a kissing noise.

'And, er, how's the other man in your life?' I asked.

'Darren's right here,' she said, and I could tell she was smiling. 'Holding my hand and listening in.'

I let out a breath. 'So you didn't mind me interfering?'

'Somebody needed to,' I heard Darren say. 'We were making a right pig's ear of it by ourselves.'

'Thank you, sis,' said Evie. 'We've talked and talked about what we each want and where we go from here.'

'And . . . ?' I held my breath.

'The most important thing is that we still love each other more than ever. And when you've got love, everything else will work itself out.'

'I'm so pleased.' I let out a breath. 'So no divorce?'

'Absolutely not,' Darren confirmed. I heard them kiss and my heart squeezed for them.

With promises to keep in touch, we ended the call and before long I was in bed. The window was open and a faint breeze blew in, tickling my face, and with it came the strains of a barn owl hooting a mournful lullaby in the distance. I lay in the middle of my big double bed, my hand resting on my stomach, and Evie's words echoed round and round in my head.

When you've got love, everything else will work itself out.

I exhaled wistfully; I only wished that applied to me too . . .

Chapter 22

The weather turned that night; the temperature dropped a few degrees and for the next few days the hills and valleys of Derbyshire were treated to some soft summer rain. But on Friday morning the blue skies returned and from eight o'clock, as the day warmed up, there was a hazy view across the vineyard and the ground steamed gently in the sunshine. It was now ten and almost time to leave for the hospital. Jensen was on his way but heavy traffic on the motorway meant he was running late, so to keep busy, I was doing a quick inspection of the grapes with Pippa. Starsky had trotted down with us but was now dozing under the bench.

'Hopefully we've seen the back of that rain,' said Pippa.

She was wearing a long hippy-style skirt, which dragged through the long grass that had grown down the centre of two rows of Pinot Noir vines. She reminded me of a modern-day Jane Austen heroine with her wide sunhat, coppery hair and freckles.

'Hopefully,' I agreed. 'It's like a jungle along here.'

It had been too wet to get the mower up here all week and the grass was bushy and dense.

Pippa sighed wistfully. 'It would have been Ted's birthday next week and he used to say that a sunny six weeks from then until the end of September was the best birthday present he could ever get.'

'You still really miss him, don't you?'

'Terribly,' she admitted, turning away from me so I couldn't see her face. 'I was painfully shy when I was young. Still am amongst strangers, really, I suppose. I had no social confidence at all when I met Ted. All I knew was books, the only friends I had were characters from books, I worked in the library where I felt at home and my only hobby was – you've guessed it – reading. It was Ted who introduced me to a world outside of books. And now I have friends who live in the real world. I'm still shy, and always will be, but there's more to me than my encyclopaedic knowledge of the classics these days.'

'Your amazing knowledge of vines, for example.' I touched her arm reassuringly, thinking not for the first time what a legacy of good deeds Ted had left behind him. Her eyes looked as damp as the leaves on the vines but she smiled and together we bent to look at the bunches of grapes, checking for any signs of mildew.

'Talking of which, I read that too much rain can alter the complexity of the finished wine,' I said.

'Correct,' said Pippa with a bright smile, pulling herself together. 'The roots transport the water to the grapes and they swell up and become fat, bursting with juice.'

I straightened up, wincing. 'Stop talking about water, I need the loo.'

'Again?' She looked at me sharply. 'Do you think you might have a bladder infection or something?'

'No, just drunk a lot of tea this morning that's all.'

I was so preoccupied with my hospital appointment that I must have done at least ten nervous wees this morning and it was getting harder to come up with excuses for dashing inside to the bathroom. My stomach had popped out a bit more this week too and my jeans were cutting into my waist; the sooner I could tell everyone what was going on the better. Even Godfrey had remarked yesterday when we were having a tea and biscuit break from bottling the Blanc de Noir, that he liked to see a young woman with a healthy appetite, and you didn't have to be a genius to read the sub-text: step away from the bourbons, Chubby.

Pippa chewed her lip. 'I don't mean to pry, but is every-thing all right?'

'Fine, fine,' I lied. I put a hand to my neck to hide the flush. 'Did you just hear a car?'

'Er . . .'

I didn't hang around to hear her reply.

The car I'd heard was Marjorie's specially adapted car. She and Betsy had arrived shortly ahead of Jensen's super whis-pery electric one. By the time I reached the yard, Betsy was unloading shopping from the back seat and looping bags over Jensen's arms.

'I'll be two minutes,' he said, pulling a face. 'Gran appears to be catering for the five thousand. Ow!'

'Got to keep my strength up,' Betsy replied, giving him a poke in the ribs, 'or else you'll put me in a home.'

They began bickering light-heartedly about Meals on Wheels and Marjorie's arm shot out of the open car window and caught my hand. She looked like she was suffering in the heat and her short frizzy hair was damp. She was wear-ing a faded T-shirt with the words 'School's out for summer' stretched across her chest and a pair of cut-off jogging bottoms.

'How's Daddy Allbright?' she asked.

'Loads better, thank you,' I replied. 'Being fussed over by a lovely German lady who runs a dog sanctuary. He says he's been treated like one of her hopeless old mutts, but I think he loves it really.'

He'd come out of hospital on Wednesday and we'd had a long chat yesterday. Agnes, he told me, as well as running a dog sanctuary, had some rough and ready camping facilities, which was how they had met when he was looking for an overnight stop-off on his way to Austria. They'd hit it off immediately and in exchange for him cutting down an overgrown fir tree that was blocking the light from her bedroom window, she'd cooked him dinner, and by the time they'd got to dessert (the best *Apfelstrudel* he'd ever tasted), he was smitten. According to Evie she was delightful, and a tiny part of me couldn't help thinking that maybe this motorbike accident was a blessing in disguise. Once Evie and Darren were happy that he was all right, they'd booked themselves into a romantic break in a spa hotel in Heidelberg.

'Good.' Marjorie gave me a watery smile and wiped the perspiration from her forehead. 'Bloody motorbikes.'

I nodded. 'He was lucky.'

'Tell him—' She bit her lip, her voice thick. 'Tell him, if he can bear it, to get back on the bike. "Back in the saddle", as they say. I would have done if I could.' We both glanced down at her legs tucked under the wheel of the car she steered with her hands alone.

'I'll tell him,' I promised.

'Careful!' Betsy tutted from the back of the car. 'That one's got the eggs in it.'

'Yes, two dozen of them,' Jensen chuckled. 'This is a lot of food, Gran, for someone who lives alone.'

Marjorie jerked her head towards the back of the car. 'You'd better go and hurry her ladyship up. It's your big day today, isn't it?'

I nodded and my insides lurched; I was definitely going to need the loo again before we left.

'Mind you don't crush the bag of spinach in that one,' Betsy instructed. She looked as cool as a cucumber in a knee-length shift dress, a row of pearls decorating her bony décolletage and her hair swept up in its habitual clip.

'Let me guess,' Jensen said, grinning at me as I approached offering to help. 'Spinach omelette for lunch?'

'Yes, actually,' she said primly, with a well-timed look at me as I reached for the last bag. 'For the iron. Lottie, take heed. And put that bag down instantly. Jensen can manage.'

'Don't worry,' he murmured apologetically to me, his blue eyes crinkling in a smile. 'I know a quick route; we won't be late.'

'Oh heavens,' said Betsy crossly, jamming her hand on her hip, 'why didn't you remind me? It's your hospital appointment today and here I am holding you up. I wondered to what I owed the pleasure of a visit from my grandson and heir on a weekday. Of course,' she shot me a sly look, 'it's not me he's here to see, is it? It's you.'

'Actually, it's neither of you.' He grinned. 'It's Lottie's baby I can't wait to see. I've always wanted to see one of those scanning machines close up. Now please hurry up, Gran, we need to get going.'

A tiny bubble of joy burst inside me and I had to turn away.

'You'll make someone a lovely husband,' said Betsy, cupping a gnarled hand to his cheek, echoing my thoughts perfectly. I watched them, wishing I was brave enough to do the same to him. She sighed heavily. 'It must be a wonderful thing to see your own child safe and sound, breathing, moving, growing . . . There was nothing like that in my day when I had Samantha. I wish . . .' She swallowed and shook her head. 'Well, I probably couldn't see it now anyway, with my useless eyes.'

'Come with us!' I said, suddenly craving safety in numbers. 'Marjorie too. And even if you can't see the screen you might hear the heartbeat.'

'Damn it. I can't, dear girl,' Marjorie said from the front seat. She was using the car's vanity mirror to pull a hair out on her chin. 'Got an important meeting with the bank.'

'Dressed as an Alice Cooper groupie,' said Betsy tartly. '*That's* got success written all over it.'

Marjorie chuckled. 'Once a rock chick always a rock chick.'

'But I'd be honoured, Lottie, really I would.' Betsy made a sprightly leap towards me and pressed a kiss to my forehead.

Jensen looked doubtful. 'Are you sure about this?'

'Definitely,' I confirmed. 'You Butterworths are the nearest I've got to family at the moment. I'm . . .' My voice went croaky for a second and I had to clear my throat. 'I'm a bit anxious about it, to be honest.'

'That's settled then.' Betsy beamed. 'Now come along, chop, chop, child, let's get this milk in the fridge before it turns into yogurt.'

Jensen rolled his eyes and he and Betsy disappeared inside. I blew out a breath. I started towards home to collect my things when Marjorie called me back. She smoothed the skin on the back of my hand with her thumbs.

'You can do this, you know.' She eyed me wisely.

'Yeah.' I looked down at the ground. 'But it's not what I'd have planned. I know it's old-fashioned, but I thought I'd fall in love, get married and then start a family. I seem to be going about it backwards.'

'Life doesn't always pan out the way we want it to,' she said, patting my hand. 'Like when Ron decided to buy a Harley-Davidson when he turned sixty. His retirement lasted all of a few months; that didn't go quite how we'd planned either.'

'Sorry, Marjorie, here I am feeling miserable when what you went through was so much worse.'

'I'm not looking for sympathy.' She waved my apology away. 'Shall I tell you my story while you wait for the others?'

I nodded and leaned on the front wing of her car while she told me that up until Ron splashed out on a Harley a wild night out for them was strolling into Fernfield for fish and chips and a bottle of dandelion and burdock. But buying that bike and riding it home was a dream come true for him and for the next month he was on top of the world. The night they had the accident everything changed; Ron lost his life and Marjorie lost the use of her legs and was too ill even to organize her beloved's funeral. Very slowly her injuries began to heal, but she didn't see the point of trying to get better: not only was Ron gone for ever, but so too was her independence because she'd never walk unaided. Eventually, she was moved to a general ward and the lady in the bed next to her had dementia and rarely remembered who she was. One day the woman's son came to visit and Marjorie overheard her telling him that she'd once had a son but he didn't come to see her any more. The woman's son had sat there sobbing by her bed.

'And in that moment I made a discovery,' Marjorie said, her bright eyes sparkling at me. 'I was still me. I was still exactly the same person on the inside. I had two choices: I could spend the rest of my life lamenting the things I couldn't do or I could focus on the things I could do and eke as much joy out of each day as possible.'

'And you chose joy.'

'You got it.' She grinned. 'And I highly recommend it. Don't worry about the "what could have beens"; focus on the lovely things in life.'

'I'll try.'

Just then Jensen appeared brandishing bottles of water and a net bag of satsumas and shouting something about vitamin C, followed closely by Betsy tapping her way towards us with her best walking stick. For some reason she had donned a hat and looked like she was off to a wedding.

Ten minutes later, Marjorie had gone, all the doors were locked, except the winery where Clare was cleaning and labelling some bottles ready for dispatch. (The virtual sales company Jensen had recommended was already proving to be a boon and stocks of the 2015 vintage were diminishing rapidly.) I'd collected my various hospital letters and the three of us were in Jensen's car. As he started a three-point turn to head towards the drive, a little white Honda hatchback glided smoothly towards us, the driver tooting the horn.

'Jensen, wait,' I said, leaning forward from the back seat. 'That's Godfrey.'

With a glance at the time, Jensen sighed and put his brakes

on and Godfrey came to a halt in front of us. He climbed out of the car and scurried over, waving a sheet of paper excitedly.

Betsy fumbled to open her passenger window and Jensen pressed a button to do it for her.

'Morning, Godfrey; be a dear and move your car,' she ordered. 'We've got to get to the hospital.'

Godfrey was breathing heavily and his smile faltered. 'Good Lord. Not another emergency?'

'No!' I said at the same time as Jensen and Betsy both said, 'Yes!'

His shoulders drooped. 'In that case I won't keep you, it can wait.'

He looked so deflated that I took pity on him and wound my own window down too. 'Godfrey, what's the letter about?'

He mopped his head with his handkerchief. 'Not a letter; an email. I logged on this morning and there it was! I read it through twice and printed out copies for you and Betsy and then decided it couldn't wait, so here I am.'

Jensen tapped the time on his digital display. 'Thanks, Godfrey, we'll read it in the car.'

Godfrey looked agitated. 'I did want to discuss it now; it really is rather urgent.'

And we really did need to leave. 'What's the gist of it?' I asked.

'You remember Olivia Channing? From the open day?'

'English Wine bod,' Betsy cut in. 'Yes, yes, what about her?'

'She's got a slot on national radio next month to talk about English wines and wants someone from Butterworth Wines to go with her.' The old man's chest was so puffed out with pride, he looked about to pop. He lowered his voice reverentially. 'In London. What do you think about that?'

'*Next month*?' Betsy gave him a withering look. 'I think it could have blasted well waited, that's what I think.'

His chin wobbled. 'But she needs an answer today or she'll offer it to another vineyard.'

'Lottie will do it, won't you?' said Betsy blithely.

'Is that wise?' I said with a gentle laugh. 'I've only been in the wine business five minutes.'

Godfrey raised a finger timidly. 'And it needs to be a Butterworth. Or family.'

Betsy turned to look at her grandson.

'No way.' He held up a hand. 'Don't even think about it; I'm not in the wine business at all.'

'Not yet.' She batted her eyelashes at him, making him laugh.

'Betsy, why don't you do it?' I suggested. 'I'll come with you to the studio, you wouldn't have to go on your own.'

'Thank you, dear, but no.' She shuddered. 'I couldn't cope with London. I just couldn't. Sorry, Godfrey.'

I frowned, racking my brains for a solution. 'We can't let this opportunity pass us by. It's too good to miss.'

Jensen gave me a mischievous look. 'So if there was a way round it, you'd do it?'

'Yes,' I said. 'In theory but—'

'Okay, got it. Godfrey,' Jensen said firmly, 'tell Olivia that Lottie will do it and that she *is* family because she's my fiancée.'

'Er . . .' I blinked at him. 'Do I get a say?'

'Of course!' Betsy hooted with laughter and clapped her hands. 'Perfect!'

'Goodness.' Godfrey stared at all three of us, looking bewildered. 'Congratulations.'

'Not a word to anyone else,' Jensen said, fixing the dear old chap with a firm look. 'It's on a need-to-know basis only.'

Godfrey tapped the side of his nose. 'Got it. Right. Leave the details with me. Oh, this is a good day, a good day indeed. Ted would be so proud.'

Betsy's smile wavered and Jensen covered her hands with one of his.

'We're over the moon,' she said, stabbing at the buttons on the inside of the door to close her window. Jensen did it for her. 'Now step on the gas, lover-boy. Today gets better and better.'

'What did you say that for?' I said when I finally found my voice, envisaging all the awkward conversations ahead.

'You said yourself,' he grinned boyishly, 'we're as close to family as you've got right now. Why not go the whole hog?'

My heart thundered wildly for the entire journey to the hospital as Marjorie's advice bounced around my head. If I should be focusing on the lovely things in life, could one of them possibly be Jensen?

Chapter 23

'Feeling comfortable?' Dulce, the sonographer, asked as she pulled my knickers down so low at the front that Jensen squirmed beside me. I had been, I thought, mortified and wishing that I'd had the foresight to consider my bikini line. I pushed my T-shirt up myself, keeping my bra covered.

But I nodded. 'Thanks so much for letting Jensen and Betsy in with me, even though they're not family.'

Dulce smiled kindly. Her gentle voice was so soothing that if it hadn't been for Betsy's frequent exclamations, and the sensuous way Jensen's thumb stroked the back of my hand, I'd have found the whole experience very soporific.

'This is your scan; you decide who to have by your side,' she said, returning to her computer to tap something in. 'Anyway, don't they say that the best people in your life are the family you'd choose for yourself?'

'Jensen, your granddad used to say something like that,' Betsy said. 'He said family are the ones who show up when you need them most.'

'Like his volunteers at Butterworth Wines,' Jensen said.

'And you, Lottie. You showed up just when we needed you.' Betsy took a packet of mints out of her handbag and offered them round before settling back on the visitor's chair as close to the screen as she could get. 'And now we're returning the favour. Right, when does the film start?'

'Behave, Gran,' Jensen warned.

'Oh shush, this is the most fun I've had in ages.'

'Ready?' Dulce held a tube over my stomach.

I nodded and then gasped as she squirted some cold gel on to my naked stomach.

'Imagine if it's twins,' Betsy said, rustling the wrapper, blithely unaware of just how many times that particular image had visited me under the shadow of darkness.

'Imagine,' I said with a faint shudder.

I'd considered almost every eventuality from it being conceived over Christmas when Harvey and I had spent most of the holiday in bed, and therefore due any day, to triplets made during our last week together in June, to being a boy in the absolute image of its father. None of those scenarios filled me with joy.

Dulce picked up a small device connected to her computer and showed it to me. 'This is a probe. See this end? It's got a sensor on it which picks up sound waves when I press . . .' She rolled it firmly across the lower part of my stomach. 'Here.'

'Whoever decided scans should be done on a full bladder must have been a sadist,' I said, gasping.

Dulce chuckled. 'Sorry. We need the bladder full to push the uterus up to get a good view of—'

'A baby!' Jensen almost collapsed on top of me in his excitement. 'It's a baby!'

'Oh my goodness!' I exclaimed. 'So it is!'

There on the screen, unmistakably, was a baby. And as Dulce rolled the probe backwards and forwards and up and down, various parts of it came into view: a disproportionally big head, an oval-shaped body, even the faint lines of its ribs. *My* baby. I couldn't drag my eyes from the screen. It was all suddenly and overwhelmingly real.

'Can you tell if everything's okay?' I asked in a whisper, hardly daring to breathe in case the picture vanished.

'Here you are, dear.' Betsy pressed a tissue into my hand;

I hadn't even realized I was crying. She was too; even Jensen had gone a bit misty-eyed.

Dulce moved the sensor to get a good look at the baby's body. 'See the heartbeat, there? One hundred and forty-seven beats per minute.'

Jensen sucked in air and gripped my hand tighter. 'That sounds very fast to me.'

She flashed him a smile. 'It's perfectly normal. I'll take some measurements and then I can work out a due date, Lottie.'

She clicked and zoomed and muttered under her breath, Betsy did her best to work out what she was seeing and while no one was looking, Jensen pressed a kiss to my cheek.

'Thanks for letting me see this. It's so amazing. That . . .' He nodded to the screen. 'That's in you. That little boy or girl is growing inside you.'

I swallowed the ball of emotion welling up in my throat.

'Good grief,' Betsy marvelled, elbowing Dulce out of the way to get closer to the monitor as the baby bucked and kicked. 'Well, it's definitely a boy; even I can make *that* out.'

Dulce's shoulders shook as she let out a tiny giggle. 'And there's baby's leg,' she corrected gently.

'Easy mistake.' Betsy folded her arms, unfazed, and we all laughed.

Half an hour later, all the tests were complete. I'd had bloods taken, produced a urine sample (gladly) and paid for my scan photographs, one of which Betsy was still squinting over. I was fourteen weeks' pregnant; my baby was due in February and was currently the size of a lemon and it might have been psychosomatic but, by the time we reached the car, Jensen reckoned that I'd already developed a bit of a waddle.

I climbed into the back, trying out an 'oof' sound as I sat down and turned on my phone. Jensen started the engine and drove us out of the car park as a text message from Evie pinged on to my screen:

Well how did it go? When will I be an auntie? IS IT
TWINS???

Just one healthy baby. Due February 10. It was the
most incredible thing I've ever seen.

So happy for you. Did you get a pic?

I sent a shot of the scan photo to her and she replied straight
back.

Oh Lottie, so cute. I think he's waving at me. Made
me cry xxx

Me too. Even Jensen shed a tear.

Jensen and Lottie sitting in a tree . . .

Shut up

Actually Darren and I have news . . .

TELL ME

We're adopting two boys . . .

The car swerved as Jensen and Betsy both whirled round at
the sound of my gasp, which turned to a swoop of laughter
as another picture appeared on my phone from Evie: two
lovely grey and white dogs, tongues lolling and doleful
brown eyes looking straight at the camera.

Meet Roni and Skipper, two English Setters rescued
by Agnes, who'll be coming to live with me and
Darren as soon as we can possibly get them home. I
love them so much – can't wait for us to be a family!

Family, I thought; we might not get to choose them, but anyone in the Allbright family was guaranteed to be cocooned in love. I rested my hand lightly on my tummy. *And that includes you.*

Later that evening Jensen found me in the vineyard crouching down, checking up on the Chardonnay vines that Sidney had advised me on. They were looking a lot healthier already.

'Should you still be working this late in the day?'

'This isn't work,' I said hastily, brushing the dried mud from my knees and hands. 'This is an evening stroll to say goodnight to the grapes.'

He grinned. 'My granddad would have loved you.'

I glanced at my watch. 'Talking of granddads, I'll be delivering the new baby news to my dad tonight.'

'I'll walk up to your cottage with you if you like,' he said, offering a hand to pull me up. 'I'm leaving now.'

I accepted his help gratefully and took hold of his strong warm hand. He steadied me with his other hand on my elbow as I half stumbled into him.

'You're not staying the night?' I said, trying not to sound too disappointed.

'I'd love to but I've got to go home and pack.' He brushed a dried leaf from the front of my T-shirt. 'I'm flying to Cape Town on Sunday for work and I've got a report to finish tomorrow.'

'Oh, in that case I'm doubly grateful that you made the time for me today. Um . . .' I opened my mouth and closed it again.

There was a question on my mind – more than one, actually – but now that I had the perfect chance to ask it, I wasn't sure I could.

He grinned. 'What are you thinking?'

I took a deep breath, working myself up to it, and he patiently took his sunglasses out of his breast pocket and polished them on his shirt.

'Okay, I'll ask, and I want you to be honest,' I said, which was only partly true. Because if he didn't feel the same as me, I wasn't sure how I was going to cope.

'I'm nervous already.' He peered down at me from under a blond curl which had flopped over one eye. I'd thought he was gorgeous the first time I met him and now I knew him, I liked him even more. It took all of my self-control not to brush my fingers through his hair and pull his face close to mine.

'Does me being pregnant change how you feel about me? I mean me and you?' I blurted out in a rush. *Please say it doesn't.* 'If it does, I'd understand. It's just that I'd rather know the truth because you asked me to dinner three weeks ago and you haven't mentioned it since. Which is absolutely fine.'

I was gabbling so much that the expression in Jensen's dark blue eyes was morphing from amused to alarmed, but I was on a roll and I couldn't stop.

'But then last Sunday you kissed me – a really good kiss, by the way, one of the best ever,' I assured him.

His lips twitched and he looked as if he was about to speak so I jumped in again swiftly.

'And now I don't know whether it was a one-off or are we regular kissers. I mean, at the hospital you kissed my cheek, which was nice, but not quite the same. And I know I'm not a great catch or anything, particularly now I'm a *primigravida*, but I'm a bit confused and I'd like to know what you're thinking. That's all.'

'That was direct.' He blinked at me. 'And long.'

'And really embarrassing.' I fanned my face. 'God, what am I thinking? Sorry, you can leave now if you want to.' *I* wanted to leave. In fact, I wanted to plunge into the nearest bushy vine and hide.

He reached for my hand and stepped closer, bringing it to his lips. It was such a tender and gentlemanly gesture that it made me feel light-headed. I looked down through the gap between us to our feet.

'I don't want to leave yet.' His breath felt warm on the back of my hand as he spoke. 'I guess soon we won't be able to do this.'

Which told me all I needed to know.

'No,' I blinked at him despondently.

'Because the baby will get in the way.'

'I know.'

His gaze was steady and my hand felt at home in his, but I couldn't tell what he was thinking. I knew he was making a joke about the size of my bump but was this also his way of telling me that my pregnancy was going to be an emotional barrier to any future relationship?

'Is that your answer to my question?'

'No, Lottie, it isn't.' He exhaled. 'I'm just not very good at this. Can we go inside?'

I let us in to my cottage, propped the door open to let in the evening air and poured us both a glass of fizzy water. Jensen leaned against the kitchen worktop and flicked through the notes I'd been making about the change in temperature and the recent rainfall – I was taking a leaf out of Ted's notebooks, so to speak.

'I'd offer you a glass of the new Blanc de Noir I've been tasting,' I said, handing him his drink, 'but you're driving and I'm trying to cut back.'

He shot me a worried look. 'Should you be drinking at all?'

'I'm joking,' I laughed. 'I've become an excellent spitter; I haven't swallowed for ages.'

He chewed his lip trying not to laugh. 'Good to know.'

'I'm ignoring that comment.' I reached into the fridge and pulled out a bottle of sparkling wine. 'But I would like you to take this home with you to try. It's the 2016 Classic Cuvée that Sidney worked on with Clare and Matt; it's the nicest fizz I've ever tasted.'

Jensen grinned. 'And to think you used to say you knew nothing about wine.'

'A lot has changed since then. If you'd have told me how

protective I'd become of this vineyard and the grapes and all the people here, well, I wouldn't have believed you. But now I'm a complete convert; I want to tell the world how fantastic Butterworth Wines are.'

He laughed softly and looked down at his feet. 'You don't make things easy for me, do you?'

My pulse raced. 'What do you mean?'

I stood beside him, leaning against the fridge, close enough to feel the heat from his skin.

'Outside you asked me a question. The truth is . . .' He sipped his water and set his glass down. 'If I could stay longer this evening I would; I'd really like to whisk you off somewhere for dinner and get to know you a bit better.'

I glanced down at my tummy. 'You've seen bits of me that have never been seen before.'

His gaze softened. 'That was amazing. I thought it would look like a little blob, but it was all there. A proper little person.'

My stomach swooped as I remembered my baby bouncing about looking like it was having a lovely time. 'It is.'

He turned to face me. 'Lottie, you being pregnant did throw me for two reasons. Firstly, because I'm worried enough about Gran here on her own and what might happen if I'm not around, but now I've got two of you to worry about.'

'Betsy and I are fine. We hardly ever climb trees or practise our knife-throwing these days,' I said, unable to resist teasing him, but secretly flattered that he cared.

'Don't joke, I'm serious.' He had a crease between his eyebrows that appeared when he was worried; it was there now.

'Sorry,' I said, meaning it. 'But I promise you we won't do anything stupid.'

His eyes held mine for a moment before he glanced away uneasily. 'There's an opening coming up at work; it would be a big step up for me and if I get it, I'll be travelling more, *a lot* more, so I need to know you're safe. Both of you.'

'Is that why you're going to Cape Town?'

He nodded. 'We're finalizing the costings for a global project. If I impress the directors, there could be another promotion in it for me.'

'Of course you'll impress them.' I nudged him playfully, even though the thought of seeing him even less than I did now was frankly depressing. 'And I'll be here, acting sensibly for as long as Betsy will have me. What's the second reason?'

He glanced at me briefly then rubbed a hand through his hair.

'Look, from what you've said, you had a great childhood, stable and loving, two parents who doted on you. I had love but no stability and I believe every child deserves both. I guess—' He faltered, as if struggling to find the right words, and gulped at his water.

My heart sank; so that was the end of that. It was obvious he didn't want things to go any further between us. He'd seen the baby as a real tangible being on the screen today and it must have made him realize just what he'd be getting himself into.

'It's okay,' I said, plastering on a smile. 'I understand. Let's say no more about it. Perhaps you should be going.'

He spluttered on his water. 'No, no, that's not what I mean!'

I frowned. 'Then I'm confused.'

'Sorry,' he smiled contritely. 'Told you I was rubbish at this sort of thing. What I mean is that I feel like I should step back and put my own feelings to one side, give you time to patch things up with your ex. Because if there was any chance you could work things out with him and be parents together, a family, I don't want to get in the way of that.'

'Are you sure you're not stepping back because I'm carrying another man's baby?' I asked quietly. 'Because no one would blame you if you were; it's a big ask. Think of all the comments we'd get in public when I get bigger; people will assume it's yours.'

'Only people who don't know us, and who cares what

they think?' His gaze softened and the look in his eyes melted my heart. 'None of that bothers me at all.'

'You are kind, Mr Butterworth.' I leaned my head against his shoulder. 'In a perfect world, I'd like to be doing this with the baby's father. But it's not going to happen.'

One corner of his mouth lifted. 'Is it really bad of me that I'm quite pleased?'

'Very bad,' I teased. 'Anyway, you kissed me last Sunday, that wasn't stepping back.'

'I'm only human.' He turned to face me, and took the glass out of my hand. 'And you are adorable.'

To my total horror I replied by burping in his face. 'I am so sorry. I'm very gassy these days.'

'Spitting and belching,' he said, laughing. 'Remind me again why you're still single?'

I shrugged playfully. 'It's a mystery.'

'To me too,' he said softly.

I held his gaze and felt my heart thump against my ribs. My feelings for this lovely man were getting harder to hide and suddenly I wanted him to know everything, to put his mind at rest about Harvey and to know with absolute certainty that he was no longer part of my life.

'Then I'll tell you: I'm single because Harvey was controlling and erratic and I was scared of him. So I left him. I don't want him to be part of my life, or the baby's. We could never be parents together.' I blew out a breath. 'So now you know.'

Jensen looked stricken and stared for a second.

'Oh my God, I had no idea. Come here.'

Then he pulled me towards him and held me tight, and I buried my head in his neck while he pressed kisses to my hair and I dared to think that maybe if he cared for me like I was beginning to care for him, then one day home for him would mean coming home to me. We stayed like that, holding each other, until the sun slipped from the sky and the owl started to hoot and he regretfully peeled himself away, made me vow to look after myself and promised to meet me before my radio interview in London and take me for lunch.

All of which was heavenly but made me very late getting round to ringing my dad.

Conscious of the time difference between England and Germany, as soon as Jensen had gone, I got comfortable on the sofa and dialled my dad's mobile number. He must have been waiting for my call because he answered on the first ring.

'Hello, Dad!'

'Hello, love. I was beginning to think you'd forgotten your old man.'

'Sorry I'm late. I've had a visitor and he's only just left.'

'A gentleman caller, eh?' Dad probed.

'Not like that,' I said vaguely, not wanting to go into details. I knew what Dad was like: he'd be wanting chapter and verse if I didn't nip it in the bud. Besides, I really wanted to tell him about the baby. 'It was my boss Betsy's grandson, Jensen. But enough about him, how are you?'

'Good, I think. At least, Agnes says I've got roses back in my cheeks.'

'She speaks good English, then?'

'She speaks four languages. She claims to be a little rusty at English, but I think she's amazing,' he said proudly. 'She used to be a translator but she's retired now. Well, I say "retired", she runs a dog rescue centre and has a field she rents out to campers.'

'She sounds lovely, not to mention very enterprising' I smiled; it was so good to hear the enthusiasm in his voice. It seemed he had found a foxy frau after all.

'I think she's marvellous, and she's great company; if I'd known how much fun you could have being retired, I'd have done it years ago. Up until my accident she was acting as my tour guide. I've been to places that tourists would never normally go to.'

Such as the inside of an operating theatre, I mused. 'And how are all your broken bits?'

'Recovering nicely,' he said briskly. 'Nothing to worry about.'

'No more motorbiking, okay?'

'Don't worry; I'll stick to Agnes's sidecar from now on.'

'You'll do no such thing!'

'I'm teasing,' he said with a chuckle.

'You do sound happy.'

'I am,' he said brightly. 'I've missed having someone who cares about me.'

'Oh Dad,' I said quietly. I cared about him and so did Evie, but I knew what he meant. He missed having someone to share life's ups and downs with, or simply someone to mull over the minutiae of the everyday. Even though I was rarely on my own for long, I missed that too and I'd only been single for a matter of weeks; Dad had been on his own for over a decade.

'And I've missed someone to fuss over in return. Not that I can do much at the moment; I'm a liability. But she calls me "Schatz" – I wasn't sure about that at first, it sounded a bit rude, but it means treasure. It's a long time since I've been anyone's treasure.'

'Evie and Darren said she's very nice.'

'She is. She's made the last couple of weeks very enjoyable.'

My heart squeezed for him and in that moment I don't think I'd ever missed Mum more. But it was good that he was moving on. He deserved happiness.

'So,' I said, remembering why I was phoning him, 'when do you think you'll be home?'

'Can't drive for another few weeks, so Agnes is stuck with me. But she's got a few jobs lined up for me; I doubt I'll have time to get bored. And,' he paused to clear his throat, 'I've heard that Munich at Christmas is lovely so I'll probably stay until at least then.'

My eyes nearly popped out on stalks; Christmas was four months away. 'Gosh, you really do like her, don't you?'

'Early days, but, yes I do.' He sounded so worried I could have hugged him. 'Do you mind?'

'Not at all; I'm thrilled . . . but, Dad . . .' I bit my lip. 'Please can you be home by February, because I'd like you to meet someone.'

'But not until February? That's very precise. You're not getting married, are you?' He chuckled. 'Is it that boy – what was his name? – Jensen?'

'It might be a boy.' I swallowed. 'Or it might be a girl. I'm having a baby, Dad.'

There was a silence down the other end of the phone. I held my breath and eventually heard him blow his nose.

'Dad, are you there?'

'Stone the crows, I'm going to be a granddad,' he cried with a watery laugh. 'Congratulations, love! I'll definitely be back for February; try keeping me away. And tell me how you are; is everything okay? Have you been poorly?'

Relieved, I told him how far along I was and that I had a tiny bump already. And that I hadn't really lost my passport, but that I'd had to go for my scan. I described how the baby had kicked and waved its arm. Then he shared the news with Agnes who came on the phone and wished me well. I heard her kiss his cheek and I shed a tear at the enormity of everything.

'And what does Harvey have to say about it?' Dad asked when things had calmed down a bit.

'He doesn't know yet.' I sighed. I would have to tell him, I knew that; but how? I didn't want to see him face to face and I couldn't imagine delivering this sort of news in a letter. 'I'm dreading him finding out; I don't want him to have anything to do with it.'

'Neither do I,' Dad growled. 'Maybe you could do nothing for now, wait until the baby's born and if you decide you want him to know then I'll go and visit him first.'

I blew out a long breath. 'Would you? I'd like that; thanks, Dad.'

'Don't mention it; you're still my little girl, you know.'

We fell silent for a few seconds and then I asked him something that had been bothering me.

'Dad, do you think Mum would have been disappointed in me, because I'm unmarried and bringing a baby into the world as a single mum?'

'Don't be soft,' he chuckled. 'She'd have your scan photo enlarged and mounted above the mantelpiece and she'd be knitting bonnets for England. She'd be as proud as Punch.'

I let out a trembly breath. 'Thank you.'

'You'd better go,' he said, and I could hear him shuffling in his chair ready to sign off. 'Goodness knows how much this call is costing you.'

'You're worth it,' I said, laughing. 'Look after yourself, *Granddad*.'

Chapter 24

'Don't throw that away,' said Marjorie indignantly as Betsy consigned another of Ted's T-shirts to the bin bag I was holding open for her. 'There's plenty of wear left in it and it might fit me.'

Betsy retrieved it and sighed dramatically. 'Here you are, Cinders, you shall go to the ball.' She tossed the faded T-shirt to her sister-in-law. 'But I will point out that I bought that on a trip to Valencia and I paid for it in Spanish pesetas. So it's at least twenty years old, and quite probably older.'

'Even better,' said Marjorie, stretching it across her bosom and twinkling her eyes at me. 'That means it's vintage. It's what all the cool kids are wearing this summer.'

Betsy tutted her disapproval and shoved a handful of men's pyjamas into the bag before Marjorie purloined those as well. Starsky had made a nest for himself in one of Ted's old jumpers and had fallen asleep on his back, paws in the air, with the most adorable doggy smile on his face. He was probably dreaming of happy days spent with his master. The thought made my eyes sting and I laughed to myself. My brain had turned to mush recently; I never used to be this soppy. I gave myself a shake and pulled a pretty white broderie anglaise dress from the pile. It had soft gathers under the bust line and three pearly buttons down the front. 'This can't be Ted's!'

Betsy looked up and tried to focus on what I'd found.

'I've thrown some of my things away too. It's a nightdress, but it was always too short to be decent on me. Might suit you, though.'

I agreed, thinking it would be perfect in the months to come.

Marjorie harrumphed. 'So Lottie gets *your* lovely cast-offs and I have to beg for Ted's old T-shirts.'

'She is going to need some bigger clothes soon,' Betsy said reprovingly, 'whereas you take great delight in dressing like a bag lady.'

Marjorie hooted with glee. 'True on both counts.'

'I need bigger clothes *now*,' I said, tugging at my T-shirt. 'For something the size of an onion, this baby certainly seems to be making its presence felt.'

'Wait until you get heartburn,' said Betsy. 'And swollen ankles.'

'You look radiant, Lottie,' Marjorie cut in. 'Don't listen to the prophet of doom over there.'

I shook my head fondly, left them bickering and went into the kitchen to make us all a drink.

It was the second week in September and four weeks since my scan; I was eighteen weeks' pregnant and according to the baby website I was addicted to, the baby only weighed 190 grams. I, on the other hand, had put on considerably more and I wouldn't have been able to hide my pregnancy even if I'd wanted to. We'd had a team meeting a couple of weeks ago and I'd told everyone my news and handed round the scan photo. I'd become almost tearful at their display of kindness and excitement, feeling much loved, and to everyone's surprise, Roger had welled up too and promptly offered his babysitting services when the time came. Matt had popped the cork on a bottle of 2015 Blanc de Noir and topped one up with a splash of orange juice for me and they'd all drunk to my health. Since then, they'd treated me with kid gloves, making sure I didn't lift anything too heavy and spying on me to check I was taking a lunch break and eating properly. It was like having a flock of aunts and uncles tucking me under their wings and I considered myself very fortunate.

My so-called housekeeping duties had never really materialized and had dried up altogether once Betsy found out I was pregnant. Things had eased on the cash flow front, she assured me. A cleaning firm with a military-style attention to detail now came in once a week to 'do' for her. At the moment I was still enjoying being in charge of the cottage garden and veg patch, although Betsy had warned me that as soon as I struggled to bend down to pick the lettuce, she was getting a gardener in. However, Marjorie had phoned yesterday to tell me that she and Betsy were planning on tackling some of the wardrobes this morning and had asked if I'd be able to carry things downstairs to make it easier for them both to manage.

I took a tray of tea back into the living room and found both ladies fanning their faces with table mats.

'Have you finished?' I said, handing Marjorie a cup.

'For now,' said Betsy, adding a drop of milk to hers. 'The wardrobe in the spare room is completely empty.'

'Three bags full for charity, two for the bin and four new T-shirts for me,' said Marjorie happily.

'Hmm,' Betsy sniffed. 'We're supposed to be sweeping away the old to make room for the new, remember?'

'They *are* new to me,' said Marjorie, crunching on a custard cream.

'Making room?' I asked. 'Are you both planning a shopping trip?'

The two old ladies looked at each other shiftily.

'Sort of,' said Betsy, twisting her wedding ring round, not meeting my eye. 'Have you heard from Jensen?'

If she was trying to distract me, it worked; my heart was pierced with a tiny dart of joy at the mention of his name. Only two weeks until I was due in London for the radio interview and, more importantly, a lunch date with Jensen.

I nodded. 'He Skyped me last night; he's there for another three days and loving every minute. Apparently Cape Town is amazing and the project is going well.'

'Drat,' said Marjorie, furrowing her brow like a cartoon baddie. 'Looks like your dastardly plan might fail, Betsy.'

Betsy sighed. 'Yes, how tedious. We really need him to hate it there.'

I smiled at their comical plotting. 'Why?'

'His boss has hinted that if he does well with this project it could lead to a promotion to head up the Cape Town office.' Betsy folded her arms crossly. 'And that would mean a permanent move to South Africa.'

'A permanent move!' I gasped, completely unable to mask my dismay.

This must have been what he'd been referring to when he'd said he might be away more in the future. I hadn't realized that he'd be away *all* the time. No wonder he hadn't repeated his offer to take me to dinner. He'd probably only invited me to lunch because I'd forced him into a corner. How embarrassing. Was it really bad of me to hope that he didn't do well with the project . . . ?

'And of course he'll do brilliantly,' said Marjorie, regarding my expression shrewdly. 'So our only hope is that he'll decide he doesn't want the job even if he's offered it.'

'Indeed,' said Betsy. 'Ted had so wanted Butterworth Wines to stay in the family but we're running out of time. If we can't persuade Jensen to come back to manage it, then . . .' Her voice petered out and her shoulders sagged.

Marjorie reached across and patted her arm. 'Chin up, old thing, it ain't over until the fat lady sings.'

'Less of the old,' grumbled Betsy.

'What about your daughter?' I said. 'Couldn't you speak to her?'

Betsy's cup rattled in the saucer as she set it down on the coffee table.

'I have spoken to Samantha about it, but she and Victor

are living a life of luxury in Shanghai. She doesn't see them returning to the UK for the foreseeable future, if at all. She did, however, order six cases of Classic Cuvée to be shipped over for a golf club gala dinner Victor is hosting, so it wasn't all bad news.' She managed a wan smile. 'Apparently the Chinese love English sparkling wine.'

'Do they?' I made a mental note to include that in my 'interesting facts about English wine' section of the presentation Godfrey and I were doing at Pippa's library next week.

'Brit Fizz they're calling it.' Betsy shuddered. 'And so do the Americans. Ted would turn in his grave; although he'd be thrilled to know his wine was being drunk on the other side of the world. So swings and roundabouts.'

'Exports are one of the areas I've been looking into,' I said thoughtfully. 'I'm hoping to pick Olivia Channing's brains about it while I'm in London.' Perhaps I should invite her along to lunch with Jensen and me, I thought; at least that would keep things on a professional level and stop me making an idiot of myself.

'Oh?' Betsy raised a hopeful eyebrow. 'What other areas?' I felt the weight of both of their stares.

'Well, I'm only here for six months, but if I had time I was thinking we could convert one of Ted's sheds into a little shop, so customers can drop in and buy direct from us.'

'I like that idea.' Marjorie's eyes glittered thoughtfully. 'A year-round income, cutting out the middle man. Very good.'

I continued, encouraged. 'And I thought about putting a wine holiday package together: accommodation nearby, a wine tour and tasting and, for those who wanted hands-on experience, a few days volunteering in the vineyard and winery. It was Olivia who gave me the idea.'

'You think people would *pay* to come and work for us?' Betsy eyed me sceptically.

'I do.' In fact, I was sure of it. Wine tourism was well established in other parts of Europe but still new in

England and owning your own vineyard was the new 'escape to the country' dream for people looking for a change of pace. The risk-free option was to try before you buy, and where better than an established vineyard where would-be winemakers could get real hands-on experience and learn from the experts. Well, expert-ish.

Marjorie slurped the last of her tea. 'Told you, Bets.'

'Told her what?' I asked.

'That you might not be a Butterworth but this place has got under your skin,' she said smugly.

'It definitely has.' I laughed. 'It's the best job I've ever had.'

'Good grief,' said Betsy drily. 'I don't know whether to feel flattered or sorry for you.'

I laughed. 'Be happy for me. Until now, I've simply drifted career-wise. And now I know that the wine business is my future. Whatever happens next, that's my goal and I've got Butterworth Wines to thank for that.'

Betsy and Marjorie exchanged excited looks.

'That's the best news I've heard since you told us you were expecting,' said Betsy, reaching for my hand to pat it.

'If I could afford to buy the business from you, I'd do it in a heartbeat,' I said. 'Although I'm not family, of course.'

'Tell Jensen your ideas when you see him in London,' said Marjorie, pursing her lips. 'He knows a profitable scheme when he sees one, he might take the bait.'

'Yes!' Betsy clapped her hands. 'If anyone can convince him to come back to Fernfield, it's you, my dear.'

My heart squeezed at the hopeful looks on their faces.

'I'll do my best,' I promised. And I meant it; after all, I realized, I wanted Jensen to come back just as much as they did.

'The grapes will be pressed on the day we pick them,' I said, smiling at my audience, 'which is usually mid-October, and the juice pumped into tanks where it will stay until February—'

'Sorry for interrupting, Lottie, the sugar levels are very high for September,' Godfrey put in, pulling his notebook from his pocket and flicking through it. 'Ah, here we are. I took readings from the Pinot Meunier this morning and the refractometer was giving me sixty-four in places. So I don't think it'll be mid-October this year.'

'I agree,' said Pippa, raising a hand. 'We've had a lot of sun this season and apart from the rain in August, we've had very few setbacks.'

'Gosh.' I pulled a face. The number was an indicator of sweetness. According to Ted's notes, we hadn't reached a reading of above sixty until the end of September last year. 'So harvest really could be very early?'

It was later that same afternoon and I'd gathered the team on the terrace under the shade of the parasol. Betsy had gone for a snooze and Marjorie had gone home and I was running through my presentation for the library wine-tasting event next week. At least, I was trying to. My audience consisted of Matt, Clare, Godfrey and Roger, most of whom couldn't resist adding in their own two penn'orth at every opportunity. Pippa was there too, acting as my assistant. She was in charge of pouring the wine samples and handing round the sheets of detailed tasting notes that Roger had prepared.

'This dry weather is certainly bringing the grapes on well,' she said now, grimacing as she eased the cork out of sparkling elderflower juice which we were using instead of the real McCoy for our practice. 'It's more like the Dordogne than Derbyshire, particularly through the Chardonnay vines: the paths are dusty and dry and the leaves are beginning to turn brown at the edges.'

'The Pinot Noir is looking good too,' said Clare, looking up from her crocheting. Apparently, she was still being harangued by the blanket committee. 'I sent Sidney some photos of the crop the other day and he reckoned they were as ripe as his.'

'Phew.' Matt pretended to wipe his brow. 'Looks like we emptied out the tanks just in time, then, Lottie.'

He and I had spent most of last Sunday evening finishing off *tirage* for the 2017 Blanc de Noir. Which meant all last year's vintage had been blended, bottled and was now on its second fermentation and could be left alone until next spring. The big stainless-steel tanks had been scrubbed and cleaned, ready to use again. I'd smelled like a barmaid's apron by the end of the night and Issy the midwife had sniffed me suspiciously when I'd gone for my check-up the following day.

'Order!' Roger banged the table with a teaspoon. 'Lottie will never get to the end of this if she keeps getting interrupted. Will you all please concentrate?'

'Thank you, Roger,' I said, soothing our resident grump. 'But everyone's points are valid and we do need to make plans for harvesting.'

'Planning will have to wait until after the radio interview in two weeks,' Godfrey said nervously. 'This is the biggest opportunity Butterworth Wines has ever had: taking part in a live panel with a chef from a Michelin-starred restaurant and the spokesperson for English Wines. This is our moment to shine!'

My stomach churned at the thought. 'Thanks for that, Godfrey.' I pressed a hand to my stomach. 'Now where was I?'

I looked to Pippa for help. She poured an inch of sparkling elderflower into a plastic cup for me.

'You said the juice will stay in the tanks until February,' she whispered discreetly.

'Oh yes.' I took a sip of my drink. It fizzed on my tongue and the next thing I knew I was thinking about how amazing bubbles were and all other thoughts had evaporated from my head. 'And by then, the, er . . .' I faltered. The only thing I could remember about February was that as of the tenth, one would become two and the thought terrified me. 'Sorry, everyone, I can't concentrate this afternoon.'

'By February, the first fermentation will have finished,'

Pippa filled in for me. 'And don't apologize, I'm in awe of you for offering to do this library event. I could never stand in front of a group of people and talk. It took me a year to speak up in front of this lot.'

'You could do it standing on your head blindfolded,' I retorted. 'You've got all the facts at your fingertips; all I've got is a head of cotton wool.'

'Baby brain. It won't last for ever,' said Clare with a chuckle, peeling the paper wrapper off a new ball of wool. 'Like baby weight. Although I'm still waiting to shift mine and Ben is twenty-five.'

'Have you thought about names yet?' said Matt, rocking back on his chair, which Betsy always told him off for. 'Matthew is good for a boy, just saying.'

'Clare means "bright and clear",' said Clare proudly. 'Beat that.'

'Apparently, Roger means "famous warrior",' said Roger with a smirk, looking up from his phone. 'So I think that trumps Clare.'

'Have you been researching the meaning of your own name, Roger?' Godfrey folded his arms smugly. 'I thought we were supposed to be concentrating.'

'Not exactly, I . . .' He went bright red and his mouth flapped open and closed like a marooned goldfish. 'Well, all right, I did.'

We all laughed but the effect of Godfrey's admonishment was diminished somewhat by his own mobile pinging with an incoming email. His eyes lit up when he saw who the sender was.

'Ah. Email from the lovely Olivia; shall I read it out?'

We agreed that he should and I took a seat, halting my presentation for the time being. Godfrey skimmed quickly through the first half of the email. Olivia thanked us again for agreeing to take part, confirmed the name of the other participants, Thomas Devine – a chef who was semi-famous, very pompous and liked the sound of his own voice – and the TV and radio presenter Fiona Love, a bubbly lady in her fifties whom everybody in the country adored.

'Phwoar. Can you get me Thomas's autograph?' said Clare, pretending to fan her face. 'He's got that sexy bad boy thing going on. Gorgeous.'

'Fiona's not bad either,' said Matt with a wolfish grin. 'She's got that sexy cougar thing going on.'

'Ahem,' Roger put in. 'Concentrate please, the pair of you.'

They giggled like teenagers and Godfrey cleared his throat.

'Olivia goes on as follows: the only fly in the ointment,' he read aloud, 'is that Thomas Devine can't make the original date and so we've had to bring our interview forward to *next Friday*. I hope this doesn't cause you too much inconvenience, but I've already accepted the alteration on your behalf.' He looked up. 'That'll be all right, won't it?'

My first thought was that it would give me an excuse to see Jensen earlier than planned; thank goodness he'd be back from his travels by then. My second was that now I had even less time to swot up.

'One week from today?' Pippa squeaked. 'Oh no!'

My mouth had gone dry and I knocked back the sparkling elderflower. 'I'll never be ready! It's a tall enough order as it is, sending me – the newbie – into a live radio interview.'

Matt topped up my glass. 'Don't be daft, Lottie, you're a natural. And don't forget what Sidney said: that he'd found a new apprentice. You'll smash it.'

'Hear, hear,' said Roger, 'as long as you do your homework, you'll be fine.'

'And Olivia will be at your side,' Godfrey added. It was fair to say that he had a colossal crush on her. 'And she is extremely knowledgeable about wine.'

Clare swatted at the men. 'Stop bullying the poor girl. If she doesn't want to do it, she doesn't have to.'

They mumbled their apologies and stared at me, waiting for me to respond.

'Thank you.' I smiled weakly and took a deep breath but before I had a chance to reply Pippa grabbed my arm.

'Are you all forgetting something? The event for the library is next Friday!' Her eyes were as big as tennis balls. 'Lottie is supposed to be the host. We can't let them down; it's a sell-out.'

'Oh, bloody hell!' Clare clamped a hand over her mouth.

'Of course we won't let them down,' said Roger calmly. 'We can just use Lottie's notes. There are enough of us to manage it between us. Not me, though, unfortunately; I'm taking the Year Sevens on a school trip for three days next week.'

'And I'm dyslexic,' said Matt, holding his hands up. 'I can't make head nor tail of the tasting notes even though I helped make the wine; I'd get all those statistics wrapped round my neck.'

'I'm not around either,' said Clare, doing a little shimmy. 'Ben's flying home for R&R on Thursday and Ian and I are picking him up from the base. I can't wait.'

'That's great news,' said Godfrey and I together.

'No. It. Is. Not!' said Pippa querulously, her pale face going pink. 'It is *not* great at all. I've never organized an event before, I've put in a lot of effort, everyone's looking forward to it and now it's doomed to fail.'

We all stared at her. I'd never heard her raise her voice before and neither had the others judging by their shocked expressions.

Godfrey raised a hand timidly. 'I'll be here to help, although I'd rather stick to pouring the wine and handling sales than doing any talking.'

'Great,' Pippa muttered ungraciously. She took a deep breath and pressed her hands to her face. 'Sorry I lost my temper. It's just that everyone at the library knows how much the vineyard means to me; I want them to see it in the best possible light.'

'You could do the presentation yourself, you know,' I said softly. 'No one knows this place better than you.'

'It's true, honey,' said Clare, fiddling with her armful of bangles. 'I bet if we took you into the middle of the vineyard blindfolded, you'd know exactly where you were.'

Pippa folded her arms and frowned. 'Well, I probably would, but speaking about it is a completely different ball game.'

'You know the wines pretty well and I can coach you on the new ones,' Matt offered. 'I was going to have a final run-through with Lottie before the radio interview; we can bring it forward a week and you can join us.'

Pippa looked out across the vines and nibbled on her lip, her chest rising and falling with nerves. We all waited with bated breath, hoping she'd push herself out of her comfort zone.

Finally, she sat up tall. 'Okay, I'll do it. I'll make a total hash of it, but I can't see that we've any choice.'

'Hooray!' I said, giving her a hug. 'I'm so proud of you. And I'm sure Ted would be too.'

'And you, Lottie,' said Roger gruffly. 'Ted always shied away from the spotlight, it wasn't his way to blow his own trumpet, but he'd be very impressed with your gumption, not to mention the amount of knowledge you've acquired in such a short time.'

A well of emotion rushed up inside me; that was the nicest thing he'd ever said to me – that and the offer of babysitting. He wasn't such an old grump after all.

'I've had some very good teachers,' I said, beaming at my colleagues. They had already become such good friends. 'I couldn't have done it without you.'

'This deserves a proper drink,' said Matt, throwing the rest of his elderflower into the rose bush.

I gathered up my notes and left them giving tips to Pippa

on how to overcome her nerves and celebrating her new-found bravery with a bottle of Blanc de Blanc that had been opened this morning for a wine blogger. As I wandered back to The Stables, it dawned on me that the change of date meant that this time next week I'd be on national radio, extolling the virtues of Butterworth Wines and that every-one seemed to have complete faith that it was me, the newbie, giving the interview and representing the company.

That was fine, I decided, aware of the bounce in my step. Before I left Harvey all those weeks ago, I'd been looking for the bright and bubbly Lottie Allbright that I'd once been, and now, I thought with a fizz of anticipation, she was back, stronger and bolder than ever.

Chapter 25

The following day, Clare and I were in the winery together. I was at the desk, transferring Ted's handwritten notes on the vineyard and the crop development into a spreadsheet and Clare was having a break after packing and dispatching the day's orders, including the consignment of sparkling wine for Betsy's daughter to China.

'I've never got to grips with spreadsheets,' said Clare, peering over my shoulder and shaking her head at the rows of numbers.

'It's a monotonous job,' I replied. 'But once the data is in, it means anyone can look up the details of any wine we've ever produced.'

I saved the document I was working on. I was up to Ted's last journal now. He had been a meticulous note taker; I'd learned so much from reading his detailed weather reports, his methods for dealing with mildew, pests and wildlife and the copious readings he'd taken with a refractometer (the device to test sugar content) from every single row of vines. It would make it so much easier to make decisions for whoever took over the vineyard once Betsy had moved on. I didn't want to think about that now, it was too depressing. I couldn't bear the idea of seeing a name on the bottle label other than Butterworth. I loved the fact that Marjorie and Betsy were plotting to persuade Jensen to leave his globe-trotting job and settle here, but much as I'd like it to happen,

I couldn't see it. He seemed to thrive on the cut and thrust of international business and global projects. A provincial vineyard where the biggest decisions were where to store all the new bottles bought in ready for the next harvest and whether we should strip more foliage off the lowest parcel of vines to get extra light to the fruit . . . Well, sadly, I didn't think Butterworth Wines had enough to interest him.

'If you say so,' said Clare, jolting me back to the present. She took the lid off a plastic tub of date and apricot flapjacks. 'Tuck in, these will do the trick to sort out that little problem you mentioned. I've added extra linseed and bran too.'

'Thank you, that's very kind.' I smiled weakly and took the smallest brown square, setting it next to the laptop. That'll teach me to mention my constipation in public. 'Actually, I think Godfrey's syrup of figs, Roger's half-tube of haemorrhoid cream and the long ramble along the river which Pippa insisted on taking me for have already produced several tricks. You've all been very kind.'

'TMI.' She snorted and took a small piece for herself. 'Just indulge me, Lottie. I never got the chance to fuss around my daughter Frankie when she was pregnant, with her living in Australia.'

I took a sip of water in readiness for a fibre hit and picked up my flapjack.

'My mum would have thrown herself into full-on nurturing mode too. I'm sure she'd approve of these; they look very healthy. Evie's fantastic, but it's not the same as having your mum around.'

Clare pulled a sad face. 'Of course it isn't. But anything you need, any advice or someone to come and hold your hand at any time, you just ask.'

Everyone knew about my family situation and had sent good wishes to my dad in Germany. Betsy had told me to invite Evie over so she could meet her properly, having only seen her and Darren arguing in the Italian restaurant on the night I moved in. Evie was coming today, in fact. She and

Darren had been back for a while but they'd been so busy re-establishing their marital home that I'd barely seen them.

'I might ask you to bake for me again,' I said through a mouthful of flapjack. 'This is really good.'

'No need to sound surprised! I was on the school PTA cake sale committee for years. My Viennese whirls are second to none. Now, tell me to keep my snout out,' Clare brushed the crumbs from her cleavage and took her ever-present crocheting from her bag, 'but you're smart, lovely and, unless you're very good at hiding things, you've got no obvious off-putting personal habits. And I can't help wondering about you being single?'

'You mean who's the baby's father and why am I not with him?'

'Well, yeah.' She looked sheepish. 'Sorry, I'm a nosy moo, but in my defence I know first-hand how tricky first babies can be.'

My face must have fallen because Clare reached across and rubbed my arm, smiling sympathetically.

'Put it this way: it's not what I'd have planned,' I admitted, smoothing my T-shirt dress down over my bump. 'But better on my own and happy than with someone who was making me miserable.'

'Abso-bloody-lutely.' Clare gave a nod of approval. 'Although to play devil's advocate, some men come into their own when they reach fatherhood and they finally grow up.'

I shuddered. 'Harvey would have to do a lot more than grow up for me to want him back in my life. I haven't seen or spoken to him since before I started here. And I don't want to either.'

I posted the last mouthful of flapjack in and chewed resolutely.

Clare frowned. 'Knowing how easy-going you are, he must have really done a number on you.' I nodded and she rolled her eyes. 'Listen to me, I'm doing it again, poking my nose in.'

'It's okay,' I said, laughing softly. 'I don't mind talking

about him. We met online and I fell for him completely; I really thought Harvey was the one and we moved down to London to start a new life together. We were ecstatically happy for a while and then gradually he started to change; bit by bit he became very controlling and jealous. By the time I realized I ought to leave him, he'd even begun to get aggressive. I don't know how I got him so wrong.'

'I hope you're not blaming yourself,' she said indignantly, offering me another flapjack. I shook my head. 'And you're right, being on your own is far better than being unhappy.'

'I must be a bad judge of character.' I sighed, wondering how I'd let Harvey manipulate me for so long.

'Oh, they're not all the same; you can't tar them all with the same brush.'

'I suppose not,' I said wistfully.

I thought about how decent Jensen had been to me, how supportive. He'd taken me to hospital twice already and I'd only known him for three months. Still there was no use getting my hopes up there, not if he was planning a move to Cape Town. Unless, of course, he asked me to go with him. They had loads of vineyards there, didn't they? Maybe I could get a job and carry on learning about viticulture. Except, I snapped myself out of my daydream, I'd have a baby in a few months. I kept forgetting that. I'd be busy getting it weighed and going to baby percussion classes or whatever people did with a new-born . . .

'If I'd thought like that,' Clare continued, picking up her crochet needle and focusing on the square of wool on her lap, 'I'd never have allowed myself to fall in love with Ian and get married again. Sometimes we don't get our happy-ever-after first time around, you know.'

'Ian's your second husband?'

She nodded. 'I'd been married for two years – *happily* married, so I thought – when I found out my first husband, Pete, was running a brothel. A brothel!' Her eyes widened. 'I couldn't believe it.'

'Gosh, even Harvey wasn't doing anything that dodgy,' I said, sipping from my water bottle.

'He told *me* he was the night manager at a hotel in Stockport. I always wondered why he said we couldn't get staff discount in the restaurant. I only found out because I'd taken a pregnancy test and couldn't wait to tell him the good news, so I got on the bus to surprise him at work. You can imagine who got the biggest surprise. I found him in a seedy room with stripy wallpaper and swirly carpet with two poor girls clad in baby-doll nighties draped round his neck.' She shuddered at the memory.

'Oh Clare,' I said in a hushed voice. 'You must have been devastated.'

'Life can change in the blink of an eye,' said Clare flippantly. 'All I'd wanted was a family. In the space of one evening I lost my home and my husband and my security. I wish someone could have told me at the time that all would be well, but right then, I thought my life had ended.'

'I've always wanted what my parents had,' I said. 'That's all. They did everything the traditional way: found the perfect match, tied the knot in church, had two children. I seem to be doing it back to front. And as to whether I'll ever get married, who knows. Some men are funny about other men's children, aren't they?' A shiver ran down my back remembering how Harvey had been so anti-fostering when I'd joked that I'd do it if I couldn't have my own.

'The right man won't be funny about it,' she said cheerily. 'My daughter, Frankie, was six months old when I met Ian. I think he fell in love with her before me. He was totally besotted with her tiny fingernails and her button nose. I was a young mother, living in the cheapest flat I could find, with very few job skills and no hope. I thought I had nothing to offer another man. When Ian proposed, he said he'd found everything he'd ever wanted in me and Frankie. I got my happy-ever-after second time around.'

'I'm so glad,' I said warmly. 'You're a lovely lady, Clare, you deserve to be happy.'

'Ditto,' she said a wide smile. 'Your happy ending is out there too. I promise.'

I hoped so, I really did, but sometimes it was difficult to imagine.

'Clare . . . ?' She looked up and I hesitated, not entirely sure if I wanted to put a voice to the niggling worry that I'd had on and off for weeks. 'Can I ask you something personal, something just between us?'

She rummaged in her wool bag and brought out a ball of the palest lemon yarn. 'Course, fire away.'

'Well. Even though you had all that going on, and things were not as you'd planned and your future wasn't certain . . .' My voice trembled and I took a deep breath before continuing. 'Even then, did you never once think that maybe you shouldn't keep the baby?'

She studied my face with concern before laying her crochet square on her knee and taking my hand in hers. My emotions felt exposed and raw and her touch absorbed them and soothed my heart. 'I've never told anyone this. Not a soul. But yes I did. At first I thought about having a termination, because I was so scared of how I was going to cope on my own and I was also worried about Pete having a personality transplant and taking an interest in his own child.'

She raised a wry eyebrow.

'But I couldn't do it. I know it's right for some, but I'd been *trying* for a baby, I couldn't give up on it just because my marriage had fallen apart.'

'And you never doubted you'd be a good parent?' I said, feeling the full weight of my words settling on my heart.

'All the time,' she said. 'All the time. I thought about all the childless couples who had everything a baby would need, like two parents and a comfortable home, who would give it the start it deserved, you know?'

I nodded. That was exactly how I felt. Even more so because of Evie and Darren's difficulties conceiving.

'But you kept her,' I said, wanting her to tell me I was doing the right thing.

'I did.' She smiled, her eyes twinkling. 'Despite everything – my circumstances, and knowing that I'd be on my own through the long nights of feeding and colic and never finishing a cup of tea while it was hot – I knew that I'd love it. And when it comes down to it, if a child knows it's loved, even by only one of its parents, the rest – the big house with a swing in the garden, the new clothes, the piles of toys – is just window dressing. That's all you need to ask yourself: can I love this baby?'

And there it was: the million-dollar question. For the last seven weeks, my focus, whether conscious or not, had been on the practical and physical things and coming to terms with actually being pregnant. Could I love Harvey's baby? Or would I be reminded of his furious face, his hand gripping my cheeks in Evie's living room whenever I looked at it?

I took a calming breath, closing my eyes for a second. Thinking like that would never do; this baby was pure and innocent and not to blame for what had happened between me and its father.

I nodded gently and a smile of relief spread across my face as I placed a hand on my stomach. 'I can; at least, I'll do my very best. This baby is part of me, the best part of me. Thanks, Clare.'

She did a comedy wink. 'You're welcome, honey. You know, perhaps I should go on a counselling course, I think I'd be good at that.'

I laughed affectionately. 'I don't know where you find the time for all these activities.'

'Multi-tasking,' she said, tapping the side of her nose. 'Why do one job when you can do three or four?'

'What are you crocheting? It's beautiful.'

Clare wove her crochet hook through the yellow wool, looping and poking and twisting, creating patterns as if by magic.

'Baby blankets. A lady at church sends them to Syria to the maternity hospital. Lots of the mothers come in with nothing for their babies, we make these little shawls and we send them with our love, so when they leave hospital with their babies wrapped up warmly, the mums are taking our good wishes with them. I'll do one for your baby if you like?'

Low down inside me, I felt a sensation like tiny bubbles fizzing and popping. I took a sharp breath in. 'I think something's on the move; the linseeds must be working already.'

Clare lowered her crochet hook and sat forward. 'Maybe. How far along are you?'

'Eighteen weeks. Ooh!'

The feeling changed from a fizz to a flickering, like the rapid fluttering of a hundred butterfly wings. I'd read about this; it wasn't wind at all . . . My child was moving inside me.

'It moved. The baby moved,' I gasped and laid a hand on my bump, laughing.

'Hello, Mummy,' said Clare in a high-pitched voice.

Mummy. Until now, I'd thought of myself as being pregnant, I'd focused on the nine months leading up to the birth, never really envisaging myself as a mother. A mum. I'd be a mum with a child of my own. For the first time since all this began, I imagined a baby in my arms, its soft body weighing nothing and yet, everything, peeping up at me from a blanket in the softest wool, and my heart leapt with an explosion of love for the life inside me. In that moment, that *very* moment, I became its mother.

'Hello, my darling one,' I murmured.

Clare's eyes misted up. 'How lovely.'

'Yes please, Clare,' I said, tears pricking at my eyes. 'We'd love one of your blankets very much.'

*

'This cottage is very sweet,' said Evie later that afternoon as she poked her head into my bathroom and made appropriate 'ooh' and 'aah' noises about everything. 'I was in too much of a flap about Dad to take it in last time I was here. You've been unbelievably fortunate, getting this.'

'I have,' I said, swallowing a sigh. 'It's going to take some beating when my job comes to an end in December.'

'Would Betsy not consider keeping you on?' She sat neatly on the sofa and kicked off her pumps. She looked so delicate and sylph-like compared to me. I was worried she'd bounce straight up in the air as soon as I plonked myself down.

'It's complicated,' I said, lowering myself gingerly on to the seat beside her.

'I'm listening,' she said, helping herself to a banana from the huge bunch in the fruit bowl and offering one to me. 'Where's all your grapes? I thought you'd get loads of free grapes as a perk of the job?'

The bananas were a gift from Pippa who'd read that they were a superfood that cured everything from constipation to cramp, something else I'd begun to suffer from.

'Our grapes aren't ready yet. I'll take you on a tour of the vines later and let you taste some. They aren't anywhere near as sweet as the table grapes you buy in the shops.'

Evie grinned. 'Lottie Allbright, Fernfield's resident grape expert: who'd have thought it?'

'I thought you were listening to my complicated story?'

'Sorry. Go on.'

And while she nibbled on her superfood, I told her about Betsy's dilemma: her worsening macular problem and reliance on others to see and read her post for her, as well as to drive her around.

'There are so many things she struggles with now,' I said. 'Eventually she won't be able to cope with simple things like the central-heating controller or the display on the washing machine.'

'Poor thing.' Evie frowned. 'And managing this place on top of losing her husband.'

'She promised to see the next harvest through, but after that I think she'll be ready to move on.'

'You can't blame her. She shouldn't be running a business at her age if she doesn't want to.'

I puffed out my cheeks. 'I wish there was a way I could afford to buy the vineyard, but I don't think I'd even get a mortgage on a house, let alone a business.'

Evie bit her lip. 'I could lend you some money, but I imagine it would be a drop in the ocean; the property must be worth a bomb, and then the vineyard on top.'

'Aw, that is so sweet of you,' I said, pressing a hand to my chest. 'But I couldn't accept your money. Betsy was hoping that Jensen would take an interest in the wine business. If he moved back here, she could hand over the reins *and* stay in her own home. That would be the perfect solution.'

She cocked an eyebrow. 'For Betsy or you?'

'I can't lie,' I said, feeling a flash of heat rise to my face. 'I really like him.'

She folded her banana skin up and laid it tidily on the coffee table. 'And what are you going to do about it?'

'Me?' I blinked at her. 'I wasn't planning on doing anything.'

'I see.' Evie stretched her legs out and put her feet up on my lap. 'Waiting for him to take the lead and decide where, when or even *if* you see him?'

She looked at me pointedly. This was where I'd gone wrong with Harvey, I realized: following blithely, going along with his plans in lieu of making my own.

'You're right,' I said firmly. 'I need to be more proactive. Not just for myself; I've got the baby to think of now too.'

Evie's mouth twisted into a grin. 'Now you're talking. So, I repeat, what are you going to do about it?'

'I'm seeing him for lunch in London next week before the

radio interview.' I shrugged. 'But there's no point doing anything at the moment; I don't even know if he's moving abroad or not. If he's not, then maybe I'll tell him how I feel.'

'And if he is?'

I forced a smile. 'Then he'll have got the big promotion he deserves, I'll congratulate him, wave him off and I won't stand in his way.'

'Just like that?' She looked very unimpressed. 'That's not very proactive.'

I sighed hopelessly; taking a firmer stance was harder than it looked. 'I'll think of something. Anyway,' I smiled brightly and patted my sister's leg, 'you look radiant. I take it you and Darren are love's young dream again?'

Her eyes sparkled with happiness. 'I love him so much. I can't believe I let him go in the first place.'

'Don't be too hard on yourself. You both went through a lot.'

'If I've learned anything from our split it's to never stop talking to one another. After losing the baby, day by day we withdrew a bit more from each other until we didn't know what the other wanted any more.'

'And now you know what you both want?'

'Yep,' she said firmly. 'We want to be parents. Together. Whatever that means.'

I was confused. 'But wasn't that always the case?'

'Darren thought that, for me, being a mother was about giving birth. Because he couldn't give me a baby, he decided that the best thing to do would be for me to find someone else to have a family with. But he was wrong about that: that was never my priority. Being pregnant is only one part of it. I would have loved to bring our biological baby into the world but it wasn't to be. But being a mother is about the relationship you have with a child. And that lasts a lifetime; pregnancy is over in the blink of an eye. He was right about fostering, though.'

'You'd get too attached to your foster children?'

She wrinkled her nose and nodded. 'So now we're focusing on adoption.'

I grinned. 'And when do Skipper and Roni arrive?'

'At the beginning of October. But that's not what I mean. We're going to register to adopt a child of our own.'

I pulled her towards me and hugged her tightly. 'That's fantastic. I'm so pleased for you. You'll be a brilliant mum.'

She dashed a tear from her cheek and beamed. 'And so will you.'

'If I wasn't pregnant I'd be proposing a toast with champagne. But I could rustle up a glass of fizzy water?'

'No thanks, but funny you should say that, I'd like to buy a nice bottle of Butterworth fizz while I'm here to go with our celebration dinner this evening. I've left Darren marinating squid in chilli and kiwi juice.'

I rubbed my chest. 'Just thinking of that is giving me heartburn.'

She gave a snort of laughter. 'In that case you would not like the main course: garlic chicken and spicy noodles.'

'Not right now, no,' I said, wincing. 'Although after the amount of fibre my colleagues have fed me today, I don't think I can face any food at all.'

Her face became serious for a second. 'You're doing so well, you know. You've completely taken pregnancy in your stride, no fuss, no drama. When I was pregnant – briefly – I was so uptight and paranoid that every little thing would damage the baby that I couldn't enjoy it. And then of course . . .' She gave me a wan smile. 'It was over.'

'I'm not that calm,' I said, stroking my tummy. 'You should have seen me earlier when the baby moved for the first time.'

'Wow.' Her eyes widened. 'Is it moving now?'

I took her hand and guided it to my bump, pressing it firmly against my jersey dress. I watched her features soften in amazement and wondered whether I'd be brave enough to do this with Jensen next week.

'That is incredible,' she whispered.

'Isn't it?' I looked at her through watery eyes. 'I'm in love with it already.'

Evie's own eyes were moist with tears when she met my gaze.

'Tell Jensen how you feel,' she said suddenly. 'Even if he's offered this new job. I didn't tell Darren how much I loved him and I nearly lost him for good. Don't make the same mistake.'

My stomach fluttered nervously, although now I didn't know which was me and which was the baby. I pictured Jensen's face as he'd watched the baby move on the scan four weeks ago; he'd been so excited. But he was excited about the prospect of this promotion in Cape Town too and it wouldn't take a genius to guess which he'd choose: a new job in South Africa in a career that he loved versus staying in England to help bring up somebody else's baby. Despite Clare's words of encouragement earlier, I couldn't see my happy ending coming any time soon . . .

Chapter 26

As the train pulled into London St Pancras station, the butterflies in my stomach had switched to turbo-mode. It wasn't the baby; it was the impending live appearance on national radio coupled with a lunch date with Jensen.

After the warmth of the train, I shivered as I stepped on to the platform. The Indian summer of the first three weeks of September had vanished overnight and autumn had arrived in all its shades of gold and red.

When I'd left home first thing this morning, the air had had a chill to it and a stiff breeze had scattered leaves like faded summer confetti along the country lanes between the vineyard and Fernfield station. Even now, hours later, it was still cool and I was glad I'd accepted Betsy's gift of one of her cosy old cardigans in soft navy cashmere. It added a touch of elegance to my denim smock dress. The dress skimmed my waist and was one of the few smartish things I owned which wasn't uncomfortable to wear; I didn't even show in this. Not that it was a secret any more, but travelling alone with bottles clinking in a cool bag had drawn a few curious looks from my fellow passengers and that was without them knowing I was pregnant.

Suddenly my stomach swooped; there he was, waiting for me on the other side of the ticket barrier.

Jensen spotted me and grinned. I drank in his dark blue eyes, his open friendly smile which lit up his face and that lovely floppy bit of hair over one eye. He was more tanned than he'd been last time I'd seen him and looked very handsome in a suit and tie. In fact, although he didn't seem to notice it, he was attracting quite a bit of attention from other women.

He opened his arms and I walked straight into them, inhaling his scent and thinking that if every train journey could end like this, I'd travel every single day of my life.

'Wow.' He kissed my cheek.

'Double wow,' I replied and then smiled to myself remembering that that had been my first thought on the day I met him. 'You've missed me then while you were living it up in Cape Town?'

'Working fourteen-hour days, you mean?' His eyes sparkled. 'But yes, I thought about you a lot while I was there. I kept thinking Lottie would like this, Lottie would love to go there . . . Pathetic, aren't I? You look great, by the way.'

He looked genuinely pleased to see me. I felt myself blush and hoped the cardigan was covering any neck rash, although thinking about it, I hadn't felt its presence for a while, perhaps pregnancy had banished it. There had to be some benefits, after all, seeing I was heavier than I've ever been in my life and couldn't fit into most of my clothes, had toothache on and off, and a brown patch of pigment on my forehead, which my midwife said was very common and would fade after the baby was born.

'Thank you, I thought I'd better make an effort,' I said with a mischievous smile. 'Seeing as I'm supposed to be your fiancée.'

'I'm flattered,' he said, taking the cool bag from me and guiding me towards the escalator with a hand in the small of my back. 'But you'd never have to dress up for me; I liked you the first time I met you with mud on your face.'

I glanced sideways at him. 'Did you?'

'Don't you remember how tongue-tied I was?' He groaned lightly. 'Even Gran noticed. I think I introduced myself to you twice.'

I stepped on to the escalator in front of him, which meant I didn't have to hide the huge smile on my face until we reached the bottom. I thought back to our first meeting in Betsy's kitchen, my first day at the vineyard. I'd been an emotional wreck then, not knowing what to do with my life. So much had changed since then.

'You're looking very nice too,' I said, as we headed towards the taxi rank outside. 'I've never seen you in a tie before.'

He looked smart and sophisticated, totally at ease amidst the bustle of London. On the other hand, all I needed to complete my country-bumpkin look was a stalk of wheat.

'It feels like a noose.' He ran a finger around his collar. 'Which is appropriate as I've been called into a board meeting at four o'clock this afternoon. The sealed bids for the project I've been working on are due in any moment and if it hasn't gone well, my neck will be on the line.'

'Oh. That sounds serious.' I blinked at him, trying to hide my dismay. My radio interview was at three o'clock and I'd hoped that he'd be able to accompany me to the radio studio. I guessed now that wouldn't be possible.

He took my hand as we exited through the big glass doors and the smell of diesel, the rush of people and the din of the traffic took my breath away. I had a sudden recollection of my last day in London, when I'd been travelling in the opposite direction, heart thudding as I left my job, my flat and my boyfriend behind. I blew out a breath to bring myself back to the moment. But that life was over and the one I'd created was on my terms, my choice.

Jensen glanced at me. 'You okay?'

We joined the queue at the taxi rank and he set the cool bag down.

'Bit nervous,' I admitted, nibbling my lip. 'But nothing compared to Pippa.'

He whistled under his breath when I told him she'd agreed to run the library event; he remembered how she used to hide amongst the vines to avoid talking to anyone when she'd first started helping his granddad out. She'd bombarded me with texts this morning, worrying about everything from the possibility of someone getting stung by a wasp to how to get rid of the visitors at the end. I'd replied as best I could and then sent Godfrey a message suggesting he give her some alcohol for Dutch courage before anyone arrived.

'I'm sorry I can't wait with you while you're on air.' Jensen squeezed my hand. 'But I'll see you get to the studio on time and I'll be listening in. I promise.'

We reached the front of the queue and I climbed into the taxi while Jensen gave the driver directions.

'Devine Kitchen, Shoreditch, please.'

I raised my eyebrows at him as he got in beside me, thrilled that he'd chosen a restaurant owned by Thomas Devine, my fellow radio guest. 'Nice touch, I'm impressed.'

He grinned. 'Good. I thought we could check out his wine list before you meet him.'

'Woe betide him if there's no English wines on it,' I said sternly.

He laughed. 'I'm sure you'll set him straight. Mind if I just check in with the office?'

I didn't mind and while he spoke to a colleague, I sat back happily, watching the streets of London go by, listening as the cabbie moaned about traffic jams and roadworks and how cycle lanes were the bane of his life.

It didn't take us long to get there. Jensen paid the fare and lifted the cool bag out of the cab and as we approached the restaurant, a man dressed head to toe in black pulled the door open for us.

'I hope he doesn't think we've brought our own picnic,' Jensen whispered.

I snorted. 'I might open a bottle of Butterworth wine if I don't like the selection.'

The smiley woman at the front desk showed us to our table and Jensen's hand was a feather-light touch on my waist as we followed behind her. In no time, we were settled at our table with a jug of iced water and menus.

'Look at the prices!' I hissed, scanning the à la carte menu. 'Twenty-five pounds for sausage and mash and they don't even serve gravy with it! That would be about eight quid at the Royal Oak and you'd get gravy thrown in.'

'Ah, but these are wild boar sausages,' said Jensen. 'And there is gravy, they just call it *jus*.'

'Humph,' I said, swapping to the wine menu. 'Blimey, look at that, their bog-standard prosecco starts at thirty quid. And I bet they buy it in from Aldi.'

He shook his head, laughing. 'I bet they don't. Anyway, to hell with the cost, this is a special occasion.'

It was. I swallowed, wishing I was brave enough to reach across and kiss him or at least tell him that it was special for me too. I pictured Evie spurring me on to speak my mind, but all I could manage was: 'Oh?' and hoped he couldn't hear the thumping of my heart.

He rolled his eyes playfully. 'We've just got engaged, remember?'

And before I had a chance to reply he whipped out a ring box from inside his jacket and snapped it open.

'Jensen!' I gasped in surprise.

Nestled inside the black velvet-lined box was a silver ring with a large green stone in the centre surrounded by tiny diamantés.

'Don't look so alarmed, it's not valuable,' he whispered. 'I bought it from Topshop for twenty quid. I thought if you were meant to be my fiancée you ought to look the part. And no one will question that it's not genuine gemstones.'

I still hadn't mustered a response so he took it out of the

box and slipped it on my finger. 'What do you think? I thought it matched your eyes.'

He'd gone shopping for me *and* he'd remembered the colour of my eyes *and* it fitted perfectly. SWOON.

I felt dazed and a little overcome. 'I think it's beautiful. And much better value than a plate of sausage and mash.'

'You hopeless romantic.' He laughed and, leaning across, placed a light kiss on my lips. 'Is that a yes?'

I was suddenly aware that the air around us had stilled and everyone had stopped talking. Other diners were holding their breath in a collective hush.

'We-ll, I'd have preferred you to get down on one knee, but . . .' I pretended to think about it. 'Seeing as it matches my eyes, it's a yes from me.'

'Ahem.'

We both looked round to see a man whose badge announced him as Didier, the maître d', beaming at us.

'Madam, sir, on behalf of my colleagues at the Devine Kitchen,' he said with a heavy French accent, 'let me be the first to congratulate you both on your engagement.'

'Thank you,' we answered together, not daring to look at each other.

'May I?' Didier indicated my new ring and, somehow managing not to giggle, I held my hand out to be inspected. If he noticed it was only a cheapie, he had the good manners not to mention it. '*Charmant.*'

'Good choice, do you reckon?' said Jensen, sending me the tiniest wink.

'Dazzling.' He released my hand and took a little bow.

'I meant my fiancée,' said Jensen.

'So did I, sir.' His lips twitched and we all laughed.

'Now,' Didier clapped his hands together, 'please choose a bottle of champagne from the wine list with our compliments.'

'That's so kind!' I exclaimed, noticing that our table was still attracting an awful lot of attention.

Jensen passed me the wine list with a flourish. 'My fiancée is the wine expert.'

I glanced at it fleetingly. 'What I'd really like is some English sparkling wine, but there's none on the list.'

Didier inclined his head. 'A very discerning choice if I may say so, madam, let me have a word with our head sommelier. In the meantime, what would you like to eat?'

Jensen looked at me questioningly and I nodded.

'We'll both have the sausage and mash please.'

'Two or three?' said Didier, leaning forward discreetly. 'They are very large, madam.'

I shrugged; I was eating for two, after all.

'Three please. With extra gravy,' I added. 'Not *jus*.'

Twenty minutes later, we were tucking in to a huge pile of sausage and mash. I took it back; the wild boar sausages were amazing, the ones at the Royal Oak weren't a patch on these. And to accompany our lunch, the maître d' had unearthed a bottle of sparkling wine from Cornwall which, according to the sommelier, was regularly served at Buckingham Palace and the Houses of Parliament.

'But not Devine Kitchen?' I asked.

Didier shrugged apologetically, bowed and left us to it. I got my phone out to take a picture to show Clare later; she'd be so impressed that we were drinking the Queen's favoured fizz.

'To us,' said Jensen, tapping his champagne flute gently against mine.

'To the Butterworths,' I said and swirled it round before inhaling it. 'That is lovely. Vibrant and full of fruit.'

'Impressive.' Jensen sniffed his, eyeing me with interest. 'You're quite good at this.'

I let the flavours develop in my mouth. 'I can see why the Queen likes it; it's like an English meadow in summer: fragrant and fresh with a hint of honey. Yum.'

He looked at me, amazed. 'How do you do that?'

'Matt taught me, and your granddad taught him. It's all about letting go of your inhibitions and letting your taste buds take over.'

Jensen sipped his sparkling wine and a tiny sigh escaped. 'I wish I'd had more time with Granddad. We think we've got all the time in the world, don't we? It's a cliché but moments really should be seized.'

'They should.' I reached over and squeezed his hand. Our eyes locked and we stayed like that for several seconds and I knew that whatever happened I'd always look back on that particular moment and remember how my heart was so full of joy that it was almost bursting with happiness.

'Ted would be thrilled with this year's harvest,' I said finally. 'I've got nothing to compare it to, of course, but the rest of the team are convinced that we've got a bumper crop on our hands.'

'I'll come and help pick if I'm around.'

'Betsy will be delighted to hear that.'

'Just Gran?' He gave me a cheeky smile.

'Me too, obviously. Many hands make light work.'

'I see. You just want me for my muscles.'

'Amongst other things,' I said coyly.

'Oh, yeah?'

'Your sausage,' said Didier smugly, appearing again and pointing to the untouched one on my plate. 'I thought it might beat you.'

He topped up our glasses with a gracious smile even though I'd barely touched mine and looked most put out when we both collapsed with laughter.

'About the harvest . . .' said Jensen carefully. 'I suppose once the grapes have been pressed and the crop is in, we ought to start thinking about putting the vineyard up for sale. Gran only wanted to stay until the end of the season.'

My stomach lurched instantly.

'I don't want to think about it. Even if you do put it on the market, the wine in the tanks will still need to be looked after, the 2016 vintage will be ready to sell, the 2017 vintage will be ready for its *dosage*, there'll be so much to do . . .' I felt a lump in my throat at the thought of leaving it all behind.

'I know, Lottie.' He gave me a sympathetic smile, checked his watch and signalled for the bill. 'But there'll always be something to do, whenever we try to find a buyer.'

'In my head I'm already planning for the 2018 vintage,' I said excitedly. 'I've been talking to Sidney—'

'You're still in touch with him?'

I nodded. 'Weekly. He's got a wealth of knowledge, and as his own family don't seem to want it he's happy to share it with me. I happened to mention that we use less Pinot Meunier in our sparkling wines than the other two varieties even though it makes up a third of our vines, and a couple of days later I received two bottles of still white wine from him: Pinot Meunier. Guess what?'

He looked amused by my eagerness. 'What?'

'It was fantastic. Flinty and just the right side of acidic with notes of currants and cherry.'

'I've never had a still Pinot Meunier.' Jensen's forehead crinkled thoughtfully.

'Exactly!' I felt a fizz of enthusiasm, maybe if I could get him to see a way to take the vineyard in a new direction, he'd see the business as a challenge instead of simply his grandfather's achievement. 'It hasn't taken off here. *Yet*. We could lead the way. And pink sparkling. Not that that's new, but we should do it. Pink is in. Look what it's done for gin!'

A waiter appeared with the bill and a card machine. I reached for my purse but Jensen waved it away so I carried on talking while he paid.

'Talking of gin, did you know we can press the grapes a second time with more pressure after we've extracted the juice for our sparkling wine and use it as a base to distil gin?'

He raised an eyebrow. 'Really?'

'Yes!' I wrinkled my nose. 'Don't ask me how, I haven't researched it too deeply. But my point is . . .'

I stood up and Jensen gallantly helped me into my cardigan and picked up the cool bag. Lots of people then congratulated us and asked to see my ring and wished us well and it wasn't until we were back outside on the pavement and he was flagging down another cab that I had the chance to finish my sentence.

'My point is that Ted has laid the groundwork for a business that could grow and grow. There's so much potential. So much we could do. You and me. Together.'

I looked at him earnestly and held my breath as Evie's advice rang in my ears. *Tell him how you feel. Tell him . . .*

Before I could utter another word Jensen sighed and pulled me to him, pressing his cheek against mine and wrapping his arms tightly around me.

'I love your enthusiasm, Lottie,' he murmured. 'And believe me, I have thought along the same lines.'

My spirits sank. 'But?'

A taxi swung over to our side of the kerb and we got in, me giving the driver the address of the radio station.

'Today's the big day for our global water project. My assistant has told me that all the sealed bids have arrived from our chosen contractors and the board directors are opening them as we speak. My company has been selected to conduct a water resilience project in five cities around the world. Each city has been chosen because it has a particular type of water issue: they all suffer from either too much or too little. The Cape Town project I've been involved with is about solving problems of severe drought. If the infrastructure we install is successful it will provide a framework to solve water problems for the whole world.' His eyes glittered with passion. 'If I get offered the job of managing that I don't think I could turn it down.'

'Of course you couldn't.' I sighed. 'It does make my gin idea seem a bit pathetic.'

He took hold of my hand with its new shiny ring and held it to his lips. 'It's a great idea. You're the best thing that

302

could have happened to Butterworth Wines. And I think you're right: together you and I could be great.' He stared down at his lap. 'But next year you'll need time off work to look after the baby, and I, well, I need to do this.'

I didn't trust myself to speak, but I managed to nod. I hadn't given a great deal of thought to maternity leave; there didn't seem much point as my job was only temporary anyway. Although if I was still around, I was sure I'd be able to do most things with a small baby in tow. But it was a moot point; if Jensen couldn't be tempted back to Derbyshire, and Betsy wanted to relinquish responsibility, the vineyard would have to be sold. Simple as that.

'Okay if I drop you here?' the cab driver called through the Perspex screen. 'Global Media is across the street.'

'Thanks for lunch and the ring,' I said, pressing a hasty kiss to Jensen's cheek as I got out.

He handed me the cool bag. 'You'll be fantastic, good luck.'

'Thanks. You too, with your meeting.' I managed a smile and shut the door of the cab.

'Lottie, I . . .' He raked a hand through his hair; for a man who might be about to land his dream job he didn't look very happy.

'Cheer up, mate,' the cabbie laughed, turning round to watch us. 'I'm sure you'll see her later.'

My heart twisted; would he? We hadn't made arrangements for after my interview. And I guessed if he did get the big job he was hoping for he'd have a lot more important things to think about than me and my plans for pink wine.

'I'd better go,' I said, half hoping he'd leap from the taxi and snog me senseless. He didn't. But at the last second, just as the cab pulled away, he launched his head out of the window.

'Lottie! Wait for me,' he yelled. 'I might be a while but wait for me here. Okay?'

'Okay!' I yelled back, my spirits soaring once again, and I

waved madly until his taxi had melted into the stream of traffic.

'Hi there?' a polite voice called from behind me. 'Lottie?'

I turned to see Olivia Channing jiggling on the spot.

'I thought it was you,' she said, darting over to give me a hug. 'Ready for the onslaught?'

'That sounds ominous.'

She took in my cool bag. 'I hope you've brought some Butterworth wines to win him round? Good effort.'

'I thought this was a friendly chat about English wine.' I stared at her. 'You're making it sound like some sort of battle.'

She laughed and looped my arm through hers. 'Thomas Devine hates English wine, everyone knows that.'

My scalp prickled with fear.

'Not everyone,' I said with a gulp.

Just what had I let myself in for this time?

Chapter 27

The last verse of 'September' by *Earth Wind and Fire* was playing across the airwaves. Fiona Love slipped her headphones back over her ears and held up a finger to silence Olivia who'd kept up a nervous chatter ever since we'd arrived in the 'Love in the Afternoon' studio. Olivia looked at me and let out a tiny squeak and my insides bubbled with nerves.

It had all been a bit of a rush since arriving. We'd signed in at reception, visited the Ladies and been ushered up to the fourth floor with just enough time to spare for Nigel, the show's producer, to dispatch an assistant to fetch champagne flutes in readiness to try the sparkling wine I'd brought.

Apparently, there had been no sign of Thomas Devine and he wasn't answering his phone, so Nigel, tearing at his already sparse hair, had hastily come up with a Plan B. Now, instead of debating the merits or otherwise of English wines and family-run vineyards as planned, Olivia and I would have a nice chat with Fiona, taste some of our sparkling wines on air and take vetted questions from callers about all things wine-related. Plan B sounded heavenly.

As the song reached its last few bars, the door opened and Thomas Devine stalked in, his phone in one hand and a bottle of champagne dripping with condensation in the other. Dressed all in black and with a thin angular face, prominent nose and slicked-back black hair, he looked like a crow. He air-kissed Fiona, nodded at us and folded his tall frame into the furthest chair from where Olivia and I were sitting on unforgiving swivel chairs.

'Phone away now, darling,' Fiona said, batting her eyelashes at Thomas who sighed wearily and slipped it into his back pocket.

'My mouth's gone dry,' Olivia rasped beside me.

'I think I need another wee,' I whispered back.

The studio was like a big goldfish bowl. One wall was almost entirely made of glass through which we could see a beaming Nigel, giving us the thumbs-up. The room itself was dominated by a huge curved white desk. Fiona sat behind it on a comfy-looking chair on wheels with various keypads and mixer panels arranged in a semicircle in front of her. I was already a bit in awe of her: she seemed eminently capable of keeping up with four different computer screens showing the programme's social media channels, national news and the show's playlist. She was a curvy Marilyn Monroe lookalike in red stilettos and red lipstick and if I could look half as sexy as she did when I reached her age, I'd be over the moon.

'Hello there and welcome to "Love in the Afternoon". I'm Fiona Love and joining me in the studio we have Olivia Channing from the English Wine Board, Lottie Allbright from Butterworth Wines and Thomas Devine, who many of you will know from his successful restaurant chain, Devine Kitchen.'

Thomas scowled and leaned into his microphone. 'It's not a chain.'

'Pardon?' Fiona gave a fluttery smile.

'Devine Kitchen is *not* a chain of restaurants.'

'Oh, Thomas.' Fiona laughed coquettishly. 'You have restaurants in five locations, surely that makes you a chain?'

He shook his head. 'To call it a chain is to dismiss the

effort we have put into each venue to make it different and special.'

'Here we go,' Olivia murmured to me under her breath. 'Arguing already.'

Fiona's smile was fixed. 'But the menu is the same in each, no?'

'Correct,' he admitted through gritted teeth.

'And the décor too?'

He exhaled so hard with frustration that I thought he was going to flounce out. 'That's hardly the point, the experience at each of our restaurants is unique and—'

'It's nothing to shy away from, Thomas,' said Fiona soothingly. 'Customers appreciate knowing what to expect, a certain quality, a guarantee of consistency.'

Thomas started to argue again but this time Fiona simply talked over him, addressing Olivia.

'Which leads us neatly into quality English wine, and Olivia Channing.' She smiled encouragingly at Olivia, who was trembling so much that I was worried the microphone would pick up the sound of her knocking knees. 'Is it fair to say that one of the problems up till now with wine from this country is the lack of consistency?'

'Um.' Olivia swallowed in vain and managed to croak out an answer. 'Not really.'

Poor Olivia; her saliva seemed to have deserted her. Fiona turned to look at Nigel through the glass and did the universal hand signal for drink.

'I'm talking about unreliable weather coupled with an industry which, let's face it,' Fiona laughed affably, 'we don't exactly have huge experience in, do we?'

An assistant glided in with a plastic cup of water for Olivia, who gulped it down in one as if she'd been stranded in a sandstorm for a week, wiped her mouth with the back of her hand and panted. Fiona was shooting looks at her, clearly waiting for an answer, and I realized I'd have to step

307

in and say something. I cleared my throat and my heart rate speeded up but luckily Olivia found her voice in time.

'Oh, that's better now I've wet my whistle,' she said with a giggle.

'Excellent,' said Fiona with a steely smile.

'It's true we're a little behind other nations in developing a commercial wine industry, but in the last decade, English wines have made a *huge* impact on the worldwide scene,' Olivia said, sounding much more confident, although there were two pink spots on her cheeks. 'And they are now being appreciated all over the world. In fact, many vineyards have won major awards at international level.'

Thomas Devine, still smarting from the restaurant chain comment, gave a derisory snort.

I smiled sweetly at him. 'Is that so difficult to believe?'

He gave me a withering glare and sat back lazily in his chair. 'Look. Let's be clear. The British are good at a lot of things. Some of our produce is the best in the world. But our grapes . . . ?' he scoffed. 'Get real. Grapes in this country are never going to thrive. English wine producers are playing at it. We're great at cider, but come on, guys, leave wine to the French.'

Fiona leaned her elbows on the desk, affording Thomas a bird's-eye view of her considerable cleavage. 'Not everyone thinks that way, do they, Thomas? Even our friends across the pond are beginning to take an interest, isn't that right, Lottie?'

'That's correct, Fiona,' I piped up. 'Several well-established French wine houses have been looking very seriously at expanding their production into the UK, and Taittinger has already planted fifty acres of vines.'

Thomas laughed. 'Yeah, yeah, let's see how that works out for them.'

I gave him my sternest stare; there weren't many people I disliked on first meeting, but he was an arrogant snob and very self-opinionated.

'And let's not forget,' said Olivia with quiet anger, 'that geologically-speaking, the Champagne region in France has an almost identical *terroir* to parts of the south-east chalk downs.'

Thomas closed his eyes for a second, took a deep breath and muttered something beginning with F. On the other side of the glass, Nigel got to his feet and must have said something in Fiona's earpiece because she looked at him sharply.

'Thomas,' Fiona pursed her lips, 'it says on your website that you source locally whenever possible. There is a well-established, award-winning vineyard within five miles of your Oxfordshire restaurant and yet you don't include it on your menu. Have you got a comment to make on that?'

'I have indeed.' He folded his arms. 'We do source locally, providing we have access to the best produce. In the case of wine, we have to go further afield to find the quality our customers demand. Even if that means importing New World wines.'

That was the final straw; I'd heard enough.

'New World wines,' I said hotly. 'Meaning that their wine industries have opened up relatively recently. Places that only a few decades ago were in the position English wine is now. I bet you'd like Butterworth sparkling wines if you tried them, but you're so far up your own—'

Olivia gasped lightly and laid a restraining hand on my arm. I took a deep breath.

'You're so predisposed not to like them,' I went on, changing tack, 'that you wouldn't admit it even if you did find them acceptable.'

Thomas looked across at my cool bag and smirked. 'Come on, then. Put your money where your mouth is, let's try them.'

'And while we get prepared for some wine-tasting in the studio, here's The Christians with their eighties hit "Harvest for the World",' said Fiona smoothly, taking a deep breath as the music kicked in.

'How long have we got?' I asked, feeling an urgent pressing on my bladder. 'I really need to go.'

'Only three minutes,' Fiona replied with a frown. 'There's no time for a comfort break.'

'I'll run.'

I scrambled off my chair, darted from the studio and broke the land speed record for going to the loo. I made it back as Fiona was fading the track out.

'Jesus, I nearly had a heart attack,' whispered Olivia, grasping at her throat as I threw myself back into my swivel chair.

'So. The moment I've been waiting for ever since my producer told me who today's guests were,' said Fiona with a smile in her voice. 'I'm about to get my first taste of English sparkling wine! Over to you, Lottie.'

Fear coursed through me. I'd brought along a Classic Cuvée 2013, a Blanc de Blanc 2016 and one of our brandnew Blanc de Noirs which had a pale pink glow to it, but I'd brought them thinking this was going to be a genteel affair, not the War of the Rosés. I could see what was going to happen: Thomas Devine would ruin us. He'd say they tasted awful when they didn't and everyone back at Butterworth Wines would be mortified. And Jensen, who said he'd be listening in . . . My legs had started to shake now and I could feel the blood pumping in my ears.

'Uh-oh, Fiona, I think she's doubting herself.' Thomas stretched his arms up and clasped his hands behind his head. The smug sod.

'Butterworth Wines is one of the most promising vineyards I've had the pleasure of visiting,' said Olivia, tilting her chin up at him. 'That's why I invited Lottie along to represent the best in English wines. No *doubt* about it.'

'And Lottie, I understand you're engaged to be married to a member of the Butterworth family, so you're marrying into a wine dynasty?' Fiona announced teasingly, obviously keen to lighten the mood.

'Um.' Dynasty was pushing it a bit, I thought, with a rush of affection towards Betsy and Starsky. 'Yes, that's right.'

'Congratulations! Can I see the ring while Olivia uncorks the first bottle?'

I held out my trembly hand with my Topshop sparkler on it.

'Start with the Blanc de Noir,' I muttered as Oliva unzipped the cool bag.

'Oh what an exquisite piece of jewellery,' Fiona gushed. 'He's a keeper, for sure.'

I pictured Jensen's face listening in and grinning about his bargain ring being mistaken for precious stones. Meanwhile, Olivia removed the first cork with a practised twist and Thomas held glasses as she poured.

'Talk us through it,' said Fiona to me, taking a glass.

Like Olivia's had been, my mouth was now completely desiccated. I took a big swig of the wine and looked round for somewhere to spit it out. There was nothing and with cheeks like a hamster I sent Olivia a frantic look.

'Do you have a spittoon?' she asked Fiona, quickly understanding my problem.

Fiona looked appalled and shook her head. 'I don't think spitting will translate well on air, nobody wants to listen to that sort of noise. You'll have to swallow it.'

I felt my face go red and shook my head.

Thomas roared with sarcastic laughter. 'Not much of an endorsement; even *she* doesn't want to swallow it.'

My eyes blazed at him as I gulped the wine down. 'That is not the case at all, I happen to be pregnant.'

I clapped a hand over my mouth; I hadn't intended for that to come out.

'A pregnant English winemaker,' Thomas hooted, slapping his thigh. 'You couldn't make it up.'

'Congratulations!' Fiona beamed. 'When is it due?'

My heart thumped. This wasn't in the script. Not that there was a script as such but no one had warned me the questions might get personal. 'February,' I said hurriedly, reaching for the cool bag again. 'I'll get the next bottle ready.'

'A winter baby, how lovely!' Fiona cried. 'Let's all toast to Lottie and Jensen.'

'Thank you,' I said quietly. I didn't like lying and I had a bad feeling about this. I also hadn't mentioned any of this ruse to my family, who I knew were listening in – even Dad and Agnes in Germany.

Olivia saw my discomfort and took over, swirling the wine in the glass and inhaling it. 'This has a slightly pinky hue, Fiona, and can you smell the red fruit?'

Thomas and Fiona both sniffed loudly. Olivia slurped it, sucking air in over her tongue to release the flavours. 'Mmm, mmm.' She swallowed it and smacked her lips like all good professionals do. 'It's got a complex toasted palate, with a lovely balanced finish.'

'I like it,' said Fiona simply, holding up her glass for a refill. 'Thomas?'

He sniffed. 'Can't say I'm bowled over. Next.'

Rude. He met my eye and shrugged, a mean grin of amusement plastered across his face. It was just as I thought; he was enjoying taking us down and there was nothing I could do about it.

I uncorked the Blanc de Blanc and poured some for everyone, including a drop for myself, explaining for the listeners' benefit that it was made solely from Chardonnay grapes, left on its lees for eighteen months and had hazelnut notes and a citrusy acidity on the palate.

Fiona and Olivia made appreciative noises while they sipped it; Thomas stared into his glass as if he'd spotted a fly in it, knocked it back in one and gave a slight shudder as he set the glass down.

Fiona noticed and shot him a warning look. 'What would you recommend to serve this with, Olivia?'

'It's elegant and the bubbles are super-fine, I think it

would work well as an aperitif and perfect with something delicate like seafood.'

'Would you agree with that, Thomas?' I asked.

'It has nothing to recommend it, I'm afraid,' he said curtly, focusing on his bottle of champagne as he whipped off the foil and removed the wire cage. 'Why don't we try the real stuff now?'

I quickly scanned the bottle but despite the work both Sidney and Matt had done with me, I didn't recognize the house it was from. Maybe it was far superior to ours, I couldn't tell, but there was a chance that Thomas wouldn't be able to tell either and at this point it was a risk I was prepared to take.

'How about a blind tasting?' I blurted out, challenging him with my stare. 'The French fizz against our Classic Cuvée. We could put a blindfold on Doubting Thomas here and ask him to name which is his favourite.'

'That would be interesting.' Olivia's eyes sparkled with mischief.

Thomas's face was a study in lemon-sucking and he shook his head dangerously at me. The tension in the air had immediately doubled.

'I love it,' cried Fiona swiftly, clapping her hands. 'We've got ninety seconds until the news, so let's make it snappy.'

Olivia and I leapt into action, uncorking the bottles while an assistant came in and tied a West Ham scarf around Thomas's face.

'Careful, not so tight.' He grimaced. 'Ugh, this rag smells of fried onions.'

Someone else appeared with fresh glasses, Fiona read out the names of the two bottles in the blind taste test and I passed Thomas his first glass.

'I'm being stitched up like a kipper here,' he muttered.

This time, with Fiona giving a running commentary, Thomas laboured over it, inhaling, swirling the liquid around, inhaling again before taking a big draft of the pale yellow sparkling wine. It was ours. I daren't speak in case I gave something away; I so wanted him to prefer it.

'It's crisp and fresh, full of minerals. I'm getting that nice brioche flavour. Creamy soft mousse. Not bad,' he said after swallowing.

I could have punched the air; Olivia and I exchanged excited smiles.

'And the second one,' I said, mildly putting a glass of French champagne into his hand. He sniffed and sipped again and smacked his lips after downing it.

'Well?' said Fiona with a hint of drawl. 'What do you think?'

'Quite lively. Fizzier than the first one and yeasty aroma. I'm tasting toasted oats and apricots.'

He pulled the scarf off and stared distrustfully at all three of us, scared of making a fool of himself.

'And the moment of truth,' said Olivia, her eyes wide with anticipation. 'Which did you prefer?'

I held my breath, crossed my fingers and prayed that he picked ours.

He scratched his chin, scowling. 'They were both passable.'

I grinned at him; however this finished, an English sparkling wine had already been deemed passable by the impossible-to-impress Mr Devine.

'We need an answer,' said Fiona, glancing as the seconds on the wall clock counted down.

Thomas gave an exasperated huff. 'Okay, I'll go with the first.'

Olivia and I jumped out of our chairs and hooted with delight.

'And the winner is the Butterworth Classic Cuvée,' said Fiona. 'We'll be back after the news; over to you, Sarah . . .'

We came off air while a reporter in the next studio read the news.

'Congratulations,' Olivia whispered, squeezing my hand.

'Thanks,' I beamed back. 'This has made my day. The Butterworth team are going to be so thrilled.'

I was so elated that I could have happily run from the studio and phoned the vineyard immediately, but we still had a few more minutes left to go to wrap things up.

Thomas's expression was as hard as granite and he folded his arms. 'Whatever. My opinion still holds. And any restaurateur who serves English wine in his restaurant is an idiot.'

'Is that so?' I said quietly.

I slid my mobile phone across the desk, displaying the photo I'd taken at his restaurant earlier. Pride of place on the table was the award-winning bottle of Cornish Brut we'd been drinking.

Thomas picked up the phone and stared at the picture in disbelief. 'Is that . . . ? How . . . ?'

'Also recommended by Her Majesty. I must admit it was the perfect accompaniment to your wild boar sausages.' I smiled innocently at him. 'An idiot, you say?'

Fiona cleared her throat. 'Thank you for that news report, Sarah,' she said easily. 'The big news here on "Love in the Afternoon" is that a sparkling wine from Derbyshire-based Butterworth's has beaten a bottle of French champagne in a taste test, according to Thomas Devine. A man who until today was a staunch believer that English sparkling wine can't compete with our European cousins and has no place on wine lists across the UK. This must be quite a triumph for the English wine world, Olivia?'

'It's certainly confirmation of what we already knew,' Olivia replied. 'And hopefully an indication of a mood swing in the restaurant world.'

'English wines are starting to appear more frequently on wine lists,' I said. 'A trend I hope to see continue.'

Thomas swallowed, his eyes darting towards the door as if contemplating his escape. Now was my moment, I mused. I could have dropped him in it. But I decided not to. I had an advantage and I was determined to press it home.

Fiona hadn't seen the photo on my phone, but she had picked up on a change in energy between Thomas and me.

'Lottie, you're obviously very passionate about your wines; what do you think the future holds?'

'Wines, not just sparkling, but still wines, are emerging from all over Britain. We might not be the most experienced winemakers in the world, we might not be able to grow the range of grape varieties that lots of other countries can. But we're learning all the time. Year after year we're getting better at what we do. And Thomas . . .' I leaned forward to hold his gaze, oblivious to the fact I was on national radio broadcasting to thousands. Right now, my audience was one man alone. 'What we need is people in influential places to help us. Having someone to believe in us makes all the difference, don't you agree? A champion?'

I'd done my research into Thomas Devine and I was paraphrasing his words from a recent newspaper interview. Thomas had been brought up in poverty. And then he'd had a spot of good fortune: aged sixteen his talent had been spotted by the millionaire owner of the local football club where'd he'd played for their junior team. Not as a footballer, his skills were only just above average, but as a kid with a fire in his belly. Thomas referred to that man as his champion; he'd supported him through college and lent him the money to set up his first burger van outside the football ground. And Thomas had repaid the man's faith in him a hundredfold.

And if Butterworth Wines and myriad other vineyards around the country were going to hit the next level, we'd benefit from that same good fortune, that same faith in us.

'Thomas?' Fiona prompted.

'Sure,' said Thomas reluctantly, ignoring her and staring narrow-eyed at me, 'as long as that belief isn't misplaced.'

Just then the baby moved; a rapid fluttering deep in my core. I pressed a hand to my stomach before replying. It may have been a fanciful thought, but having someone real to fight for made me sit up straight and return his stare.

'We English winemakers aren't playing at it. Far from it. It's a multi-million-pound business now, and as exports flourish, the future looks even brighter.'

Olivia jumped in in support. 'Over a million new vines are being planted per year at the moment, can you believe it!' she gushed. 'And global warming has increased mean temperatures by up to one and a half degrees in some areas, which has a big impact on ripening grapes.'

'Hurray,' said Thomas sarcastically, 'who cares about the polar ice cap when it means we can have more inferior wine!'

I turned my back on him. 'Fiona, supporting home-grown wine by asking for it in shops and restaurants isn't just helping wine producers like Butterworth. There is a whole host of industries that we rely on: printers, manufacturers of bottles, steel tanks, valves, hoses, specialist equipment for our labs such as refractometers and hydrometers, and a thousand and one others.'

Fiona nodded. 'Gosh, I'd never considered that.'

'We're setting our sights on the world stage,' I said excitedly. 'My goal for next year is to conquer the Chinese market.'

I paused for a second as I absorbed what I'd just said. *You're having a baby*, a little voice in my head reminded me. *None of this is going to happen*. It couldn't.

'Really?' Fiona nodded encouragingly. 'Why China?'

I dragged myself back from my thoughts.

'The Chinese people are falling in love with sparkling wine,' I explained. 'Consumption has gone up by twenty per cent in the last three years. Within the next couple of years, they'll be the second largest market in the world after the United States. Vineyards are starting to pop up in China, but it will be a long time before supply can match demand. In the meantime,' I spread my hands and grinned, 'it's Butterworth Wines to the rescue.'

'Well, that's very ambitious of you,' said Fiona, looking impressed.

'Not really,' I said lightly, 'it's a combination of risk, optimism and fact. We can succeed there and I believe we will.'

'Actually, I'd second that,' Thomas said, sounding surprised to be agreeing with me. 'China has a huge hunger for British brands. In fact, Devine Kitchen will be opening up in Beijing next spring.'

'And will you have the Butterworth Classic Cuvée on your wine list?' I asked, holding my breath.

Our eyes connected and I saw something in him shift; somehow, incredibly, it looked like I'd won him over. His face relaxed, he inclined his head towards me and the first genuine smile I'd seen from him lit up his face. 'Why not? Hell, I might even serve it at our official opening party.'

My smile was so big I nearly turned myself inside out. 'I'll hold you to that.'

He laughed. 'I don't doubt it for one second.'

'Thank you to my guests this afternoon: Olivia Channing from the English Wine Board,' said Fiona, 'Thomas Devine from Devine Kitchen and Lottie Allbright from Butterworth Wines, whom I think we'll be hearing an awful lot more from in the future.'

Once our slot was over, the production assistant wasted no time in escorting us back down to reception and signing us out and within minutes I was back on the pavement in Leicester Square. After surprisingly amicable farewells, both Olivia and Thomas had jumped in taxis and zoomed away. It was four o'clock; Jensen would be heading into his meeting so I had some time to kill. My head was buzzing from my exchange with Thomas Devine and I couldn't wait to talk to Jensen about it. I walked round to stretch my legs for a while, merged with the crowd to watch a bare-chested fire eater and then headed to a coffee shop and ordered a skinny decaff latte.

Beating the French champagne had given me an incredible boost. The truth was that our wines were amazing and the company ethos was fantastic. Ted Butterworth had created a legacy which was simply too awe-inspiring to let it slide into someone else's hands. Fiona was right when she said I was ambitious for wanting to expand into China and grow the Butterworth brand internationally; I'd meant every word.

It was a tall order given my current circumstances, I acknowledged, stroking my baby bump, and Betsy's circumstances too. But right now, I felt I could conquer the world and maybe if I could somehow persuade Jensen to help me do it, I actually would.

Chapter 28

Alone at a window table, watching a continuous stream of tourists, city workers and fast-food delivery guys pass by, I sipped my latte and turned on my phone. A barrage of notifications flashed up on the screen but before I had a chance to open any of them a call came through from Pippa.

'The library event went SO WELL!' she squealed. 'It was amazing, they loved it, they loved ME!'

'Of course they did,' I replied, thrilled for her. 'You're an expert on Butterworth Wines and people recognize passion when they see it.'

'Do you know,' she said, sounding perky, 'I think you might be right. I was shaking like a leaf to begin with and gripped Godfrey's arm so tightly that his wrist turned white, but then I got into my stride and . . . Oh, the power, I had the audience in the palm of my hand. I felt like a celeb. And then Clare turned up at the end with her son Ben. My eyes nearly popped out; he's so handsome. I went all tongue-tied again.'

That was probably the longest speech I'd ever heard from her and her excitement made my heart fill with joy.

'So we'll be booking more events, then?' I smiled.

'Definitely. I'm thinking of ringing *Good Morning Derbyshire* to see if they'd like to come for a tour.'

'The TV news show?' I stared at the phone in disbelief.

This was the woman who wouldn't say boo to a goose only a week ago.

'Absolutely. Butterworth Wines has been hiding in the shadows far too long,' she said determinedly. 'And so have I.'

'I'll drink to that,' I said, slurping the last of my coffee.

As soon as Pippa signed off, a call came through from my dad.

'Hi, Dad!'

'Not disturbing you, am I?'

'Not at all, it's lovely to hear from you!'

The two middle-aged ladies sharing a strawberry tart at the next table smiled at me and then each other indulgently.

'Just wanted to say congratulations, love. Agnes and I have just listened to your interview on the internet.'

'Ah, thank you!' I said with a wave of love, imagining them both listening avidly in Germany. 'I've never been so nervous in my life.'

There was a pause down the line.

'I'm not surprised.' He sounded hurt. 'In my day, a young fellow asked the father's permission before proposing to his girlfriend. Fancy me finding out from the radio that my daughter's engaged to be married.'

I laughed. 'I promise you, Dad, if a man were really to ask for my hand in marriage, you'd be the first to know.'

'So you're not engaged?'

'No it was just a ruse, don't worry.'

He sighed and I could picture him scratching his beard. 'I'm confused.'

It took me a few minutes to convince him about my fake engagement and the two ladies at the next table didn't even bother to hide the fact that they were totally enthralled by my tale. But eventually Dad saw the funny side, at which point I heard his voice tremble and he told me how proud he'd been to hear me talk on the radio.

'And I didn't realize you were so passionate about wine, love?'

321

'It's taken me by surprise too. I've never been so passionate about anything before,' I said. 'Until I started working at the vineyard, I didn't think of myself as a career woman. After Mum died and I dropped out of university, I lost my purpose. Now I've found something I love and I know I'm having a baby and it won't be easy but I want to go back to uni, Dad, and learn how to do it properly. I really think I could make a go of this. As well as motherhood, that is.'

There was a silence down the line that went on a beat too long for comfort; for a moment I thought the line had gone dead.

'Are you still there?' I asked.

'Lottie, there's something I want to say that I should have said long ago,' he said haltingly. 'I leaned on you far too heavily when your mum died. A stronger man would have insisted that you live your own life and not put your aspirations on hold to look after a grieving father. Then I was selfish again when I encouraged you to join Allbright Tree Services. You should have been out in the world ploughing your own furrow instead of helping me with mine. I loved having you so close, but even at the time I felt guilty about it. I'm sorry, love.'

'But, Dad, I was happy with the choices I made,' I insisted.

And I meant it; maybe Mum's death had been the reason I'd put my future on hold, an excuse to stay in the bosom of my family and take the easy path through life. But maybe that was because I hadn't known what I'd wanted out of life. Now I had found something that made me happy and that was all that mattered.

He let out a long whistling breath. 'You don't know how relieved I am to hear that. But listen, love, about university, me and your mum supported Evie through her studies, and I'll do the same for you if that's what you want to do.'

'Wow!' I gasped. 'I feel like I should be standing on my own two feet by now, but that would be amazing, thank you.'

'Really. I want you to be happy.'

I felt a lump form in my throat; I had been wondering how I was going to fund myself. My heart melted a little bit more when Dad went on to suggest that he'd give Adam and Nicky three months' notice on his house so that I'd have somewhere more permanent to bring the baby home to.

'I'm so lucky having you as my dad,' I said.

'And I'm lucky to have you and Evie and now Agnes too,' he said softly. 'Meeting her has opened up a whole new world.'

I smiled. 'And meeting the Butterworths has done the same for me.'

'Does that include this Jenson fellow?' Dad asked with the perception that can only come with several decades of parenthood.

'He's lovely,' I said with a sigh, glancing up as a clock struck five. 'But I imagine, as we speak, he's probably accepting a job in South Africa.'

Over the next fifteen minutes it felt like I spoke or sent messages to everyone I knew. I'd never experienced such praise in my life. I knew how Pippa felt after her success at the library; it was very flattering to be appreciated. The loveliest call was from Betsy and Marjorie who were having a day out together but had managed to work out the speaker phone function on Betsy's special big button phone in order to both hear the conversation.

'Ted couldn't have done a better job himself,' said Betsy with a tremor in her voice.

'And I bet Jensen's impressed,' Marjorie added. 'All that stuff about China; Betsy and I were flabbergasted.'

'I haven't spoken to him yet. And Betsy, it was you who gave me the idea of looking into it,' I said, 'when you mentioned about Samantha ordering our Classic Cuvée for the golf club.'

'Do you really think it's possible, dear girl?' Betsy asked. 'Could we send Butterworth wines to China?'

'It would entail a lot of work, but it *would* be possible,' I said carefully. 'Although, I thought you were planning on selling up after the harvest? Are you thinking you might like to carry on for another year? Because if you were, I'd happily stay on.'

My heart thumped with hope; even one more year would be amazing . . .

'But what about the baby?' said Marjorie.

'And maternity leave?' Betsy added.

'If Emmeline Pankhurst can do it, so can I,' I reminded them.

I heard some hissed comments volley between the two of them but couldn't make out the words.

'Just spit it out,' I heard Marjorie insist.

'Oh bother,' Betsy grumbled. 'I wanted to talk to you properly about this, face to face, but seeing as it's come up, I'll give you a condensed version.'

My stomach twisted nervously; whatever it was it sounded like bad news.

'Okay,' I said with a gulp.

'Marjorie and I have decided to buy a bungalow together,' she said.

'Oh, that's wonderful!' I said, meaning it. 'What a great idea.'

They made a great team, they clearly adored each other; together they'd be happy and safe and really that's what we all longed for in our old age, wasn't it? Health, happiness and a good laugh every day.

'It's a new development for the over fifty-fives,' said Marjorie. 'All mod cons and a live-in warden, so if Betsy overdoes the sherry, help will be at hand.'

'It wasn't me who shot herself in the eye with a cork last night.'

I jumped in quickly to ask for more details before they began quibbling in earnest and found out that the cul-de-sac of twenty properties was still a building site but the first ones should be habitable by January. And the beauty of it was that it was only a couple of miles away from the vineyard. It sounded perfect and I was thrilled for them.

'See, I knew she'd be happy for us,' said Marjorie.

'She's just being kind, Mar, that's all.'

I didn't pick up on the inference straight away, not thinking through what this would mean for me.

'You'll finally get that new kitchen you've always wanted,' I said, remembering the conversation we'd had on the day I'd moved in, just before Jensen had arrived and spun her around in the air. He'd put me in a spin that day, too; in fact, I was still spinning. I glanced at my watch again. Surely he'd be out of his meeting soon?

'So in answer to your question, Lottie, I'm sorry, but unless Jensen should have a change of heart and decide to move back to Fernfield and take over, the vineyard will go up for sale after this year's harvest.'

I nodded, letting the news sink in. It was the right thing to do, the only logical thing to do for Betsy. She deserved to enjoy the rest of her life without having the demands of Butterworth Wines hanging around her neck. As her sight failed, she'd need life to become as straight forward as possible. I understood that. And as for Jensen having a change of heart; I'd seen the way his face came alive when he talked about his work. He wasn't ready to settle for the good life in the country yet.

From the depths of my disappointment I managed to smile as I spoke. 'I'm very happy for you both and I'll support you whatever you decide to do.'

My phone beeped suddenly and Jensen's name flashed across the screen. I said goodbye to the ladies and opened his message:

Meet me outside Leicester Square tube station in fifteen minutes. J xx

With a nervous flutter in my stomach, I gathered my things and left the café. Had he been offered the job? And where would that leave Butterworth Wines, and me? And what about *him* and me? The quicker I found out the better . . .

I was walking behind a crowd of Italian students when I saw him and a rush of affection welled up inside me. He was leaning back against the wall by the circular red underground sign, hands thrust deep in his jacket pockets, scanning the stream of pedestrians left and right as they approached him. I care for this man, I thought. He'd got under my skin in a hundred different ways: the love he showed Betsy, his kindness towards me, the sweet things he'd said about the baby, even the passion with which he'd described his job. All these things added up to one special man and I hoped – regardless of what it would mean for me – with all my heart that he'd heard what he'd wanted to hear in the boardroom today.

He spotted me and his face broke into that wide friendly smile I'd come to treasure. He pushed through the students and grabbed hold of me, lifting me on to my tiptoes, pressing his cheek to mine and rocking me side to side.

'You superstar,' he laughed. 'Lottie, you're an absolute legend.'

I felt myself melt into his arms. The noise of the traffic fell away, the hustle and bustle of the people on one of the world's busiest streets disappeared. It was just him and me, wrapped up in each other. I closed my eyes and breathed him in, feeling his heart beating against mine.

'You should probably put me down,' I said.

'Oh crikey!' He lowered me immediately and looked down at my tummy. 'Have I squashed the lemon?'

An elderly man with a tiny white poodle under his arm did a double take as he walked by and we both burst out laughing.

I shook my head. 'Not at all. And it's the size of a pomegranate now; lemons are so last week.'

We grinned at each other for a few seconds, enjoying each other's company.

'You were fantastic on the radio, so calm and confident.' His eyes danced with pride. 'And when you put that dickhead Devine in his place, I spat out my coffee on my desk.'

We both laughed. Someone shouted at us to get a room and we stepped out of the flow of humans towards the wall.

'It was a risk,' I admitted, pulling a face. 'If he'd said he preferred the French wine, it could have ended very differently indeed.'

He shook his head. 'I loved the fact that you were so confident that he'd prefer ours. I had every faith you'd pull it off.'

'Thanks,' I said. 'But your granddad's wine is pretty amazing, it was that *I'd* got my faith in.'

'And all that stuff you said about supporting the growth of the wine industry and exporting Granddad's products to China,' he marvelled. 'He'd have been chuffed.'

I suppressed a sigh. 'There are no shortage of opportunities.'

'You'll be a heroine when you get back to Fernfield. I've already spoken to Gran and Aunt Marjorie; they couldn't say enough good things about you.'

A look of discomfort passed across his face and I guessed they'd also told him their bungalow news. I didn't want to think about that now. I shook the thought from my head and looked at him, daring myself to kiss away his anxious expression with a feather-light kiss to his cheek.

'Those two are adorable. Now let's talk about you.' I took a step closer and held his hand. 'How did you get on?'

His eyes flashed with excitement.

'We've chosen a contractor from the sealed bids, so we can push the button on the water resilience project. All systems go, as they say. Everyone is thrilled.'

Of course they were; I mustered up a smile. 'Does that mean you've been offered that promotion?'

His eyes darted away and he scratched his nose before answering.

'Yep. Managing director of the Cape Town office. They want a decision after the weekend.'

'Jensen, that's fantastic!' I threw my arms round his neck and hugged him tight. 'Congratulations!'

'Even though it had been implied, I can't believe my boss has actually followed through with it,' he said in such a calm tone he could have been talking about a new stapler rather than a fancy new job.

I peered into his eyes. 'Why don't I get the impression that you're over the moon about it?'

He blew out a long breath. 'They want me out there on the first of October.'

I stiffened. 'That's the date of my next scan.'

He looked at the floor. 'I know. The date was already in my diary. I was hoping to come with you.'

My stomach looped the loop; that was just like him to be organized. I'd be twenty-one weeks' pregnant by then. The thought of him being so far away filled me with sadness, but I wasn't going to let it show. This was his moment to shine, the moment he'd been working so hard towards.

'You can be ready to leave by then, can't you?'

'Well, I suppose.' He looked at me sadly. 'Although I won't be able to help with the harvest.'

'Don't worry about that,' I said brightly. 'We can find someone else to take your place.'

'Oh.' His body seemed to slump a little. 'Of course you can.'

'But we'll miss you. Especially me. I'll miss you a lot.'

I glanced at my watch. I'd been planning on asking him whether he'd got time to go for a drink somewhere, but now it seemed better to leave as soon as possible; I didn't think I could keep up my 'I'm so delighted for you' act for too much longer.

'Do you have to go?' he asked, brushing the hair from my face with his fingertip.

I felt my breath quicken as the urge to fold myself into his arms grew stronger and stronger. My head was whirling with all the things I wanted to say but didn't dare. It wasn't fair to say anything that might change his mind, however much I wanted him to turn down the job.

'There's a train in forty minutes,' I said. 'If I leave now, I won't have to rush.'

'I'm not ready to say goodbye,' he said, his blue eyes holding mine.

I swallowed, forcing back the ball of emotion in my throat. 'Me neither.'

'Then stay.' The pad of his thumb stroked my cheek. 'Stay the night with me.'

It was all I needed to hear.

I answered by grabbing hold of his hand, leading him to the kerb and flagging down an oncoming taxi.

'Where to, love?' called the cabbie.

I laughed and climbed into the back. 'His place.'

'It's very neat,' I said, choosing my words with care as Jensen let me into his flat on the top floor of a modern apartment block in Farringdon. 'And minimalist.'

'You can be honest,' he said, dumping his keys in a glass bowl on a glass console table in the hall. He showed me into an open-plan kitchen and living area and gestured for me to sit down. 'I know it's a bit boring. My previous girlfriend was a fan of owls: pottery owls, stuffed owls, candles, pictures, cushions in the shape of owls ... I moved into this place on my own after we split up and relished being clutter-free. It's become a habit.'

He put the kettle on to make tea while I kicked off my shoes, sat down on the sofa and tucked my feet underneath me.

'I know something you could do to make it less boring.'

'Oh?'

I patted the cushion next to me. 'Come over here and I'll show you.'

He didn't need asking twice . . .

It was a perfect evening filled with laughter and, on my part at least, the first sparks of love. Jensen was the perfect gentleman, insisting on making up a bed for me in the spare room while we waited for our Chinese food to arrive later that night. (Despite my huge sausage and mash lunch, the adrenalin-filled day had made me ravenous.) We kissed and talked and held each other as we watched night fall across London. The conversation was light and easy and we swapped funny stories about our childhoods and our dating disasters, talked about our first gigs, our first kisses, favourite films . . . each of us building a picture of the other. I knew I'd remember this night for the rest of my life.

By eleven o'clock my eyelids were fluttering with sleepiness. Jensen and I were curled up together on the sofa, my cheek nestled into his chest, his hand resting casually on my hip. Jason Mraz was crooning a love song to us from the sound system and the night had become very mellow.

'You know,' Jensen began, his voice barely more than a whisper, 'if you didn't want me to accept this new job, I'd turn it down.'

I sat up, shocked. 'I'd never put you in that position; I'm not going to be the one to keep you from achieving your goals.'

He twirled a lock of my hair through his fingers and took a deep breath. 'There's something I haven't mentioned yet. I wouldn't be entitled to any leave for six months, other than a couple of days at Christmas. It's part of the deal and non-negotiable. By the time I'd be able to come back, you'll have had the baby.'

A pang of sadness hit me and I nodded in agreement, not daring to speak. It was on the tip of my tongue to tell him how I felt about him, that I cared about him more deeply than I'd ever done for anyone else, that in a perfect world I'd like him to be there at my side holding my hand at the moment when this baby made its way into the world. That the thought of not seeing him for so long was too awful to contemplate. But I couldn't do that to him. I remembered Dad's words only a couple of hours or so ago, how he'd felt guilty for holding me back. I didn't want that same burden. If Jensen wanted to go, he should go. He deserved this promotion and there'd be no pressure from me either way.

'Lottie, I know it's early days, you and me, and maybe you'll think I'm crazy to be even thinking this far ahead,' he hesitated and took my hand, bringing it to his lips, 'but I'd been planning to say that if you needed anyone around, you know, when the baby comes, I can be there. I'd *like* to be there.'

I stared at him. 'What exactly are you offering?'

'To take you to hospital, carry your bag, keep your spirits up.' He grinned bashfully. 'And be nothing like a second doctor at all. But only if you thought it was appropriate and there was no one else you'd rather have at your side.'

'There is no one else.' My throat burned with the effort of holding back a sob. 'And if circumstances were different, I'd love you to be there in the labour suite mopping my brow and reminding me to breathe and closing your ears when I swear. But it would mean turning down the Cape Town job and I won't let you do that for me.'

He tucked a lock of hair behind my ear, his fingers grazing my cheek. 'If I'm going to be part of your life, and the baby's, I'd like to be there from the beginning.'

'Even though it's not yours?'

He shook his head, laughing softly. 'Even though. I've told you that before and I meant it; it doesn't matter to me. If your ex was still on the scene wanting to play the father role, I might hesitate to be involved. But he isn't.' Jensen shrugged. 'To be honest, I'm quite excited about it. What do you say?'

My heart skipped a beat; I wasn't sure what I'd done to deserve this man, but whatever it was I was grateful for it. 'How about I sleep on it?'

'Sure.' He slipped his arm around me and brought his lips to mine, kissing me with such tenderness that I could no longer hold back the tears. My hands wove through his hair and I felt his desire as I pressed my body against his.

'In fact,' I said, when we came up for air, 'I think I'm ready for bed now.'

I wasn't talking about the spare room.

Chapter 29

I was disorientated for a second when I awoke the next morning. And then a shimmer of happiness spread through me: I was *chez* Butterworth, in Jensen's bed. Judging by the humming coming from the kitchen, he was feeling pretty pleased with himself too. I reached across to the bedside table and drank most of a glass of water; my mouth was dry and tingly from the Chinese food last night. The bedroom blinds were still closed but a shaft of light pierced the semi-darkness and landed on the ring Jensen had given me yesterday. The diamantés twinkled and the central green stone glowed beautifully. I slipped the ring on to my finger and rolled on to my back to look at it. I knew it was only make-believe, but for a moment I allowed my mind to wander and imagine what it would be like to wake up like this every day.

My heart swelled at the thought. Harvey had left such an unpleasant taste in my mouth that I'd assumed I'd be put off men for years. But there had been something about Jensen's manner that had attracted me the first time I saw him. He was one of the loveliest men I'd ever met, he was kind and thoughtful, funny and clever and – I smiled to myself at the memory – a very generous lover. My mum would have adored him. He'd been there for me when I'd needed a friend over the last few months and he had come to mean so much more than that. Maybe he was the one: the partner with whom I could create the same loving relationship as my parents had had.

Except that I had to let him go . . .

The bedroom door opened silently and Jensen, wearing only boxer shorts, crept in carrying a tray. My heart jolted at the sight of him.

His face lit up with a smile when he saw I was awake. 'Good morning, beautiful!'

'Don't know about that.' I smiled back and covered my left hand with my right, feeling silly that he'd caught me admiring the ring. 'I've probably got panda eyes and hair like a bird's nest.'

'If you're trying to put me off you, it's not working.'

He kissed me firmly on the lips before setting the tray on my lap. My scalp prickled with nerves; he was nearer the mark than he knew. After our cosy conversations last night, the things I was going to say this morning weren't going to be easy.

'How are you feeling?' he asked, perching on the bed beside me.

I bit my lip and cast my eyes down to the ring on my finger. 'Awful, I'd been planning on waiting until our wedding night, to, you know . . .'

He shot me such a worried look that I couldn't hold back a giggle. 'Your face!'

'You minx,' he tutted. 'Now, ideally I'd have brought you a really nice tea tray with flowers and fresh croissants but I was worried about you waking up and finding the flat deserted, so I've improvised.'

My insides went wobbly when I saw what he'd done. He'd made tea in a proper pot, put milk in a jug and found two matching mugs. But the *pièce de résistance* was a rose he must have made himself from twisted silver foil.

I picked up the flower and twirled it round. 'It's perfect.'

Blind to my wobbly lip, Jensen continued, 'I haven't got much in to eat, I'm afraid. I thought we could go and get breakfast somewhere. Or brunch, if we don't make it until later. So in the meantime, it was either a dish of leftover noodles or these . . .'

He held up the two fortune cookies which had been tucked into our Chinese takeaway last night and swapped one for the silver rose in my hand. 'Open yours while I pour the tea.'

The shiny wrapper crinkled as I turned it over in my palm. Jensen lifted the teapot lid, a frown of concentration on his face as he stirred the contents before pouring us both a mugful.

It was so lovely. *He* was so lovely. But I'd lain awake and watched him sleep for hours last night and I'd come to a decision. My stomach twisted; this was so hard.

'Jensen,' I began hesitantly.

He held out my tea. 'Hurry up and read what your cookie says, then you can take this mug off me.'

Reluctantly, I tore open the wrapper, broke the little horseshoe-shaped biscuit in half and unfurled the slip of paper inside.

'What does it say?'

I swallowed, not daring myself to speak. If I'd needed a sign that I'd made the right decision, this was it. The motto in my cookie couldn't have been clearer.

There is no greater pleasure than seeing your loved ones prosper.

I held it up for him to read.

'True,' he said with a grin. He handed me my mug 'Now let me read mine.'

But before he'd even picked up his fortune cookie I set my mug down and took hold of his hands.

'Promise me something.'

He blinked at me. 'What is it?'

'Just promise.'

He shrugged and gave a soft laugh. 'Sure, fire away.'

I took in a deep breath. 'I want you to take this job in Cape Town.'

'But Lottie, that would mean not seeing each other until next April?' he said, frowning.

I nodded and with a huge amount of will-power managed to blink away the tears. 'But it would also mean you taking the promotion you deserve. I don't want to be the one who stands in your way.'

His eyes shifted sideways to the spot in the bed he'd vacated less than fifteen minutes ago. 'What's changed?'

I shook my head. 'Nothing. If anything I love . . .' The word stuck in my throat, I was setting him free, the last thing I should be telling him is that I thought I loved him. 'I've loved the time we've spent together. But I want you to go. Your gran has told you her plans?'

'To move in with Marjorie, yes, but—'

'So then you can go off and do amazing things with your water project, safe in the knowledge that she'll be okay.'

His lips twisted to one side and I could almost see the cogs whirring in his brain; he knew I was right.

I gripped his hands tighter. 'Don't you see? This is the perfect opportunity for you to take your career to the next level. And you must. Do it for me. Please?'

His troubled eyes met mine. 'And what about you, would you be okay too?'

'I'll be fine,' I said with a lightness my heart didn't feel. 'I'll work at the vineyard for as long as I'm needed and once the baby comes I'll take a few months off. Then in the autumn I'm hoping to start a course in viticulture.'

The university course I'd mentioned to Dad was at a college just outside Brighton which specialized in all things wine-related and, providing everything was well with Baby Allbright, maybe I'd be joining the student ranks as a distance learner in September.

'Sounds like you've got it all planned out,' he said. 'And us?'

He looked so crestfallen that I almost backtracked and begged him to stay after all, but that would be selfish.

'Jensen, I really like you; you make me very happy.' *Understatement of the century.* My throat was beginning to ache with the effort of not collapsing into tears. 'And I think you and I might have something special, but we're so new. If we're meant to be, then six months apart won't change anything. I know it means you won't be there when the baby is born, but we can Skype and FaceTime and talk every day.'

He took a deep breath. 'It probably sounds crazy to you, but I'm really looking forward to this baby. Talking every day won't be the same.'

'No,' I conceded, 'but the time will fly by.'

He stared at our hands entwined for a long moment before exhaling sadly. 'You're probably right. And it is a good opportunity.'

'There you go, then.' I kissed him gently. 'It's a plan. And when you're back in the spring we can spend some proper time together, the three of us, and you can decide whether the reality of being with a tiny baby and a frazzled new mother lives up to your expectations.'

He gave me a lopsided smile. 'Deal. So now what? Do you want to go for breakfast, or . . . ?'

My heart ached at the flatness of his voice; the sooner I got out of his sight the better. I made a show of looking at the time on my phone.

'I think I'll just head off, if that's okay,' I said bravely, pushing the duvet back, ready to get out of bed. 'I'm sure you've got a lot of organizing to do.'

'It can wait a bit longer. Come here.'

He folded me into his arms and held me tight. I clung on to him, imprinting the feel of his stubble and the smell of his skin and the warmth of his affection into my memory. This was going to be the longest six months of my life . . .

Three hours later, the train pulled into the station at Fernfield. I collected my belongings, which didn't amount to much – I'd even left my cool bag in Fiona Love's studio – and stepped on to the platform. The crisp air was a good few degrees cooler than London and I shivered as I headed for the car park.

There'd been a couple of messages on my phone, including one from Evie to say that she and Darren were bringing home Roni and Skipper, their rescue dogs, today and would I like to call round later to say hello. There hadn't been any message from Jensen.

I paid the parking fee and climbed into the van. Before I started the engine I called Betsy.

'It's Lottie,' I said brightly when she answered. 'I'm in the village and on my way home; do you need anything from the shops while I'm out?'

'Oh, there you are!' she said. 'We knocked at your cottage but there was no reply.'

'*We*? Is Marjorie with you?'

'No!' Her voice was brimming with excitement. 'You've got a visitor. A handsome *male* visitor.'

Jensen! I almost gasped with delight. He had obviously raced me back to declare he loved me and that he wasn't going to take the job in Cape Town because he couldn't bear us to be apart. To hell with my principles, I thought; this time I wasn't going to argue.

'How on earth did he manage to make it back from London before me?' I said, laughing. 'Tell him I'll be there as soon as I can.'

'Will do.' Betsy half-covered the mouthpiece and called out loudly, 'Harvey, dear, she's on her way.'

My blood turned to ice with terror and I ended the call without saying another word. My heart was pounding so hard I couldn't think. I gripped the steering wheel and forced myself to breathe.

What the hell was he doing here? What was I going to do? Evie. I'd call Evie. With fumbling fingers, I searched my phone for her number. She answered on the first ring.

'Hey, it's my celebrity sister!' she said gaily. It sounded as if she was driving; it was a bad line and there was a lot of noise in the background. 'Star of national radio and queen of English champagne. I'm honoured!'

Normally I'd correct her on the champagne thing and tell her that only French stuff was allowed to be called that, but wine terminology was the last thing on my mind.

'Harvey's come back. I've just got off the train and he's at the vineyard waiting for me.' The words tumbled out in a rush. 'He must have heard me on the radio yesterday, so he knows where I live. Oh my GOD! And that I'm pregnant.'

'Shit,' Evie gasped. 'If he knows all that, he's going to know you're engaged to be married too.'

A wave of nausea hit me, I could just imagine him listening in and getting more and more angry.

'But I'm not, not really!' My voice was trembling. I threw open the van door to get some fresh air, worried I might be sick.

'I know, sis, I spoke to Dad last night.' The line cracked for a moment. 'There, I've put you on hands-free so Darren can hear this as well.'

'Lottie, Evie told me what happened last time this thug came to visit.' Darren's voice was firm but calm. 'He's obviously dangerous; think of the baby.'

'*His* baby,' I yelped. 'I am so cross with myself. I should never have done that interview; I knew as soon as I mentioned being pregnant that it was a mistake.'

'Phone the police,' Evie ordered.

'Can't you and Darren come over?' I pleaded. 'There's safety in numbers; I'm sure he wouldn't try anything on with another man there. And maybe he just wants to talk.'

Darren and Evie both groaned.

'Oh, honey, I'm so sorry but we can't,' said Evie.

'We're on our way to Dover to collect the dogs,' Darren explained. 'Agnes organized a specialist animal transport company to bring them over on the ferry.'

'And we're nearly there – we can't get out of it now,' Evie added.

My heart sank. 'No, of course not.'

'Just don't go back to the vineyard,' Evie suggested.

I blew out a breath. 'Harvey's expecting me any minute, he might get suspicious if I don't arrive and I can't leave Betsy to deal with him alone.'

'The police then,' Evie said firmly. 'Call them now and keep me posted. I love you.'

I ended the call and started the engine. There was no time to call the police, besides it wasn't as though it was an emergency, just an unpleasant situation. Harvey might be an idiot, but he'd never hurt his own child, would he? I shuddered and gave myself a shake. Of course not. Anyway, by the time they turned up, I could have sorted out the situation myself. Probably.

'Okay, little one, time to face the music,' I said bravely.

The sooner this was over, the better.

Chapter 30

By the time I turned into the driveway at Butterworth Wines, I was shaking like a leaf. The doors to the winery were closed and there were no cars in the yard. Even if I'd been planning on calling in reinforcements from the rest of the team, I wouldn't have been able to. Maybe I was being a bit foolhardy, but this was my mess and I was going to be the one to clear it up. Before getting out of the van, I slipped off Jensen's ring and shut it into the glove box.

Harvey might have been controlling and a little forthright in his views at times, I told myself firmly, as I made my way up the path towards Betsy's front door, but he had never been a violent man. Well, not until I'd left him unexpectedly with only a note to let him know why. Mind you, there was that time when he'd pulled my hair. Still, inside he was a good man, someone I'd loved and who'd loved me. He wouldn't lay a finger on a pregnant woman.

As I reached the front step, I touched my tummy soothingly in case the baby was feeling my anguish.

'We'll be fine, I promise,' I murmured under my breath and raised my hand to knock on the door.

Before my knuckles had even made contact, the door opened and Harvey stood in front of me.

My heart rattled with fear and instinctively I took a step back.

'Surprise, surprise,' he said with a wolfish smile. He leaned casually against the frame of the door, arms folded.

The blood drained from my head and for a moment I was worried I might faint. I reached a hand out to lean on the wall and inhaled sharply.

'There's no need to look so petrified,' he said.

'Isn't there?' My mouth was so dry I could scarcely get my words out. I rubbed my tongue over my teeth.

Ignoring my question, his eyes roamed down to my stomach. Even though the dress was loose fitting he knew my body well enough to notice the changes. The thought of that made me feel sick.

'There's a bit more of you than the last time I saw you,' he said in a dangerously low voice.

I took in his appearance properly. Ironically there was less of him. He looked like the old Harvey. His black hair was longer, like it had been when I'd first met him, and he'd lost a lot of the muscle that had built up on his neck, shoulders and arms, which had made him appear quite bullish. He looked much better for it.

'Yes, well, I don't have to have those awful breakfast shakes any more,' I said defiantly.

'Don't joke.' He leaned forward and his eyes glittered with anger.

I stumbled backwards, regretting my flippancy, and he caught hold of my wrist and grabbed me back.

'Let go!'

He released me and held his hands up. 'Just didn't want you to fall in your condition.'

'Lottie, dear! You're back!'

Behind Harvey, Betsy was making her way along the corridor, trailing her fingers along the wall to keep herself steady. 'Where are you? Let me see your lovely face. You were marvellous yesterday, absolutely marvellous. I can't wait for us to have a proper catch-up about it all. Do you know the phone and online orders have gone through the roof? We've even got a waiting list for this year's vintage.'

Which would be the last Butterworth vintage. I felt a sob forming in my throat as my emotions became too much for me to keep in. I pushed past Harvey and into Betsy's arms.

'I'm so pleased,' I said through my tears. 'I've been so happy here; you don't know what this place has done for me.'

'Oh, silly, the pleasure and the privilege is all ours.' Betsy patted my back and peered at me. 'Harvey has been telling me how you two met and about your lovely flat in London. Quite the romantic, isn't he? I must admit I was surprised when he turned up, but I'm very happy for you.' She lowered her voice. 'If that's what you want?'

'I . . . well, yes, I'm surprised too,' I said, wondering what sort of cock and bull story Harvey must have told her.

'I thought Lottie could give me a tour, Mrs Butterworth,' Harvey said as politely as a Boy Scout. 'Get some fresh air into her lungs after that train journey.'

'Of course, good idea.' Betsy looked disappointed at not having me to herself.

'Actually, I want to go and freshen up first,' I said. I pressed a kiss to her soft cheek. 'Perhaps we can catch up later with a cup of tea?'

Betsy and I arranged to have afternoon tea at three and Harvey and I set off across the yard to my cottage. I was all fingers and thumbs and after several attempts to unlock my front door, Harvey took the key from my hand.

I stood back, expecting him to open the door, but he twirled the keyring round on his finger and closed it into his palm. He nodded at my stomach.

'Due in February, then?'

I licked my lips, wondering whether I had the guts to lie and pretend it wasn't due for another six months, thereby automatically eliminating him as the father. But I couldn't do it; whatever the relationship was between us now, at the time we'd made this baby, we'd loved each other.

'That's right,' I said, summoning up all my bravado to look him in the eye. 'I conceived sometime in May.'

He raised an eyebrow. 'Who's the father?'

I was taken aback. 'You, of course! We didn't split up until June.'

He laughed meanly under his breath. 'There's no "of course" about it. I heard you on the radio yesterday, Lottie, boasting that you were engaged. I googled this Jensen Butterworth, he works for a firm near Tower Bridge. And I googled this place. A bit weird, isn't it, that as soon as you do the dirty on me, you get a job here and five minutes later you're engaged and expecting?' He placed himself between me and my front door. 'So this is what I think: you were seeing him behind my back in London and when you realized you were pregnant you ran. Bitch.'

A surge of anger propelled me towards him.

'It wasn't like that. It *isn't* like that,' I yelled at him furiously, trying to wrestle the key back out of his hands. 'I didn't meet Jensen until I started working here. This is your baby. I left you because you scared me. Like you're scaring me now. Please go. Leave me alone before I call the police.'

He stepped away from me and tossed the key to the ground. 'I'm sorry. I'm sorry. Don't call the police.'

I picked up the key, put it in the lock, turned it and, heart pounding, pushed inside, locking the door behind me.

He knocked on the door. 'We need to talk. Open the door.'

'What's left to say?' I shouted.

He can't touch me now. I repeated it over and over in my head as I poured myself a glass of water and gulped it down.

'I was taking steroids,' Harvey shouted from outside.

344

'The pressure to build muscle at that gym was huge. So I started taking pills. And they worked. Everyone commented on what good shape I was in. Even you.'

That was true. At least it had been at first. Then he went too far; he looked out of proportion, like a triangle.

'But what they don't tell you about steroids is the mood swings,' he said. His voice had calmed down now and I could tell he was leaning against the door. 'I'd get this red mist, this flood of anger, and my heart would speed up. The slightest thing would set me off. It was uncontrollable.'

It made sense. Our relationship had been much better before he'd started working at that gym. Not perfect, I accepted. I realized now that he had always had his own interests at heart; what I wanted had always come second. And I was worth more than that. I knew that now. It had taken Jensen's thoughtfulness to show me that there was a different way to be loved.

I moved closer to the door. 'And you've stopped taking them?'

'Yes.' I heard him exhale. 'I got into a fight. I was charged with assault and I lost my job. I've had a shit time, Lottie. But it was the wake-up call I needed.'

'And yet you stormed up here, fists clenched and accused me of sleeping with someone else behind your back?' I said archly, braver now there was a thick oak door between us.

'I learned my ex-girlfriend was pregnant and engaged to someone new. I learned that I might be about to be a father. And I found out all this from a radio show. How did you expect me to react? When exactly were you going to tell me?'

My stomach churned. I supposed he did have a right to be annoyed at least about the baby. But my private life was none of his business any more.

'I'm not engaged to Jensen; that was made up for the radio programme. Long story,' I added as he started to protest. 'And my dad was going to tell you about the baby once it was born, because I was frightened about how you'd react.'

He was quiet for such a long time, I wondered if he'd gone.

'That makes me feel very ashamed,' he said finally. 'Please open the door; I want to talk to you properly.'

'No, Harvey.'

'Please, just for five minutes, then I'll leave you in peace.'

I bit my lip. He did sound much more subdued now and if he stayed outside shouting, Betsy might hear him and get worried.

'Okay, but only for five minutes,' I said, against my better judgement. 'And I'll have my phone in my hand the whole time and if you even lay a finger on me, I'll call the police.'

'I won't, I promise.'

I unlocked the door. Harvey smiled grimly and stepped inside. 'Thank you.'

He walked closer and I retreated to the other side of the kitchen table, holding my phone where he could see it.

'So how are you?' he asked, wiping beads of sweat from his forehead. 'Is the pregnancy going okay, I mean?'

I nodded. 'I was ill to begin with, but now I'm full of beans again. I'm nineteen weeks so the baby is starting to get quite mobile.'

It was on the tip of my tongue to tell him that I had a scan coming up but I didn't want to risk him wanting to see the baby for himself. Not having Jensen there was going to feel bad enough, but having Harvey there in his place would have felt extra cruel.

'And you're looking forward to being a mum?'

I nodded warily. 'I am now. It took some getting used to, seeing as it was an accident.'

Harvey's lips twisted into a smirk.

'Actually, it wasn't a complete surprise to me.'

346

I frowned questioningly. 'How come?'

'I pierced the condoms a couple of times.'

I stared at him. 'You did what?'

He sniggered and I felt my anger rise again. 'I thought I'd better check you were working properly, seeing as your sister is barren.'

Shock snatched the air from my lungs.

'How dare you make those sort of decisions on behalf of someone else? There is nothing wrong with my sister,' I spat at him. 'And quite clearly, there is nothing wrong with me. You're insane.'

'Yeah, well, all's well that ends well,' he said as if bored by the conversation. 'You just said you're happy, so you win. Whereas I've moved into a squat and have had to get a dead-end job at a call centre because no one will employ me now I've got a criminal record.'

I shook my head in disbelief. What had I ever seen in him? He was looking at me, waiting for me to say something. I floundered around trying to think of something.

'At least you're off the steroids,' I said. 'Well done on that.'

'Anyway, blossom,' he made a point of looking around the cottage approvingly, 'you look like you've landed on your feet here so don't bother chasing me for child maintenance, or anything, because half of zero is zero. I'm skint.'

I stiffened. 'Don't call me blossom. My dad called my mum that, and hearing it come from you taints that memory I have of them together.'

He laughed cruelly. 'Yeah, I know that. Why do you think I called you that in the first place?'

I'd never told him that. I blinked at him. 'I don't follow you?'

He rolled his eyes. 'You posted a photo of your folks on Facebook once. Some soppy thing about wanting to find a man who loved you as much as your dad loved her. Someone to call you blossom and bring you flowers, all that shit.'

My head started to spin. 'That was years before I met you.'

'I know, I read everything you'd ever posted. And when I got to that bit I thought, you've hit the jackpot, mate, that's a guaranteed shortcut into her knickers.' He gave me an evil grin. 'I was right, wasn't I?'

'You're sick. I hate you. Get out!' I launched myself at him, punching his chest, but he was far too strong for me.

'Please,' I begged. 'Please leave us alone.'

'Us?' He barked with laughter. 'It isn't born yet. But okay, I'm going. And remember, I'm not paying for it, or having anything to do with it.'

'Can I have that in writing?' I swiped the tears from my face. 'Because I never want to set eyes on you again.'

He opened the door and hesitated in the doorway before pulling me roughly towards him.

'One last kiss for old times' sake, eh?'

'Don't you dare!' I gasped, struggling against him.

Before I could escape, he crushed his lips against mine. Our teeth clashed and I tried to scream as I tasted blood. But his hand was gripping the back of my head too tightly.

Finally, he ended the kiss and I staggered backwards, tears blinding my eyes. But he hadn't finished. With one hand squeezing my arm, he ran his other hand down over my breasts and circled my bump.

'I made that, remember,' he said, his eyes glinting.

The shock of such a violation sucked the air from my lungs. My mouth was open in horror but no sound could escape. With a slight shove he released me and ran lightly down the path.

My blood thundering in my ears, I collapsed against the door frame, and as my breathing began to steady, I became aware of a car parked outside Betsy's house, its engine still running.

Jensen.

It was Jensen. He'd come for me. Thank the Lord.

A sob rose in my throat. I wanted to run to him but my legs had turned to jelly. Instead, I stepped clear of my front door and waved wildly, tears coursing down my cheeks.

But to my horror, Jensen reversed the car, span it around and drove off. I caught a glimpse of his stony expression as he passed but he didn't even look my way.

I was devastated; presumably he'd driven all the way up from London to see me, only to witness what Harvey had just done. No wonder he had jumped to the wrong conclusion – who wouldn't?

I watched uselessly as he disappeared out of sight, passing Harvey on his way up the drive. With shaking hands, I dialled Jensen's number, but even though I knew he had a hands-free device in his car, he didn't answer. I tried again but this time he sent the call to voicemail. I rang a third time and this time pulled myself together enough to leave him a message.

'Please come back. What you saw was just Harvey being an idiot. Please come back and let me explain.'

I waited on the doorstep for ten minutes but Jensen didn't return. Eventually, my bones weary with exhaustion, I trailed back inside and shut the world out.

I could scarcely take it in. Everything about my relationship with Harvey had been fake: from stalking me on Facebook to pretending to take care of contraception. Even his body, courtesy of steroids, was fake.

And my shock pregnancy – it wasn't unplanned at all; at least not as far as Harvey was concerned. How dare he play Russian roulette with my body? I would never forgive him for this, never. If I had needed further convincing that I didn't want Harvey to have any part in my baby's life, this would have been more than enough to do it. But Jensen wasn't to know that. He'd been honest with me: if my ex was on the scene, he'd back away. And that was exactly what he'd done. And if he wouldn't take my calls, he'd never know the truth. I'd just have to hope that he'd listen to the message I'd left for him and trust me.

It was only early afternoon and the day had gone on far too long for my liking. I headed for my bed and pulled the covers over me.

Stop the world, someone, I want to get off.

Chapter 31

For the next few days I stumbled around like a zombie. I told everyone who'd listen that I'd had an unwanted visit from my ex-boyfriend but that he was now out of my life for good in the vain hope that it would somehow get back to Jensen. But he didn't get in touch and after leaving him five messages, I resigned myself to the fact that he wasn't going to. I put our pretend engagement ring in a drawer and tried to forget how golden that day in London had been from start to finish.

Betsy had no knowledge of her grandson's fleeting visit on Saturday and wasn't aware of how things had spiralled and subsequently plummeted between us and there didn't seem any point in involving her in the whole sorry tale. She informed me on Monday morning that he would soon be heading off to South Africa to take on an exciting new role and wouldn't be back for a while. She passed on his regards and good-luck wishes with the baby, at which point her eyes had filled with tears and she'd admitted that although she couldn't have been more proud she'd miss him terribly.

You and me both, I'd thought desolately.

The only bright spot had been on Sunday, the day after Harvey had paid me a visit, when Darren and Evie had called in while they were out walking their new dogs. The two English Setters had made themselves at home straight away and it had warmed my heart to see my sister and brother-in-law so happy. And while Starsky sniffed warily

351

around both of the bigger dogs, Darren told me that they'd made an appointment with an adoption agency and that, fingers crossed, they'd soon be on the waiting list for a child of their own. It seemed that they had got their happy ending after all and I was so pleased for them that I buried my face in Evie's shoulder and we'd both cried. I'd already told her what Harvey had said and done, and both of them had been furious and horrified on my behalf, agreeing that I should try to put him out of my mind for good.

It would be a long time before I could forget or forgive his actions, but I was determined not to let him mar the baby's future – or mine, for that matter. I could manage perfectly well on my own if I had to. And thanks to Harvey, it looked as if I might. Before they left, Evie offered to come to my next scan with me. She also suggested I put everything I wanted to say to Jensen in a letter, that way at least he'd know how I felt. And deciding that I'd got nothing to lose, I'd done just that.

I wrote that I'd heard he'd taken the promotion and that I was happy for him and wished him every success. I explained that the things Harvey told me had cast a huge question mark over our relationship. But one thing was certain: I never wanted to see him again as long as I lived. And I tried to express how much Jensen meant to me . . .

You said that me having another man's baby didn't matter to you as long as that man isn't in my life. I promise you he isn't, but I understand if you feel differently now. But for me, nothing has changed. You have captured my heart in a way that no one else has ever done. I shall be counting down the months and weeks until you come home, and will pray with all my strength that you feel the same way.

Love always,
Lottie xxx

So Jensen knew how I felt and knew where to find me and yet by Friday afternoon, a week after the radio show, I still hadn't heard a word from him. The only possible conclusion was that I'd misread the signs. So even though I still felt as if I'd been run over by the Coca-Cola Christmas truck, I knew I had to pull myself together. The grapes were almost ready to be harvested; there were a million and one things to be done and no time to be moping around feeling sorry for myself.

Elsewhere, a celebratory mood still hovered over the vineyard following our triumph on the radio show and that, coupled with the promise of a decent harvest, meant that I couldn't keep my lovely volunteers away and everyone had put in extra hours all week.

Roger, who must have bolted for the school gates as soon as the afternoon bell had gone, had taken Godfrey and Pippa straight out amongst the vines. They'd each got refractometers and notebooks and were taking readings from all four corners of the vineyard. Matt and Clare, meanwhile, were having a sort-out in the winery and hosing down the tanks ready for the pressing of the grapes – whenever that might be.

When to harvest the crop was keeping me awake almost as much as my heartache over the Jensen/Harvey fiasco. And despite the fact that all the others had been here longer than me, no one else seemed to want to make the decision for me. The consensus was that the longer we could leave the grapes on the vine, the sweeter and juicier they'd be. But we were almost into October. The evenings were getting cooler and darker and the dew was staying on the grapes longer in the mornings. We couldn't pick the crop when it was wet or damp, picking in the dark wasn't ideal and a sudden run of bad weather could scupper us completely. I was hoping the readings we took today would help me at least schedule in the first day of harvesting.

I put my coat on, made up a tray of tea and biscuits, and trudged down the path to take it to the team in the vineyard.

A strong breeze had picked up since this morning and as I walked past the line of tall slim conifers at the edge, a layer of amber vine leaves at my feet, I heard the unmistakable creak of branches. I looked up to see that the third tree along was looking decidedly brown and a large section of it had broken off from the trunk and was hanging at a precarious angle. I made a mental note to call Adam to come and remove the tree as soon as he could. The last thing we needed was that falling on top of someone.

I carried on, setting the tray down on the bench in the centre of the vineyard and shouted, 'Tea time!'

Roger appeared first, wearing a waterproof jacket and walking boots. He strode towards me, tapping his notebook.

'There's a big variation within the Pinot Meunier vines,' he said, pointing out the range of numbers written on the page. 'The top corner has definitely benefited from being sheltered by the wall; the readings are much higher there than, say, the lower section, over here.' He wafted an arm towards the middle of the vines.

I studied the readings while he spooned sugar into a mug of tea.

'This is my favourite time of year at the vineyard,' said Pippa, arriving next, full of smiles. Her hair was tousled from the wind, her cheeks were rosy and with her thigh-length cable-knit jumper over a long floral skirt and tan ankle boots, she looked like a model for Burberry. 'Ooh, tea; excellent.'

She helped herself and handed me the readings she'd taken from the Pinot Noir. I scanned the numbers.

'Not bad, are they?' she said, dunking a biscuit. 'I'm sure we harvested at lower sugar levels than those last year?'

I nodded. 'So that gives us a starting point; we pick the Pinot Noir before the Pinot Meunier.'

Godfrey, who'd been working at the very bottom of the vineyard, came into view, wheezing uphill towards us from the lowest parcel of Chardonnay vines. Wisps of his white hair were escaping from under his hat just above his ears and his face was pink from the wind.

I had his tea ready to hand him by the time he reached us. 'I'd say the Chardonnay could do with another week,' he said breathlessly. 'A bit more sunshine would make all the difference.'

'If we get any more sun,' said Roger. He pulled at the zip at the front of his jacket, frowning at the sky, which was looking as grey as my mood this afternoon. 'This weather is getting a bit too cool for my liking.'

I plucked a red grape off the nearest vine, popped it into my mouth and chewed thoughtfully. The taste was sharp but definitely sweeter than it had been only a week ago. 'Okay, I'll go and look at the long-range weather forecast and if it looks dry enough, how about we plan to start picking from next Monday at noon?'

'The first of October,' Godfrey nodded. 'Sounds like the perfect day to me.'

My heart sank. It was the day of my scan, which was okay because the appointment was early morning, I could be there and back before harvest got underway. But it was also the day Jensen was due to start his new job. For all I knew, he might have already arrived in Cape Town to sort out accommodation and get organized for his new life. Which was what I'd wanted him to do, but I'd thought then that we'd have a chance at a long-distance relationship. Now all I had from him was distance.

Was it really only a week since we'd had such fun over lunch together, him slipping a ring on to my finger and the other diners smiling and wishing us well? And then later on, that perfect night spent in his arms . . .

Pippa clapped her hands, bringing me crashing back to earth. 'How exciting! I can't wait! Harvest time is better than sex. Actually, no it's not. Oh, that reminds me—' She stopped mid-sentence and blushed. We all waited.

'Reminds you what?' said Roger bluntly.

She shook her head timidly. 'Nothing.'

'I'm excited too, Pippa,' said Godfrey fondly.

'Moving on . . .' Roger tutted impatiently and then rubbed his hands together. 'Reinforcements. That's the key to smooth operations. We'll need to rally the troops asap.'

'Righto.' Godfrey slurped the last of his tea. 'I'll email round the regulars, Matt can put up a poster in the pub and I'll post a notice on the village website.'

'Brilliant. Thanks, everyone,' I said, mustering a smile as I collected in the mugs and picked up the tray. 'I think I'll go and run our plan by Sidney and see what he makes of our latest readings.'

They breathed a collective sigh of relief, glad to be let off the hook as far as the final decision was concerned. I started back towards the winery and Pippa caught me up, insisting on taking the tray out of my hands.

'I think Clare's son Ben might be interested in helping with the harvest,' she said coyly. 'And he's very strong.'

'Is he still on leave?'

She twirled a lock of hair around her fingers and nodded. 'For another week.'

'Great, the more the merrier; I'll mention it to Clare.'

She giggled. 'It's okay, I'm seeing him tonight; I'll ask him.'

'Fabulous.' I grinned at her, suddenly understanding her 'harvest is better than sex' comment. 'Good for you, Pippa. It's lovely to see you so happy.'

'It's all down to you.' She smiled shyly. 'Your attitude has inspired me.'

'Me?' My current attitude wavered between misery, defeat and despair. 'You're too generous.'

'You don't let anything stand in your way or get you down,' Pippa continued firmly. 'You know what you want and you go for it. You should be proud of yourself.'

Her words of praise were incredibly well timed and when we parted in the yard there was a spring in my step as I unlocked my cottage door, thinking that maybe I wasn't such a failure after all.

I sent Sidney a message asking if he was free for a chat and seconds later we were facing each other on Skype via our screens. He looked relaxed and tanned in a short-sleeved shirt. I, on the other hand, having just come in from a windy Derbyshire hillside, looked like I'd spent the night in a hedge.

'Harvest has already started here,' he said, uncorking a plain bottle and pouring some pale juice into a glass. 'Our Chardonnay Cuvée. Cheers!' His bright eyes crinkled at the corners as he smiled and held his glass up to the screen. 'Delicious. How is your crop doing?'

He listened carefully, stroking his moustache as I mentioned the readings the team had taken from various rows and told him of our plan to start picking on Monday.

'You're doing great, Lottie, but ideally you need another warm dry week,' he said, leaning back in his chair. 'Is that likely?'

I glanced through the window of my cottage. There was a blanket of unbroken cloud overhead. When the wind dropped it wasn't too cold, and there'd been little or no rain for a few days so the ground was dry.

'Checking out the long-range forecast is my next job,' I said, rubbing a hand over my tummy distractedly. I didn't know if it was coincidence or not but the baby had been very active since Harvey's visit and it had crossed my mind several times that maybe I'd managed to transmit my anxiety and the baby was unsettled too. 'What would Ted do, do you reckon?'

'Ted was a risk taker,' said Sidney. 'He'd leave harvesting until the last possible moment. What is your gut saying?'

'I don't know.' I nibbled my lip. 'I don't feel experienced enough to take risks. On the other hand, if we're going to give a still wine a shot, the riper the better.'

'If you can wait until next Friday, I should be able to get a flight over and help you out.'

I could have wept with relief. 'That would be amazing! But *please*, let your family know this time.'

Our laughter was interrupted by an urgent rapping at the door immediately followed by Matt bursting in, out of breath.

'Sorry to barge in, boss.' He raised a hand in greeting to Sidney on my laptop. 'There's just been an urgent weather warning on the radio. Storm Sandra is on its way across from Siberia.'

Panic gripped my lungs like a vice. 'How bad?'

'Gale force winds, torrential rain, the lot,' he said gravely. 'According to the weather man, it should hit Derbyshire late on Monday.'

I groaned. 'This is my worst nightmare. Now what am I going to do?'

'Hey, don't panic, you're not on your own, you know.' Matt put an arm roughly around my shoulders and squeezed me to him.

'Thank you,' I mumbled, peeling my face from his stubbly jaw.

Sidney moved closer to his computer so that his face filled the screen. 'Well, that's taken the decision out of your hands. You've got Saturday, Sunday and Monday to get the grapes in. Whatever's left on the vines after then will probably be destroyed.'

It looked as if my scan would have to be delayed; I'd been so looking forward to seeing the baby again, but it couldn't be helped.

I nodded numbly. 'Three days.'

'Lottie, listen to me,' Sidney's voice had taken on an urgent tone, 'the priority is the grapes. Pick them in as soon as possible, get everything in place today and start tomorrow.'

'Understood. I'll organize as many pickers as I can lay my hands on,' I said. 'The quadbike has just come back from being serviced and we've had a delivery of new plastic crates.

I'll have to buy up Fernfield's entire stock of secateurs, but that's easily arranged.'

'Good stuff.' Sidney gave me an encouraging smile. 'Matt?'

'Yes, mate?' Matt leaned closer.

'I was hoping to come and oversee the pressing for you, but it's unlikely I'll make it on time now. Do you think you can handle it alone?'

He puffed out his chest. 'I can run that press blindfolded. So can Clare. We'll manage just fine.'

'Just one last thing, Lottie: has Betsy mentioned anything about—'

The screen went black. He'd gone. Mentioned what? I wondered. But the internet had gone down again and I had no time to waste fiddling with the connection now. It was Butterworth Wines versus Storm Sandra and this was a battle I had no intention of losing.

It was harvest time.

Chapter 32

The next morning dawned bright and clear, if a little chilly. The moon had been muffled behind a thick layer of cloud last night, which had kept the temperatures mild and the dew to a minimum. I was just grateful that Storm Sandra hadn't gathered any extra speed overnight.

'Welcome to Butterworth Wines, everyone, and thank you so much for coming.' I stood at the top of the south-facing slope with the gate behind me where the assembled crowd could all see me. Starsky was wandering amongst them hopefully, trying to sniff out any dog owners on the off chance they might harbour treats in their pockets. He was having reasonable success and looked like he was having a far more relaxing time than me. 'It's lovely to have so many victims – I mean *volunteers* – here to help us today.'

My little joke raised a laugh as I'd hoped it would. I needed them to enjoy themselves because that way they might not notice how back-breaking picking grapes was.

'Today we'll be harvesting Pinot Noir, which is one of our red varieties. If you'd all like to turn around, Roger will demonstrate how we'd like the bunches to be picked.'

The group did as they were told, and while Roger ran through the instructions about where to snip, and which grapes to leave on the vine, Clare and I handed out secateurs and gardening gloves.

My team had risen to the challenge as usual and had been hard at it preparing the groundwork since eight this morning. Pippa had a morning shift at the library but would be heading down here with Ben as soon as she'd checked on her dog and changed into her grape-picking clothes. Between us, we'd assembled twenty pickers, including Olivia Channing and her girlfriend Sazzle who'd come up at the crack of dawn this morning and were staying in Betsy's spare room, five people who'd come to our open day in July, some from the library, a couple from Clare's blanket committee, Issy the midwife's mum and her best friend and several members of the darts team from Matt's pub.

When Roger was happy that he'd drilled the instructions into everyone's heads, I cleared my throat to speak.

'Before we start,' I said, 'I just want to introduce you to Olivia.'

Olivia dutifully put up her hand.

'She's going to be live tweeting today's harvest on behalf of the English Wine Board, so if anyone is a fugitive or a felon or would just rather not be in the photos, speak up.' I meant it jokingly but two of the darts team looked a bit shifty, so I moved swiftly on, dividing the group into two and nominating Roger and Godfrey as team leaders.

'Any questions see either myself or one of the Butterworth team,' I said, clapping my hands together. 'Good luck, everyone. Harvest 2018 is officially on!'

'Action stations!' Roger yelled. 'My team, follow me to the low slopes.'

Everyone whooped and cheered, and within seconds the crowd had dispersed.

'Any jobs for an old codger like me?' The gruff voice from behind me made my breath catch in my throat. It couldn't be . . . I whirled around and gasped.

'Dad!' I froze, unable to believe what I was seeing. 'Oh my God, Dad! What on earth . . . ?'

He opened his arms and I didn't need asking twice. I buried my face in his jumper and bit back tears, determined to show him how strong I was being.

'Your sister told us you've been having a rough time of it, love, so I thought it was time I came home and gave my little girl some support.'

I swallowed the lump in my throat. 'It certainly hasn't been boring, that's for sure.'

The hug went on for ages. He couldn't take his eyes off my baby bump and I couldn't get over how well he looked. I couldn't remember the last time I'd seen him so relaxed and happy.

'Hey,' he said finally, 'as I came down the path I could hear a young woman giving orders and motivating her team. Imagine my delight when I realized it was you. I'm very proud of you, love, very proud indeed. Seems like you've taken to this job like a duck to water.'

'I do love it,' I said, beaming. I had done well, I thought proudly; I'd taken the challenges that the vineyard had thrown at me in my stride, coped with an unexpected pregnancy and dispatched an unwelcome ex-boyfriend. Okay, so maybe my love life wasn't smooth sailing, but at least my career seemed to have taken off at last.

'But when did you get here? And how?' I was bewildered; I'd only spoken to him a couple of days ago and he'd definitely been in Germany then.

'Agnes and I flew back this morning. Darren and Evie picked us up from the airport.'

I nodded. 'Ah, so that was why Evie sounded so mysterious and giggly on the phone last night.'

Darren had volunteered to help tomorrow and Evie had put her name down for Monday, both pleading other commitments today. Another thought occurred to me.

'So Agnes is here?'

Dad nodded, the smile on his face a mix of pride and

nerves. 'Would you like to meet her? She's waiting in the winery with a huge lad who looks like a pirate.'

'That's Matt,' I laughed. 'We'd better get back; he'll have made her taste half a dozen wines by now.'

I checked round quickly to make sure I wasn't needed and headed to the yard, arm in arm with Dad, sneaking glances at him as we walked. I felt like pinching myself to check I wasn't dreaming; it was so good to see him. He was completely recovered from his injuries now and had, he told me, been keeping himself busy making new dog runs for Agnes's dog rescue operation. There was no mention of continuing his European tour and it was obvious he'd found what he was looking for in Germany.

Agnes was leaning on the door frame and, as predicted, she had a glass of sparkling wine in her hand. She was wearing multicoloured harem trousers, a leather biker jacket and Crocs and stood up straight when she spotted us. Matt was nowhere to be seen, but I could hear him singing and clattering about in the winery.

'Agnes,' said Dad reverently, 'may I introduce you to my youngest daughter, Lottie.'

Agnes smiled. 'Hallo, Lottie.'

My stomach flipped as I smiled back; this was the lady who'd captured my dad's heart. The only woman he'd shown an interest in since Mum died. I knew she must be special.

'It's lovely to meet you face to face, Agnes.' I'd seen her via Skype and FaceTime, but a digital image was a poor substitute for the real thing. 'I love your jacket.'

She set the hardly touched glass down on the ground with a trembling hand. Bless her, she was just as nervous as I was.

'It is very good to meet you too.' Her English was perfect even if her German accent made her sound stiff. She edged towards me with her hand outstretched.

Her eyes slid sideways to Dad's and he gave her an

encouraging smile and my heart twisted with happiness for them both. Ignoring her hand, I hugged her warmly.

'Thank you.' I kissed her cheek, hoping I hadn't overstepped some strict code of German etiquette.

She looked puzzled. 'For what?'

'For making my dad so happy.'

Dad slipped a casual arm around her waist and Agnes laughed shyly. 'I was so nervous that you would be angry at me for taking your father away from you.'

And then an odd thing happened. I got the peculiar feeling that someone was at my shoulder and I could feel their warm breath on the back of my neck. Far from being creepy, it was a lovely sensation and I knew without doubt that Mum was giving her blessing.

I shook my head and felt a peace that I hadn't felt in days.

'I don't feel like that at all,' I said, smiling at them both. 'In fact, I'd go as far as to say you've actually brought him back.'

Agnes's gaze held mine. 'Your mother did a wonderful job with her daughters.'

'Ahem,' said Dad, pretending to be insulted. 'It's hard work being a dad too.'

I hugged him. 'But you rose to the challenge, just like you will when you're a granddad.'

He rocked forward and back on his heels, looking smug. 'I suppose I will.'

'And talking of hard work,' Agnes thrust her shoulders back, 'we're not here to party. Give us a job.'

'You and I, Agnes,' I said, looping my arm through hers, 'are going to get on very well. How does picking fifty kilograms of grapes sound?'

'Heavy,' Dad muttered.

'Stop moaning!' said Agnes and I at the same time and we laughed all the way back to the vineyard.

*

The clear weather held and for the rest of Saturday and all of Sunday we worked like demons. The yard was a hive of activity, cars coming and going as more people heard about Storm Sandra and turned up to help us hit our deadline. Pippa and Ben were kept busy on the quadbike, pulling the trailer piled high with full crates of grapes to the winery and then heading straight back with empty ones to give to the pickers. Betsy was thoroughly enjoying the drama and on Sunday Marjorie arrived to stay over for the night to keep her sister-in-law out of trouble because we kept finding her lost amongst the vines insisting she wanted to be useful.

Matt and Clare had pressed the first load of grapes on Saturday, working through the night to get the juice pumped into tanks ready for the press to be used again on Sunday. It was hard physical work and by Sunday lunchtime Clare was flagging so Ben swapped places with her. He took over the job of tipping the grapes into the big funnel on top of the wine press and his mum spent the rest of the day with secateurs in hand, chatting to her friends amongst the Pinot Meunier grapes.

Ben was a lovely guy. It was easy to see why Clare was so proud of her son and why Pippa had fallen for him in a matter of days. He was laid back and softly spoken, which suited Pippa perfectly, had an easy smile and could turn his hand to anything. He was also incredibly strong and Matt was enjoying having someone else to help with the heavy lifting.

Having Dad and Agnes here gave me such a boost. Not only was Agnes extremely industrious and a quick learner, but she was a great team player too. She fussed round making sure everyone was all right, and wasn't hungry or thirsty and I noticed she kept a close eye on Dad's right side which he'd injured in the summer. It was wonderful to see Dad so happy. I'd got used to not having him close when I was living in London, but spending a couple of days in his presence made me realize how much I loved him. Darren had helped yesterday and after we'd finished, Dad and Agnes had taken him and Evie out to the pub for Sunday dinner. I'd been invited too, but there'd be no pub visits for me until the harvest was in; it was all hands to the deck amongst the Butterworth team for now.

And the good news was that our hard work was paying off. The first two days of harvest couldn't have gone any better. The winery was working at full throttle, pressing grapes virtually round the clock. By midnight on Sunday, there were forty thousand litres of juice already pumped into the tanks, most of the red grapes were harvested and the first load of Chardonnay grapes had been pressed too. And when I eventually fell into bed in the early hours of Monday morning, I'd actually begun to believe we could do this. All we needed was the next day's picking to go as well as the last day and then Storm Sandra could do what she liked; Butterworth Wines 2018 vintage would be safe.

On Monday morning I was woken up early by a persistent noise. I threw back the covers and dashed to the door, thinking I had a visitor, but there was nobody there. Instead, a vicious wind was blowing through the yard, rattling at window frames, stealing under gaps around doors, scooping up all the fallen leaves and sending them spinning in ever tighter circles. The sky looked ominous: huge grey clouds scudded by so fast it was like watching a time-lapse film. I was almost glad I'd rearranged my scan; I really didn't fancy driving in this weather. I took one last look and shut the door.

Storm Sandra was on the way.

At least it was dry. Although how long it would remain that way was anybody's guess.

We decided to start picking as soon as we could. It would be hard going amongst the vines today; we'd lost most of the remaining leaves overnight and if we weren't careful we were going to lose the grapes too. I'd been worried that support would have dropped off by day three, but I needn't have been: there were more pickers than ever when they assembled at the top of the vineyard ready to receive the day's instructions. Retired couples mostly, I noticed. Roger had had to go into school but Pippa had booked the day off from the library to help out. Godfrey was here but the poor dear was aching all over and we'd given him a sit-down job in the winery for a few hours. Clare had got blisters on her feet so she was driving the quadbike for a change and Matt was being team leader along with Pippa. Everyone on the team was suffering to a certain degree. I wasn't too bad because no one had allowed me to do anything strenuous; even so my ankles were swollen and I was tired from having been on the go so much over the last forty-eight hours.

'Okay, guys, listen up.' I was on the bottom step today, starting the day with my usual pep talk. The wind was stealing my words and I had to shout to make myself heard. 'Thank you so much for being here, we couldn't manage without you.'

'Louder please!' Evie raised a hand and I laughed and stuck my tongue out. My sister was glowing, there was no other word for it. She was blaming it on the fresh air thanks to walking the dogs, but she wasn't fooling me. She and Darren were more in love than ever and it showed in her face. I looked across at Dad who was tucking a strand of white hair behind Agnes's ear and I felt infused with warmth that my family were so happily loved up. I sent the baby a mental message: And I love you too, little one; we've got each other.

I raised my voice a bit more. 'It's Chardonnay picking time. So far the rain has held off. Fingers crossed we get lucky today too but time is of the essence,' I stressed. 'I don't have to tell you it's very windy and vine branches can be very painful if they whip you in the eye. Any injuries, come to the winery, we have a full first-aid box. Please stay safe.'

'That includes you,' said Agnes, stepping forward and zipping up my jacket over my bump. She touched my cheek. 'I have not seen you rest since I have been here.'

I dredged up a smile. 'I'll rest as soon as these grapes are in, I promise.'

Just then a strong gust of wind lifted my hood up and over my face and we both laughed.

'I just hope we've got enough time,' I added.

I left Pippa and Matt to divide the group into two teams and headed back to report in to Betsy and Marjorie. I didn't get far; they were crossing the garden and coming towards me, heads bowed, protecting themselves from the wind.

'Right hand down, Parker,' bellowed Marjorie, one hand clasping her chest and the other gripping the handrail of her wheelchair. 'You nearly upended me in the potato patch.'

'Oh, these damn eyes,' said Betsy testily. 'They're even worse in this dreadful gust. I could have sworn I was on the path, I was just rushing to see who'd come to help. Who's Parker anyway?'

'Lady Penelope's servant in *Thunderbirds*.'

'Servant? I'm nothing like him. Thin beaky fellow, nick-named Nosey.'

'Exactly, if the cap fits,' Marjorie drawled, tucking her chin into a thick fleece I distinctly remembered being consigned to the pile marked 'rubbish' when we'd had that clear-out. She looked more fragile than usual; the wind was making furrows in her grey hair and I could see her pale scalp.

'Cheek.' Betsy halted in her tracks to tuck the ends of her pink headscarf into the collar of her bright yellow raincoat and squinted as I approached. 'Pippa, is that you?'

'It's Lottie,' Marjorie chuckled. 'You can tell because she's *not* mooning about like a lovesick puppy but she *does* huff and puff when she walks.'

'I do not,' I said, pausing to catch my breath.

Marjorie and Betsy exchanged know-it-all looks.

'Anyway,' said Betsy, wiping her watery eyes with the back of her hand, 'we're reporting for duty. What shall we do?'

'Take it easy and watch from the window,' I said simply.

'Enjoy being inside while the rest of us feel like we're in the black-and-white bit of *The Wizard of Oz* when the hurricane hits Kansas.'

'How tedious,' said Marjorie.

'I will not be written off just because I'm mature,' said Betsy crossly. 'You're being ageist.'

'I'm being practical,' I said, touching her arm. 'Look at me – I'd love to be out there getting stuck in but I can't. My back's already aching and it's only ten o'clock.'

'She's right, Bets.' Marjorie sighed. 'It's just such a great Dunkirk spirit out there. We're missing out on all the fun.'

They looked dejected and I felt a pang of guilt for dismissing their efforts so swiftly.

'Look,' I said, thinking that no one had said I'd need the skills of a UN peacekeeper to do this job, 'there's a gang of people down there who are going to be freezing to death if we don't look after them. What about making some soup and sandwiches for them?'

'Consider it done,' said Betsy, brightening instantly. 'Tell everyone we'll eat in my dining room. It'll be a squash but we can just about manage it.'

Marjorie pouted. 'I hate cooking.'

I thought on my feet, making up the teeniest lie. 'I've been expecting a letter from the hospital about some blood tests and it hasn't arrived. It might have got mixed up in the post for the house. Could you have a quick scan through the office for me?'

'No problem,' said Marjorie. 'I might do a bit of tweeting while I'm at it. Pick up where Olivia left off. Hashtag English wine, hashtag harvest 2018.'

Olivia had taken Sazzle home last night, but not before Marjorie had cornered her and asked her to explain social media. Unfortunately, Marjorie had pressed something while Olivia's back was turned and Marjorie's entire camera roll had uploaded to Facebook. Olivia had been a nervous wreck when she left.

'Go for it,' I grinned as Betsy span the wheelchair back round.

'Oi, that's the potato patch again!' Marjorie yelped.

'Hashtag you don't say,' said Betsy gleefully. 'Pull up a plant or two while we're here, Mar, we'll have vichyssoise.'

'Urgh. Isn't that cold soup?'

Betsy snorted. 'Not when I make it.'

It was almost lunchtime and Evie and I were working together near the centre of the vineyard in one of the most exposed spots.

'Up until today, my image of picking the grape harvest was all "*du pain, du vin, du Boursin*", basking under a hot Mediterranean sky,' she said through chattering teeth.

'It was nice last week, unfortunately Storm Sandra had other ideas.' I snipped a perfect bunch of grapes and dropped them in our crate.

'Ooh.' Evie paused to circle her shoulders. 'Perhaps you could get a job somewhere warmer next year.'

I wrinkled my nose. 'Nah. I like it here. For as long as it lasts. Mind you, I'd like it even more if a certain person hadn't gone incommunicado on me.'

She smiled sympathetically, before bumping the crate along the ground to the next vine. 'I know this is clichéd coming from me, but things have a way of working out. Don't give up hope. You never know: he might turn up out of the blue.'

I sighed, trudging after her. 'The only blue he's interested in at the moment is the wide blue sky over Table Mountain.'

'So go to him.' She blinked at me as if it was the obvious answer. I had actually googled flights to Cape Town, but there was too much work for me to do here at the moment and by the time it calmed down, my pregnancy would probably be too advanced for me to get permission to fly. Also, I was too scared he'd send me away.

I shook my head. 'He's ignored all my attempts to

370

communicate. I've tried telling him that there's nothing going on between Harvey and me, but I think seeing us together coupled with the fact that I insisted he take this new job has hurt his feelings beyond repair.'

'Hmm.' Evie's eyes glittered.

'No way,' I said, recognizing the signs. 'Don't interfere.'

She raised her eyebrows innocently. 'Like you *didn't* interfere with Darren?'

'That was different,' I said quietly. 'I knew Darren loved you. No one loves me.'

Evie dropped her secateurs to the ground and flung her arms around me. 'I do. Dad does.'

Moments later we heard Agnes's strident shout from the top of the vineyard telling us that lunch was ready. Evie went on ahead and I caught up with Matt in the winery who was unloading full crates of grapes from the back of the trailer.

He pulled off his black beanie and ruffled his hair. 'You look wiped out,' he said, frowning with concern. 'Sit down before you fall down. Godfrey's inside.'

My legs did feel a bit wobbly and although I was hungry and ready for lunch, it was a relief to be out of the wind for a moment so I headed for the desk where Godfrey was sitting and flopped down on the spare chair just as my stomach gave a loud rumble. The radio was on low thankfully: Godfrey was into jazz music, which to me always sounded like the musicians couldn't agree on which tune to play so they all played something different.

'It's a mixed blessing having such a good harvest,' said Godfrey, taking the lid off his lunchbox and offering me a sandwich. 'Five years ago if we'd worked this hard with a team this large we'd have our feet up by now. But this year we've got such a big yield.'

'I dream of putting my feet up.' I helped myself to a ham and pickle sandwich. There was frilly lettuce hanging out of it and the bread was thick, soft and crumbly. 'Oh Godfrey, this is heavenly.'

'Home-made bread,' he beamed.

'And I know it's hard work, but it'll be worth it when we're bottling lots of lovely wine next year.'

Godfrey's eyes flicked briefly to my stomach and I felt my face heat up; I knew what he was thinking: that I'd be more concerned with baby bottles than wine bottles by then. But I couldn't think that far ahead at the moment.

'The lunch break will have to be short and sweet,' Matt said grimly, joining us. 'We haven't got enough grapes to fill the press yet. And I want to get another load in and pressed before I go to bed tonight.'

The pile of plastic crates overflowing with juicy green grapes looked huge, but even I could tell we were working at a slower rate than yesterday.

'It's this wind,' I said, looking out at the sky. Still no sign of rain, thank heavens. 'It's slowing us all down. Walking back uphill was such an effort.'

'Then you shouldn't be doing it.' Matt frowned so deeply that his black eyebrows met in the middle.

I held up a hand to silence him and whacked up the volume on the radio just in time for a weather report. 'Shush and listen.'

Storm Sandra is tightening its grip on the UK as it wreaks havoc on the road and rail system in the north-east of England. Thousands of homes are without power and two deaths have already been reported in storm-related accidents. Winds of up to seventy miles per hour have been recorded in Northumberland and the hurricane-force gusts are showing no signs of abating. The Met Office is warning people to stay off the roads as Storm Sandra heads south through Yorkshire, Derbyshire and the Midlands . . .

My heart pounded and I jumped up. 'It's heading our way. Come on, we'll have to crack on. I'll go and tell the others.'

Matt caught my arm. 'They need a break or they won't have the strength to carry on this afternoon.'

I took a breath. 'You're right. How about more volunteers? That would help, wouldn't it?'

Godfrey swallowed his sandwich. 'I'll call Roger, see if he can rope in any of the staff at school.'

Matt was already pulling out his phone. 'I should be able to get hold of a few pub regulars.'

'And I'll ask the volunteers who are already here if they can all invite their friends.'

I jogged out of the winery and across the yard, glad to be doing something positive. We'd all put so much into the vineyard; I couldn't let us fall at the last hurdle. Betsy's dining room was packed with hungry workers and they'd spilled out into the kitchen. In the centre was the lady of the house herself, regaling anyone who'd listen with tales of previous harvests. Marjorie was sitting with Agnes swapping motorbike stories. Pippa and Ben were feeding each other crisps and most of the retired couples were standing around, glass in hand, chatting. It was such a convivial, sociable scene but for a moment I stood at the edge of it, observing and feeling completely isolated and alone.

'Lottie,' cried Evie, spotting me and patting the chair next to her. 'You need food, come and sit here.'

Everyone turned and I used the opportunity to attract their attention.

'Sorry to interrupt your lunch,' I shouted above the chatter and clatter, 'but the weather is worsening and we could do with more help with the harvest. Please call anyone and everyone you can to come and help. And remember there's a bottle of wine in it for everyone who turns up.'

Immediately I finished, the conversation roared into action and everyone began throwing out suggestions of suitable grape-pickers. Pippa was on her phone first, calling the radio station to let them know about our dilemma.

'I do not have anyone to call,' said Agnes, sidling up to me and wrapping an arm around my waist, 'but there is something I can do.'

'Oh?' I blinked at her tiredly.

'I can make you go to bed and take a nap. Ah, ah, ah!' She

held up a finger as I started to protest and steered me to the door. 'I am very bossy and also used to dealing with your father. You Allbrights are all stubborn. Come.'

Suddenly the thought of my bed was so appealing that I didn't have the energy to fight. I let Agnes guide me back to The Stables. She took my jacket from me and tugged off my shoes.

'I will make you some tea.' She pulled back the covers. 'And then you will sleep.'

I opened the alarm clock on my phone. 'Fine, but only for thirty minutes. Because if new volunteers arrive—'

'If they arrive, someone else can deal with them.'

'Okay then, forty minutes.' My eyelids were already drooping; this was a great idea.

I heard Agnes slide a mug on to my bedside cupboard and then the front door closed as she let herself out. I was in that delicious state – almost asleep – when I suddenly thought about Jensen and wondered where he was. Had he landed in Cape Town ready to start his new job, or was he flying today and hoping his flight wouldn't be affected by the storm? I reached a hand out from under the covers and opened my bedside cupboard. My fingers felt around until they found what I was looking for. I slid his ring on to the third finger of my left hand and closed my eyes again.

Safe travels wherever you are . . .

Chapter 33

Sometime later, a knock at the door woke me up. I glanced at my phone as I blinked myself awake. An hour had gone by. A whole hour! Damn, I'd slept through my alarm.

The person at the door knocked again.

'Lottie? Are you in there?' It was Marjorie's voice, although I could hardly hear her over the wind.

'Coming.' I opened the door. 'Gosh, look at all those cars.'

While I'd been asleep, our cry for help had obviously been heeded.

'You should see the vineyard,' said Marjorie, pulling her hood back up. 'There are so many bodies down there it looks like we've been invaded by locusts.'

Just then Clare sailed by on the quadbike, head down against the wind. It was so blowy that loose grapes were blowing off the back of the trailer and on to the ground. Starsky was running behind her, barking into the turbulent air and snapping at the falling fruit. He seemed to be the only one enjoying this weather.

'Are you going to leave me here to freeze?' Marjorie yelled.

I shook myself. 'Sorry. I'm not used to seeing you without Betsy pushing you.'

'Don't look so shocked.' She wheeled herself over the threshold and came in. 'I can manoeuvre myself, you know. I've lived alone since Ron died.'

'Of course.' I closed the door after her and breathed a sigh of relief at shutting out the bad weather. I automatically walked to the kettle. 'I hope I've got time for a cup of tea, I'm desperate. Do you want one?'

She pulled a face. 'I'm awash with the stuff. No, I came to give you this letter.'

She reached into her fleece, retrieved a rather bent envelope and handed it over to me.

'So there really was a letter for me!' I said before realizing my mistake.

She looked confused. 'Well, you did ask me to check Ted's office. I suppose we should stop calling it that now. And I managed to send some tweets. Olivia immediately retweeted them and we've had some new followers . . .'

I sank on to a dining chair, not really listening; the envelope was too interesting. It was handwritten and postmarked London. I tore it open with a mix of dread and anticipation. I didn't recognize the handwriting which meant it wasn't likely to be from Harvey, but I wouldn't have put it past him to disguise his writing. Or it could be from Jensen.

Please let it be from Jensen.

I pulled two sheets of paper from the envelope clumsily, desperate to see who it was from.

It was from Jensen.

My heart swelled with joy. He *had* written to me after all. I tuned back into Marjorie, willing her to go so I could read the letter in private. She'd stopped talking and her eyes were wide open in surprise.

'The ring!' She pointed at my fake engagement ring.

I fiddled with it, feeling my cheeks heat up. Now I was going to have to explain why I was wearing it and make an idiot of myself in the process. 'Pretty, isn't it?'

She nodded. 'It's the Butterworth ring.'

I frowned. 'Well, Jensen gave it to me, but he just got it from T—'

'Ted,' Marjorie supplied before I could say Topshop. 'His granddad left it to him. It's very valuable. Oh, Lottie.'

Her expression had gone all dreamy and she pulled her bottom lip between her teeth.

'But . . .' I stared down at the ring I'd casually chucked in my drawer when I got back from London ten days ago.

Now that I looked at it, it was obviously the real thing. How could I ever have thought it was costume jewellery? It was heavy and felt solid but more than that . . . it was exquisite. Oh God. My spirits sank. That was probably what he was writing to me about: he wanted the family heirloom back. I slipped it off my finger and put it on the table.

'I had no idea,' I said in a voice barely above a whisper.

Marjorie could hardly keep the lid on her excitement.

'That ring has been passed down the Butterworth male line for several generations. Ted and Ron's father gave it to their mother when he proposed to her.' She pressed a hand to her chest. 'And now Jensen has given it to you. I must admit, Betsy and I did wonder when we heard that radio presenter, Fiona Thingumabob talking about it.'

'Please don't read anything into it.' My mouth had gone dry. 'Really. We had to pretend to be engaged so that I'd be eligible to do the radio interview, that was all. We're just friends.'

Friends who currently weren't speaking, although perhaps this letter might provide me with some answers . . .

'If you say so.' She pursed her lips mischievously. 'Now I'm going to take myself back across the yard and batten down the hatches. And if you've got any sense, you'll do the same.'

She refused my offer of help but I opened the door for her and watched her battle against the wind across the yard to Betsy's before shutting it and swooping down on Jensen's letter like a starling on a juicy grape.

It had been posted a week ago. My insides clenched: poor man, he must have thought I'd received it and hadn't cared enough to reply. But by the time I got to the bottom, my own heart was in shreds and tears were dripping down my face. I'd never before received a love letter that doubled up as a 'goodbye'.

Dearest Lottie,

Thank you for your messages and for the letter. I've loved hearing your voice on my answerphone and reading your texts, even though it does make it harder to get over you. I wish things were different. But we are where we are and I need to put some distance between us and forget what might have been.

In case you're unsure what you mean to me, I'm going to tell you one last time.

You rocked up in a van of all things, with those adorable green eyes and glossy hair that makes me want to bury my face in it, and from the moment you arrived on Gran's doorstep, the sun came out. Not just at Butterworth Wines but in my life too. The crazy girl who can fill potholes, wield a chainsaw and climb trees stole my heart and there'll never be anyone else like you. You claim not to be ambitious, but your natural optimism and determination come through in everything you do and everyone around you is swept along in your tide of enthusiasm. This is a great gift and I know it will stand you in good stead in the months to come.

Lottie, you're going to be a great mum. And on February the tenth I'll be holding my breath for you and wishing you and the baby every happiness.

Now the tough bit. When I saw you with Harvey, kissing on your doorstep, it tore me apart. I was surprised after what you'd told me about him but I was glad too. Glad that you were giving your relationship another chance. In other circumstances, I'd have

378

fought for you, tried to convince you that we could be good together, but I know how much a happy family life means to you, and to me too. And this isn't just about us. Your baby is the most important person right now. And if you two have got a hope of giving that kid two loving parents, then I'm not going to stand in your way. So even though it hurts like hell, I'm doing the honourable thing and stepping aside.

I'm leaving for Cape Town on October the first and after that, I'd ask you to only get in contact with me if it's to do with Gran's health. Be happy.

Ek is lief vir jou
Jensen xxx

It was the first today. I wondered what time his flight was; he'd probably already gone. My lungs felt crushed and I fought for breath, gulping in air while my brain was whirring wondering how I could stop this from happening. He cared about me. As much as I cared for him. Why hadn't he believed me when I'd promised that there was nothing between me and Harvey any more? There was no need for him to step aside; he was single, I was single and there was absolutely no reason why we couldn't be together. There had to be a way to sort this out. I wasn't going to give up on us. And what on earth did *Ek is lief vir jou* mean?

The baby started to kick. It was less of a tickly sensation these days and more like having a bouncy ball flung repeatedly at my insides. Maybe there was still time. I grabbed my phone and called his number, pacing back and forth while I waited for it to connect and rubbing my other hand over my tummy in circles, as if the baby would be my good-luck charm.

Come on, Jensen, pick up.

I tried three times, and each time it went straight to voice-mail. Now what? My heart was thumping so hard I could

379

hardly hear myself think ... If I lived nearer to Heathrow, I'd hightail it to the airport like something out of a film. I'd yell, 'I LOVE YOU, DON'T GO!' across the barriers and the crowds would part like the Red Sea until it was just him and me and the most amazing make-up kiss ...

The door banged open, literally swinging on its hinges and startling the life out of me, as Evie blew in.

'Jeez. It's unbelievable out there.' She slammed it shut, panting. 'I think you should call a halt to the grape-picking, Lottie, it's too dangerous. There are loose twigs and debris flying about all over the place ... Lottie, are you okay? You're rubbing your stomach really hard.'

Was I? I looked down; my T-shirt was all crumpled.

'I'm fine,' I said vaguely as a stab of guilt hit me; I'd been so caught up with Jensen's letter that I'd deserted my post and ignored all the kind volunteers who were out there braving the elements.

'Sure?' Evie frowned, unconvinced.

'You're right,' I said, shoving my arms in my coat. 'People's safety is more important than grapes.'

'Tuck your hair in or you won't be able to see,' she said, reaching for the door. 'Ready?'

I nodded, scooping my hair up into a ponytail.

She opened the door and we both stepped outside. The wind whistled round my ears so loudly that although I could see Evie's mouth moving, I couldn't hear a thing. Above us, the sky was charcoal grey and menacing. The noise of the trees blowing and bending so violently sounded like the roar of the sea. In the distance I heard a rumble and I felt a wave of fear ripple through me.

'Is that thunder?' I yelled, but Evie didn't hear me. I grabbed her arm to lead her to the double gates at the side entrance to the vineyard. Matt came running up behind us and tapped my shoulder. I spun around to read his lips.

'The rain will be here in minutes,' he bellowed, holding his palms up.

I nodded. It wasn't raining yet, but it was in the air, I could feel it. 'I'm calling the harvest off now.'

He stuck his thumb up. 'Just tell people to pick up a crate, even if it's only half-full and bring it to the winery.'

Evie shouted as loud as she could. 'I'll run right to the bottom and let as many know as I can. Lottie, you focus on the top section.' She sprinted off and I envied how nimble she was. Even if I hadn't been pregnant, my feet were aching too much to run like that.

'Where's Clare and the quadbike?' I yelled.

He pointed to the path. 'She and Ben are loading up the trailer with the last full crates.'

Overhead there was a second thunder roll and the two of us separated: me towards the vineyard and Matt back to the winery.

'Stay safe,' he warned, calling over his shoulder.

The quadbike was heading towards me between the line of conifers and the first row of vines. The tall thin evergreens were swaying dangerously from side to side and even from a distance, I could see Clare was frightened. She was clinging on for dear life, lying almost flat over the steering wheel and driving at a snail's pace so as not to tip up the trailer and lose the precious cargo. She hadn't even spotted me so I stepped back, pressing myself into the trees out of her way as she passed by.

Just then Godfrey appeared at the end of the row, staggering under the weight of a full crate, with Starsky yapping at his feet. The dog ran out in front of the quadbike and I yelped in horror.

'STOP!' I cried, barely able to look.

Clare spotted the dog at the last second and jammed on the brakes. I don't think she'd even heard me, although Starsky had. He scampered up to me unharmed.

'You silly dog!' I said, scooping him up out of harm's way.

Godfrey heaved the crate on to the trailer and waved at Clare to carry on.

'I'm done in,' he shouted, his plump frame being buffeted by the wind as he approached. 'Absolutely cream-crackered.'

I put Starsky down and kissed the old man's cheek. 'We're all stopping now,' I yelled back. 'Would you mind letting Betsy know? Perhaps she and Marjorie could sort out some tea and biscuits.'

He nodded and patted his leg to attract Starsky's attention. 'Come on, fella, let's go in.'

The two of them set off uphill and I headed across the top of the rows of vines to look for the others. I was halfway across the width of the vineyard when I heard an almighty cracking sound followed by a long creak and a crash.

I froze: my experience as a tree surgeon told me a tree was coming down. Someone shouted and then I heard the dog bark again.

I turned and retraced my steps, running as fast as I could to the edge of the vineyard, cursing my own forgetfulness. It was that third tree along; I could see the gap it had left already. How stupid of me not to have got it cut down before the storm came. It was an accident waiting to happen. Thank goodness Clare had already got through safely.

Still running, I rounded the edge of the row but Roger overtook me. The dead tree had gone straight down across the first two rows, taking the vines, posts and wires with it. Starsky was barking like mad, and trapped underneath the trunk, face down, was Godfrey.

My heart missed a beat and I surged forward, joining Roger as he dived to the ground. 'Godfrey, are you all right, old chap, can you hear me?'

'I'm fine,' Godfrey wheezed. 'I dropped my glove, bent down to pick it up and the next second, I'd been knocked over. Actually, my legs feel a bit sore.'

Roger and I exchanged a glance; they looked worse than 'a bit sore'. Roger tried to lift the trunk but he couldn't shift it.

'Where is everybody?' I cried. 'We need help!'

'Where's your chainsaw?' Dad shouted as he and Agnes ran towards us. 'And ropes?'

'Your van,' I said, relieved. 'It's open.'

Dad jogged off and thankfully Starsky scampered after him out of harm's way. Agnes knelt down beside Godfrey. 'We will have this tree off you very quickly. Do not worry.'

Right on cue, just as I thought the situation couldn't get any worse, the sky cracked with an ear-splitting roll of thunder, the heavens opened and the rain started. Within seconds it was torrential.

Godfrey was moaning with pain.

'We need to call an ambulance,' I said, trying to think straight. 'But I left my phone inside the cottage.'

'I don't have one either. Hang on in there, old thing,' Roger shouted.

'I do not also.' Agnes shook her head.

Godfrey was sweating and he screwed his eyes up. Agnes and I exchanged worried looks. Next would come lightning and given our current run of luck, the last thing we needed was to be struck by that too.

Agnes looked up. 'Here come some more people.'

It was Matt and three other men I hadn't seen before who must have arrived while I was sleeping.

'Call an ambulance,' I yelled and one of the men did.

'If we can lift the tree a little, we might be able to pull him free,' Matt shouted.

'The tree's been dead for a while,' I yelled, shivering. 'We might manage to move it between us.'

'You're not lifting anything,' Matt warned. 'Out of the way.'

'Be quick,' shouted Agnes, brushing water from her face. 'He is very grey.'

Roger leaned over Godfrey who'd stopped making any noise. 'Hang on in there, chum, have you out in a jiffy.'

'If we take some of the weight off here,' I said, gesturing to the mid-section of the trunk, 'we can ease him out.'

'I've got it!' It was Dad. He was wearing a hard hat with ear defenders attached and had found the chainsaw and a length of rope.

I let out a shaky breath. This would soon be over. Thank heavens Dad was here.

'What's happening?' Clare gasped breathlessly, sliding on the wet grass as she joined us.

'Godfrey's hurt and I think he might be drifting in and out of consciousness,' I said. 'Can you wait in the yard and direct the ambulance?'

She nodded and ran back uphill, slithering in the mud.

I grabbed hold of the rope, threaded it under the trunk and tied a knot.

'Everyone out of the way,' Dad ordered and started up the chainsaw. The roar of it made everyone take a step backwards.

He sliced into the trunk. I dug my feet into the slippery ground and pulled on the rope. There were alarm bells going off in my head; I knew I was being foolish, but I couldn't let anything happen to Godfrey. And anyway I wasn't alone; behind me, Matt grabbed the rope and several others behind him did the same. With a concerted effort, we pulled the top section of the tree clear of Godfrey's legs. My arms ached, my thighs were quivering and my stomach was taut from clenching my muscles; I was exhausted – physically and mentally.

'Careful!' Agnes cried, trying to protect the old man from falling branches.

'Uhhhhh.' Godfrey's eyes flickered open.

'Godfrey!' I sank to the muddy floor in relief and sobbed as if my heart would break. 'Thank goodness.'

I was wet through and covered in mud. Storm Sandra was in full force and I didn't have the energy to fight her any more. I put my hand on my tummy to soothe the baby, but it was still, at least it had stopped head-butting me. *You're tired too, eh? Like Mummy. I'm so tired, so very tired . . .*

There was a stabbing pain along my side. I pressed my

hand into it, flopping over on to my hip, and winced. I'd probably strained a muscle lifting that tree trunk. Still, no harm done, crisis over. Around me the activity continued: Dad sawing the tree into pieces and everyone rolling sections of the trunk away. I vaguely registered the sound of a siren and then someone leaning over me.

'Lottie? Lottie, it's Evie, don't cry, lovely girl. Come on, let's get you inside. Godfrey's going to be okay, a paramedic has arrived.'

The roar of the chainsaw stopped and I heard people running and Godfrey groaning and Agnes's voice soothing him. The rain and the wind were relentless. Evie brushed strands of my hair from my face and then swore under her breath.

'What the hell?' said a gruff male voice. It was vaguely familiar, but I was too tired to open my eyes.

'Everything's going to be fine now, Lottie,' Evie murmured. 'Let's get you inside, you need some rest.'

Someone lifted me up roughly. I didn't register who it was or have the words to whisper my thanks. I tried to say that they'd got the wrong person – it was Godfrey not me who needed to go to hospital – but it was too much effort. I closed my eyes and a coat was laid over me, covering most of my face to protect it from the downpour. I was being carried now, back uphill, and even though my body was shivering uncontrollably, I felt warmer, safer already, and I turned into the man's chest. The smell of him was so vivid, so particular, that its effect was like smelling salts. I inhaled again and felt a sob forming in my throat. The paramedic wore the same cologne as the man I'd fallen in love with. The smell reminded me of happy times, chasing starlings through the vines, seeing my baby for the first time on the scanner, snuggling together on his sofa . . .

My eyes sprang open and I gasped.

'Jensen?' I blinked. This must be a dream, a delicious dream. 'I thought you were on a flight to . . . ?' Where was it again? My brain felt all fuzzy.

'Just as well I'm not.' His voice was strained. Partly with anger but also from struggling through this rain and mud with me in his arms. 'What the hell did you think you were doing?'

'Harvesting grapes before Storm Sandra hit? It got a bit messy that's all.'

'*That's all*? Huh!' His jaw was set like stone. 'I arrive to tell you— Well, anyway, that can wait, and I find you in a tug-of-war contest with a tree while your dad's waving a chainsaw literally millimetres from your unborn child.'

I swallowed. When he put it like that, it did seem a bit rash.

'I thought you liked it when I did crazy stuff?' I murmured, attempting to make him smile. What had he come to tell me?

He shook his head. 'I am so mad with you right now.'

I looped my arms around his neck and clung on. I didn't care; I was still glad to see him.

He carried me across the yard, where a man in a neon yellow waterproof coat was lifting medical kit out of the back of an ambulance car.

'Is she for us too?' he shouted. 'Because we've only got the car. The emergency call rate goes through the roof in bad weather like this. All the rigs are out.'

'No,' Jensen yelled back, 'I can deal with this one myself.'

'I'm fine,' I said crossly, feeling stronger already. 'You fuss more than your gran. And you still haven't said what you're doing here.'

He pushed open the door of my cottage and put me down on the sofa. He took off his shoes and coat, peeled my wet coat and shoes off me and handed me a towel from the bathroom. The letter that Marjorie had given me earlier was still on the table and I saw him look at it. I wrapped the towel around my hair.

'What does that bit at the end mean?' I asked. 'The bit in the strange language?'

'It can wait,' he said gruffly. 'I'll make you a hot drink, you're shivering.'

I started to take off my clothes; the situation between us was anything but clear and it did seem a bit weird stripping off in front of him, but it wasn't as if there was anything he hadn't seen before. I pulled my jogging bottoms off and dumped them in a soggy pile on the floor.

He put the kettle on and caught my eye.

I smiled weakly. 'You're supposed to say, "Let's get you out of those wet things."'

'And *you're* supposed to . . .' His voice tailed off and the colour drained from his face. 'Lottie, darling.'

My heart bloomed in my chest: he called me *darling*. Then I followed his gaze. The tops of my inner thighs were streaked with blood. 'Oh no, that's not good.'

I looked at Jensen in horror and felt my stomach. Still no movement.

'I haven't felt the baby move for ages.' I whispered hoarsely.

'Right.' He jumped to his feet and held his palms up. 'Let's not panic.'

'Get help.'

'I'll get help.' Jensen seized my face, planted a kiss on my lips and darted out of the door.

I stood there, frozen to the spot, staring at the mess on my legs.

'Hang on in there, tiddler,' I whispered, stroking my tummy. 'It's okay.'

The pain down my side was still there. More of a dull ache now than a stabbing pain and I stumbled back on to the sofa, wishing more than anything that Mum was here to hold my hand and tell me everything was going to be all right. It would be all right, wouldn't it?

Chapter 34

I was probably only alone for a minute but to me it felt like time had stood still. I reached a hand between my legs. It felt warm and sticky and I didn't need to look to know what was happening. The towel I'd used to dry my face and hair was on the floor by my feet. I reached down and hitched myself up, sliding it underneath me to protect the sofa. Thinking about the sofa was much easier than thinking about anything else.

I heard voices and several pairs of feet running towards the cottage. Evie came through the door first, bringing a gust of wind and rain with her followed by one of the paramedics. Lastly Jensen appeared and shut the door.

'How's Godfrey?' I managed to say.

The paramedic stuck his thumb up. 'No bones broken; my colleague's treating him for shock.'

Evie skittered across the room towards me and grabbed my hand. 'I'm not letting this happen to you. I'm not.'

She was soaked to the skin, her blonde hair plastered across her tear-stained cheeks. We stared at each other, and I knew she was thinking of her miscarriage and how her chance of motherhood had ebbed away. But this wasn't the same; she'd done nothing wrong, whereas I'd behaved irresponsibly, without thought to my baby.

'I'm sure I'm fine,' I sniffed, giving her a thin smile as she brushed the tears away from my face. 'Probably a storm in a teacup.'

'Sure.' She nodded and swallowed, her own eyes brimming with tears. 'I'll get you a tissue.'

'Loo roll in the bathroom,' I said.

The paramedic was a big, broad-shouldered redhead with a beard. He calmly knelt beside me and felt for my pulse. 'I'm Hugh.'

Jensen hovered around, fidgeting. 'What can I do? Boil a kettle, fetch towels?'

Hugh grinned at me. 'Somebody's been watching too much *Call the Midwife*.'

I tried to laugh but it came out as a shaky sob. 'Just hold me please, Jensen.'

He sat down, wrapped one arm around my shoulders and held my hand tightly.

'Let's see what's going on then, shall we?' The paramedic opened a big bag and took out a stethoscope. 'Do you mind lifting your top up?'

I did as I was asked and Hugh put the ends of the stethoscope in his ears. I looked at the pale curve of my tummy. *I promise to put you first from now on, little one. Please give me a kick, hard as you can.*

'Ek is lief vir jou,' Jensen whispered, pressing a kiss to the side of my face.

'That's what you said in the letter,' I said weakly. 'What does it mean?'

'I love you.'

I thought my heart would explode. 'I love you too.'

'And I love you too,' Evie cried, collapsing on to a chair.

I drew in a breath as Hugh moved the cold stethoscope across my skin, a slight frown on his face. He nodded, pulled the earpiece from his ears and grinned.

'The heart's beating like a drum. Baby sounds fine.'

'Thank God.' I squeezed my eyes tight and let out the breath I'd been holding. I'd been such a fool, taking my health for granted. From now on, I promised myself, I'd be a model mother-to-be.

Beside me I heard Jensen exhale steadily too as his grip on my hand tightened. Evie burst into tears and I reached out to rub her arm.

'If anything had happened,' she began, gulping noisily.

'But it hasn't,' said Jensen in a shaky voice. 'It hasn't.'

'And the bleeding?' I asked, pulling my T-shirt back down. 'Are you sure the baby is not in danger?'

Hugh sat back on his heels. 'Could be due to a number of things. Best get to hospital and have it checked out. But in my opinion, there's no immediate risk to the baby.'

Jensen and I exchanged looks, although I could barely see him through my veil of tears and his eyes looked moist too.

Just then the radio clipped to the edge of Hugh's coat crackled into life.

'Go ahead?' said Hugh, pressing a button.

'Mr Hallam is in the car, are you ready to go?'

'Yep. On my way.' He released the radio and got to his feet. 'We can take you, Lottie, but there'd be no room for anyone else.'

'I'm taking her,' said Jensen.

Hugh patted my arm. 'Then I'll leave you in your boy-friend's capable hands.'

Evie wiped her face. 'I'll go and let Dad know. He'll be having kittens by now.'

Then it was just Jensen, me and the bump. Outside Storm Sandra continued to rage; wind whistled down the chimney, the roof creaked and the windows were being buffeted with incessant rainfall. But inside my cottage, and to be more precise, here on my sofa, my world felt warm, safe and complete.

'Thank you for coming back,' I said, gazing at him. I knew my love for him was written all over my face but I couldn't help it. I was tired of being coy about my feelings and not wanting to admit how much I cared for fear of it not being reciprocated. I thought back to what Evie had said about how she and Darren had stopped communicating; I wasn't going to make that mistake.

He smiled.

'I think I'm destined to be your second doctor, whether you like it or not.' He kissed the top of my head and started to get up. 'I'll get you some dry clothes.'

I held on to his arm to stop him from moving.

'Did you mean it?' I swallowed. 'What you said earlier?'

'About being really mad with you?' His lips twitched. 'A bit. I thought I'd lost you.'

I smiled. 'No. The other thing. Did you mean that?'

His eyes softened and he cupped a hand to my face. 'Did you?'

'I asked first.'

He covered my lips with his. 'I love you, Lottie. With all my heart. Satisfied?'

I traced a line down his beautiful face with my fingertip. 'Completely.'

The sonographer opened the door to the same ultrasound room I'd been in last time.

'Miss Allbright?' she said.

'Call me Lottie,' I said.

She smiled and ushered us in.

'Hop on the bed and make yourself comfy,' she said. If she knew this was an emergency appointment due to an unspecified bleed, her tone gave nothing away. She was calm and unhurried, which was very reassuring. 'I'm Rachel. And you are?'

'Jensen, apparently I'm called the birth-partner.' His eyes sparkled as he tugged my trainers off for me. 'I can't wait to see him again.'

'Or her.' I smiled back, even though my heart was crashing against my ribs with nerves.

'I don't mind what it is, do you?' he said, plumping up the pillow before I lay back.

My heart leapt with hope. That sounded like the sort of thing, well, that a father might say. I shook my head. 'Just as long as it's healthy.'

This scan was just a precaution and as I'd been booked in tomorrow for a slightly belated routine twenty-week scan, it was agreed they'd fit me in while I was at the hospital. So far this evening, I'd been examined and poked and prodded and roundly told off for overdoing it. But I didn't mind. The amazing thing was that the baby's heart was beating as it should be. And the second amazing thing was that Jensen was here, by my side, not as a friend as he'd been last time, but as someone I loved and who loved me.

His eyes locked on mine and we stared at each other, grinning inanely while Rachel eased the waistband of my leggings down, tucked a piece of tissue below the elastic and squirted the cold gel on to my tummy. Then I felt a pressure on my stomach and gasped with shock.

'There's baby.' The sonographer leaned back so we had a good look at the screen. 'He's waving to you, look!'

Sure enough one arm was raised and waving.

'Hello, darling thing!' I said through a blur of tears. 'I'm so happy to see you.'

'Nothing wrong with this little fellow,' Rachel laughed. She patted her head. 'Oh, not again. I've put my glasses down somewhere. Excuse me a second.'

She got up and left the room, leaving us with an image of the baby on the screen.

Jensen walked around to the far side of the bed, leaned over and kissed me. 'I thought I'd lost you.' Then he touched his fingertip to the screen. 'And you.'

I sat up and pulled him close. 'I'm so glad you didn't.'

We kissed again, slowly and tenderly, and I thought my heart would melt.

He smiled. 'You asked me earlier why I came back.'

I stared at him, my breath catching in my throat, praying he wasn't just here to say goodbye after all. 'And?'

He dug his fingers into his pocket and pulled out a strip of paper. 'We didn't finish reading out the fortune cookies.'

I frowned. He was right. I'd read mine. Something about getting pleasure from seeing your loved ones prosper. It had confirmed my decision to set him free to take the promotion. Except he hadn't, had he? He was still here. Thank heavens.

'So I'm going to read mine out. Ready?'

I nodded.

'If you have someone good in your life, don't let them go.' He cupped my face in his hands and kissed me again. 'And as I figured you're the best thing in my life, why would I let you go?'

His kisses tasted of sunshine and happiness and above all home, but there was still something I needed to be certain of. I ended the kiss and ran my fingertips over his lovely face.

'And the baby?' I asked quietly.

Jensen's face split into the widest smile. 'Is the second best thing.'

'Sorry, sorry, sorry!' Rachel arrived back in the room looking flustered. 'My reading glasses have gone AWOL. I've had to borrow someone else's or I won't be able to type my notes.'

As I lay back down I caught hold of Jensen's hand, marvelling at how magical my life had become and wondering what I'd done to deserve it and a thought struck me.

'Rachel, you've referred to the baby as "he" and "little fellow". Are you trying to tell us something?'

She shook her head. 'No, don't worry, we always use the masculine, I wouldn't tell you the baby's sex unless you asked. Do you want to know?'

Jensen and I looked at each other. He raised an eyebrow as if to say that it was up to me and my heart began to thump.

'Yes please!'

Rachel picked up the probe again but Jensen quickly put a hand on her arm to stop her.

'I just need to ask a question first.' Out of his pocket he pulled the engagement ring that I'd left on the table at home and held it up. 'Lottie, I love you very much. Will you marry me? For real this time?'

'YES PLEASE!'

He slipped the ring on to my finger and I reached around his neck and kissed him with all my heart.

'I've seen some things in this room,' said Rachel with a sniff, 'but that was the best ever.'

Jensen puffed his chest out. 'I'm quite pleased with it myself.'

'Now,' said Rachel, dabbing a tissue to her eyes, 'ready to find out the sex?'

'Do you know?' I said suddenly. 'I think I've had enough surprises for one day.'

'Don't blame you.' Rachel chuckled, wiping the gel from my tummy.

'Then shall we go home?' Jensen held out a hand to me. 'You and me.'

I laced my fingers through his. 'And baby makes three.'

For a moment we just looked at each other as if we couldn't quite believe what had happened and my heart swelled with love for this man.

There was still so much to talk about: his job, my job, the future of the vineyard and what was going to happen when the baby came along.

But none of that mattered. What mattered was that he loved me and I loved him. And when you've got love anything is possible.

Epilogue

'There. It's finished.' I pressed the earth firmly around the base of the rose bush and brushed the loose specks of dirt from the brass plaque.

'Don't dig it up again, Starsky,' Jensen said fondly, as the little dog sniffed around the newest plant in the vineyard. Starsky scampered off and took a flying leap into Marjorie's lap.

'Muddy paw prints!' she said drily. 'Just what I've always wanted.'

I peeled off my gardening gloves and thought about standing up. The problem was that at seven and a half months' pregnant I was so top heavy that I didn't dare. The thought of toppling over in front of the assembled crowd didn't appeal.

'Here, allow me.' Jensen, anticipating my dilemma as usual, offered me a hand and pulled me up.

'Why thank you, kind sir.' I snuggled into him and we wrapped an arm around each other.

'Read it out to me again,' said Betsy, squinting in the low winter sunlight.

It was only a few days until Christmas and although the grass still retained its coat of frost in the most shadowy corners, the sunlight felt warm on my face.

'In memory of Ted Butterworth.' Marjorie leaned forward in her wheelchair. 'Forever loved, much missed and never forgotten. Nothing brings people together like good wine and nobody achieved that better than Ted.'

'That's lovely.' Betsy pressed the corner of her hanky to her eye. 'Perfect. Thank you, Lottie.'

'You'll be able to sit here and talk to him, or just enjoy being here,' I said, releasing Jensen to give her a hug. 'The wooden bench will go just there, behind us, in Ted's favourite spot. You can come and breathe it all in anytime.'

She looked at me with her watery pale blue eyes and my heart ached for her. In the six months I'd known her, her sight had already deteriorated. But she was moving in with Marjorie in the New Year and it would be the start of a new adventure for both of them. As long as they had each other, they'd be happy.

'He'd love it.' Sidney twirled the end of his moustache and winked at me. 'And such a practical solution too.'

The rose bush *was* a memorial to Ted and his ashes would be sprinkled here too when Betsy felt up to it. But the plan was to plant a rose at the end of every row of vines which would look beautiful in summer but would also serve another purpose. Sidney told me that this was what they did in his estate in Reims as a way of detecting possible diseases early and now I was adopting it here too.

Betsy cleared her throat. 'And talking of practical solutions . . .'

She turned to Marjorie, who lifted up one buttock and removed two envelopes from under her.

'With our warmest wishes, literally,' she said, shooting Marjorie a look, before handing Jensen and me an envelope each.

We glanced at each other curiously and tore into them.

Mine was a letter from a solicitor, stating that I'd been given a ten per cent share in Butterworth Wines.

I opened my mouth to protest, but Betsy shushed me. 'You're part of the family now, Lottie, and Ted would want you to have it. Besides, you've run this place almost single-handedly this year, I've no doubt you'll go from strength to strength.'

'It's a lovely gesture, Gran,' said Jensen, tapping his own letter into his palm, 'as is giving me an even bigger stake in the business, but Lottie is going to have her hands full next year; I don't think it's fair to expect too much.'

Betsy pursed her lips imperiously. 'I'm well aware of that, which is why I've sold another share to Sidney. In exchange for a lump sum – which I've used to buy the bungalow with Marjorie – Sidney will be our Master Winemaker.'

I laughed with delight and kissed Sidney's cheek. 'That's fantastic news!'

'The others have each been given a small share too,' Betsy continued. 'So that when we're making a profit they'll be rewarded for their loyalty and hard work.'

Sidney's eyes twinkled. 'I've been bursting to tell you. I'm not going to interfere but we can work on that still wine we were talking about and I've got some ideas for pest control I'd like to discuss with you too. But you're still the boss.'

I grinned. 'I like the sound of that. And you needn't worry about maternity cover, Betsy, because I'll still be able to come over every day from Fernfield with the baby through spring and everyone says they'll pitch in. And Pippa will be back in February from her travels.'

Pippa had handed her notice in at the library and was spending the winter touring vineyards in New Zealand and Australia. I'd decided to postpone doing a viticulture course for a year, but Pippa was going to do it instead, so Butterworth Wines would still benefit from the new knowledge. Adam and Nicky would be moving out of the Allbright family home in a couple of weeks and I'd have just enough time to get a room ready for the baby before it arrived.

'No need to be in Fernfield,' Betsy said with a sniff. 'I'll be gone so there'll be plenty of empty rooms here. A much easier commute, don't you think?'

I blinked at her. 'Well, I do think, but—'

'That's a relief!' Marjorie clapped a hand to her chest. 'Because we've already told your father, love, and he's told his tenants they can stay.'

Jensen and I gazed at each other in amazement.

'And it'll be rent-free, of course,' Betsy continued. 'Perk of the job. I was going to offer the house to Jensen anyway but, dear boy, I know you're still firmly rooted in London for the time being.'

'Actually,' he scratched his head self-consciously, 'I've resigned. From January I'm going to be setting up my own business.' He squeezed me to his side. 'I can be based wherever I like. And I quite like it here.'

This had been entirely his decision, although I might have sown the tiniest seed by suggesting that because he wanted to be around when the baby came, to be a hands-on dad, perhaps now might be a good time to do his own thing, like he'd always planned.

'Bravo!' cried Marjorie, punching the air.

'Well . . . !' Betsy gasped, speechless for once.

'And there's one more piece of news.' I checked with Jensen who nodded.

'We've set the date for the wedding,' I said excitedly. 'Easter Saturday.'

Jensen threaded his fingers through mine and drew me closer. 'So the baby can be there with us.'

'It's perfect,' Betsy sniffed, pulling her hanky back out of her sleeve. 'Just perfect.'

'And not only that,' said Sidney, rubbing his hands together, 'it's also the perfect excuse to pop open a bottle of the new vintage.'

'I'll drink to that,' said Marjorie, waggling her eyebrows.

Jensen reached for the bottle that had been sitting on the bottom step, put there earlier in readiness for just this moment. He peeled off the foil cap and wire and with an expert twist of his wrist the cork came out with a refined 'phut'.

'Just a small one for me,' said Betsy, twisting a finger through her pearls, and we all laughed.

It was good to know that some things, at least, never changed.

'Why don't we let the next Mrs Butterworth propose a toast?' said Marjorie, when we'd all got a drink.

I took a breath and glanced down to the valley below. The low sun lent a silvery glow to the winter landscape, completely different to the view on a summer's day, but it had a beauty all of its own. The vines were bare now, and it was almost impossible to imagine that only a couple of months ago they'd been green and bowed down with fruit. But they'd bud again in spring, new shoots would appear, and the circle of life would begin again. This vineyard had brought me so much more than just a job: it was my haven, my happy place and the start of a new chapter in my life. My hand stole to my stomach and I felt our baby, who we reckoned was nine-parts boxer and one-part acrobat, move beneath my fingers. And next year, another new chapter, a new family and home.

'Not like you to be short of words,' Jensen whispered playfully.

There was love in his voice as his hand crept over mine and I felt his warmth wrap itself around me like a blanket. My heart skipped a beat; even now I had to pinch myself that he was mine.

I looked into his eyes as I raised my glass.

'To new life, love and another vintage summer.'

The Thank Yous

Thank you to my talented, patient and wise agents for helping me through this book. I was lucky enough to have two in 2018 – Caroline Hardman and Hannah Ferguson from Hardman Swainson. I thank you (and congratulate you) both from the bottom of my heart for doing such a good job on my behalf.

Thanks as ever to the wonderful team at Transworld who have helped put the fizz into *A Vintage Summer* (see what I did there): Francesca Best, Molly Crawford, Julia Teece, Sophie Bruce and Hannah Bright.

My interest in vineyards began ten years ago on an unforgettable holiday at Chateau Bauduc near Bordeaux with my friends Lucy Nicholson and Linda Lawler. So thank you, ladies, for planting that initial seed which took ten years to mature!

Once I'd got my story premise, I needed to research the English wine industry and three vineyards in particular have been extremely helpful. Special thanks to Helenka Brown at Hanwell Wines, who gave up a lot of her time to answer my questions and let me join in with the 2017 harvest! Thank you to Helenka's parents, Tony and Veronica Skuriat, owners of Eglantine Vineyard, who showed me their winery and gave me lots of useful details about tending vines. A big thank you to Ben Hunt at Halfpenny Green Wine Estate who let me into his lab and taught me lots of technical stuff to do with making sparkling wine. Any errors are all mine!

Thank you to two ladies who helped with my questions about pregnancy: Issy Bourton and Hannah Barker. Apologies for the weird questions and for making Hannah over-share. While we're on health matters, thank you to my lovely Nanna for helping me with Betsy's story and her struggle with macular degeneration. Also thank you to Lisa Ward for her in-depth knowledge of ambulances!

Last year I set up a Facebook group called Cathy Bramley's Book Club. This warm-hearted and friendly community has helped me enormously, not only by helping me with details such as character names, but by encouraging me with their kind messages and glowing reviews. Thank you so much, dear members, it is lovely to have your support.

To the Literary Hooters: what wonderful friends you are, I am lucky to have you and cherish our little club dearly. Thank you for your love, wisdom and ability to make me laugh through everything.

Lastly, to Tony, Phoebe and Isabel, my thanks and love always.

Cathy xxx

*You can enjoy another irresistible
love story from Cathy Bramley*

A MATCH
MADE IN DEVON

Nina has always dreamed of being a star. Unfortunately
her agent thinks she's more girl-next-door than leading
lady and her acting career isn't going quite as planned.
Then, after a series of very public blunders and to escape
a gathering storm of paparazzi, Nina is forced to flee
the city, leaving nothing but an empty bottle of
hair dye and a tiny bedroom behind.

Her plan is to lay low with a friend in Devon, in
beautiful Brightside Cove. But soon Nina learns that
more drama can be found in a small village than
on a hectic television set.

And when a gorgeous man (and his adorable dog)
catches her eye, it's not long before London and
showbiz start to lose their appeal.

Will Nina choose to return to the bright lights or
has she met her match in Brightside Cove?

Available now

THE LEMON TREE CAFÉ

When Rosie Featherstone finds herself unexpectedly
jobless, the offer to help her beloved Italian
grandmother out at the Lemon Tree Café –
a little slice of Italy nestled in the rolling hills
of Derbyshire – feels like the perfect
way to keep busy.

Surrounded by the rich scent of espresso, delicious
biscotti and juicy village gossip, Rosie soon
finds herself falling for her new way of life. But
she is haunted by a terrible secret, one that even
the appearance of a handsome new face can't
quite help her move on from.

Then disaster looms and the café's fortunes are
threatened . . . and Rosie discovers that her *nonna*
has been hiding a dark past of her own. With
surprises, betrayal and more than one secret
brewing, can she find a way to save the
Lemon Tree Café and help both herself and
Nonna achieve the happy ending they deserve?

Sometimes you have to revisit the past to
truly move forwards . . .

Available now

HETTY'S
FARMHOUSE BAKERY

Thirty-two-year-old Hetty Greengrass is the star
around which the rest of her family orbits. Marriage,
motherhood and helping Dan run Sunnybank
Farm have certainly kept her hands full for
the last twelve years. But when her daughter
Poppy has to choose her inspiration for a school
project and picks her aunt, not her mum,
Hetty is left full of self-doubt.

Hetty's always been generous with her time and, until
now, her biggest talent – baking deliciously moreish
shortcrust pastry pies – has been limited to charity
work and the village fete. But taking part in a
competition run by Cumbria's Finest to find the
very best produce from the region might be just
the thing to make her daughter proud . . . and
reclaim something for herself.

Except that life isn't as simple as producing the
perfect pie. Changing the status quo isn't easy – and
with cracks appearing in her marriage and
shocking secrets coming to light, Hetty must
decide where her priorities really lie . . .

Available now

White Lies & Wishes

Flirtatious, straight-talking **Jo Gold** says she's got no time for love; she's determined to save her family's business.

New mother **Sarah Hudson** has cut short her maternity leave to return to work. She says she'll do whatever it takes to succeed.

Self-conscious housewife **Carrie Radley** says she just wants to shift the pounds – she'd love to finally wear a bikini in public.

The unlikely trio meet by chance one winter's day, and in a moment of 'Carpe Diem' madness, embark on a mission to make their wishes come true by September.

Easy. At least it would be, if they hadn't been just the teensiest bit stingy with the truth . . .

With hidden issues, hidden talents, and hidden demons to overcome, new friends Jo, Carrie and Sarah must admit to what they really, really want, if they are ever to get their happy endings.

Available now

Wickham Hall

Holly Swift has just landed the job of her dreams: events co-ordinator at Wickham Hall, the beautiful manor home that sits proudly at the heart of the village where she grew up. Not only does she get to organize for a living and work in stunning surroundings, but it will also put a bit of distance between Holly and her problems at home.

As Holly falls in love with the busy world of Wickham Hall – from family weddings to summer festivals, firework displays and Christmas grottos – she also finds a place in her heart for her friendly (if unusual) colleagues.

But life isn't as easily organized as an event at Wickham Hall (and even those have their complications . . .). Can Holly learn to let go and live in the moment?

After all, that's when the magic happens . . .

Available now

the Plumberry School of Comfort Food

Verity Bloom hasn't been interested in cooking anything more complicated than the perfect fish-finger sandwich, ever since she lost her best friend and baking companion two years ago.

But an opportunity to help a friend lands her right back in the heart of the kitchen. The Plumberry School of Comfort Food is due to open in a few weeks' time and needs the kind of great ideas that only Verity could cook up. And with new friendships bubbling and a sprinkling of romance in the mix, Verity finally begins to feel like she's home.

But when tragedy strikes at the very heart of the cookery school, can Verity find the magic ingredient for Plumberry while still writing her own recipe for happiness?

Available now

Appleby Farm

Freya Moorcroft has wild red hair, mischievous green eyes, a warm smile and a heart of gold. She's been happy working at the café round the corner from Ivy Lane allotments and her romance with her new boyfriend is going well, she thinks, but a part of her still misses the beautiful rolling hills of her Cumbrian childhood home: Appleby Farm.

Then a phone call out of the blue and a desperate plea for help change everything . . .

The farm is in financial trouble, and it's taking its toll on the aunt and uncle who raised Freya. Heading home to lend a hand, Freya quickly learns that things are worse than she first thought. As she summons up all her creativity and determination to turn things around, Freya is surprised as her own dreams for the future begin to take shape.

Love makes the world go round, according to Freya. Not money. But will saving Appleby Farm and following her heart come at a price?

Available now

Ivy Lane

Tilly Parker needs a fresh start, fresh air and a fresh attitude if she is ever to leave the past behind and move on with her life. As she seeks out peace and quiet in a new town, taking on a plot at Ivy Lane allotments seems like the perfect solution.

But the friendly Ivy Lane community has other ideas and gradually draw Tilly in to their cosy, comforting world of planting seedlings, organizing bake sales and planning seasonal parties.

As the seasons pass, will Tilly learn to stop hiding amongst the sweetpeas and let people back into her life – and her heart?

Available now